The Sins of the Father

THE SINS
OF THE FATHER

A ROMANCE OF THE SOUTH

By Thomas Dixon

With an Introduction by
Steven Weisenburger

THE UNIVERSITY PRESS OF KENTUCKY

Publication of this volume was made possible in part by a grant from the National Endowment for the Humanities.

Scholarly publisher for the Commonwealth, serving Bellarmine University, Berea College, Centre College of Kentucky, Eastern Kentucky University, The Filson Historical Society, Georgetown College, Kentucky Historical Society, Kentucky State University, Morehead State University, Murray State University, Northern Kentucky University, Transylvania University, University of Kentucky, University of Louisville, and Western Kentucky University.

Editorial and Sales Offices: The University Press of Kentucky
663 South Limestone Street, Lexington, Kentucky 40508-4008
www.kentuckypress.com

Frontispiece: Thomas Dixon Jr. (1864–1946). Image courtesy of Library of Congress, Prints and Photographs Division (reproduction number: LC-USZ62-110941)

04 05 06 07 08 5 4 3 2 1

Library of Congress Cataloging-in-Publication Data

Dixon, Thomas, 1864-1946.
The sins of the father : a romance of the South / by Thomas Dixon ;
with an introduction by Steven Weisenburger.
p. cm.
Includes bibliographical references.
ISBN 0-8131-9117-3 (pbk. : alk. paper)
1. Reconstruction (U.S. history, 1865-1877)—Fiction. 2. White supremacy movements—Fiction. 3. Ku-Klux Klan (1866-1869)—Fiction. 4. Newspaper editors—Fiction. 5. North Carolina—Fiction. I. Weisenburger, Steven. II. Title.
PS3507.I93S56 2004
813'.52—dc22
2004017744

This book is printed on acid-free recycled paper meeting the requirements of the American National Standard for Permanence in Paper for Printed Library Materials.

Manufactured in the United States of America.

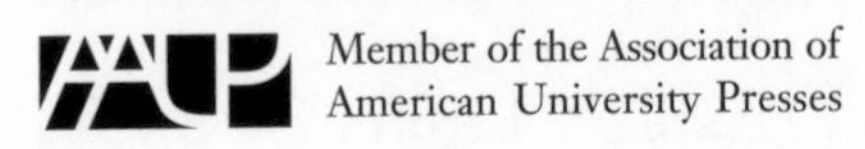

Member of the Association of American University Presses

To the memory of Randolph Shotwell
of North Carolina—
soldier, editor, clansman, patriot

To the Reader

I wish it understood that I have not used in this novel the private life of Captain Randolph Shotwell, to whom this book is dedicated. I have drawn the character of my central figure from the authentic personal history of Major Daniel Norton himself, a distinguished citizen of the far South, with whom I was intimately acquainted for many years.

Thomas Dixon
New York
March 8, 1912

Contents

Book Two: Atonement

Introduction

The Sins of the Father opens with a scene of writing and humiliation as the story's protagonist, Raleigh, North Carolina, newspaper editor Daniel Norton, gazes out his office window at a "horror" perpetrated on "the conquered South." In the city square recently freed slaves are auctioning the labor of aging white men and women bankrupted during the Civil War, and Norton recognizes one of those white-haired, newly indentured bondsmen as "the son of a hero of the American Revolution" (4). Thus gazing on what he considers a pantomime of the racially upside-down world created by Reconstruction-era carpetbaggers and scalawags, Norton finds himself "brushing a tear from his cheek" (4). His crying strikes the first mournful note in a relentlessly racist melodrama that novelist Thomas Dixon sustains for more than three hundred action-packed pages. Yet tears express only half of the message in Dixon's opening scene. Soon Norton has "turned again to his desk," to complete an editorial that summons Confederate veterans to overthrow the "horror" outside and to redeem their state in the name of white supremacy. Crying suggested effeminate weakness. In contrast, Norton's writing is "a man's work for men. When he struck the blow he saw the dent of the hammer on the iron, and heard it ring to the limits of the state" (9).

As one of the most popular American novelists of the early twentieth century, Thomas Dixon was deeply invested in writing as hammer blows, as masculine work directed at reforming the American polity right down to its foundations. He had come to a writing career at age thirty-eight after first having left the doctoral program in political science at Johns Hopkins in his twenties and briefly trying stage acting in New York; returning to North Carolina to study and practice law; serving a term as state legislator; taking a post as minister of a Baptist church in Raleigh; and finally returning to New York and achieving extraordinary success in the ministry—which he precipitously abandoned in 1899 to travel the country as a highly paid chautauqua speaker, work he just as precipitously quit in order to write novels. His first novel, *The Leopard's Spots* (1902), climbed the lower rungs of best-seller lists, while its proudly expressed white supremacy, and especially its revisionist representations of Reconstruction-era Ku Klux Klan violence, sparked a firestorm of controversies. A third novel, *The Clansman*, part two of his Klan Trilogy, attained a number one best-seller ranking soon after its release in early 1905. Within months Dixon had capitalized on the novel's huge success with a dramatic script melding and condensing the story line of his trilogy's first two novels (*The Traitor*, the closing volume in the series, would appear in 1907). As a stage drama, *The Clansman* played to record audiences in New York and led in its own turn to a script adaptation for director D.W. Griffith's pioneering and infamously racist 1915 film, *The Birth of a Nation.* Then in a triumphant moment, in February 1915, Dixon gave the film a private, White House debut to former Johns Hopkins graduate school classmate Woodrow Wilson, who supposedly hailed the film afterward, saying, "It is like writing history with lightning."[1]

The president's remark testifies to the enduring but long-unexamined power of race melodrama in American culture. Dismissed by generations of critics for using stock characters, programmatic story lines, and overwrought sentiments circling around spectacles of bodily suffering, melodrama assumed a more significant literary/historical guise when feminist critics of the 1980s fought to restore to the American canon of masterworks Harriet Beecher Stowe's 1852 novel, *Uncle Tom's Cabin.* Stowe's book required feminists to think differently about the ways in which melodrama represents the home as an iconic space of innocence and purity opposite which the pat representatives of rapine and evil from The Slave Power might be figured. These figurations constituted not an aberrant, archaic, or excessive mode of writing, but rather a vital way for Americans to work through the intense moral dilemma of race. Additionally, studying the dozens of "anti-Tom" novels published after 1852 compelled critics to consider the ways in which melodrama was also a mobile form that was adaptable to profoundly racist as well as racially progressive ideologies. It is also, Susan Gillman finds in *Blood Talk*, a deeply protean representational mode capable of absorbing for its various needs contemporary historical, legal, social/scientific, and scientific discourses, as well as the narrative conventions of sentimental, regional, and fantasy fiction. As for its durability, in *Playing the Race Card* Linda Williams studies race melodrama's powerful influence in the 1990s and the O.J. Simpson trial.[2]

Race melodramas bore the burden of expressing as well as critiquing the legitimizing myth of white supremacy, especially during the period of Jim Crow segregation from 1890 to 1950. Melodrama's elemental convention has always been its Manichean morality, its world of good and evil that is so easily adaptable to the apparently black-and-white domain of race relations. But scholars working on melodrama have also always noted its tendency toward excess, its desire to render a dualistic ethos in terms so overdetermined, so hyperlegible that the excessiveness spills over into illegibility and even contradiction.[3] Signs of this excessiveness can be found in the ways in which melodrama abounds with instances of mistaken, disguised, and doubled identities, and American race melodramas certainly specialize in such instances. Plots of long-hidden or mistakenly attributed interracial intimacies generate erroneously raced, illicitly, and perhaps even incestuously, coupled characters, that in turn generate social crises that bring secret societies and militias like the Klan into conflicts verging on race wars. The formula works as well for an antiracist novel, such as Charles Chesnutt's *The Marrow of Tradition* (1902), as it does for a work like Dixon's first novel, *The Leopard's Spots*, which is explicitly composed as an anti-Tom novel. Therefore, Linda Williams argues, in reading either kind we do well to keep a critical eye fastened on how the story specifies evil's victims, for melodrama's spectacles of racially marked suffering focus like a laser beam its political and moral argument. Whether Stowe's figure of the tortured black male body, Uncle Tom in *Uncle Tom's Cabin*, or Dixon's figure of the virginal white victim of interracial rape, Marion Lenoir in *The Clansman*, these iconic scenes are composed to represent social grievances that demand not just adjudication but immediate action. American race melodramas are always calls to arms, and that power is what drew Thomas Dixon to the form.

With his steady output of novels and plays, and by his relentless self-promotion, Thomas Dixon amassed a small fortune, lost it in the panic of 1907, then just as quickly recouped and handsomely surpassed his losses. But the wealth merely indexed the more significant fact: by late 1915, when his novels and the Griffith film had inspired William Simmons to inaugurate the modern Klan with an elaborately staged cross burning at Stone Mountain, Georgia (a rebirth that Dixon ironically disliked), the novelist had secured his position as the imaginative genius—or demon—of an American white supremacist dogma that reached its zenith in the early twentieth century.[4] Writing had thus bestowed upon him Daniel Norton's fictional power to strike blows that profoundly affected racial customs, laws, institutions, and statecraft.

So Thomas Dixon wrote a great deal of himself into Daniel Norton. The fictional hero stands a tall and narrow "six feet three," with high cheekbones and a "gaunt and serious" look (5), much like Dixon. Or, for that matter, like Abraham Lincoln, a figure the novelist worked tirelessly to reclaim for the South and, relying on several scant yet widely circulated Lincoln quotes about the supposed social incompatibility of whites and blacks, to recruit as an icon for the white supremacist cause.[5] Certainly Norton functions as a virtual mouthpiece for Dixon's racial ideology. Moreover, Norton's story is flush with details from Dixon's biography.

Dixon dedicates *The Sins of the Father* to "The Memory of Randolph Shotwell of North Carolina, Soldier, Editor, Clansman, Patriot." But then in a complicated dodge, Dixon warns us that he drew Norton's character not from Shotwell's "private life," but from the "authentic personal history" of a Major Daniel Norton, with whom he was "intimately acquainted for many years." In fact, a scouring of North Carolina records suggests that no such man ever existed.

Randolph Abbott Shotwell (1844–1885) was a Confederate officer who survived Pickett's Charge at Gettysburg and a lengthy prisoner-of-war internment at Fort Delaware. After the Civil War he returned to his farm near the town of Shelby, the Dixon family seat in the North Carolina piedmont.[6] In 1868 Shotwell started up a "rickety Democratic weekly" in nearby Rutherfordton that quickly went bankrupt. He then moved to Asheville, where he edited another short-lived newspaper. Returning to the Shelby area, Shotwell got himself installed as "chief" over the unruly Rutherfordton Klan, a den whose three hundred or so members soon acquired a reputation for terrorizing freedmen involved in Republican politics, nighttime whippings of white men who kept black mistresses, and sexual assaults on black girls. Historian Allen Trelease also notes that Shotwell was notorious for running up "whisky bills with a group of equally aimless men."[7]

The man who installed Shotwell as chief of the Rutherford Klan was Colonel Leroy McAfee, maternal uncle and "boyhood idol of novelist Thomas Dixon." By all accounts McAfee presided over a much larger and better disciplined Klan based in Shelby—a den eight-hundred strong with a reputation for sweeping in on local black residents as they slept, confiscating firearms and threatening retaliation against all who sought to exercise their voting franchise. In late 1870, McAfee's den was responsible for the lynching, just beyond the Dixon family doorstep, of a black man involved in Republican politics. Inquiries never determined if Dixon's uncle Leroy directly authorized the lynching, but the well-known fact that he had worked tirelessly to regulate unsanctioned raids by his men kept suspicions alive for some years. In any case, by 1871 McAfee was already the subject of a state investigation into Klan violence. His response: to strong-arm state legislators of the piedmont region into supporting the (successful) impeachment of North Carolina governor William Holden, whose main offense was crucial state support for federal anti-Klan prosecutions. Soon after Holden's removal, McAfee was tried for Klan activities and was convicted and fined. His more careless and loose-lipped compatriot Shotwell was prosecuted in federal courts, convicted, fined heavily, and sentenced to six years hard labor at a New York penitentiary.[8]

These tumultuous events must have burned themselves into young Thomas Dixon's memory. Certainly they forged in his thoughts an ironclad link between politics and domestic life, establishing for him that all politics are not just local but also familial. Throughout his writings Dixon would represent the nuclear family as the basis for all world-historical struggles, partly because, on this view, bourgeois domesticity modeled white patriarchal authority and the subordinate relations of all its dependents: women, children, racial underlings, and animals. Indeed, when biographer Raymond Cook notes that Dixon's Klansman father used his Baptist ministry in Shelby to dictate the voting allegiances and racist beliefs of his congregants, we ought to make a connection between that and later information about how the elder Thomas Dixon homeschooled young Thomas until age twelve—training that undoubtedly fixed in the boy's mind those power relations and white supremacist beliefs. Four decades later, when Dixon had drawn Daniel Norton's fictional character as a composite of his father, uncle, and a family friend, the dedicatory attribution to an "authentic" figure served to deflect attention from Norton's more problematic autobiographical and historical origins.

In the Klan Trilogy, Dixon represents the Klan's resistance to Radical Reconstruction as the first half of the larger saga treating a politically, ethically, and spiritually righteous movement for restoring white men's supposedly natural authority. Repeatedly in *The Leopard's Spots*, *The Clansman*, and *The Traitor* Dixon represents elite Klan leaders (such as his uncle Leroy) struggling to discipline riotous rank-and-file Klansmen (such as Shotwell) who betray the restoration cause by using their anonymity as white-sheeted nightriders for personal vendettas. In Dixon's revisionist history these poor whites thus neglected the overarching problem. First Emancipation, and then the Fourteenth and Fifteenth Amendments, had been (he believed) unleashed on the prostrated South legions of black men staking their claims to the ballot, and hence claims for "social equality" among white neighbors. In the logic of white supremacist phobias, such claims inexorably lead to desires for interracial sexual relations whose ghastly outcome, given the phobic presupposition of white women's revulsion at the mere prospect of *any* contact with black men, was black-on-white rape. Thus practical politics translates into a domestic ultimate, because Dixon generally figures white women as fragile vessels bearing the future of white "civilization." He insists that white men can only answer the crisis with final solutions—total segregation, lynchings, or a terminal race war.

The second half of Dixon's saga unfolds two decades after white race-traitors and federal intervention had thwarted the restoration of elite white authority. Drawing again from state history, Dixon fictionalizes the Democrats' 1898 white supremacy campaign to "redeem" North Carolina from a Republican and Populist Party coalition, or "Fusion," that had produced disastrous 1894 and 1896 election campaigns for Democrats, as Fusion candidates won the state house, grabbed state legislative seats, took control of local governments along North Carolina's heavily black eastern seaboard, and installed African American appointees in post offices and customs houses. Among the "redeemers" were some of Thomas Dixon's closest friends, including Raleigh *News & Observer* editor Josephus Daniels and Democratic Party chairman Furnifold Simmons, men who were—along with Dixon and Walter Hines Page, the publisher of Dixon's novels—founding members of the Raleigh-based Watauga Club, a kind of think tank for white racial conservatives.[9] Daniels and Simmons spearheaded the campaign. Drawing from sensationalized reporting from across the South, they fomented panic around the issue of black-on-white rape. They argued, for example, that white farmers and laborers had become so fearful of leaving their wives and daughters alone during the day, as easy prey for roving "black beasts," that the men could no longer leave home for work. Simmons and Daniels employed South Carolina's infamous white supremacist governor, "Pitchfork Ben" Tillman, as well as future Georgia senator Rebecca Latimer Felton to raise the specter of rape and race war and to urge, if necessary, the extermination of the Carolinas' black population in defense of white womanhood.

Following Daniels's lead, North Carolina newspapers depicted the state's African American population as an "incubus" feeding upon and polluting the blood of Carolina whites. The result, historian Glenda Gilmore has shown, was that Democrats not only claimed victory in the balloting of November 8, 1898, but also unleashed in the "hypermasculine" cant of their demagoguery a bloodthirsty rage on their own side that culminated, two days later, in elite white men commanding white militias in the massacre of black citizens of Wilmington.[10] Two years later the Democrats who reclaimed the statehouse fulfilled their promises to North Carolina white supremacists with legislation that effected the near-total disfranchisement of eligible black voters. Jim Crow repression descended on the state for decades to come. George White, an African American congressman formerly representing the eastern shore Second District, fled to New Jersey because he understood how the ballot was taken from blacks virtually at gunpoint. Thomas Dixon worked from the same understanding.

Simply put, there is no overstating the importance of these two historical movements for Dixon's fictions. *The Leopard's Spots* historicizes in considerable detail the 1898 white supremacy campaign and Wilmington massacre, *The Clansman* narrates extensively the Reconstruction-era saga of the Klan's rise, while *The Traitor* concentrates on the Klan's undoing. But each novel frames its story by using the same arc: from the Klan's 1871 demise to the Democrat's 1898 redemption. *The Sins of the Father* does this as well, but in a much more effective condensed form; additionally, Dixon wove fascinating thematic changes into his 1912 novel. Most important, in the trilogy Dixon had given narrative form to that party line according to which the "incubus" or black male rapist demanded violent solutions. *The Sins of the Father* inverts those gender roles, assigning the ultimate threat against white racial purity to the figure of an alluring but dangerous mixed-race woman preying upon white supremacist leadership—none other than soldier-Klansman-editor-politician Daniel Norton.

Why the change? Following the publication of *The Leopard's Spots* and *The Clansman*, African American thinkers had met Dixon's representations of rape and lynching with vigorous and vehement critiques that need further study. For example, an anonymous poem published as "A Reply to Thos. Dixon, Jr." in the Cleveland *Journal* referred to the novelist as one of "Satan's angels to be vanquished."[11] In February 1906, when *The New York Age* editor T. Thomas Fortune refused to shake Dixon's hand at a public debate on the topic "What Shall We Do With The Negro?"—because the novelist not only refused to back away from his radical racism but claimed he hadn't said enough on the subject—newspapers reported the slight nationwide.[12] Novelist Sutton Griggs used a supplementary essay at the back of his novel, *The Hindered Hand*, to counter that Dixon's representations of rape and lynching were based on fantasies that "the ultra radical element of Southern whites" had put in the service of a cynical politics. Griggs concluded that Humanity "claims him not as one of her children."[13] Critiquing the white supremacist triumvirate of South Carolina governor Ben Tillman, Mississippi governor James K. Vardaman, and North Carolina novelist Dixon, W.E.B. DuBois argued that concerns about African American voting rescripted as nightmares about black-on-white rape had demonized black men and made Dixon into a writer "more widely read than Henry James."[14]

Among the most hard-hitting of these critiques was a 1905 pamphlet by Kelly Miller. Born to a formerly enslaved South Carolina mother, Miller studied mathematics and physics at Howard University and Johns Hopkins (where Dixon had studied alongside the future president). Back at Howard in the mid-1890s, Miller brought sociology into the curriculum as a discipline for scientific studies of United States race relations and staked out a middle ground among African American intellectuals, somewhere between the conservatism of Booker T. Washington and the radicalism of DuBois. In the pamphlet, however, Miller pulled no punches. He asked, rhetorically, why Dixon would have "unfrocked" himself "as a priest of God" in order to work as a hellhound "preaching the doctrine of hate." Cannily intuiting that some deep personal complex must be driving his phobia over the sexual "amalgamation" of American whites and blacks, Miller counters first that Dixon's race-baiting only compelled light-skinned African Americans into "crossing the color line" as whites, threatening still more of the "amalgamation" Dixon rants against.[15] But where did those passers come from? In his next breath Miller counters that "this stream of white blood" courses through "the veins of some six out of ten million Negroes" because of white men's relations with black women during and after slavery.[16]

Such charges had a general currency. Months before the 1898 massacre, Alexander Manly, editor of the Wilmington *Daily Record*, had launched a quite similar attack on leaders of the white supremacy campaign.[17] And for working the same theme in her 1892 antilynching crusade, whites had forced Ida B. Wells to abandon her Memphis home or face a lynch mob herself, although in reply Wells only refined her argument in books treating the lynching crisis, *A Red Record* and *Southern Horrors*.[18] But in taking on Dixon, Miller's *Open Letter* cut close to the bone. He insists that "the loud-mouthed advocates of race-purity" among white supremacists are hypocrites who speak and write so compulsively on the subject because no amount of compensatory rhetoric will erase the plain fact that their fathers, and perhaps they themselves, have ventured sexually over a "color line" they insist is absolute.[19]

Dixon closely followed these critical responses to his work.[20] In fact Dixon's appearances at public debates with African American activists such as Fortune, in addition to his spiteful representations of them in his novels (even of apologists such as Booker T. Washington), were contributions to a complex and long-running dialogue in turn-of-the-century American struggles over race. *The Sins of the Father* may be read, in some part, as an important piece of that historically significant dialogue—in terms both public and, for Dixon, intensely private. Even after *Sins* was published the dialogue continued, as African American novelist Thomas H. Walker published a 1915 novel, *J. Johnson, or The Unknown Man*, whose subtitle specified that it was "An Answer to Mr. Thos. Dixon's *Sins of the Fathers*.[21]

Kelly Miller had cut deep in a place where Dixon was exceedingly tender, where Joel Williamson identifies "a very deep emotional problem."[22] For Tom Dixon's complex involved a mother who, Dixon believed, had been terribly violated while she was still a girl. Amanda McAfee Dixon had been married in 1847 at the age of thirteen, "before her *mensus* had appeared" (her son Tom later recalled), to a Thomas Dixon Sr., who was then twenty-seven. Dixon insisted that this sexual trauma had caused miscarriages both before his mother successfully bore Dixon's brother in 1855 and again before his own 1864 birth; he also claimed that these births led finally to a "painful collapse" of his mother's health, leaving her weak and invalided but also enabling little Tom to develop an especially close relationship with her. Certainly Williamson is right to read into these facts and Dixon's construction of them an intensely oedipal family, where the son ought to hold his father liable for violating the girlish innocence of his mother, whom he has placed on a pedestal and thus imagines himself as her protector or vindicator. Nonetheless, Dixon showed no outward "sign of remarkable hostility toward his father" and even "overtly revered the man." Moreover, as Glenda Gilmore has further discovered, Dixon sustained that reverence despite, or perhaps because of, the surfacing in New York City of a biracial man who claimed publicly after *The Leopard's Spots* appeared in 1902 that he was the novelist's half brother, a claim that circulated widely in African American periodicals and that Kelly Miller would certainly have recalled in 1905. As for Dixon, he acknowledged knowing "that darkey" whose mother was the Dixon family cook while also vehemently denying the man's claim of a filial relation.[23] But as the 2003 revelations about South Carolina senator Strom Thurmond's "shadow family" remind us, the wall of silence that elite white men typically erected between themselves and charges of "miscegenation" was always just a veil through which true facts might still be known. Thus supposing the New York man spoke the truth, Thomas Dixon's deeper problem becomes clear. His father had not only violated and thereby invalided Amanda Dixon, he had allegedly taken sexual solace with a woman of color—once again despite, and probably also because of, how Amanda was invalided, and with careless disregard for how it would further pollute the ideal of white womanhood she embodied.

From these complicated skeins of memory, history, and contemporary debate Dixon wove a story playing out themes of miscegenation and incest. In working up the plot of *Sins* he turned once again to the North Carolina Klan's demise during Reconstruction for historical framing, and then to the state's "Redemption" by white supremacists in the campaigns of 1898–1900. In *Sins,* however, he managed to give that material a much tighter narration than the sprawling trilogy had managed. This happened because—reversing the earlier process of going from novel to dramatic script—his 1912 story first took shape as stage drama. Indeed, bowing unmistakably to the plot's historical background Dixon premiered his play in September 1910 at Norfolk, Virginia. Days later when the troupe took it to Wilmington, North Carolina, the leading man was (incredibly) eaten by a shark while swimming off nearby Wrightsville beach and Dixon himself took up the Daniel Norton role, thus creatively working through his father's "sins."[24] For the rest of its thirty-week run Dixon toured with the show and then, during the following year, transformed the stage script into the novel reprinted in this edition.

As an X-ray of white supremacist complexes and contradictions, *The Sins of the Father* gives us a matchless composition for study. Daniel Norton's beautiful but "delicate" wife Jean, a "petted invalid" with an enigmatic yet potentially fatal throat ailment (13), stands as the epitome of idealized, elite white womanhood. She would have been the focal point of rape phobias in any of Dixon's prior novels. *Sins*, in contrast, displaces those fears on Norton, figuring him as powerless before the leonine sexual wiles of the light-skinned "octoroon" nurse, Cleo, he reluctantly hires to care for the toddler—so interestingly named Tom—whose birth had apparently invalided Jean several years before. Consciously Norton had "always loathed the Southern white man who stooped" to having intimacies with "such women," but their attraction he also recognized as something "instinctive and irresistible." "Why?" Norton asks himself (16). It looms as a key "paradox" of Dixon's narrative, for how *can* a supposedly "natural" and profoundly moral "repugnance" bred instinctively into any elite white man collapse before the equally instinctual lure of black women's mere sexuality (24)? In part, Dixon's answer is that Norton battles but succumbs to Cleo's seductions not only because of her *proximity*, a representation that explicitly points to the novel's insistence on total racial segregation, but also because of "the beast that slumbered within" Norton himself (28), a representation tied to an implicitly expressed and problematic logic. As a symbol of elemental manliness, Norton's beastly nature accounts for the warrior's prowess that had elevated him to the rank of major during the war and then to a reputation in state politics that brings him (in part 1, which is titled "Sins,") to the brink of a governorship—after spearheading the campaign to impeach the sitting governor. But it equally accounts for how Norton surrenders to Cleo, or (as Dixon might insist) to an elemental manhood he cannot fully deny. In this sense, defining Norton's "beast within" as equal parts blessing and bane is fully consistent with turn-of-the-century constructions of masculinity.[25] Partly, too, Dixon answers the question about why Norton surrenders by representing the "half-savage"

Cleo as overmastering Norton because she offers, paradoxically, to act her more "natural" role—at least in matters of sex—as his "slave" (67, 129). The idea is to paint Norton as a victim and thus counter the charges of critics such as Kelly Miller, though it required ascribing a great deal of rationality and conspiratorial wiliness to beastly Cleo.

After Jean discovers his unfaithfulness, a panicked and penitent Daniel Norton plans to confess his "tragic sin" and, in phrasing that resonates eerily with the key white-supremacist metaphor of the 1898 campaign, promise her a "redeemed life" (101). But Dixon stages two interventions: First, the Norton family physician argues that Norton "never had a chance" against Cleo because generations of illicit intimacies over the color line had "bred [miscegenation] into the bone and sinew of succeeding generations" like Norton's (84, 85). And second, Dixon introduces Jean's mother into the story with another argument which reveals that Jean's father had made frequent forays over the color line with his slave women and had even "died in the cabin of a mulatto girl he had played with as a boy" (93). Worse, she explains to Jean, is that Cleo's mother was one of those slaves; so we realize Norton committed "miscegenation" with Jean's second cousin—foreshadowing the incest specter that Dixon raises in book 2 ("Atonement") of the novel. But if these disclosures up the ante thematically they also raise the rhetorical stakes, for how could this great leader of white civilization have unleashed such beastly horrors within himself, his family, and society? Explaining it as best he can, Jean's doctor reasons that however highly refined he is, when a white man acts "civilized" in his "relations to women it is not by inheritance" for he is still at rock bottom a "primeval man" who is vulnerable to the "enfolding animal magnetism" of a "free primeval woman who is unafraid" (105). Doctor Williams concludes that even the nation's natural-born leaders wither before interracial temptation when, like Norton, they have also been "bred" to that sin. Book 1 of *The Sins of the Father* thus characterizes white civic identity in the United States as a hive of contradictions whose main threat, if left unresolved, is to the very survival of fragile white wives and therefore white racial destiny. This is why, in her elaborately staged death scene, Jean lays on Norton a solemn duty to break the paternal chain of miscegenation in raising little Tom. After her funeral Norton makes a grieving departure for New York. Cleo also leaves the state, only to stun Norton months later with news of their illegitimate daughter's birth.

Book 2 opens two decades later with the onset of North Carolina's 1898 white supremacy campaign and Daniel Norton reentering politics as its "natural leader."[26] But why bring Cleo back into the story? Those twenty years earlier, Norton had made provisions for supporting their child at a convent school. And back then Norton's only initial reason for allowing Cleo into the household was to take his invalided wife's role as little Tom's loving nurse. But now the boy is a full-grown, self-reliant gentleman who resembles—and therefore raises in Norton's memory the ghost of—the mother and wife killed by his racial sin. This makes it all the more inexplicable that Norton assents to Cleo's return. Still, Dixon requires Cleo in order to stage for readers a terminal struggle of their opposing wills. Each of his trilogy novels had developed that black-and-white battle through rape/lynching scenarios that are always represented as prefiguring total racewar, should elite white men fail to resolve the nation's "Negro Problem." In contrast, *Sins* reroutes the aggression formerly directed against the black-beast rapist toward a light-skinned but legally black woman that Dixon is bent on demonizing. This revised gendering of the principal figures in a white fantasy of racial conflict is unique and quite remarkable for its time—when American mass culture was ascribing mythic status to the black mammy's great nurturing powers.[27] In most respects Dixon's characterization of Cleo fits the historical mammy's profile that Cheryl Thurber summarizes: not an old, plus-size, head-rag-wearing mammy of myth, but rather a young, well-mannered mammy with a cultivated sense of caste relations—including her own superiority—and a tireless devotion to bestowing playful, loving attention on the white children in her care.[28] The key difference is that bestial licentiousness that casts Cleo, instead, as Mammy's evil counterpart, the jezebel. In fact, by casting Cleo as a vicious, crypto-jezebel in a mammy's disguise, Dixon's eliminationist racial program launches a truly daring assault, for despite a contemporary popular movement to mythify Mammy, to erect monuments glorifying her beneficence, her epitomizing "the good negro," *Sins* unmasks Mammy as a domestic security threat that must be eliminated.

Cleo's strategy is to once more use the white man's sexual weakness against him, but rather than focus on the man, she would target the boy to whom she had once been a surrogate mother. By waiting until Norton is away campaigning and then introducing to the Major's household a lovely young girl, Helen, whom we can only take to be their daughter, Cleo sets in motion the incest plot foreshadowed in book 1. In retrospect, readers will recognize signs scattered throughout the narrative indicating Helen's true, all-white lineage. Nevertheless, Dixon counts on the apparent incest's tragic inevitability to speed his novel's action past those signs, as Helen exclaims to Tom, "I feel as if I've known you all my life" (166), and a horrified Major Norton feels "the steel bars of an inexorable fate close on his own throat" (176). Dixon tries to rest the novel's tragic push during a few comic interludes involving the major's black servants Andy and Minerva.

Yet even these scenes contribute to the novel's eliminationist project by mocking his African American characters' capacity for conjugal love. This is represented as merely imitating whites' romantic conventions and therefore showing that African American people lack any capacity for domestic harmony and productivity. Thus even the comic scenes drive Dixon's story toward the tragic finale prophesied in his book's title—in Euripides, "the gods visit the sins of the father upon the children." In the novel's penultimate chapter, Norton and Tom—haunted by Jean Norton's spirit and seemingly doomed by a history of interracial conjugality that is national as well as familial—agree on a mutual suicide pact.[29]

By this juncture Dixon has spared no opportunity to use that looming tragedy in backlighting his novel's white supremacist message. Observing young Tom and Helen together, Major Norton's cook, Minerva, proclaims young love a "sweet wonderful foolishness" that "makes us all akin" (248). But precisely there is love's danger: unchecked under a racially progressive regime—or within anything resembling a loving community—interracial intimacies threaten "extinction of the National character" (139). This is why Major Norton campaigns "for the first time in the history of the [Democratic] party" (151) on behalf of repealing the Fifteenth Amendment, and for disfranchising all black voters, imposing strict antimiscegenation laws, then in due course—Norton argues—mandating the "complete separation of the races" by removing "the negro [to] a nation of his own" (141). The novel's penultimate chapter, with the suicide pact between father and son, and then the obligatory scene of horror with Daniel Norton and his son both lying dead on the floor, were meant to prove that "complete separation" can't arrive soon enough. This is why Dixon's brief final chapter depicts Tom Norton, his life having been miraculously spared, taking up just where the novel opened. Using his father's newspaper, now with a rapidly burgeoning national audience, Tom editorializes "for the purity of the race" (317) and the absolute removal of all African-descended people from the United States.

So Dixon's conclusion to *The Sins of the Father* simply rebuilds the familiar white supremacist platform: repeal, antimiscegenation, disfranchisement, and total separation leading to elimination. But we arrive there via complexly realized innovations on stock elements of prior white racial melodramas. No black-beast incubi threatening white women, with northern carpetbaggers abetting the horrors; no elite white Southern men arriving just-too-late on the rape scene, and therefore no self-righteous lynching scenarios. This novel turns around and upside down every gendered position in that familiar race melodrama. Responding to multiple, complex, contemporary phenomena such as the mammy craze and the nationwide slowdown of disfranchisement efforts after numerous southern successes from 1890 to 1905, Dixon determined to go at his readers with the most persuasive combination of themes in the arsenal—miscegenation and incest. A vigorous public dialogue with African American intellectuals, as well as psychological and biographical complexes and revelations turned loose by that dialogue also increased that determination. There's nothing like it until William Faulkner fully develops those same themes in *Absalom, Absalom!* (1936) and *Go Down, Moses* (1942). At key points in the 1936 novel, Faulkner references Dixon's title and, Werner Sollors notes, "specifically revises" the 1912 novel's plot.[30]

Connecting Dixon to Faulkner this way reminds us how formal innovation, sublimated history, dialogical responses to contemporary voices, and psychological depth are qualities critics perennially locate in canonical literature in the "masterworks." Dixon once claimed that he disregarded such distinctions, but *The Sins of the Father* clearly aspires to that level of achievement.[31] In studying how it does so, we might recognize not only that *Sins* is in many ways Dixon's most "literary" achievement but it also stands squarely amid a "white canon" of best-selling and prize-winning fiction published during the early modern era. Other popular novels in that canon, best-sellers such as Thomas Nelson Page's *Red Rock* (1898), Benjamin Rush Davenport's *Blood Will Tell* (1902), and Robert Lee Durham's *The Call of the South* (1908), overtly express their white supremacist ideology through narrative condemnations of interracial marriages; and Durham's self-consciously melodramatic tale about an interracial marriage in the U.S. president's family also vaguely hints at incest.[32]

Then we have a range of best sellers such as Edgar Rice Burrough's *Tarzan of the Apes* (1914), E.M. Hull's *The Sheik* (1917), Zane Grey's *The Vanishing American* (1925), and Oliver LaFarge's *Laughing Boy* (1929), fiction that mystifies racial ideology by transporting the story to nonwhite worlds, only to work through the same phobias about interraciality, the same plots of quasimiscegenation, and even—in the example of T.S. Stribling's much more racially progressive 1922 novel, *Birthright*—the threat (once again) of incest. Hull's tale of Englishwoman Diana Mayo's romantic Arabian sojourn plays in remarkably blunt ways with the motif of black-on-white rape, partly exculpated by revelations that the novel's deeply-tanned "Sheik" turns out to be an aristocratic Englishman exploring his dark, sensuous side in the desert heat—a plot that inverts the gender roles in *The Sins of the Father*, where Dixon's ending allows readers to exhale a sigh of relief in recognizing the supposedly "dark" Helen as lily white.

Resituating Thomas Dixon's work within the heart of this canon enables us to understand more fully the vigorous early twentieth-century dialogue between white supremacists and African American thinkers and artists such as Kelly Miller, Charles Chesnutt, Pauline Hopkins, T. Thomas Fortune, Sutton Griggs, Thomas H.B. Walker, Oscar Micheaux, and Pauline Hopkins. Micheaux's 1920 film *Within Our Gates* barely averts an incestuous interracial white-on-black rape, in Armand Girdlestone's sexual assault on his daughter Sylvia Landry. And Hopkins's 1902 novel *Of One Blood* also concentrates on the themes of "black blood" spreading invisibly through the dominant white population and therefore threatening miscegenative incest, themes that Dixon plies toward an opposite sociopolitical message: not one of tolerant assimilationism but one of a segregationist fantasy backlit with images of a looming race war.

Moreover, resituating Dixon's novel within a core of popular white racialist fiction ought to send students and scholars once more into the canon of twentieth-century American masterworks. The forthrightness of Dixon's ideology enables us to reread as race melodramas not only the great Faulkner novels but a range of other literary fiction. Fitzgerald's *The Great Gatsby* (1925) and Hemingway's *The Sun Also Rises* (1926) simply read differently when set alongside Dixon.[33] In foregrounding the amorous pursuits of elite white women by putatively nonwhite men such as the crypto-Jewish James Gatz, the overtly Jewish Robert Cohn, and dark-skinned Pedro Romero, Hemingway and Fitzgerald turn their narratives around interracial promiscuities and the resulting corruptions of domestic virtues, the overwrought affective responses to such "sins," and the irruptions of violence that function cathartically to restabilize a white-male-dominated social contract threatened by chaos. These are Dixon's great themes. Thus, moving his 1912 novel from its place on the far margin of "Modern American Literature" back toward the center enables readers to clarify the insidious, the carefully masked, and occulted formulas essential to United States fantasies in black-and-white.

Steven Weisenburger
Southern Methodist University

NOTES

1. So Dixon and Griffith claimed, in promoting *Birth*. But in *Playing the Race Card: Melodramas of Black and White from Uncle Tom to O.J. Simpson* (Princeton, N.J.: Princeton University Press, 2001) Linda Williams cautions that Wilson's statement was "apparently apocryphal." The president's actual words to Dixon: "I congratulate you on an excellent production" (see pp. 98 and 327n2).

2. See Susan Gillman, *Blood Talk: American Race Melodrama and the Culture of the Occult* (Chicago, Ill.: University of Chicago Press, 2003), 3–4; and Williams, *Playing the Race Card.*

3. See Peter Brooks, *The Melodramatic Imagination: Balzac, Henry James, Melodrama, and the Mode of Excess* (New Haven, Conn.: Yale University Press, 1976).

4. Historian Joel Williamson, for example, regards *The Leopard's Spots* as "the one work nearest to a codification of Radical [white supremacist] dogma" that we have; see his *A Rage for Order: Black/White Relations in the American South Since Emancipation* (New York: Oxford University Press, 1986), 98.

5. Although Lincoln figures in each of his race melodramas, Dixon followed *The Sins of the Father* with *The Southerner: A Romance of the Real Lincoln* (New York: Grossett and Dunlap, 1913). The book was "Dedicated to Our First Southern-Born President since Lincoln, my Friend and Collegemate Woodrow Wilson," and like *Sins* it was another work of revisionist history. The story depicts an agonized Lincoln forced into the war and then into Emancipation by northern senators ("Radical theorists of Congress") who anticipate plundering the postwar South. It further represents the president planning, on the eve of his assassination, to "remove negro soldiers from the country as quick as possible," then to pass laws ensuring "that two such races as the Negro and Caucasian could not live side by side in a free democracy" (543).

6. R.A. Shotwell Biography, Finding Aid for Shotwell Family Papers, Southern Historical Collection, University of North Carolina, Chapel Hill, 1–4.

7. Allen W. Trelease, *White Terror: The Ku Klux Klan Conspiracy and Southern Reconstruction* (Baton Rouge: Louisiana State University Press, 1995), 339.

8. McAfee served two years of his sentence before he was pardoned by President Grant. For details on McAfee's Klan activities, work on the Holden impeachment, and the McAfee and Holden trials and convictions, see Trelease, pp. 339–46 (also the source of the "boyhood idol" quote). On the lynching outside the Dixon home, and for many of details on Dixon's life, see the Raymond A. Cook biography, *Fire from the Flint: The Amazing Careers of Thomas Dixon* (Winston-Salem, N.C.: John F. Blair, 1968).

9. See Glenda Elizabeth Gilmore, *Gender and Jim Crow: Women and the Politics of White Supremacy in North Carolina, 1896–1920* (Chapel Hill, N.C.: University of North Carolina Press, 1996), 66.

10. See Gilmore, *Gender and Jim Crow*, especially chapters 3 and 4. On the Wilmington racial massacre, see also H. Leon Prather Sr.'s, *We Have Taken a City: Wilmington Racial Massacre and Coup of 1898* (Rutherford, N.J.: Fairleigh Dickinson University Press, 1984).

11. See "We Are Rising:" in the Cleveland *Journal* 3.35 (November 11, 1905), 1.

12. See for example, "Negro Editor Insults Thomas Dixon, Jr.," New York *Times*, January 30, 1906, 3; "T. Thomas Fortune Spurns Hand of Vulgar Dixon," in the Cleveland *Journal*, February 3, 1906, 1; and an untitled sidebar note in the New Orleans *Times Picayune*, February 1, 1906, 2.

13. Sutton E. Griggs, "A Hindering Hand: A Review of the Anti-Negro Crusade of Mr. Thomas Dixon, Jr.," in *The Hindered Hand: Or, The Reign of the Repressionist*, 3rd ed. (1905; repr., New York: AMS Press, 1969), 332–33.

14. W.E.B. DuBois, "The Problem of Tillman, Vardaman, and Thomas Dixon, Jr.," [Kansas City] *Central Christian Advocate* 49 (October 18, 1905); reprinted in Herbert Aptheker, ed., *Writings by W.E.B. DuBois in Periodicals Edited by Others, Volume 1, 1891–1909* (Millwood, N.Y.: Kraus-Thomson Organization, 1982), 265.

15. Kelly Miller, *As to "The Leopard's Spots": An Open Letter to Thomas Dixon, Jr.* (Washington, D.C.: Hayworth, 1905), 16.

16. Miller, 17.

17. See Gilmore, 105–7.

18. See Philip Dray, *At the Hands of Persons Unknown: The Lynching of Black America* (New York: Modern Library/Random House, 2002), 59–65.

19. Miller, 17.

20. John David Smith, "'My books are hard reading for a Negro': Tom Dixon and his African American Critics, 1905–1939" in Michele Gillespie and Randal Hall, eds., *Thomas Dixon Jr. and the Making of Modern America* (forthcoming).

21. Thomas Hamilton Beb Walker, *J. Johnson, or, "The Unknown Man": An Answer to Mr. Thos. Dixon's "Sins of the Fathers"* (De Land, Fla.: E.O. Painter Printing Co., 1915).

22. Williamson, *A Rage for Order*, 106. The following discussion draws from his fascinating biographical interpretation of Dixon's life, 106–16.

23. Gilmore, 68.

24. For information on the stage play's premier, see Williamson, *A Rage for Order*,. 114.

25. "Primitive Masculinity" is Anthony Rotundo's name for this formation, see *American Manhood: Transformations in Masculinity from the Revolution to the Modern Era* (New York: Basic Books, 1993), 227–32. Gail Bederman writes that "By about 1912, a new and 'savage' note began to sound more frequently in popular expressions of middle-class manhood. Increasingly, male power and authority were being described as wild, primitive, not all endangered by overcivilized decadence," and thus *a good thing* for the unified expression of white American civic identity and for its projection globally. See *Manliness and Civilization: A Cultural History of Gender and Race in the United States, 1880–1917* (Chicago, Ill.: University of Chicago Press, 1995), 157–67.

26. The year is clearly indexed when Dixon explains that Norton waited to launch his campaign until "a torpedo under an American warship lying in Havana harbor shook the nation" (197), a reference to the February 1898 attack on the battleship *Maine*. The North Carolina white supremacy campaign commenced in July of that summer. The reader's problem is that Dixon's math doesn't add up: book 1, "Sins," ends around 1871–72, with the successful impeachment of the state's governor; book 2, "Atonement," begins after "twenty years" have passed (135).

27. See Cheryl Thurber, "The Development of the Mammy Image and Mythology," in *Southern Women: Histories and Identities*, ed. Virginia Bernhard (Columbia: University of Missouri Press, 1992), 87-108; and Kenneth W. Goings, *Mammy and Uncle Mose: Black Collectibles and American Stereotyping* (Bloomington: Indiana University Press, 1994). Beginning in the 1890s, the mammy craze peaked, and Thurber finds that between 1906 and 1912 it then enters a period of "gradual decline" (96). Indeed a sign of mammy's peaking popularity were increasing calls after 1910 for public "memorials to mammy," a social movement that culminated (Thurber found) in 1923 with the United Daughters of the Confederacy proposing a mammy monument for the capital mall in Washington, D.C. (99).

28. Thurber, "The Development of the Mammy Image and Mythology," 103–5.

29. The singular ("father") suggests the title's possible origin in Euripides (from *Phrixus*, Frag. 970, according to *Bartlett's Familiar Quotations*) as well as the more familiar scripture

in Deuteronomy 5.9: "for I the Lord your God am a jealous God, visiting the sins of the fathers upon the children to the third and fourth generation of those who hate me."

30. Werner Sollors, *Neither Black Nor White Yet Both: Thematic Explorations of Interracial Literature* (Cambridge, Mass.: Harvard University Press, 1997), 330.

31. After the *New York Times* gave *The Clansman* a less than favorable review, on February 22, 1905, Dixon wrote back: "Whether *The Clansman* is literature or trash is a question about which I am losing no sleep"; quoted in Anthony Slide, *American Racist: The Life and Films of Thomas Dixon* (Lexington, Ky: University Press of Kentucky, 2004), 45.

32. Durham's novel involves complex genealogies. His black protagonist John Hayward Graham traces his "blood" through a white father descended from South Carolina planters; so does Graham's wife, Helen, the president's daughter who also descended from South Carolina elite. These details, coupled with character descriptions revealing shared facial and other physiological characteristics, suggest to readers that Helen's first attraction to Graham grows from their likeness. Interestingly, too, Durham uses that same device of the secret and secretively consummated marriage that Dixon will use in *Sins* (see Lewis Becke's *The Call of the South* [Boston: L.C. Page, 1908], 244–45) but with an added twist: Graham's belated consummation of their marriage occurs when he mistakes Helen's swoon during a terrible storm for her passionate surrender to "the demon of the [black] blood" within him (290). In effect then, he rapes her, proof of the novel's key racist warning: "What's bred in the bone will come out in the blood . . . and bad blood is more assertive than good" (69). Throughout this tale Durham's narrator and his characters refer to its great "melodrama" (for examples, see pp. 66, 128, 131, 313).

33. This is exactly the potential Walter Benn Michaels explores, through his readings of racial formations in a range of American novels from the early modern period; see his *Our America: Nativism, Modernism, and Pluralism* (Durham, N.C.: Duke University Press, 1995).

Suggestions for Further Reading

Cook, Raymond A. *Fire from the Flint: The Amazing Careers of Thomas Dixon.* Winston-Salem, N.C.: John F. Blair, 1968.

Gillman, Susan. *Blood Talk: American Race Melodrama and the Culture of the Occult.* Chicago, Il.: University of Chicago Press, 2003.

Gilmore, Glenda Elizabeth. *Gender and Jim Crow: Women and the Politics of White Supremacy in North Carolina, 1896–1920.* Chapel Hill, N.C.: University of North Carolina Press, 1996.

Gunning, Sandra. *Race, Rape, and Lynching: The Red Record of American Literature, 1890–1912.* New York: Oxford University Press, 1996.

Michaels, Walter Benn. *Our America: Nativism, Modernism, and Pluralism.* Durham, N.C.: Duke University Press, 1995.

Slide, Anthony. *American Racist: The Life and Films of Thomas Dixon.* Lexington, Ky.: University Press of Kentucky, 2004.

Sollors, Werner. "Incest and Miscegenation." *Neither Black Nor White Yet Both: Thematic Explorations of Interracial Literature.* Cambridge, Mass.: Harvard University Press, 1997, 285–335.

Williams, Linda. *Playing the Race Card: Melodramas of Black and White from Uncle Tom to O. J. Simpson.* Princeton, N.J.: Princeton University Press, 2001.

Williamson, Joel. *A Rage for Order: Black-White Relations in the American South Since Emancipation.* New York: Oxford University Press, 1986.

A Note on the Text

In March 1912, *The Sins of the Father* was published simultaneously in two editions: one by D. Appleton & Company of New York and London and one by Grosset and Dunlap Publishers of New York—the base-text for this edition. The editions are identical except for the quality of their binding and paper.

Obvious errors of spelling and punctuation were corrected for this edition. Otherwise, the editor has let stand the original text's occasional archaic spellings and locutions: for example, "marvellous" instead of "marvelous," "clew" instead of "clue," "mould" instead of "mold," and "to-day" instead of "today." Also, like many racist writers and editors prior to the 1950s, Dixon refused African American leaders' requests to show respect by capitalizing "Negro," and this edition sustains his practice.

As to still more substantive matters in the text, careful readers will note that Dixon could be careless in tallying story time. Book 2, "Atonement," unfolds its action during the summer and fall of 1898, after the successful United States' invasion of Cuba. During that period Daniel Norton thinks of himself as "scarcely forty-nine years old" (301), which would have made him a twelve-year-old boy when the Civil War began and a sixteen-year-old "major" by the war's end—claims contradicted by the statement that he had enlisted in the Confederate "ranks at eighteen" (5). Still worse, the jump of "twenty years" (135) after book 1 would have book 2 unfolding in 1887 rather than 1898. Insofar as these errors seem to derive from Dixon's larger thematic and historical intentions for the book, the editor leaves them intact for readers.

Steven Weisenburger

Book One

SIN

Chapter I

The Woman in Yellow

The young editor of *The Daily Eagle and Phoenix* straightened his tall figure from the pile of papers that smothered his desk, glanced at his foreman who stood waiting, and spoke in the quiet drawl he always used when excited:

"Just a moment—'til I read this over——"

The foreman nodded.

He scanned the scrawled pencil manuscript twice and handed it up without changing a letter:

"Set the title in heavy black-faced caps—*black*—the blackest you've got."

He read the title over again musingly, his strong mouth closing with a snap at its finish:

THE BLACK LEAGUE AND THE KU KLUX KLAN
DOWN WITH ALL SECRET SOCIETIES

The foreman took the manuscript with a laugh:

"You've certainly got 'em guessing, major——"

"Who?"

"Everybody. We've all been thinking until these editorials began that you were a leader of the Klan."

A smile played about the corners of the deep-set brown eyes as he swung carelessly back to his desk and waved the printer to his task with a friendly sweep of his long arm:

"Let 'em think again!"

A shout in the Court House Square across the narrow street caused him to lift his head with a frown:

"Salesday—of course—the first Monday—doomsday for the conquered South—God, the horror of it all!"

He laid his pencil down, walked to the window and looked out on the crowd of slouching loafers as they gathered around the auctioneer's block. The negroes outnumbered the whites two to one.

A greasy, loud-mouthed negro, as black as ink, was the auctioneer.

"Well, gemmen an' feller citizens," he began pompously, "de fust piece er property I got ter sell hain't no property 'tall—hit's dese po' folks fum de County Po' House. Fetch 'em up agin de wall so de bidders can see 'em——"

He paused and a black court attendant led out and placed in line against the weatherbeaten walls fifty or sixty inmates of the County Poor House—all of them white men and women. Most of them were over seventy years old, and one with the quickest step and brightest eye, a little man of eighty-four with snow-white hair and beard, was the son of a hero of the American Revolution. The women were bareheaded and the blazing Southern sun of August beat down piteously on their pinched faces.

The young editor's fists slowly clinched and his breath came in a deep quivering draught. He watched as in a trance. He had seen four years' service in the bloodiest war in history—seen thousands swept into eternity from a single battlefield without a tear. He had witnessed the sufferings of the wounded and dying until it became the routine of a day's work. Yet no event of all that fierce and terrible struggle had stirred his soul as the scene he was now witnessing—not even the tragic end of his father, the editor of the *Daily Eagle*—who had been burned to death in the building when Sherman's army swept the land with fire and sword. The younger man had never referred to this except in a brief, hopeful editorial in the newly christened *Eagle and Phoenix*, which he literally built on the ashes of the old paper. He had no unkind word for General Sherman or his army. It was war, and a soldier knew what that meant. He would have done the same thing under similar conditions.

Now he was brushing a tear from his cheek. A reporter at work in the adjoining room watched him curiously. He had never before thought him capable of such an emotion. A brilliant and powerful editor, he had made his paper the one authoritative organ of the white race. In the midst of riot, revolution and counter revolution his voice had the clear ring of a bugle call to battle. There was never a note of hesitation, of uncertainty or of compromise. In the fierce white heat of an unconquered spirit, he had fused the souls of his people as one. At this moment he was the one man hated and feared most by the negroid government in power, the one man most admired and trusted by the white race.

And he was young—very young—yet he had lived a life so packed with tragic events no one ever guessed his real age, twenty-four. People took him to be more than thirty and the few threads of gray about his temples, added to the impression of age and dignity. He was not handsome in the conventional sense. His figure was too tall, his cheek bones too high, the nostrils too large and his eyebrows too heavy. His great height, six feet three, invariably made him appear gaunt and serious. Though he had served the entire four years in the Confederate army, entering a private in the ranks at eighteen, emerging a major in command of a shattered regiment at twenty-two, his figure did not convey the impression of military training. He walked easily, with the long, loose stride of the Southener, his shoulders slightly stooped from the habit of incessant reading.

He was lifting his broad shoulders now in an ominous way as he folded his clenched fists behind his back and listened to the negro auctioneer.

"Come now, gemmens," he went on; "what's de lowes' offer ye gwine ter start me fer dese folks? 'Member, now, de lowes' bid gets 'em, not de highes'! 'Fore de war de black man wuz put on de block an' sole ter de *highes'* bidder! Times is changed——"

"Yas, Lawd!" shouted a negro woman.

"Times is changed, I tells ye!—now I gwine ter sell dese po' white folks ter de lowes' bidder. Whosomever'll take de Po' House and bode 'em fer de least money gits de whole bunch. An' you has de right ter make 'em all work de Po' farm. Dey kin work, too, an' don' ye fergit it. Dese here ones I fotch out here ter show ye is all soun' in wind and limb. De bedridden ones ain't here. Dey ain't but six er dem. What's de lowes' bid now, gemmens, yer gwine ter gimme ter bode 'em by de month? Look 'em all over, gemmens, I warrants 'em ter be sound in wind an' limb. Sound in wind an' limb."

The auctioneer's sonorous voice lingered on this phrase and repeated it again and again.

The watcher at the window turned away in disgust, walked back to his desk, sat down, fidgeted in his seat, rose and returned to the window in time to hear the cry:

"An' sold to Mister Abum Russ fer fo' dollars a month!"

Could it be possible that he heard aright? Abe Russ the keeper to the poor!—a drunkard, wife beater, and midnight prowler. His father before him, "Devil Tom Russ," had been a notorious character, yet he had at least one redeeming quality that saved him from contempt—a keen sense of humor. He had made his living on a ten-acre red hill farm and never used a horse or an ox. He hitched himself to the plow and made Abe seize the handles. This strange team worked the fields. No matter how hard the day's task the elder Russ never quite lost his humorous view of life. When the boy, tired and thirsty, would stop and go to the spring for water, a favorite trick of his was to place a piece of paper or a chunk of wood in the furrow a few yards ahead. When the boy returned and they approached this object, the old man would stop, lift his head and snort, back and fill, frisk and caper, plunge and kick, and finally break and run, tearing over the fields like a maniac, dragging the plow after him with the breathless boy clinging to the handles. He would then quietly unhitch himself and thrash Abe within an inch of his life for being so careless as to allow a horse to run away with him.

But Abe grew up without a trace of his father's sense of humor, picked out the strongest girl he could find for a wife and hitched her to the plow! And he permitted no pranks to enliven the tedium of work except the amusement he allowed himself of beating her at mealtimes after she had cooked his food.

He had now turned politician, joined the Loyal Black League and was the successful bidder for Keeper of the Poor. It was incredible!

The watcher was roused from his painful reverie by a reporter's voice:

"I think there's a man waiting in the hall to see you, sir."

"Who is it?"

The reporter smiled:

"Mr. Bob Peeler."

"What on earth can that old scoundrel want with me? All right—show him in."

The editor was busy writing when Mr. Peeler entered the room furtively. He was coarse, heavy and fifty years old. His red hair hung in tangled locks below his ears and a bloated double chin lapped his collar. His legs were slightly bowed from his favorite mode of travel on horseback astride a huge stallion trapped with tin and brass bespangled saddle. His supposed business was farming and the raising of blooded horses. As a matter of fact, the farm was in the hands of tenants and gambling was his real work.

Of late he had been displaying a hankering for negro politics. A few weeks before he had created a sensation by applying to the clerk of the court for a license to marry his mulatto housekeeper. It was common report that this woman was the mother of a beautiful octoroon daughter with hair exactly the color of old Peeler's. Few people had seen her. She had been away at school since her tenth year.

The young editor suddenly wheeled in his chair and spoke with quick emphasis:

"Mr. Peeler, I believe?"

The visitor's face lighted with a maudlin attempt at politeness

"Yes, sir; yes, sir!—and I'm shore glad to meet you, Major Norton!"

He came forward briskly, extending his fat mottled hand.

Norton quietly ignored the offer by placing a chair beside his desk:

"Have a seat, Mr. Peeler."

The heavy figure flopped into the chair:

"I want to ask your advice, major, about a little secret matter"—he glanced toward the door leading into the reporters' room.

The editor rose, closed the door and resumed his seat:

"Well, sir; how can I serve you?"

The visitor fumbled in his coat pocket and drew out a crumpled piece of paper which he fingered gingerly:

"I've been readin' your editorials agin' secret societies, major, and I like 'em—that's why I made up my mind to put my trust in you——"

"Why, I thought you were a member of the Loyal Black League, Mr. Peeler?"

"No, sir—it's a mistake, sir," was the smooth lying answer. "I hain't got nothin' to do with no secret society. I hate 'em all—just run your eye over that, major."

He extended the crumpled piece of paper on which was scrawled in boyish writing:

"We hear you want to marry a nigger. Our advice is to leave this country for the more congenial climate of Africa.

"By order of the Grand Cyclops, KU KLUX KLAN."

The young editor studied the scrawl in surprise:

"A silly prank of schoolboys!" he said at length.

"You think that's all?" Peeler asked dubiously.

"Certainly. The Ku Klux Klan have more important tasks on hand just now. No man in their authority sent that to you. Their orders are sealed in red ink with a crossbones and skull. I've seen several of them. Pay no attention to this—it's a fake."

"I don't think so, major—just wait a minute, I'll show you something worse than a red-ink crossbones and skull."

Old Peeler tipped to the door leading into the hallway, opened it, peered out and waved his fat hand, beckoning someone to enter.

The voice of a woman was heard outside protesting:

"No—no—I'll stay here——"

Peeler caught her by the arm and drew her within

"This is Lucy, my housekeeper, major."

The editor looked in surprise at the slender, graceful figure of the mulatto. He had pictured her coarse and heavy. He saw instead a face of the clean-cut Aryan type with scarcely a trace of negroid character. Only the thick curling hair, shining black eyes and deep yellow skin betrayed the African mother.

Peeler's eyes were fixed in a tense stare on a small bundle she carried. His voice was a queer muffled tremor as he slowly said:

"Unwrap the thing and show it to him."

The woman looked at the editor and smiled contemptuously, showing two rows of perfect teeth, as she slowly drew the brown wrapper from a strange object which she placed on the desk.

The editor picked the thing up, looked at it and laughed.

It was a tiny pine coffin about six inches long and two inches wide. A piece of glass was fitted into the upper half of the lid and beneath the glass was placed a single tube rose whose peculiar penetrating odor already filled the room.

Peeler mopped the perspiration from his brow.

"Now, what do you think of that?" he asked in an awed whisper.

In spite of an effort at self-control, Norton broke into a peal of laughter:

"It does look serious, doesn't it?"

"Serious ain't no word for it, sir! It not only looks like death, but I'm damned if it don't smell like it—smell it!"

"So it does," the editor agreed, lifting the box and breathing the perfume of the pale little flower.

"And that ain't all," Peeler whispered, "look inside of it."

He opened the lid and drew out a tightly folded scrap of paper on which was written in pencil the words:

> "You lying, hypocritical, blaspheming old scoundrel—unless you leave the country within forty-eight hours, this coffin will be large enough to hold all we'll leave of you.
>
> K. K. K."

The editor frowned and then smiled.

"All a joke, Peeler," he said reassuringly.

But Peeler was not convinced. He leaned close and his whiskey-laden breath seemed to fill the room as his fat finger rested on the word "blaspheming:"

"I don't like that word, major; it sounds like a preacher had something to do with the writin' of it. You know I've been a tough customer in my day and I used to cuss the preachers in this county somethin' frightful. Now, ye see, if they should be in this Ku Klux Klan—I ain't er skeered er their hell hereafter, but they sho' might give me a taste in this world of what they think's comin' to me in the next. I tell you that thing makes the cold chills run down my back. Now, major, I reckon you're about the level-headest and the most influential man in the countym—the question is, what shall I do to be saved?"

Again Norton laughed:

"Nothing. It's a joke, I tell you——"

"But the Ku Klux Klan ain't no joke!" persisted Peeler. "More than a thousand of 'em—some say five thousand—paraded the county two weeks ago. A hundred of 'em passed my house. I saw their white shrouds glisten in the moonlight. I said my prayers that night! I says to myself, if it don't do no good, at least it can't do no harm. I tell you, the Klan's no joke. If you think so, take a walk through that crowd in the Square to-day and see how quiet they are. Last court day every nigger that could holler was makin' a speech yellin' that old Thad Stevens was goin' to hang Andy Johnson, the President, from the White House porch, take every foot of land from the rebels and give it to the Loyal Black League. Now, by gum, there's a strange peace in Israel! I felt it this mornin' as I walked through them crowds—and comin' back to this coffin, major, the question is—what shall I do to be saved?"

"Go home and forget about it," was the smiling answer. "The Klan didn't send that thing to you or write that message."

"You think not?"

"I know they didn't. It's a forgery. A trick of some devilish boys."

Peeler scratched his red head:

"I'm glad you think so, major. I'm a thousand times obliged to you, sir. I'll sleep better to-night after this talk."

"Would you mind leaving this little gift with me, Peeler?" Norton asked, examining the neat workmanship of the coffin.

"Certainly—certainly, major, keep it. Keep it and more than welcome! It's a gift I don't crave, sir. I'll feel better to know you've got it."

The yellow woman waited beside the door until Peeler had passed out, bowed her thanks, turned and followed her master at a respectful distance.

The editor watched them cross the street with a look of loathing, muttering slowly beneath his breath:

"Oh, my country, what a problem—what a problem!"

He turned again to his desk and forgot his burden in the joy of work. He loved this work. It called for the best that's in the strongest man. It was a man's work for men. When he struck a blow he saw the dent of his hammer on the iron, and heard it ring to the limits of the state.

Dimly aware that some one had entered his room unannounced, he looked up, sprang to his feet and extended his hand in hearty greeting to a stalwart farmer who stood smiling into his face:

"Hello, MacArthur!"

"Hello, my captain! You know you weren't a major long enough for me to get used to it—and it sounds too old for you anyhow——"

"And how's the best sergeant that ever walloped a recruit?"

"Bully," was the hearty answer.

The young editor drew his old comrade in arms down into his chair and sat on the table facing him:

"And how's the wife and kids, Mac?"

"Bully," he repeated evenly and then looked up with a puzzled expression.

"Look here, Bud," he began quietly, "you've got me up a tree. These editorials in *The Eagle and Phoenix* cussin' the Klan——

"You don't like them?"

"Not a little wee bit!"

The editor smiled:

"You've got Scotch blood in you, Mac—that's what's the matter with you——"

"Same to you, sir."

"But my great-great-grandmother was a Huguenot and the French, you know, had a saving sense of humor. The Scotch are thick, Mac!"

"Well, I'm too thick to know what you mean by lambastin' our only salvation. The Ku Klux Klan have had just one parade—and there hasn't been a barn burnt in this county or a white woman scared since, and every nigger I've met to-day has taken off his hat——"

"Are you a member of the Klan, Mac?" The question was asked with his face turned away.

The farmer hesitated, looked up at the ceiling and quietly answered:

"None of your business—and that's neither here nor there—you know that every nigger is organized in that secret Black League, grinning and whispering its signs and passwords—you know that they've already begun to grip the throats of our women. The Klan's the only way to save this country from hell—what do you mean by jumpin' on it?"

"The Black League's a bad thing, Mac, and the Klan's a bad thing——"

"All right—still you've got to fight the devil with fire——"

"You don't say so?" the editor said, while a queer smile played around his serious mouth.

"Yes, by golly, I do say so," the farmer went on with increasing warmth, "and what I can't understand is how you're against 'em. You're a leader. You're a soldier—the bravest that ever led his men into the jaws of death—I know, for I've been with you—and I just come down here to-day to ask you the plain question, what do you mean?"

"The Klan *is* a band of lawless night raiders, isn't it?"

"Oh, you make me tired! What are we to do without 'em, that's the question?"

"Scotch! That's the trouble with you"—the young editor answered carelessly. "Have you a pin?"

The rugged figure suddenly straightened as though a bolt of lightning had shot down his spine.

"What's—what's that?" he gasped.

"I merely asked, have you a pin?" was the even answer, as Norton touched the right lapel of his coat with his right hand.

The farmer hesitated a moment, and then slowly ran three trembling fingers of his left hand over the left lapel of his coat, replying:

"I'm afraid not."

He looked at Norton a moment and turned pale. He had been given and had returned the signs of the Klan. It might have been an accident. The rugged face was a study of eager intensity as he put his friend to the test that would tell. He slowly thrust the fingers of his right hand into the right pocket of his trousers, the thumb protruding.

Norton quietly answered in the same way with his left hand.

The farmer looked into the smiling brown eyes of his commander for a moment and his own filled with tears. He sprang forward and grasped the outstretched hand:

"Dan Norton! I said last night to my God that you couldn't be against us! And so I came to ask—oh, why—why've you been foolin' with me?"

The editor tenderly slipped his arm around his old comrade and whispered:

"The cunning of the fox and the courage of the lion now, Mac! It was easy for our boys to die in battle while guns were thundering, fifes screaming, drums beating and the banners waving. You and I have something harder to do—we've got to live—our watchword, '*The cunning of the fox and the courage of the lion!*' I've some dangerous work to do pretty soon. The little Scalawag Governor is getting ready for us——"

"I want that job!" MacArthur cried eagerly.

"I'll let you know when the time comes."

The farmer smiled:

"I *am* a Scotchman—ain't I?"

"And a good one, too!"

With his hand on the door, the rugged face aflame with patriotic fire, he slowly repeated:

"The cunning of the fox and the courage of the lion!—And by the living God, we'll win this time, boy!"

Norton heard him laugh aloud as he hurried down the stairs. Gazing again from his window at the black clouds of negroes floating across the Square, he slowly muttered:

"Yes, we'll win this time!—but twenty years from now—I wonder!"

He took up the little black coffin and smiled at the perfection of its workmanship:

"I think I know the young gentleman who made that and he may give me trouble."

He thrust the thing into a drawer, seized his hat, strolled down a side street and slowly passed the cabinet shop of the workman whom he suspected. It was closed. Evidently the master had business outside. It was barely possible, of course, that he had gone to the galleries of the Capitol to hear the long-expected message of the Governor against the Klan. The galleries had been packed for the past two sessions in anticipation of this threatened message. The Capital city was only a town of five thousand white inhabitants and four thousand blacks. Rumors of impending political movements flew from house to house with the swiftness of village gossip.

He walked to the Capitol building by a quiet street. As he passed through the echoing corridor the rotund figure of Schlitz, the Carpetbagger, leader of the House of Representatives, emerged from the Governor's office.

The red face flushed a purple hue as his eye rested on his arch-enemy of the *Eagle and Phoenix*. He tried to smile and nodded to Norton. His smile was answered by a cold stare and a quickened step.

Schlitz had been a teamster's scullion in the Union Army. He was not even an army cook, but a servant of servants. He was now the master of the Legislature of a great Southern state and controlled its black, ignorant members with a snap of his bloated fingers. There was but one man Norton loathed with greater intensity and that was the shrewd little Scalawag Governor, the native traitor who had betrayed his people to win office. A conference of these two cronies was always an ill omen for the state.

He hurried up the winding stairs, pushed his way into a corner of the crowded galleries from which he could see every face and searched in vain for his young workman.

He stood for a moment, looked down on the floor of the House and watched a Black Parliament at work making laws to govern the children of the men who had created the Republic—watched them through fetid smoke, the vapors of stale whiskey and the deafening roar of half-drunken brutes as they voted millions in taxes, their leaders had already stolen.

The red blood rushed to his cheeks and the big veins on his slender swarthy neck stood out for a moment like drawn cords.

He hurried down to the Court House Square, walked with long, leisurely stride through the thinning crowds, and paused before a vacant lot on the opposite side of the street. A dozen or more horses were still tied to the racks provided for the accommodation of countrymen.

"Funny," he muttered, "farmers start home before sundown, and it's dusk—I wonder if it's possible!"

He crossed the street, strolled carelessly among the horses and noted that their saddles had not been removed and the still more significant fact that their saddle blankets were unusually thick. Only an eye trained to observe this fact would have noticed it. He lifted the edge of one of the blankets and saw the white and scarlet edges of a Klan costume. It was true. The young dare-devil who had sent that message to old Peeler had planned an unauthorized raid. Only a crowd of youngsters bent on a night's fun, he knew; and yet the act at this moment meant certain anarchy unless he nipped it in the bud. The Klan was a dangerous institution. Its only salvation lay in the absolute obedience of its members to the orders of an intelligent and patriotic chief. Unless the word of that chief remained the sole law of its life, a reign of terror by irresponsible fools would follow at once. As commander of the Klan in his county he must subdue this lawless element. It must be done with an iron hand and done immediately or it would be too late. His decision to act was instantaneous.

He sent a message to his wife that he couldn't get home for supper, locked his door and in three hours finished his day's work. There was ample time to head these boys off before they reached old Peeler's house. They couldn't start before eleven, yet he would take no chances. He determined to arrive an hour ahead of them.

The night was gloriously beautiful—a clear star-gemmed sky in the full tide of a Southern summer, the first week in August. He paused inside the gate of his home and drank for a moment the perfume of the roses on the lawn. The light from the window of his wife's room poured a mellow flood of welcome through the shadows beside the white, fluted columns. This home of his father's was all the wreck of war had left him and his heart gave a throb of joy to-night that it was his.

Behind the room where the delicate wife lay, a petted invalid, was the nursery. His baby boy was there, nestling in the arms of the black mammy who had nursed him twenty odd years ago. He could hear the soft crooning of her dear old voice singing the child to sleep. The heart of the young father swelled with pride. He loved his frail little wife with a deep, tender passion, but this big rosy-cheeked, laughing boy, which she had given him six months ago, he fairly worshipped.

He stopped again under the nursery window and listened to the music of the cradle. The old lullaby had waked a mocking bird in a magnolia beside the porch and he was answering her plaintive wail with a thrilling love song. By the strange law of contrast, his memory flashed over the fields of death he had trodden in the long war.

"What does it matter after all, these wars and revolutions, if God only brings with each new generation a nobler breed of men!"

He tipped softly past the window lest his footfall disturb the loved ones above, hurried to the stable, saddled his horse and slowly rode through the quiet streets of the town. On clearing the last clump of negro cabins on the outskirts his pace quickened to a gallop.

He stopped in the edge of the woods at the gate which opened from Peeler's farm on the main road. The boys would have to enter here. He would stop them at this spot.

The solemn beauty of the night stirred his soul to visions of the future, and the coming battle which his Klan must fight for the mastery of the state. The chirp of crickets, the song of katydids and the flash of fireflies became the martial music and the flaming torches of triumphant hosts he saw marching to certain victory. But the Klan he was leading was a wild horse that must be broken to the bit or both horse and rider would plunge to ruin.

There would be at least twenty or thirty of these young marauders to-night. If they should unite in defying his authority it would be a serious and dangerous situation. Somebody might be killed. And yet he waited without a fear of the outcome. He had faced odds before. He loved a battle when the enemy outnumbered him two to one. It stirred his blood. He had ridden with Forrest one night at the head of four hundred daring, ragged veterans, surrounded a crack Union regiment at two o'clock in the morning, and forced their commander to surrender 1800 men before he discovered the real strength of the attacking force. It stirred his blood to-night to know that General Forrest was the Commander-in-Chief of his own daring Clansmen.

Half an hour passed without a sign of the youngsters. He grew uneasy. Could they have dared to ride so early that they had reached the house before his arrival?

He must know at once. He opened the gate and galloped down the narrow track at a furious pace.

A hundred yards from Peeler's front gate he drew rein and listened. A horse neighed in the woods, and the piercing shriek of a woman left nothing to doubt. They were already in the midst of their dangerous comedy.

He pressed cautiously toward the gate, riding in the shadows of the overhanging trees. They were dragging old Peeler across the yard toward the roadway, followed by the pleading voice of a woman begging for his worthless life.

Realizing that the raid was now an accomplished fact, Norton waited to see what the young fools were going to do. He was not long in doubt. They dragged their panting, perspiring victim into the edge of the woods, tied him to a sapling and bared his back. The leader stepped forward holding a lighted torch whose flickering flames made an unearthly picture of the distorted features and bulging eyes.

"Mr. Peeler," began the solemn muffled voice behind the cloth mask, "for your many sins and blasphemies against God and man the preachers of this county have assembled to-night to call you to repentance——"

The terror-stricken eyes bulged further and the fat neck twisted in an effort to see how many ghastly figures surrounded him, as he gasped:

"Oh, Lord—oh, hell—are you all preachers?"

"All!" was the solemn echo from each sepulchral figure.

"Then I'm a goner—that coffin's too big——"

"Yea, verily, there'll be nothing left when we get through—Selah!" solemnly cried the leader.

"But, say, look here, brethren," Peeler pleaded between shattering teeth, "can't we compromise this thing? I'll repent and join the church. And how'll a contribution of fifty dollars each strike you? Now what do you say to that?"

The coward's voice had melted into a pious whine.

The leader selected a switch from the bundle extended by a shrouded figure and without a word began to lay on. Peeler's screams could be heard a mile.

Norton allowed them to give him a dozen lashes and spurred his horse into the crowd. There was a wild scramble to cover and most of the boys leaped to their saddles. Three white figures resolutely stood their ground.

"What's the meaning of this, sir?" Norton sternly demanded of the man who still held the switch.

"Just a little fun, major," was the sheepish answer.

"A dangerous piece of business."

"For God's sake, save me, Major Norton!" Peeler cried, suddenly waking from the spell of fear. "They've got me, sir—and it's just like I told you, they're all preachers—I'm a goner!"

Norton sprang from his horse and faced the three white figures.

"Who's in command of this crowd?"

"I am, sir!" came the quick answer from a stalwart masquerader who suddenly stepped from the shadows.

Norton recognized the young cabinet-maker's voice, and spoke in low tense tones:

"By whose authority are you using these disguises, to-night?"

"It's none of your business!"

The tall sinewy figure suddenly stiffened, stepped close and peered into the eyes of the speaker's mask: "Does my word go here to-night or must I call out a division of the Klan?"

A moment's hesitation and the eyes behind the mask fell:

"All right, sir—nothing but a boyish frolic," muttered the leader apologetically.

"Let this be the end of such nonsense," Norton said with a quiet drawl. "If I catch you fellows on a raid like this again I'll hang your leader to the first limb I find—good night."

A whistle blew and the beat of horses' hoofs along the narrow road told their hurried retreat.

Norton loosed the cords and led old Peeler to his house. As the fat, wobbling legs mounted the steps the younger man paused at a sound from behind and before he could turn a girl sprang from the shadows into his arms, and slipped to her knees, sobbing hysterically.

"Save me!—they're going to beat me—they'll beat me to death—don't let them—please—please don't let them!"

By the light from the window he saw that her hair was a deep rich red with the slightest tendency to curl and her wide dilated eyes a soft greenish grey.

He was too astonished to speak for a moment and Peeler hastened to say:

"That's our little gal, Cleo—that is—I—mean—of—course—it's Lucy's gal! She's just home from school and she's scared to death and I don't blame her!"

The girl clung to her rescuer with desperate grip, pressing her trembling form close with each convulsive sob.

The man drew the soft arms down, held them a moment and looked into the dumb frightened face. He was surprised at her unusual beauty. Her skin was a delicate creamy yellow, almost white, and her cheeks were tinged with the brownish red of ripe apple. As he looked in to her eyes he fancied that he saw a young leopardess from an African jungle looking at him through the lithe, graceful form of a Southern woman.

And then something happened in the shadows that stood out forever in his memory of that day as the turning point of his life.

Laughing at her fears, he suddenly lifted his hand and gently stroked the tangled red hair, smoothing it back from her forehead with a movement instinctive and irresistible as he would have smoothed the fur of a yellow Persian kitten.

Surprised at his act, he turned without a word and left the place.

And all the way home, through the solemn starlit night, he brooded over the strange meeting with this extraordinary girl. He forgot his fight. One thing only stood out with increasing vividness—the curious and irresistible impulse that caused him to stroke her hair. Personally he had always loathed the Southern white man who stooped and crawled through the shadows to meet such women. She was a negress and he knew it, and yet the act was instinctive and irresistible.

Why?

He asked himself the question a hundred times, and the longer he faced it the angrier he became at his stupid folly. For hours he lay awake, seeing in the darkness only the face of this girl.

Chapter II

Cleo Enters

The conference of the carpetbagger with the little Governor proved more ominous than even Norton had feared. The blow struck was so daring, so swift and unexpected it stunned for a moment the entire white race.

When the editor reached his office on the second morning after the raid, his desk was piled with telegrams from every quarter of the state. The Governor had issued a proclamation disarming every white military company and by wire had demanded the immediate surrender of their rifles to the negro Adjutant-General. The same proclamation had created an equal number of negro companies who were to receive these guns and equipments.

The negroid state Government would thus command an armed black guard of fifty thousand men and leave the white race without protection.

Evidently His Excellency was a man of ambitions. It was rumored that he aspired to the Vice-Presidency and meant to win the honor by a campaign of such brilliance that the solid negro-ruled South would back him in the National Convention.

Beyond a doubt, this act was the first step in a daring attempt inspired by the radical fanatics in Congress to destroy the structure of white civilization in the South.

And the Governor's resources were apparently boundless. President Johnson, though a native Southerner, was a puppet now in the hands of his powerful enemies who dominated Congress. These men boldly proclaimed their purpose to make the South negro territory by confiscating the property of the whites and giving it to the negroes. Their bill to do this, House

Bill Number Twenty-nine, introduced by the government leader, Thaddeus Stevens, was already in the calendar and Mr. Stevens was pressing for its passage with all the skill of a trained politician inspired by the fiercest hate. The army had been sent back into the prostrate South to enforce the edicts of Congress and the negro state government could command all the Federal troops needed for any scheme concocted.

But the little Governor had a plan up his sleeve by which he proposed to startle even the Black Radical Administration at Washington. He was going to stamp out "Rebellion" without the aid of Federal troops, reserving his right to call them finally as a last resort. That they were ready at his nod gave him the moral support of their actual presence.

That any man born of a Southern mother and reared in the South under the conditions of refinement and culture, of the high ideals and the courage of the old régime, could fall so low as to use this proclamation, struck Norton at first as impossible. He refused to believe it. There must be some misunderstanding. He sent a messenger to the Capitol for a copy of the document before he was fully convinced.

And then he laughed in sheer desperation at the farce-tragedy to which the life of a brave people had been reduced. It was his business as an editor to record the daily history of the times. For a moment in imagination he stood outside his office and looked at his work.

"Future generations simply can't be made to believe it!" he exclaimed. "It's too grotesque to be credible even to-day."

It had never occurred to him that the war was unreasonable. Its passions, its crushing cost, its bloodstained fields, its frightful cruelties were of the great movements of the race from a lower to a higher order of life. Progress could only come through struggle. War was the struggle which had to be when two great moral forces clashed. One must die, the other live. A great issue had to be settled in the Civil War, an issue raised by the creation of the Constitution itself, an issue its creators had not dared to face. And each generation of compromisers and interpreters had put it off and put it off until at last the storm of thundering guns broke from a hundred hills at once.

It had never been decided by the builders of the Republic whether it should be a mighty unified nation or a loose aggregation of smaller sovereignties. Slavery made it necessary to decide this fundamental question on which the progress of America and the future leadership of the world hung.

He could see all this clearly now. He had felt it dimly true throughout every bloody scene of the war itself. And so he had closed the eyes of the lonely dying boy with a reverent smile. It was for his country. He had died for what he believed to be right and it was good. He had stood bareheaded in solemn court martials and sentenced deserters to death, led them out in the gray morning to be shot and ordered them dumped into shallow trenches without a doubt or a moment's liesitation. He had walked over battlefields at night and heard the groans of the wounded, the sighs of the dying, the curses of the living, beneath the silent stars and felt that in the end it must be good. It was war, and war, however cruel, was inevitable—the great High Court of Life and Death for the nations of earth.

But this base betrayal which had followed the honorable surrender of a brave, heroic army—this wanton humiliation of a ruined people by pot-house politicians—this war on the dead, the wounded, the dying, and their defenseless women—this enthronement of Savagery, Superstition, Cowardice and Brutality in high places where Courage and Honor and Chivalry had ruled—these vandals and camp followers and vultures provoking violence and exciting crime, set to rule a brave people who had risked all for a principle and lost—this was a nightmare; it was the reduction of human society to an absurdity!

For a moment he saw the world red. Anger, fierce and cruel, possessed him. The desire to kill gripped and strangled until he could scarcely breathe.

Nor did it occur to this man for a moment that he could separate his individual life from the life of his people. His paper was gaining in circulation daily. It was paying a good dividend now and would give his loved ones the luxuries he had dreamed for them. The greater the turmoil the greater his profits would be. And yet this idea never once flashed through his mind. His people were of his heart's blood. He had no life apart from them. Their joys were his, their sorrows his, their shame his. This proclamation of a traitor to his race struck him in the face as a direct personal insult. The hot shame of it found his soul.

When the first shock of surprise and indignation had spent itself, he hurried to answer his telegrams. His hand wrote now with the eager, sure touch of a master who knew his business. To every one he sent in substance the same message:

"Submit and await orders."

As he sat writing the fierce denunciation of this act of the Chief Executive of the state, he forgot his bitterness in the thrill of life that meant each day a new adventure. He was living in an age whose simple record must remain more incredible than the tales of the Arabian Nights. And the spell of its stirring call was now upon him.

The drama had its comedy moments, too. He could but laugh at the sorry figures the little puppets cut who were strutting for a day in pomp and splendor. Their end was as sure as the sweep of eternal law. Water could not be made to run up hill by the proclamation of a Governor.

He had made up his mind within an hour to give the Scalawag a return blow that would be more swift and surprising than his own. On the little man's reception of that counter stroke would hang the destiny of his administration and the history of the state for the next generation.

On the day the white military companies surrendered their arms to their negro successors something happened that was not on the programme of the Governor.

The Ku Klux Klan held its second grand parade. It was not merely a dress affair. A swift and silent army of drilled, desperate men, armed and disguised, moved with the precision of clockwork at the command of one mind. At a given hour the armory of every negro military company in the state was broken open and its guns recovered by the white and scarlet cavalry of the "Invisible Empire."

Within the next hour every individual negro in the state known to be in possession of a gun or pistol was disarmed. Resistance was futile. The attack was so sudden and so unexpected, the attacking party so overwhelming at the moment, each black man surrendered without a blow and a successful revolution was accomplished in a night without a shot or the loss of a life.

Next morning the Governor paced the floor of his office in the Capitol with the rage of a maddened beast, and Schlitz, the Carpetbagger, was summoned for a second council of war. It proved to be a very important meeting in the history of His Excellency.

The editor sat at his desk that day smiling in quiet triumph as he read the facetious reports wired by his faithful lieutenants from every district of the Klan. An endless stream of callers had poured through his modest little room and prevented any attempt at writing. He had turned the columns over to his assistants and the sun was just sinking in a smother of purple glory when he turned from his window and began to write his leader for the day.

It was an easy task. A note of defiant power ran through a sarcastic warning to the Governor that found the quick. The editorial flashed with wit and stung with bitter epigram. And there was in his consciousness of power a touch of cruelty that should have warned the Scalawag against his next act of supreme folly.

But His Excellency had bad advisers, and the wheels of Fate moved swiftly toward the appointed end.

Norton wrote this editorial with a joy that gave its crisp sentences the ring of inspired leadership. He knew that every paper in the state read by white men and women would copy it and he already felt in his heart the reflex thrill of its call to his people.

He had just finished his revision of the last paragraph when a deep, laughing voice beside his chair slowly said:

"May I come in?"

He looked up with a start to find the tawny figure of the girl whose red hair he had stroked that night bowing and smiling. Her white, perfect teeth gleamed in the gathering twilight and her smile displayed two pretty dimples in the brownish red cheeks.

"I say, may I come in?" she repeated with a laugh.

"It strikes me you are pretty well in," Norton said good-humoredly.

"Yes, I didn't have any cards. So I came right up. It's getting dark and nobody saw me——"

The editor frowned and moved uneasily.

"You're alone, aren't you?" she asked.

"The others have all gone to supper, I believe."

"Yes, I waited 'til they left. I watched from the Square 'til I saw them go."

"Why?" he asked sharply.

"I don't know. I reckon I was afraid of 'em."

"And you're not afraid of me?" he laughed.

"No."

"Why not?"

"Because I know you."

Norton smiled:

"You wish to see me?"

"Yes."

"Is there anything wrong at Mr. Peeler's?"

"No, I just came to thank you for what you did and see if you wouldn't let me work for you?"

"Work? Where—here?"

"Yes. I can keep the place clean. My mother said it was awful. And, honest, it's worse than I expected. It doesn't look like it's been cleaned in a year."

"I don't believe it has," the editor admitted.

"Let me keep it decent for you."

"Thanks, no. It seems more home-like this way."

"Must it be so dirty?" she asked, looking about the room and picking up the scattered papers from the floor.

Norton, watching her with indulgent amusement at her impudence, saw that she moved her young form with a rhythmic grace that was perfect. The simple calico dress, with a dainty little check, fitted her perfectly. It was cut low and square at the neck and showed the fine lines of a beautiful throat. Her arms were round and finely shaped and bare to an inch above the elbows. The body above the waistline was slender, and the sinuous free movement of her figure showed that she wore no corset. Her step was as light as a cat's and her voice full of good humor and the bubbling spirits of a perfectly healthy female animal.

His first impulse was to send her about her business with a word of dismissal. But when she laughed it was with such pleasant assurance and such faith in his friendliness it was impossible to be rude.

She picked up the last crumpled paper and laid it on a table beside the wall, turned and said softly:

"Well, if you don't want me to clean up for you, anyhow, I brought you some flowers for your room—they're outside."

She darted through the door and returned in a moment with an armful of roses.

"My mother let me cut them from our yard, and she told me to thank you for coming that night. They'd have killed us if you hadn't come."

"Nonsense, they wouldn't have touched either you or your mother!"

"Yes, they would, too. Goodness—haven't you anything to put the flowers in?"

She tipped softly about the room, holding the roses up and arranging them gracefully.

Norton watched her with a lazy amused interest. He couldn't shake off the impression that she was a sleek young animal, playful and irresponsible, that had strayed from home and wandered into his office. And he loved animals. He never passed a stray dog or a cat without a friendly word of greeting. He had often laid on his lounge at home, when tired, and watched a kitten play an hour with unflagging interest. Every movement of this girl's lithe young body suggested such a scene—especially the velvet tread of her light foot, and the delicate motions of her figure followed suddenly by a sinuous quick turn and a childish laugh or cry. The faint shadows of negro blood in her creamy skin and the purring gentleness of her voice seemed part of the gathering twilight. Her eyes were apparently twice the size as when first he saw them, and the pupils, dilated in the dusk, flashed with unusual brilliance.

She had wandered into the empty reporters' room without permission looking for a vase, came back and stood in the doorway laughing:

"This is the dirtiest place I ever got into in my life. Gracious! Isn't there a thing to put the flowers in?"

The editor, roused from his reveries, smiled and answered:

"Put them in the pitcher."

"Why, yes, of course, the pitcher!" she cried, rushing to the little washstand.

"Why, there isn't a drop of water in it—I'll go to the well and get some."

She seized the pitcher, laid the flowers down in the bowl, darted out the door and flew across the street to the well in the Court House Square.

The young editor walked carelessly to the window and watched her. She simply couldn't get into an ungraceful attitude. Every movement was instinct with vitality. She was alive to her finger tips. Her body swayed in perfect rhythmic unison with her round, bare arms as she turned the old-fashioned rope windlass, drew the bucket to the top and dropped it easily on the wet wooden lids that flapped back in place.

She was singing now a crooning, half-savage melody her mother had taught her. The low vibrant notes of her voice, deep and tender and quivering with a strange intensity, floated across the street through the gathering shadows. The voice had none of the light girlish quality of her age of eighteen, but rather the full passionate power of a woman of twenty-five. The distance, the deepening shadows and the quiet of the town's lazy life, added to the dreamy effectiveness of the song.

"Beautiful!" the man exclaimed. "The negro race will give the world a great singer some day——"

And then for the first time in his life the paradox of his personal attitude toward this girl and his attitude in politics toward the black race struck him as curious. He had just finished an editorial in which he had met the aggressions of the negro and his allies with the fury, the scorn, the defiance, the unyielding ferocity with which the Anglo-Saxon conqueror has always treated his inferiors. And yet he was listening to the soft tones of this girl's voice with a smile as he watched with good-natured indulgence the light gleam mischievously from her impudent big eyes while she moved about his room.

Yet this was not to be wondered at. The history of the South and the history of slavery made such a paradox inevitable. The long association with the individual negro in the intimacy of home life had broken down the barriers of personal race repugnance. He had grown up with negro boys and girls as playmates. He had romped and wrestled with them. Every servant in every home he had ever known had been a negro. The first human face he remembered bending over his cradle was a negro woman's. He had fallen asleep in her arms times without number. He had found refuge there against his mother's stern commands and sobbed out on her breast the story of his fancied wrongs and always found consolation. "Mammy's darlin'" was always right—the world cruel and wrong! He had loved this old nurse since he could remember. She was now nursing his own and he would defend her with his life without a moment's hesitation.

And so it came about inevitably that while he had swung his white and scarlet legions of disguised Clansmen in solid line against the Governor and smashed his negro army without the loss of a single life, he was at the same moment proving himself defenseless against the silent and deadly purpose that had already shaped itself in the soul of this sleek, sensuous young animal. He was actually smiling with admiration at the beautiful picture he saw as she lifted the white pitcher, placed it on the crown of red hair, and crossed the street.

She was still softly singing as she entered the room and arranged the flowers in pretty confusion.

Norton had lighted his lamp and seated himself at his desk again. She came close and looked over his shoulder at the piles of papers.

"How on earth can you work in such a mess?" she asked with a laugh.

"Used to it," he answered without looking up from the final reading of his editorial.

"What's that you've written?"

The impudent greenish gray eyes bent closer.

"Oh, a little talk to the Governor——"

"I bet it's a hot one. Peeler says you don't like the Governor—read it to me!"

The editor looked up at the mischievous young face and laughed aloud:

"I'm afraid you wouldn't understand it."

The girl joined in the laugh and the dimples in the reddish brown cheeks looked prettier than ever. "Maybe I wouldn't," she agreed.

He resumed his reading and she leaned over his chair until he felt the soft touch of her shoulder against his. She was staring at his paste-pot, extended her tapering, creamy finger and touched the paste.

"What in the world's that?" she cried, giggling again.

"Paste."

Another peal of silly laughter echoed through the room.

"Lord, I thought it was mush and milk—I thought it was your supper!—don't you eat no supper?"

"Sometimes."

The editor looked up with a slight frown and said:

"Run along now, child, I've got to work. And tell your mother I'm obliged for the flowers."

"I'm not going back home——"

"Why not?"

"I'm scared out there. I've come in town to live with my aunt."

"Well, tell her when you see her."

"Please let me clean this place up for you?" she pleaded.

"Not to-night."

"To-morrow morning, then? I'll come early and every morning—please—let me—it's all I can do to thank you. I'll do it a month just to show you how pretty I can keep it and then you can pay me if you want me. It's a bargain, isn't it?"

The editor smiled, hesitated, and said:

"All right—every morning at seven."

"Thank you, major—good night!"

She paused at the door and her white teeth gleamed in the shadows. She turned and tripped down the stairs, humming again the strangely appealing song she had sung at the well.

Chapter III

A Beast Awakes

Within a week Norton bitterly regretted the arrangement he had made with Cleo. Not because she had failed to do her work properly, but precisely because she was doing it so well. She had apparently made it the sole object of her daily thought and the only task to which she devoted her time.

He couldn't accustom his mind to the extraordinary neatness with which she kept the office. The clean floor, the careful arrangement of the chairs, the neat piles of exchanges laid on a table she had placed beside his desk, and the vase of fresh flowers he found each morning, were constant reminders of her personality which piqued his curiosity and disturbed his poise.

He had told her to come at seven every morning. It was his habit to reach the office and begin reading the exchanges by eight-thirty and he had not expected to encounter her there. She had always managed, however, to linger over her morning tasks until his arrival, and never failed to greet him pleasantly and ask if there were anything else she could do. She also insisted on coming at noon to fill his pitcher and again just before supper to change the water in the vase of flowers.

At this last call she always tried to engage him in a few words of small talk. At first this program made no impression on his busy brain except that she was trying to prove her value as a servant. Gradually, however, he began to notice that her dresses were cut with remarkable neatness for a girl of her position and that she showed a rare talent in selecting materials becoming to her creamy yellow skin and curling red hair.

He observed, too, that she had acquired the habit of hanging about his desk when finishing her tasks and had a queer way of looking at him and laughing.

She began to make him decidedly uncomfortable and he treated her with indifference. No matter how sullen the scowl with which he greeted her, she was always smiling and humming snatches of strange songs. He sought for an excuse to discharge her and could find none. She had the instincts of a perfect servant—intelligent, careful and loyal. She never blundered over the papers on his desk. She seemed to know instinctively what was worthless and what was valuable, and never made a mistake in rearranging the chaotic piles of stuff he left in his wake.

He thought once for just a moment of the possibility of her loyalty to the negro race. She might in that case prove a valuable spy to the Governor and his allies. He dismissed the idea as preposterous. She never associated with negroes if she could help it and apparently was as innocent as a babe of the nature of the terrific struggle in which he was engaged with the negroid government of the state.

And yet she disturbed him deeply and continuously, as deeply sometimes when absent as when present.

Why?

He asked himself the question again and again. Why should he dislike her? She did her work promptly and efficiently, and for the first time within his memory the building was really fit for human habitation.

At last he guessed the truth and it precipitated the first battle of his life with the beast that slumbered within. Feeling her physical nearness more acutely than usual at dusk and noting that she had paused in her task near his desk, he slowly lifted his eyes from the paper he was reading and, before she realized it, caught the look on her face when off guard. The girl was in love with him. It was as clear as day now that he had the key to her actions the past week. For this reason she had come and for this reason she was working with such patience and skill.

His first impulse was one of rage. He had little of the vanity of the male animal that struts before the female. His pet aversion was the man of his class who lowered himself to vulgar association with such girls. The fact that, at this time in the history of the South, such intrigues were common made his determination all the more bitter as a leader of his race to stand for its purity.

He suddenly swung in his chair, determined to dismiss her at once with as few words as possible.

She leaped gracefully back with a girlish laugh, so soft, low and full of innocent surprise, the harsh words died on his lips.

"Lordy, major," she cried, "how you scared me! I thought you had a fit. Did a pin stick you—or maybe a flea bit you?"

She leaned against the mantel laughing, her white teeth gleaming.

He hesitated a moment, his eyes lingered on the graceful pose of her young figure, his ear caught the soft note of friendly tenderness in her voice and he was silent.

"What's the matter?" she asked, stepping closer.

"Nothing."

"Well, you made an awful fuss about it!"

"Just thought of something—suddenly——"

"I thought you were going to bite my head off and then that something bit you!"

Again she laughed and walked slowly to the door, her greenish eyes watching him with studied carelessness, as a cat a mouse. Every movement of her figure was music, her smile contagious, and, by a subtle mental telepathy, she knew that the man before her felt it, and her heart was singing a savage song of triumph. She could wait. She had everything to gain and nothing to lose. She belonged to the pariah world of the Negro. Her love was patient, joyous, insistent, unconquerable.

It was unusually joyous to-night because she felt without words that the mad desires that burned a living fire in every nerve of her young body had scorched the man she had marked her own from the moment she had first laid eyes on his serious, aristocratic face—for back of every hysterical cry that came from her lips that night in the shadows beside old Peeler's house lay the sinister purpose of a mad love that had leaped full grown from the deeps of her powerful animal nature.

She paused in the doorway and softly said:

"Good night."

The tone of her voice was a caress and the bold eyes laughed a daring challenge straight into his.

He stared at her a moment, flushed, turned pale and answered in a strained voice:

"Good night, Cleo."

But it was not a good night for him. It was a night never to be forgotten. Until after twelve he walked beneath the stars and fought the Beast—the Beast with a thousand heads and a thousand legs; the Beast that had been bred in the bone and sinew of generations of ancestors, wilful, cruel, courageous conquerors of the world. Before its ravenous demands the words of mother, teacher, priest and lawgiver were as chaff before the whirlwind—the Beast demanded his own! Peace came at last with the vision of a baby's laughing face peeping at him from the arms of a frail little mother.

He made up his mind and hurried home. He would get rid of this girl to-morrow and never again permit her shadow to cross his pathway. With other men of more sluggish temperament, position, dignity, the responsibility of leadership, the restraints of home and religion might be the guarantee of safety under such temptations. He didn't propose to risk it. He understood now why he was so nervous and distracted in her presence. The mere physical proximity to such a creature, vital, magnetic, unmoral, beautiful and daring, could only mean one thing to a man of his age and inheritance—a temptation so fierce that yielding could only be a question of time and opportunity.

And when he told her the next morning that she must not come again she was not surprised, but accepted his dismissal without a word of protest.

With a look of tenderness she merely said:

"I'm sorry."

"Yes," he went on curtly, "you annoy me; I can't write while you are puttering around, and I'm always afraid you'll disturb some of my papers."

She laughed in his face, a joyous, impudent, good-natured, ridiculous laugh, that said more eloquently than words:

"I understand your silly excuse. You're afraid of me. You're a big coward. Don't worry, I can wait. You'll come to me. And if not, I'll find you—for I shall be near—and now that you know and fear, I shall be very near!"

She moved shyly to the door and stood framed in its white woodwork, an appealing picture of dumb regret.

She had anticipated this from the first. And from the moment she threw the challenge into his eyes the night before, saw him flush and pale beneath it, she knew it must come at once, and was prepared. There was no use to plead and beg or argue. It would be a waste of breath with him in this mood.

Besides, she had already found a better plan.

So when he began to try to soften his harsh decision with kindly words she only smiled in the friendliest possible way, stepped back to his desk, extended her hand, and said:

"Please let me know if you need me. I'll do anything on earth for you, major. Good-by."

It was impossible to refuse the gracefully outstretched hand. The Southern man had been bred from the cradle to the most intimate and friendly personal relations with the black folks who were servants in the house. Yet the moment he touched her hand, felt its soft warm pressure and looked into the depths of her shining eyes he wished that he had sent her away with downright rudeness.

But it was impossible to be rude with this beautiful young animal that purred at his side. He started to say something harsh, she laughed and he laughed.

She held his hand clasped in hers for a moment and slowly said:

"I haven't done anything wrong, have I, major?"

"No."

"You are not mad at me for anything?"

"No, certainly not."

"I wonder why you won't let me work here?"

She looked about the room and back at him, speaking slowly, musingly, with an impudence that left little doubt in his mind that she suspected the real reason and was deliberately trying to tease him.

He flushed, hurriedly withdrew his hand and replied carelessly:

"You bother me—can't work when you're fooling around."

"All right, good-bye."

He turned to his work and she was gone. He was glad she was out of his sight and out of his life forever. He had been a fool to allow her in the building at all.

He could concentrate his mind now on his fight with the Governor.

Chapter IV

The Arrest

The time had come in Norton's fight when he was about to be put to a supreme test.

The Governor was preparing the most daring and sensational movement of his never-to-be-forgotten administration. The audacity and thoroughness with which the Klan had disarmed and made ridiculous his army of fifty thousand negroes was at first a stunning blow. In vain Schlitz stormed and pleaded for National aid.

"You must ask for Federal troops without a moment's delay," he urged desperately.

The Scalawag shook his head with quiet determination.

"Congress, under the iron rule of Stevens, will send them, I grant you——"

"Then why hesitate?"

"Because their coming would mean that I have been defeated on my own soil, that my administration of the state is a failure."

"Well, isn't it?"

"No; I'll make good my promises to the men in Washington who have backed me. They are preparing to impeach the President, remove him from office and appoint a dictator in his stead. I'll show them that I can play my part in the big drama, too. I am going to deliver this state bound hand and foot into their hands, with a triumphant negro electorate in the saddle, or I'll go down in ignominious defeat."

"You'll go down, all right—without those troops—mark my word," cried the Carpetbagger.

"All right, I'll go down flying my own flag."

"You're a fool!" Schlitz roared. "Union troops are our only hope!"

His Excellency kept his temper. The little ferret eyes beneath their bushy brows were drawn to narrow lines as he slowly said:

"On the other hand, my dear Schlitz, I don't think I could depend on Federal troops if they were here."

"No?" was the indignant sneer.

"Frankly I do not," was the even answer. "Federal officers have not shown themselves very keen about executing the orders of Reconstruction Governors. They have often pretended to execute them and in reality treated us with contempt. They hold, in brief, that they fought to preserve the Union, not to make negroes rule over white men! The task before us is not to their liking. I don't trust them for a moment. I have a better plan——"

"What?"

"I propose to raise immediately an army of fifty thousand loyal white men, arm and drill them without delay——"

"Where'll you get them?" Schlitz cried incredulously.

"I'll find them if I have to drag the gutters for every poor white scamp in the state. They'll be a tough lot, maybe, but they'll make good soldiers. A soldier is a man who obeys orders, draws his pay, and asks no questions——"

"And then what?"

"And then, sir!——"

The Governor's leathery little face flushed as he sprang to his feet and paced the floor of his office in intense excitement.

"I'll tell you what then!" Schlitz cried with scorn.

The pacing figure paused and eyed his tormentor, lifting his shaggy brows:

"Yes?"

"And then," the Carpetbagger answered, "the Ku Klux Klan will rise in a night, jump on your mob of ragamuffins, take their guns and kick them back into the gutter."

"Perhaps," the Governor said, musingly, "if I give them a chance! But I won't!"

"You won't? How can you prevent it?"

"Very simply. I'll issue a proclamation suspending the *writ* of *habeas corpus*——"

"But you have no right," Schlitz gasped. The ex-scullion had been studying law the past two years and aspired to the Supreme Court bench.

"My right is doubtful, but it will go in times of revolution. I'll suspend the *writ*, arrest the leaders of the Klan without warrant, put them in jail and hold them there without trial until the day after the election."

Schlitz's eyes danced as he sprang forward and extended his fat hand to the Scalawag:

"Governor, you're a great man! Only a great mind would dare such a plan. But do you think your life will be safe?"

The little figure was drawn erect and the ferret eyes flashed:

"The Governor of a mighty commonwealth—they wouldn't dare lift their little finger against me."

Schlitz shook his head dubiously.

"A pretty big job in times of peace—to suspend the civil law, order wholesale arrests without warrants by a ragged militia and hold your men without trial——"

"I like the job!" was the quick answer. "I'm going to show the smart young man who edits the paper in this town that he isn't running the universe."

Again the adventurer seized the hand of his chief:

"Governor, you're a great man! I take my hat off to you, sir."

His Excellency smiled, lifted his sloping shoulders, moistened his thin lips and whispered:

"Not a word now to a living soul until I strike——"

"I understand, sir, not a word," the Carpetbagger replied in low tones as he nervously fumbled his hat and edged his way out of the room.

The editor received the Governor's first move in the game with contempt. It was exactly what he had expected—this organization of white renegades, thieves, loafers, cut-throats, and deserters. It was the last resort of desperation. Every day, while these dirty ignorant recruits were being organized and drilled, he taunted the Governor over the personnel of his "Loyal" army. He began the publication of the history of its officers and men. These biographical stories were written with a droll humor that kept the whole state in a good-humored ripple of laughter and inspired the convention that nominated a complete white man's ticket to renewed enthusiasm.

And then the bolt from the blue—the Governor's act of supreme madness!

As the editor sat at his desk writing an editorial congratulating the state on the brilliant ticket that the white race had nominated and predicting its triumphant election, in spite of negroes, thieves, cut-throats, Scalawags and Carpetbaggers, a sudden commotion on the sidewalk in front of his office stopped his pencil in the midst of an unfinished word.

He walked to the window and looked out. By the flickering light of the street lamp he saw an excited crowd gathering in the street.

A company of the Governor's new guard had halted in front. An officer ripped off the palings from the picket fence beside the building and sent a squad of his men to the rear.

The tramp of heavy feet on the stairs was heard and the dirty troopers crowded into the editor's room, muskets in hand, cocked, and their fingers on the triggers.

Norton quietly drew the pencil from his ear, smiled at the mottled group of excited men, and spoke in his slow drawl:

"And why this excitement, gentlemen?"

The captain stepped forward:

"Are you Major Daniel Norton?"

"I am, sir."

"You're my prisoner."

"Show your warrant!" was the quick challenge.

"I don't need one, sir."

"Indeed! And since when is this state under martial law?"

"Will you go peaceable?" the captain asked roughly.

"When I know by whose authority you make this arrest."

The editor walked close to the officer, drew himself erect, his hands clenched behind his back and held the man's eye for a moment with a cold stare.

The captain hesitated and drew a document from his pocket.

The editor scanned it hastily and suddenly turned pale:

"A proclamation suspending the *writ* of *habeas corpus*—impossible!"

The captain lifted his dirty palms:

"I reckon you can read!"

"Oh, yes, I can read it, captain—still it's impossible. You can't suspend the law of gravitation by saying so on a scrap of paper——"

"You are ready to go?"

The editor laughed:

"Certainly, certainly—with pleasure, I assure you."

The captain lifted his hand and his men lowered their guns. The editor seized a number of blank writing pads, a box of pencils, put on his hat and called to his assistants:

"I'm moving my office temporarily to the county jail, boys. It's quieter over there. I can do better work. Send word to my home that I'm all right and tell my wife not to worry for a minute. Every man to his post now and the liveliest paper ever issued! And on time to the minute."

The printers had crowded into the room and a ringing cheer suddenly startled the troopers.

The foreman held an ugly piece of steel in his hand and every man seemed to have hold of something. "Give the word, chief!" the foreman cried.

The editor smiled:

"Thanks, boys, I understand. Go back to your work. You can help best that way."

The men dropped their weapons and crowded to the door, jeering and howling in derision at the awkward squad as they stumbled down the stairs after their commander, who left the building holding tightly to the editor's arm, as if at any moment he expected an escape or a rescue.

The procession wended its way to the jail behind the Court House through a crowd of silent men who merely looked at the prisoner, smiled and nodded to him over the heads of his guard.

An ominous quiet followed the day's work. The Governor was amazed at the way his sensational coup was received. He had arrested and thrown into jail without warrant the leaders of the white party in every county in the state. He was absolutely sure that these men were the leaders of the Ku Klux Klan, the one invisible but terrible foe he really feared.

He had expected bluster, protests, mass meetings and fiery resolutions. Instead his act was received with a silence that was uncanny. In vain his Carpetbagger lieutenant congratulated him on the success of his Napoleonic move.

His little ferret eyes snapped with suppressed excitement.

"But what the devil is the meaning of this silence, Schlitz?" he asked with a tremor.

"They're stunned, I tell you. It was a master stroke. They're a lot of cowards and sneaks, these night raiders, anyhow. It only took a bold act of authority to throw them into a panic."

The Scalawag shook his head thoughtfully:

"Doesn't look like a panic to me—I'm uneasy——"

"The only possible mistake you've made was the arrest of Norton."

"Yes, I know public sentiment in the North don't like an attempt to suppress free speech, but I simply had to do it. Damn him, I've stood his abuse as long as I'm going to. Besides his dirty sheet is at the bottom of all our trouble."

When the Governor scanned his copy of the next morning's *Eagle and Phoenix* his feeling of uneasiness increased.

Instead of the personal abuse he had expected from the young firebrand, he read a long, carefully written editorial reviewing the history of the great *writ* of *habeas corpus* in the evolution of human freedom. The essay closed with the significant statement that no Governor in the records of the state or the colony had ever dared to repeal or suspend this guarantee of Anglo-Saxon liberty—not even for a moment during the chaos of the Civil War.

But the most disquieting feature of this editorial was the suggestive fact that it was set between heavy mourning lines and at the bottom of it stood a brief paragraph enclosed in even heavier black bands:

> "We regret to announce that the state is at present without a chief executive. Our late unlamented Governor passed away in a fit of insanity at three o'clock yesterday."

When the little Scalawag read the sarcastic obituary he paled for a moment and the hand which held the paper trembled so violently he was compelled to lay it on the table to prevent his secretary from noting his excitement.

For the first time in the history of the state an armed guard was stationed at the door of the Governor's mansion that night.

The strange calm continued. No move was made by the negroid government to bring the imprisoned men to trial and apparently no effort was being made by the men inside the jails to regain their liberty.

Save that his editorials were dated from the county jail, no change had occurred in the daily routine of the editor's life. He continued his series of articles on the history of the state each day, setting them in heavy black mourning lines. Each of these editorials ended with an appeal to the patriotism of the reader. And the way in which he told the simple story of each step achieved in the blood-marked struggle for liberty had a punch in it that boded ill for the little man who had set himself the task of dictatorship for a free people.

No reference was made in the *Eagle and Phoenix* to the Governor. He was dead. The paper ignored his existence. Each day of this ominous peace among his enemies increased the terror which had gripped the little Scalawag from the morning he had read his first obituary. The big black rules down the sides of those editorials seemed a foot wide now when he read them.

Twice he seated himself at his desk to order the editor's release and each time cringed and paused at the thought of the sneers with which his act would be greeted. He was now between the devil and the deep sea. He was afraid to retreat and dared not take the next step forward. If he could hold his ground for two weeks longer, and carry the election by the overwhelming majority he had planned, all would be well. Such a victory, placing him in power for four years and giving him an obedient negro Legislature once more to do his bidding, would strike terror to his foes and silence their assaults. The negro voters far outnumbered the whites, and victory was a certainty. And so he held his ground—until something happened!

It began in a semi-tropical rain storm that swept the state. All day it poured in blinding torrents, the wind steadily rising in velocity until at noon it was scarcely possible to walk the streets.

At eight o'clock the rain ceased to fall and, by nine glimpses of the moon could be seen as the fast flying clouds parted for a moment. But for these occasional flashes of moonlight the night was pitch dark. The Governor's company of nondescript soldiers in camp at the Capitol, drenched with rain, had abandoned their water-soaked tents for the more congenial atmosphere of the low dives and saloons of the negro quarters.

The minute the rain ceased to fall, Norton's wife sent his supper—but to-night by a new messenger. Cleo smiled at him across the little table as she skillfully laid the cloth, placed the dishes and set a tiny vase of roses in the center.

"You see," she began, smiling, "your wife needed me and I'm working at your house now, major."

"Indeed!"

"Yes. Mammy isn't well and I help with the baby. He's a darling. He loved me the minute I took him in my arms and hugged him."

"No doubt."

"His little mother likes me, too. I can pick her up in my arms and carry her across the room. You wouldn't think I'm so strong, would you?"

"Yes—I would," he answered slowly, studying her with a look of increasing wonder at her audacity.

"You're not mad at me for being there, are you? You can't be—mammy wants me so"—she paused—"Lordy, I forgot the letter!"

She drew from her bosom a note from his wife. He looked curiously at a smudge where it was sealed and, glancing at the girl who was busy with the tray, opened and read:

> "I have just received a message from MacArthur's daughter that your life is to be imperilled to-night by a dangerous raid. Remember your helpless wife and baby. Surely there are trusted men who can do such work. You have often told me that no wise general ever risks his precious life on the firing line. You are a soldier, and know this. Please, dearest, do not go. Baby and little mother both beg of you!"

Norton looked at Cleo again curiously. He was sure that the seal of this note had been broken and its message read by her.

"Do you know what's in this note, Cleo?" he asked sharply.

"No, sir!" was the quick answer.

He studied her again closely. She was on guard now. Every nerve alert, every faculty under perfect control. He was morally sure she was lying and yet it could only be idle curiosity or jealous interest in his affairs that prompted the act. That she should be an emissary of the Governor was absurd.

"It's not bad news, I hope?" she asked with an eagerness that was just a little too eager. The man caught the false note and frowned.

"No," he answered carelessly. "It's of no importance." He picked up a pad and wrote a hurried answer:

> "Don't worry a moment, dear. I am not in the slightest danger. I know a soldier's duty and I'll not forget it. Sleep soundly, little mother and baby mine!"

He folded the sheet of paper and handed it to her without sealing it. She was watching him keenly. His deep, serious eyes no longer saw her. His body was there, but the soul was gone. The girl had never seen him in this mood. She was frightened. His life *was* in danger. She knew it now by an unerring instinct. She would watch the jail and see what happened. She might do something to win his friendship, and then—the rest would be easy. Her hand trembled as she took the note.

"Give this to Mrs. Norton at once," he said, "and tell her you found me well and happy in my work."

"Yes, sir," the soft voice answered mechanically as she picked up the tray and left the room watching him furtively.

Chapter V

The Rescue

Cleo hurried to the house, delivered the message, rocked the baby to sleep and quietly slipped through the lawn into the street and back to the jail.

A single guard kept watch at the door. She saw him by a flash of moonlight and then passed so close she could have touched the long old-fashioned musket he carried loosely across his shoulder.

The cat-like tread left no echo and she took her stand in the under-brush that had pushed its way closer and closer until its branches touched the rear walls of the jail. For two hours she stood amid the shadows, her keen young ears listening and her piercing eyes watching. Again and again she counted the steps the sentinel made as he walked back and forth in front of the entrance to the jail.

She knew from the sound that he passed the corner of the building for three steps in full view from her position, could she but see him through the darkness. Twice she had caught a glimpse of his stupid face as the moon flashed a moment of light through a rift of clouds.

"The Lord help that idiot," she muttered, "if the major's men want to pass him to-night!"

She turned with a sharp start. The bushes softly parted behind her and a stealthy step drew near. Her heart stood still. She was afraid to breathe. They wouldn't hurt her if they only knew she was the major's friend. But if they found and recognized her as old Peeler's half-breed daughter, they might kill her on the spot as a spy.

She hadn't thought of this terrible possibility before. It was too late now to think. To run meant almost certain death. She flattened her figure against the wall of the jail and drew the underbrush close completely covering her form.

She stood motionless and as near breathless as possible until the two men who were approaching a step at a time had passed. At the corner of the jail they stopped within three feet of her. She could hear every word of their conference.

"Now, Mac, do as I tell you," a voice whispered. "Jump on him from behind as he passes the corner and get him in the gills."

"I understand."

"Choke him stiff until I get something in his mouth."

"Ah, it's too easy. I'd like a little excitement."

"We'll get it before morning——"

"Sh! what's that?"

"I didn't hear anything!"

"Something moved."

A bush had slipped from Cleo's hand. She gripped the others with desperation. Ten minutes passed amid a death-like silence. A hundred times she imagined the hand of one of these men feeling for her throat. At last she drew a deep breath.

The men began to move step by step toward the doomed sentinel. They were standing beside the front corner of the jail now waiting panther-like for their prey. They allowed him to pass twice. He stopped at the end of his beat, blew his nose and spoke to himself:

"God, what a lonely night!"

The girl heard him turn, his feet measure three steps on his return and stop with a dull thud. She couldn't see, but she could feel through the darkness the grip of those terrible fingers on his throat. The only sound made was the dull thud of his body on the wet ground.

In two minutes they had carried him into the shadows of a big china tree in the rear and tied him to the trunk. She could hear their sharp order:

"Break those cords now or dare to open your mouth and, no matter what happens, we'll kill you first—just for luck."

In ten minutes they had reported the success of their work to their comrades who were waiting and the men who had been picked for their dangerous task surrounded the jail and slowly took up their appointed places in the shadows.

The attacking group stopped for their final instructions not five feet from the girl's position. A flash of moonlight and she saw them—six grim white and scarlet figures wearing spiked helmets from which fell a cloth mask to their shoulders. Their big revolvers were buckled on the outside of their disguises and each man's hand rested on the handle.

One of them quietly slipped his robe from his shoulders, removed his helmet, put on the sentinel's coat and cap, seized his musket and walked to the door of the jail.

She heard him drop the butt of the gun on the flagstone at the steps and call:

"Hello, jailer!"

Some one stirred inside. It was not yet one o'clock and the jailer who had been to a drinking bout with the soldiers had not gone to bed. In his shirt sleeves he thrust his head out the door:

"Who is it?"

"The guard, sir."

"Well, what the devil do you want?"

"Can't ye gimme a drink of somethin'? I'm soaked through and I've caught cold——"

"All right, in a minute," was the gruff reply.

The girl could hear the soft tread of the shrouded figures closing in on the front door. A moment more and it opened. The voice inside said:

"Here you are!"

The words had scarcely passed his lips, and there was another dull crash. A dozen masked Clansmen hurled themselves into the doorway and rushed over the prostrate form of the half-drunken jailer. He was too frightened to call for help. He lay with his face downward, begging for his life.

It was the work of a minute to take the keys from his trembling fingers, bind and gag him, and release Norton. The whole thing had been done so quietly not even a dog had barked at the disturbance.

Again they stopped within a few feet of the trembling figure against the wall. The editor had now put on his disguise and stood in the centre of the group giving his orders as quietly as though he were talking to his printers about the form of his paper.

"Quick now, Mac," she heard him say, "we've not a moment to lose. I want two pieces of scantling strong enough for a hangman's beam. Push one of them out of the center window of the north end of the Capitol building, the other from the south end. We'll hang the little Scalawag on the south side and the Carpetbagger on the north. We'll give them this grim touch of poetry at the end. Your ropes have ready swinging from these beams. Keep your men on guard there until I come."

"All right, sir!" came the quick response.

"My hundred picked men are waiting?"

"On the turnpike at the first branch——"

"Good! The Governor is spending the night at Schlitz's place, three miles out. He has been afraid to sleep at home of late, I hear. We'll give the little man and his pal a royal escort for once as they approach the Capitol—expect us within an hour."

A moment and they were gone. The girl staggered from her cramped position and flew to the house. She couldn't understand it all, but she realized that if the Governor were killed it meant possible ruin for the man she had marked her own.

A light was still burning in the mother's room. She had been nervous and restless and couldn't sleep. She heard the girl's swift, excited step on the stairway and rushed to the door:

"What is it? What has happened?"

Cleo paused for breath and gasped:

"They've broken the jail open and he's gone with the Ku Klux to kill the Governor!"

"To kill the Governor?"

"Yessum. He's got a hundred men waiting out on the turnpike and they're going to hang the Governor from one of the Capitol windows!"

The wife caught the girl by the shoulders and cried:

"Who told you this?"

"Nobody. I saw them. I was passing the jail, heard a noise and went close in the dark. I heard the major give the orders to the men."

"Oh, my God!" the little mother groaned. "And they are going straight to the Governor's mansion?"

"No—no—he said the Governor's out at Schlitz's place, spending the night. They're going to kill him, too——"

"Then there's time to stop them—quick—can you hitch a horse?"

"Yessum!"

"Run to the stable, hitch my horse to the buggy and take a note I'll write to my grandfather, old Governor Carteret—you know where his place is—the big red brick house at the edge of town?"

"Yessum——"

"His street leads into the turnpike—quick now—the horse and buggy!"

The strong young body sprang down the steps three and four rounds at a leap and in five minutes the crunch of swift wheels on the gravel walk was heard.

She sprang up the stairs, took the note from the frail, trembling little hand and bounded out of the house again.

The clouds had passed and the moon was shining now in silent splendor on the sparkling refreshed trees and shrubbery. The girl was an expert in handling a horse. Old Peeler had at least taught her that. In five more minutes from the time she had left the house she was knocking furiously at the old Governor's door. He was eighty-four, but a man of extraordinary vigor for his age.

He came to the door alone in his night-dress, candle in hand, scowling at the unseemly interruption of his rest.

"What is it?" he cried with impatience.

"A note from Mrs. Norton."

At the mention of her name the fine old face softened and then his eyes flashed:

"She is ill?"

"No, sir—but she wants you to help her."

He took the note, placed the candle on the old-fashioned mahogany table in his hall, returned to his room for his glasses, adjusted them with deliberation and read its startling message.

He spoke without looking up:

"You know the road to Schlitz's house?"

"Yes, sir, every foot of it."

"I'll be ready in ten minutes."

"We've no time to lose—you'd better hurry," the girl said nervously.

The old man lifted his eyebrows:

"I will. But an ex-Governor of the state can't rush to meet the present Governor in his shirt-tail—now, can he?"

Cleo laughed:

"No, sir."

The thin, sprightly figure moved quickly in spite of the eighty-four years and in less than ten minutes he was seated beside the girl and they were flying over the turnpike toward the Schlitz place.

"How long since those men left the jail?" the old Governor asked roughly.

"About a half-hour, sir."

"Give your horse the rein—we'll be too late, I'm afraid."

The lines slacked over the spirited animal's back and he sprang forward as though lashed by the insult to his high breeding.

The sky was studded now with stars sparkling in the air cleared by the rain, and the moon flooded the white roadway with light. The buggy flew over the beaten track for a mile, and as they suddenly plunged down a hill the old man seized both sides of the canopy top to steady his body as the light rig swayed first one way and then the other.

"You're going pretty fast," he grumbled.

"Yes, you said to give him the reins."

"But I didn't say to throw them on the horse's head, did I?"

"No, sir," the girl giggled.

"Pull him in!" he ordered sharply.

The strong young arms drew the horse suddenly down on his haunches and the old man lurched forward.

"I didn't say pull him into the buggy," he growled.

The girl suppressed another laugh. He was certainly a funny old man for all his eighty odd winters. She thought that he must have been a young devil at eighteen.

"Stop a minute!" he cried sharply. "What's that roaring?"

Cleo listened:

"The wind in the trees, I think."

"Nothing of the sort—isn't this Buffalo creek?"

"Yes, sir."

"That's water we hear. The creek's out of banks. The storm has made the ford impassable. They haven't crossed this place yet. We're in time."

The horse lifted his head and neighed. Another answered from the woods and in a moment a white-masked figure galloped up to the buggy and spoke sharply:

"You can't cross this ford—turn back."

"Are you one of Norton's men?" the old man asked angrily.

"None of your damned business!" was the quick answer.

"I think it is, sir! I'm Governor Carteret. My age and services to this state entitle me to a hearing tonight. Tell Major Norton I must speak to him immediately—immediately, sir!" His voice rose to a high note of imperious command.

The horseman hesitated and galloped into the shadows. A moment later a tall shrouded figure on horseback slowly aproached.

"Cut your wheel," the old Governor said to the girl. He stepped from the buggy without assistance. "Now turn round and wait for me." Cleo obeyed, and the venerable statesman with head erect, his white hair and beard shining in the moonlight calmly awaited the approach of the younger man.

Norton dismounted and led his horse, the rein hanging loosely over his arm.

"Well, Governor Carteret"—the drawling voice was low and quietly determined.

The white-haired figure suddenly stiffened:

"Don't insult me, sir, by talking through a mask—take that thing off your head."

The major bowed and removed his mask.

When the old man spoke again, his voice trembled with emotion, he stepped close and seized Norton's arm:

"My boy, have you gone mad?"

"I think not," was the even answer. The deep brown eyes were holding the older man's gaze with a cold, deadly look. "Were you ever arrested, Governor, by the henchmen of a peanut politician and thrown into a filthy jail without warrant and held without trial at the pleasure of a master?"

"No—by the living God!"

"And if you had been, sir?"

"I'd have killed him as I would a dog—I'd have shot him on sight—but you—you can't do this now, my boy—you carry the life of the people in your hands to-night! You are their chosen leader. The peace and dignity of a great commonwealth are in your care——"

"I am asserting its outraged dignity against a wretch who has basely betrayed it."

"Even so, this is not the way. Think of the consequences to-morrow morning. The President will be forced against his wishes to declare the state in insurrection. The army will be marched back into our borders and martial law proclaimed."

"The state is under martial law—the *writ* has been suspended."

"But not legally, my boy. I know your provocation has been great—yes, greater than I could have borne in my day. I'll be honest with you, but you've had better discipline, my son. I belong to the old régime and an iron will has been my only law. You must live in the new age under new conditions. You must adjust yourself to these conditions."

"The man who calls himself Governor has betrayed his high trust," Norton broke in with solemn emphasis. "He has forfeited his life. The people whom he has basely sold into bondage will applaud his execution. The Klan to-night is the high court of a sovereign state and his death has been ordered."

"I insist there's a better way. Your Klan is a resistless weapon if properly used. You are a maniac to-night. You are pulling your own house down over your head. The election is but a few weeks off. Use your men as an army to force this election. The ballot is force—physical force. Apply that force. Your men can master that rabble of negroes on election day. Drive them from the polls. They'll run like frightened sheep. Their enfranchisement is a crime against civilization. Every sane man in the North knows this. No matter how violent your methods, an election that returns the intelligent and decent manhood of a state to power against a corrupt, ignorant and vicious mob will be backed at last by the moral sentiment of the world. There's a fiercer vengeance to be meted out to your Scalawag Governor——"

"What do you mean?" the younger man asked.

"Swing the power of your Klan in solid line against the ballot-box at this election, carry the state, elect your Legislature, impeach the Governor, remove him from office, deprive him of citizenship and send him to the grave with the brand of shame on his forehead!"

The leader lifted his somber face, and the older man saw that he was hesitating:

"That's possible—yes——"

The white head moved closer:

"The only rational thing to do, my boy—come, I love you and I love my granddaughter. You've a great career before you. Don't throw your life away to-night in a single act of madness. Listen to an old man whose sands are nearly run"—a trembling arm slipped around his waist.

"I appreciate your coming here to-night, Governor, of course."

"But if I came in vain, why at all?" there were tears in his voice now. "You must do as I say, my son—send those men home! I'll see the Governor to-morrow morning and I pledge you my word of honor that I'll make him revoke that proclamation within an hour and restore the civil rights of the people. None of those arrests are legal and every man must be released."

"He won't do it."

"When he learns from my lips that I saved his dog's life to-night, he'll do it and lick my feet in gratitude. Won't you trust me, boy?"

The pressure of the old man's arm tightened and his keen eyes searched Norton's face. The strong features were convulsed with passion, he turned away and the firm mouth closed with decision:

"All right. I'll take your advice."

The old Governor was very still for a moment and his voice quivered with tenderness as he touched Norton's arm affectionately:

"You're a good boy, Dan! I knew you'd hear me. God! how I envy you the youth and strength that's yours to fight this battle!"

The leader blew a whistle and his orderly galloped up:

"Tell my men to go home and meet me to-morrow at one o'clock in the Court House Square, in their everyday clothes, armed and ready for orders. I'll dismiss the guard I left at the Capitol."

The white horseman wheeled and galloped away. Norton quietly removed his disguise, folded it neatly, took off his saddle, placed the robe between the folds of the blanket and mounted his horse.

The old Governor waved to him:

"My love to the little mother and that boy, Tom, that you've named for me!"

"Yes, Governor—good night."

The tall figure on horseback melted into the shadows and in a moment the buggy was spinning over the glistening, moonlit track of the turnpike.

When they reached the first street lamps on the edge of town, the old man peered curiously at the girl by his side.

"You drive well, young woman," he said slowly. "Who taught you?"

"Old Peeler."

"You lived on his place?" he asked quickly.

"Yes, sir."

"What's your mother's name?"

"Lucy"

"Hm! I thought so."

"Why, sir?"

"Oh, nothing," was the gruff answer.

"Did you—did you know any of my people, sir?" she asked.

He looked her squarely in the face, smiled and pursed his withered lips:

"Yes. I happen to be personally acquainted with your grandfather and he was something of a man in his day."

Chapter VI

A Traitor's Ruse

The old Governor had made a correct guess on the line of action his little Scalawag successor in high office would take when confronted by the crisis of the morning.

The Clansmen had left the two beams projecting through the windows of the north and south wings of the Capitol. A hangman's noose swung from each beam's end.

When His Excellency drove into town next morning and received the news of the startling events of the night, he ordered a double guard of troops for his office and another for his house.

Old Governor Carteret called at ten o'clock and was ushered immediately into the executive office. No more striking contrast could be imagined between two men of equal stature. Their weight and height were almost the same, yet they seemed to belong to different races of men. The Scalawag official hurried to meet his distinguished caller—a man whose administration thirty years ago was famous in the annals of the state.

The acting Governor seemed a pigmy beside his venerable predecessor. The only prominent feature of the Scalawag's face was his nose. Its size should have symbolized strength, yet it didn't. It seemed to project straight in front in a way that looked ridiculous—as if some one had caught it with a pair of tongs, tweaked and pulled it out to an unusual length. It was elongated but not impressive. His mouth was weak, his chin small and retreating and his watery ferret eyes never looked any one straight in the face. The front of his head was bald and sloped backward at an angle. His hair was worn in long, thin, straight locks which he combed often in a vain effort to look the typical long-haired Southern gentleman of the old school.

His black broadcloth suit with a velvet collar and cuffs fitted his slight figure to perfection and yet failed to be impressive. The failure was doubtless due to his curious way of walking about a room. Sometimes sideways like a crab or a crawfish, and when he sought to be impressive, straight forward with an obvious jerk and an effort to appear dignified.

He was the kind of a man an old-fashioned negro, born and bred in the homes of the aristocratic régime of slavery, would always laugh at. His attempt to be a gentleman was so obvious a fraud it could deceive no one.

"I am honored, Governor Carteret, by your call this morning," he cried with forced politeness. "I need the advice of our wisest men. I appreciate your coming."

The old Governor studied the Scalawag for a moment calmly and said:

"Thank you."

When shown to his seat the older man walked with the unconscious dignity of a man born to rule, the lines of his patrician face seemed cut from a cameo in contrast with the rambling nondescript features of the person who walked with a shuffle beside him. It required no second glance at the clean ruffled shirt with its tiny gold studs, the black string tie, the polished boots and gold-headed cane to recognize the real gentleman of the old school. And no man ever looked a second time at his Roman nose and massive chin and doubted for a moment that he saw a man of power, of iron will and fierce passions.

"I have called this morning, Governor," the older man began with sharp emphasis, "to advise you to revoke at once your proclamation suspending the *writ* of *habeas corpus.* Your act was a blunder—a colossal blunder! We are not living in the Dark Ages, sir—even if you were elected by a negro constituency! Your act is four hundred years out of date in the English-speaking world."

The Scalawag began his answer by wringing his slippery hands:

"I realize, Governor Carteret, the gravity of my act. Yet grave dangers call for grave remedies. You see from the news this morning the condition of turmoil into which reckless men have plunged the state."

The old man rose, crossed the room and confronted the Scalawag, his eyes blazing, his uplifted hand trembling with passion:

"The breed of men with whom you are fooling have not submitted to such an act of tyranny from their rulers for the past three hundred years. Your effort to set the negro up as the ruler of the white race is the act of a madman. Revoke your order to-day or the men who opened that jail last night will hang you——"

The Governor laughed lamely:

"A cheap bluff, sir, a schoolboy's threat!"

The older man drew closer:

"A cheap bluff, eh? Well, when you say your prayers to-night, don't forget to thank your Maker for two things—that He sent a storm yesterday that made Buffalo creek impassable and that I reached its banks in time!"

The little Scalawag paled and his voice was scarcely a whisper:

"Why—why, what do you mean?"

"That I reached the ford in time to stop a hundred desperate men who were standing there in the dark waiting for its waters to fall that they might cross and hang you from that beam's end you call a cheap bluff! That I stood there in the moonlight with my arm around their leader for nearly an hour begging, praying, pleading for your damned worthless life! They gave it to me at last because I asked it. No other man could have saved you. Your life is mine to-day! But for my solemn promise to those men that you would revoke that order your body would be swinging at this moment from the Capitol window—will you make good my promise?"

"I'll—I'll consider it," was the waning answer.

"Yes or no?"

"I'll think it over, Governor Carteret—I'll think it over," the trembling voice repeated. "I must consult my friends——"

"I won't take that answer!" the old man thundered in his face. "Revoke that proclamation here and now, or, by the Lord God, I'll send a message to those men that'll swing you from the gallows before the sun rises to-morrow morning!"

"I've got my troops——"

"A hell of a lot of troops they are! Where were they last night—the loafing, drunken cowards? You can't get enough troops in this town to save you. Revoke that proclamation or take your chances!"

The old Governor seized his hat and walked calmly toward the door. The Scalawag trembled, and finally said:

"I'll take your advice, sir—wait a moment until I write the order."

The room was still for five minutes, save for the scratch of the Governor's pen, as he wrote his second famous proclamation, restoring the civil rights of the people. He signed and sealed the document and handed it to his waiting guest:

"Is that satisfactory?"

The old man adjusted his glasses, read each word carefully, and replied with dignity:

"Perfectly—good morning!"

The white head erect, the visitor left the executive chamber without a glance at the man he despised.

The Governor had given his word, signed and sealed his solemn proclamation, but he proved himself a traitor to the last.

With the advice of his confederates he made a last desperate effort to gain his end of holding the leaders of the opposition party in jail by a quick shift of method. He wired orders to every jailer to hold the men until warrants were issued for their arrest by one of his negro magistrates in each county and wired instructions to the clerk of the court to admit none of them to bail no matter what amount offered.

The charges on which these warrants were issued were, in the main, preposterous perjuries by the hirelings of the Governor. There was no expectation that they would be proven in court. But if they could hold these prisoners until the election was over the little Scalawag believed the Klan could be thus intimidated in each district and the negro ticket triumphantly elected.

The Governor was explicit in his instructions to the clerk of the court in the Capital county that under no conceivable circumstances should he accept bail for the editor of the *Eagle and Phoenix.*

The Governor's proclamation was issued at noon and within an hour a deputy sheriff appeared at Norton's office and served his warrant charging the preposterous crime of "Treason and Conspiracy" against the state government.

Norton's hundred picked men were already lounging in the Court House Square. When the deputy appeared with his prisoner they quietly closed in around him and entered the clerk's room in a body. The clerk was dumfounded at the sudden packing of his place with quiet, sullen looking, armed men. Their revolvers were in front and the men were nervously fingering the handles.

The clerk had been ordered by the Governor under no circumstances to accept bail, and he had promised with alacrity to obey. But he changed his mind at the sight of those revolvers. Not a word was spoken by the men and the silence was oppressive. The frightened official mopped his brow and tried to leave for a moment to communicate with the Capitol. He found it impossible to move from his desk. The men were jammed around him in an impenetrable mass. He looked over the crowd in vain for a friendly face. Even the deputy who had made the arrest had been jostled out of the room and couldn't get back.

The editor looked at the clerk steadily for a moment and quietly asked:

"What amount of bail do you require?"

The officer smiled wanly:

"Oh, major, it's just a formality with you, sir; a mere nominal sum of $500 will be all right."

"Make out your bond," the editor curtly ordered. "My friends here will sign it."

"Certainly, certainly, major," was the quick answer. "Have a seat, sir, while I fill in the blank."

"I'll stand, thank you," was the quick reply.

The clerk's pen flew while he made out the forbidden bail which set at liberty the arch enemy of the Governor. When it was signed and the daring young leader quietly walked out the door, a cheer from a hundred men rent the air.

The shivering clerk cowered in his seat over his desk and pretended to be very busy. In reality he was breathing a prayer of thanks to God for sparing his life and registering a solemn vow to quit politics and go back to farming.

The editor hurried to his office and sent a message to each district leader of the Klan to secure bail for the accused men in the same quiet manner.

Chapter VII

The Irony of Fate

His political battle won, Norton turned his face homeward for a struggle in which victory would not come so easily. He had made up his mind that Cleo should not remain under his roof another day. How much she really knew or understood of the events of the night he could only guess. He was sure she had heard enough of the plans of his men to make a dangerous witness against him if she should see fit to betray the facts to his enemies.

Yet he was morally certain that he could trust her with this secret. What he could not and would not do was to imperil his own life and character by a daily intimate association with this willful, impudent, smiling young animal.

His one fear was the wish of his wife to keep her. In her illness she had developed a tyranny of love that brooked no interference with her whims. He had petted and spoiled her until it was well-nigh impossible to change the situation. The fear of her death was the sword that forever hung over his head.

He hoped that the girl was lying when she said his wife liked her. Yet it was not improbable. Her mind was still a child's. She could not think evil of any one. She loved the young and she loved grace and beauty wherever she saw it. She loved a beautiful cat, a beautiful dog, and always had taken pride in a handsome servant. It would be just like her to take a fancy to Cleo that no argument could shake. He dreaded to put the thing to an issue—but it had to be done. It was out of the question to tell her the real truth.

His heart sank within him as he entered his wife's room. Mammy had gone to bed suffering with a chill. The doctors had hinted that she was suffering from an incurable ailment and that her days were numbered. Her death might occur at any time.

Cleo was lying flat on a rug, the baby was sitting astride of her back, laughing his loudest at the funny contortions of her lithe figure. She would stop every now and then, turn her own laughing eyes on him and he would scream with joy.

The little mother was sitting on the floor like a child and laughing at the scene. In a flash he realized that Cleo had made herself, in the first few days she had been in his house, its dominant spirit.

He paused in the doorway sobered by the realization.

The supple young form on the floor slowly writhed on her back without disturbing the baby's sturdy hold, his little legs clasping her body tight. She drew his laughing face to her shoulder, smothering his laughter with kisses, and suddenly sprang to her feet, the baby astride her neck, and began galloping around the room.

"W'oa! January, w'oa, sir!" she cried, galloping slowly at first and then prancing like a playful horse.

Her cheeks were flushed, eyes sparkling and red hair flying in waves of fiery beauty over her exquisite shoulders, every change of attitude a new picture of graceful abandon, every movement of her body a throb of savage music from some strange seductive orchestra hidden in the deep woods!

Its notes slowly stole over the senses of the man with such alluring power, that in spite of his annoyance he began to smile.

The girl stopped, placed the child on the floor, ran to the corner of the room, dropped on all fours and started slowly toward him, her voice imitating the deep growl of a bear.

"Now the bears are going to get him!—Boo-oo-oo."

The baby screamed with delight. The graceful young she-bear capered around her victim from side to side, smelling his hands and jumping back, approaching and retreating, growling and pawing the floor, while with each movement the child shouted a new note of joy.

The man, watching, wondered if this marvelous creamy yellow animal could get into an ungraceful position.

The keen eyes of the young she-bear saw the boy had worn himself out with laughter and slowly approached her victim, tumbled his happy flushed little form over on the rug and devoured him with kisses.

"Don't, Cleo—that's enough now!" the little mother cried, through her tears of laughter.

"Yessum—yessum—I'm just eatin' him up now—I'm done—and he'll be asleep in two minutes."

She sprang to her feet, crushing the little form tenderly against her warm, young bosom, and walked past the man smiling into his face a look of triumph. The sombre eyes answered with a smile in spite of himself.

Could any man with red blood in his veins fight successfully a force like that? He heard the growl of the Beast within as he stood watching the scene. The sight of the frail little face of his invalid wife brought him up against the ugly fact with a sharp pain.

Yet the moment he tried to broach the subject of discharging Cleo, he hesitated, stammered and was silent. At last he braced himself with determination for the task. It was disagreeable, but it had to be done. The sooner the better.

"You like this girl, my dear?" he said softly.

"She's the most wonderful nurse I ever saw—the baby's simply crazy about her!"

"Yes, I see," he said soberly.

"It's a perfectly marvellous piece of luck that she came the day she did. Mammy was ready to drop. She's been like a fairy in the nursery from the moment she entered. The kiddy has done nothing but laugh and shriek with delight."

"And you like her personally?"

"I've just fallen in love with her! She's so strong and young and beautiful. She picks me up, laughing like a child, and carries me into the bathroom, carries me back and tucks me in bed as easily as she does the baby."

"I'm sorry, my dear," he interrupted with a firm, hard note in his voice.

"Sorry—for what?" the blue eyes opened with astonishment.

"Because I don't like her, and her presence here may be very dangerous just now——"

"Dangerous—what on earth can you mean?"

"To begin with that she's a negress——"

"So's mammy—so's the cook—the man—every servant we've ever had—or will have——"

"I'm not so sure of the last," the husband broke in with a frown.

"What's dangerous about the girl, I'd like to know?" his wife demanded.

"I said, to begin with, she's a negress. That's perhaps the least objectionable thing about her as a servant. But she has bad blood in her on her father's side. Old Peeler's as contemptible a scoundrel as I know in the county——"

"The girl don't like him—that's why she left home."

"Did she tell you that?" he asked quizzically.

"Yes, and I'm sorry for her. She wants a good home among decent white people and I'm not going to give her up. I don't care what you say."

The husband ignored the finality of this decision and went on with his argument as though she had not spoken.

"Old Peeler is not only a low white scoundrel who would marry this girl's mulatto mother if he dared, but he is trying to break into politics as a negro champion. He denies it, but he is a henchman of the Governor. I'm in a fight with this man to the death. There's not room for us both in the state——"

"And you think this laughing child cares anything about the Governor or his dirty politics? Such a thing has never entered her head."

"I'm not sure of that."

"You're crazy, Dan."

"But I'm not so crazy, my dear, that I can't see that this girl's presence in our house is dangerous. She already knows too much about my affairs—enough, in fact, to endanger my life if she should turn traitor."

"But she won't tell, I tell you—she's loyal—I'd trust her with my life, or yours, or the baby's, without hesitation. She proved her loyalty to me and to you last night."

"Yes, and that's just why she's so dangerous." He spoke slowly, as if talking to himself. "You can't understand, dear, I am entering now the last phase of a desperate struggle with the little Scalawag who sits in the Governor's chair for the mastery of this state and its life. The next two weeks and this election will decide whether white civilization shall live or a permanent negroid mongrel government, after the pattern of Haiti and San Domingo, shall be established. If we submit, we are not worth saving. We ought to die and out civilization with us! We are not going to submit, we are not going to die, we are going to win. I want you to help me now by getting rid of this girl."

"I won't give her up. There's no sense in it. A man who fought four years in the war is not afraid of a laughing girl who loves his baby and his wife! I can't risk a green, incompetent girl in the nursery now. I can't think of breaking in a new one. I like Cleo. She's a breath of fresh air when she comes into my room; she's clean and neat ; she sings beautifully; her voice is soft and low and deep; I love her touch when she dresses me; the baby worships her—is all this nothing to you?"

"Is my work nothing to you?" he answered soberly.

"Bah! It's a joke! Your work has nothing to do with this girl. She knows nothing, cares nothing for politics—it's absurd!"

"My dear, you must listen to me now——"

"I won't listen. I'll have my way about my servants. It's none of your business. Look after your politics and let the nursery alone!"

"Please be reasonable, my love. I assure you I'm in dead earnest. The danger is a real one, or I wouldn't ask this of you—please——"

"No—no—no—no!" she fairly shrieked.

His voice was very quiet when he spoke at last:

"I'm sorry to cross you in this, but the girl must leave to-night."

The tones of his voice and the firm snap of his strong jaw left further argument out of the question and the little woman played her trump card.

She sprang to her feet, pale with rage, and gave way to a fit of hysteria. He attempted to soothe her, in grave alarm over the possible effects on her health of such a temper.

With a piercing scream she threw herself across the bed and he bent over her tenderly:

"Please, don't act this way!"

Her only answer was another scream, her little fists opening and closing like a bird's talons gripping the white counterpane in her trembling fingers.

The man stood in helpless misery and sickening fear, bent low and whispered:

"Please, please, darling—it's all right—she can stay. I won't say another word. Don't make yourself ill. Please don't!"

The sobbing ceased for a moment, and he added:

"I'll go into the nursery and send her here to put you to bed."

He turned to the door and met Cleo entering.

"Miss Jean called me?" she asked with a curious smile playing about her greenish eyes.

"Yes. She wishes you to put her to bed."

The girl threw him a look of triumphant tenderness and he knew that she had heard and understood.

Chapter VIII

A New Weapon

From the moment the jail doors opened the Governor felt the chill of defeat. With his armed guard of fifty thousand "Loyal" white men he hoped to stem the rising tide of Anglo-Saxon fury. But the hope was faint. There was no assurance in its warmth. Every leader he had arrested without warrant and held without bail was now a firebrand in a powder magazine. Mass meetings, barbecues and parades were scheduled for every day by his enemies in every county.

The state was ablaze with wrath from the mountains to the sea. The orators of the white race spoke with tongues of flame.

The record of negro misrule under an African Legislature was told with brutal detail and maddening effects. The state treasury was empty, the school funds had been squandered, millions in bonds bad been voted and stolen and the thieves had fled the state in terror.

All this the Governor knew from the first, but he also knew that an ignorant negro majority would ask no questions and believe no evil of their allies.

The adventurers from the North had done their work of alienating the races with a thoroughness that was nothing short of a miracle. The one man on earth who had always been his best friend, every negro now held his bitterest foe. He would consult his old master about any subject under the sun and take his advice against the world except in politics. He would come to the back door, beg him for a suit of clothes, take it with joyous thanks, put it on and march straight to the polls and vote against the hand that gave it.

He asked no questions as to his own ticket. It was all right if it was against the white man of the South. The few Scalawags who trained with negroes to get office didn't count.

The negro had always despised such trash. The Governor knew his solid black constituency would vote like sheep, exactly as they were told by their new teachers.

But the nightmare that disturbed him now, waking or dreaming, was the fear that this full negro vote could not be polled. The daring speeches by the enraged leaders of the white race were inflaming the minds of the people beyond the bounds of all reason. These leaders had sworn to carry the election and dared the Governor to show one of his scurvy guards near a polling place on the day they should cast their ballots.

The Ku Klux Klan openly defied all authority. Their men paraded the county roads nightly and ended their parades by lining their horsemen in cavalry formation, galloping through the towns and striking terror to every denizen of the crowded negro quarters.

In vain the Governor issued frantic appeals for the preservation of the sanctity of the ballot. His speeches in which he made this appeal were openly hissed.

The ballot was no longer a sacred thing. The time was in American history when it was the badge of citizen kingship. At this moment the best men in the state were disfranchised and hundreds of thousands of negroes, with the instincts of the savage and the intelligence of the child, had been given the ballot. Never in the history of civilization had the ballot fallen so low in any republic. The very atmosphere of a polling place was a stench in the nostrils of decent men.

The determination of the leaders of the Klan to clear the polls by force if need be was openly proclaimed before the day of election. The philosophy by which they justified this stand was simple, and unanswerable, for it was founded in the eternal verities. Men are not made free by writing a constitution on a piece of paper. Freedom is inside. A ballot is only a symbol. That symbol stands for physical force directed by the highest intelligence. The ballot, therefore, is force—physical force. Back of every ballot is a bayonet and the red blood of the man who holds it. Therefore, a minority submits to the verdict of a majority at the polls. If there is not an intelligent, powerful fighting unit back of the scrap of paper that falls into a box, there's nothing there and that man's ballot has no more meaning than if it had been deposited by a trained pig or a dog.

On the day of this fated election the little Scalawag Governor sat in the Capitol, the picture of nervous despair. Since sunrise his office had been flooded with messages from every quarter of the state begging too late for troops. Everywhere his henchmen were in a panic. From every quarter the stories were the same.

Hundreds of determined, silent white men had crowded the polls, taken their own time to vote and refused to give an inch of room to the long line of panic-stricken negroes who looked on helplessly. At five o'clock in the afternoon less than a hundred blacks had voted in the entire township in which the Capital was located.

Norton was a candidate for the Legislature on the white ticket, and the Governor had bent every effort to bring about his defeat. The candidate against him was a young negro who had been a slave of his father, and now called himself Andy Norton. Andy had been a house-servant, was exactly the major's age and they had been playmates before the war. He was endowed with a stentorian voice and a passion for oratory. He had acquired a reputation for smartness, was good-natured, loud-mouthed, could tell a story, play the banjo and amuse a crowd. He had been Norton's bodyservant the first year of the war.

The Governor relied on Andy to swing a resistless tide of negro votes for the ticket and sweep the county. Under ordinary conditions, he would have done it. But before the hurricane of fury that swept the white race on the day of the election, the voice of Andy was as one crying in the wilderness.

He had made three speeches to his crowd of helpless black voters who hadn't been able to vote. The Governor sent him an urgent message to mass his men and force their way to the ballot box.

The polling place was under a great oak that grew in the Square beside the Court House. A space had been roped off to guard the approach to the boxes. Since sunrise this space had been packed solid with a living wall of white men. Occasionally a well-known old negro of good character was allowed to pass through and vote and then the lines closed up in solid ranks.

One by one a new white man was allowed to take his place in this wall and gradually he was moved up to the tables on which the boxes rested, voted, and slowly, like the movement of a glacier, the line crowded on in its endless circle.

The outer part of this wall of defense which the white race had erected around the polling place was held throughout the day by the same men—twenty or thirty big, stolid, dogged countrymen, who said nothing, but every now and then winked at each other.

When Andy received the Governor's message he decided to distinguish himself. It was late in the day, but not too late perhaps to win by a successful assault. He picked out twenty of his strongest buck negroes, moved them quietly to a good position near the polls, formed them into a flying wedge, and, leading the assault in person with a loud good-natured laugh, he hurled them against the outer line of whites.

To Andy's surprise the double line opened and yielded to his onset. He had forced a dozen negroes into the ranks when to his surprise the white walls suddenly closed on the blacks and held them as in a steel trap.

And then, quick as a flash, something happened. It was a month before the negroes found out exactly what it was. They didn't see it, they couldn't hear it, but they knew it happened. They *felt* it.

And the silent swiftness with which it happened was appalling. Every negro who had penetrated the white wall suddenly leaped into the air with a yell of terror. The white line opened quickly and to a man the negro wedge broke and ran for life, each black hand clasped in agony on the same spot.

Andy's voice rang full and clear above his men's:

"Goddermighty, what's dat!"

"Dey shot us, man!" screamed a negro.

The thing was simple, almost childlike in its silliness, but it was tremendously effective. The white guard in the outer line had each been armed with a little piece of shining steel three inches long, fixed in a handle—a plain shoemaker's pegging awl. At a given signal they had wheeled and thrust these awls into the thick flesh of every negro's thigh.

The attack was so sudden, so unexpected, and the pain so sharp, so terrible, for the moment every negro's soul was possessed with a single idea, how to save his particular skin and do it quickest. All *esprit de corps* was gone. It was each for himself and the devil take the hindmost! Some of them never stopped running until they cleared Buffalo creek, three miles out of town.

Andy's ambitions were given a violent turn in a new direction. Before the polls closed at sundown he appeared at the office of the *Eagle and Phoenix* with a broad grin on his face and asked to see the major.

He entered the editor's room bowing and scraping, his white teeth gleaming.

Norton laughed and quietly said:

"Well, Andy?"

"Yassah, major, I des drap roun' ter kinder facilitate ye, sah, on de 'lection, sah."

"It does look like the tide is turning, Andy."

"Yassah, hit sho' is turnin,' but hit's gotter be a purty quick tide dat kin turn afore I does, sah."

"Yes?"

"Yassah! And I drap in, major, ter 'splain ter you dat I'se gwine ter gently draw outen politics, yassah. I makes up my min' ter hitch up wid de white folks agin. Brought up by de Nortons, sah, I'se always bin a gemman, an' I can't afford to smut my hands wid de crowd dat I been 'sociating wid. I'se glad you winnin' dis 'lection, sah, an' I'se glad you gwine ter de Legislature—anyhow de office gwine ter stay in de Norton fambly—an' I'se satisfied, sah. I know you gwine ter treat us far an' squar——"

"If I'm elected I'll try to represent all the people, Andy," the major said gravely.

."If you'se 'lected?" Andy laughed. "Lawd, man, you'se dar right now! I kin des see you settin' in one dem big chairs! I knowed it quick as I feel dat thing pop fro my backbone des now! Yassah, I done resigned, an' I thought, major, maybe you got a job 'bout de office or 'bout de house fer er young likely nigger 'bout my size?"

The editor smiled:

"Nothing just now, Andy, but possibly I can find a place for you in a few days."

"Thankee, sah. I'll hold off den till you wants me. I'll des pick up er few odd jobs till you say de word—you won't fergit me?"

"No. I'll remember."

"An', major, ef you kin des advance me 'bout er dollar on my wages now, I kin cheer myself up ter-night wid er good dinner. Dese here loafers done bust me. I hain't got er nickel lef!"

The major laughed heartily and "advanced" his rival for Legislative honors a dollar.

Andy bowed to the floor:

"Any time you'se ready, major, des lemme know, sah. You'll fin' me a handy man 'bout de house, sah."

"All right, Andy, I may need you soon."

"Yassah, de sooner de better, sah," he paused in the door. "Dey gotter get up soon in de mornin', sah, ter get erhead er us Nortons—yassah, dat dey is——"

A message, the first news of the election, cut Andy's gabble short. It spelled Victory! One after another they came from every direction—north, south, east and west—each bringing the same magic word—victory! victory! A state redeemed from negroid corruption! A great state once more in the hands of the children of the men who created it!

It had only been necessary to use force to hold the polls from hordes of ignorant negroes in the densest of the black counties. The white majorities would be unprecedented. The enthusiasm had reached the pitch of mania in these counties. They would all break records.

A few daring men in the black centres of population, where negro rule was at its worst, had guarded the polls under his direction armed with the simple device of a shoemaker's awl, and in every case where it had been used the resulting terror had cleared the place of every negro. In not a single case where this novel weapon had been suddenly and mysteriously thrust into a black skin was there an attempt to return to the polls. A long-suffering people, driven at last to desperation, had met force with force and wrested a commonwealth from the clutches of the vandals who were looting and disgracing it.

Now he would call the little Scalawag to the bar of justice.

Chapter IX

The Words That Cost

It was after midnight when Norton closed his desk and left for home. Bonfires were burning in the squares, bands were playing and hundreds of sober, gray-haired men were marching through the streets, hand in hand with shouting boys, cheering, cheering, forever cheering! He had made three speeches from the steps of the *Eagle and Phoenix* building and the crowds still stood there yelling his name and cheering. Broad-shouldered, bronzed men had rushed into his office one by one that night, hugged him and wrung his hands until they ached. He must have rest. The strain had been terrific and in the reaction he was pitifully tired.

The lights were still burning in his wife's room. She was waiting with Cleo for his return. He had sent her the bulletins as they had come and she knew the result of the election almost as soon as he. It was something very unusual that she should remain up so late. The doctor had positively forbidden it since her last attack.

"Cleo and I were watching the procession," she exclaimed. "I never saw so many crazy people since I was born."

"They've had enough to drive them mad the past two years, God knows," he answered, as his eye rested on Cleo, who was dressed in an old silk kimono belonging to his wife, which a friend of her grandfather had sent her from Japan.

She saw his look of surprise and said casually:

"I gave it to Cleo. I never liked the color. Cleo's to stay in the house hereafter. I've moved her things from the servants' quarters to the little room in the hall. I want her near me at night. You stay so late sometimes."

He made no answer, but the keen eyes of the girl saw the silent rage flashing from his eyes and caught the look of fierce determination as he squared his shoulders and gazed at her for a moment. She knew that he would put her out unless she could win his consent. She had made up her mind to fight and never for a moment did she accept the possibility of defeat.

He muttered an incoherent answer to his wife, kissed her good night, and went to his room. He sat down in the moonlight beside the open window, lighted a cigar and gazed out on the beautiful lawn.

His soul raged in fury over the blind folly of his wife. If the devil himself had ruled the world he could not have contrived more skillfully to throw this dangerous, sensuous young animal in his way. It was horrible! He felt himself suffocating with the thought of its possibilities! He rose and paced the floor and sat down again in helpless rage.

The door softly opened and closed and the girl stood before him in the white moonlight, her rounded figure plainly showing against the shimmering kimono as the breeze through the window pressed the delicate silk against her flesh.

He turned on her angrily:

"How dare you?"

"Why, I haven't done anything, major!" she answered softly. "I just came in to pick up that basket of trash I forgot this morning"—she spoke in low, lingering tones.

He rose, walked in front of her, looked her in the eye and quietly said:

"You're lying."

"Why, major——"

"You know that you are lying. Now get out of this room—and stay out of it, do you hear?"

"Yes, I hear," came the answer that was half a sob.

"And make up your mind to leave this place to-morrow, or I'll put you out, if I have to throw you head foremost into the street."

She took a step backward, shook her head and the mass of tangled red hair fell from its coil and dropped on her shoulders. Her eyes were watching him now with dumb passionate yearning.

"Get out!" he ordered brutally.

A moment's silence and a low laugh was her answer.

"Why do you hate me?" she asked the question with a note of triumph.

"I don't," he replied with a sneer.

"Then you're afraid of me!"

"Afraid, of you?"

"Yes."

He took another step and towered above her, his fists clenched and his whole being trembled with anger:

"I'd like to strangle you!"

She flung back her rounded throat, shook the long waves of hair down her back and lifted her eyes to his:

"Do it! There's my throat! I want you to. I wouldn't mind dying that way!"

He drew a deep breath and turned away.

With a sob the straight figure suddenly crumpled on the floor, a scarlet heap in the moonlight. She buried her face in her hands, choked back the cries, fought for self-control, and then looked up at him through her eyes half blinded by tears:

"Oh, what's the use! I won't lie any more. I didn't come in here for the basket. I came to see you. I came to beg you to let me stay. I watched you to-night when she told you that I was to sleep in that room there, and I knew you were going to send me away. Please don't! Please let me stay! I can do you no harm, major! I'll be wise, humble, obedient. I'll live only to please you. I haven't a single friend in the world. I hate negroes. I loathe poor white trash. This is my place, here in your home, among the birds and flowers, with your baby in my arms. You know that I love him and that he loves me. I'll work for you as no one else on earth would. My hands will be quick and my feet swift. I'll be your slave, your dog—you can kick me, beat me, strangle me, kill me if you like, but don't send me away—I—I can't help loving you! Please—please don't drive me away."

The passionate, throbbing voice broke into a sob and she touched his foot with her hand. He could feel the warmth of the soft, young flesh. He stooped and drew her to her feet.

"Come, child," he said with a queer hitch in his voice, "you—you—mustn't stay here another moment. I'm sorry——"

She clung to his hand with desperate pleading and pressed close to him:

"But you won't send me away?"

She could feel him trembling.

He hesitated, and then against the warning of conscience, reason, judgment and every instinct of law and self-preservation, he spoke the words that cost so much:

"No—I—I—won't send you away!"

With a sob of gratitude her head sank, the hot lips touched his hand, a rustle of silk and she was gone.

And through every hour of the long night, maddened by the consciousness of her physical nearness—he imagined at times he could hear her breathing in the next room—he lay awake and fought the Beast for the mastery of life.

Chapter X

MAN TO MAN

Cleo made good her vow of perfect service. In the weeks which followed she made herself practically indispensable. Her energy was exhaustless, her strength tireless. She not only kept the baby and the little mother happy, she watched the lawn and the flowers. The men did no more loafing. The grass was cut, the hedges trimmed, every dead limb from shrub and tree removed and the old place began to smile with new life.

Her work of housekeeper and maid-of-all-work was a marvel of efficiency. No orders were ever given to her. They were unnecessary. She knew by an unerring instinct what was needed and anticipated the need.

And then a thing happened that fixed her place in the house on the firmest basis.

The baby had taken a violent cold which quickly developed into pneumonia. The doctor looked at the little red fever-scorched face and parched lips with grave silence. He spoke at last with positive conviction:

"His life depends on a nurse, Norton. All I can do is to give orders. The nurse must save him."

With a sob in her voice, Cleo said:

"Let me—I'll save him. He can't die if it depends on that."

The doctor turned to the mother.

"Can you trust her?"

"Absolutely. She's quick, strong, faithful, careful, and she loves him."

"You agree, major?"

"Yes, we couldn't do better," he answered gravely, turning away.

And so the precious life was given into her hands. Norton spent the mornings in the nursery executing the doctor's orders with clock-like regularity, while Cleo slept. At noon she quietly entered and took his place. Her meals were served in the room and she never left it until he relieved her the next day. The tireless, greenish eyes watched the cradle with death-like stillness and her keen young ears bent low to catch every change in the rising and falling of the little breast. Through the long watches of the night, the quick alert figure with the velvet tread hurried about the room filling every order with skill and patience.

At the end of two weeks, the doctor smiled, patted her on the shoulder and said:

"You're a great nurse, little girl. You've saved his life."

Her head was bending low over the cradle, the baby reached up his hand, caught one of her red curls and lisped faintly:

"C-l-e-o!"

Her eyes were shining with tears as she rushed from the room and out on the lawn to have her cry alone. There could be no question after this of her position.

When the new Legislature met in the old Capitol building four months later, it was in the atmosphere of the crisp clearness that follows the storm. The thieves and vultures had winged their way to more congenial climes. They dared not face the investigation of their saturnalia which the restored white race would make. The wisest among them fled northward on the night of the election.

The Governor couldn't run. His term of office had two years more to be filled. And shivering in his room alone, shunned as a pariah, he awaited the assault of his triumphant foes.

And nothing succeeds like success. The brilliant young editor of the *Eagle and Phoenix* was the man of the hour. When he entered the hall of the House of Representatives on the day the Assembly met, pandemonium broke loose. A shout rose from the floor that fairly shook the old granite pile. Cheer after cheer rent the air, echoed and re-echoed through the vaulted arches of the hall. Men overturned their desks and chairs as they rushed pellmell to seize his hand. They lifted him on their shoulders and carried him in procession around the Assembly Chamber, through the corridors and around the circle of the Rotunda, cheering like madmen, and on through the Senate Chamber where every white Senator joined the procession and returned to the other end of the Capitol singing "Dixie" and shouting themselves hoarse.

He was elected Speaker of the House by his party without a dissenting voice, and the first words that fell from his lips as he ascended the dais, gazed over the cheering House, and rapped sharply for order, sounded the death knell to the hopes of the Governor for a compromise with his enemies. His voice rang clear and cold as the notes of a bugle:

"The first business before this House, gentlemen, is the impeachment and removal from office of the alleged Governor of this state!"

Again the long pent feelings of an outraged people passed all bounds. In vain the tall figure in the chair rapped for order. He had as well tried to call a cyclone to order by hammering at it with a gavel. Shout after shout, cheer after cheer, shout and cheer in apparently unending succession!

They had not only won a great victory and redeemed a state's honor, but they had found a leader who dared to lead in the work of cleansing and rebuilding the old commonwealth. It was ten minutes before order could be restored. And then with merciless precision the Speaker put in motion the legal machine that was to crush the life out of the little Scalawag who sat in his room below and listened to the roar of the storm over his head.

On the day the historic trial opened before the high tribunal of the Senate, sitting as judges, with the Chief Justice of the state as presiding officer, the Governor looked in vain for a friendly face among his accusers. Now that he was down, even the dogs in his own party whom he had reared and fed, men who had waxed fat on the spoils he had thrown them, were barking at his heels. They accused him of being the cause of the party's downfall.

The Governor had quickly made up his mind to ask no favors of these wretches. If the blow should fall, he knew to whom he would appeal that it might be tempered with mercy. The men of his discredited party were of his own type. His only chance lay in the generosity of a great foe.

It would be a bitter thing to beg a favor at the hands of the editor who had hounded him with his merciless pen from the day he had entered office, but it would be easier than an appeal to the ungrateful hounds of his own kennel who had deserted him in his hour of need.

The Bill of Impeachment which charged him with high crimes and misdemeanors against the people whose rights he had sworn to defend was drawn by the Speaker of the House, and it was a terrible document. It would not only deprive him of his great office, but strip him of citizenship, and send him from the Capitol a branded man for life.

The defense proved weak and the terrific assaults of the Impeachment managers under Norton's leadership resistless. Step by step the remorseless prosecutors closed in on the doomed culprit. Each day he sat in his place beside his counsel in the thronged Senate Chamber and heard his judges vote with practical unanimity "Guilty" on a new count in the Bill of Impeachment. The Chief Executive of a million people cowered in his seat while his accusers told and re-told the story of his crimes and the packed galleries cheered.

But one clause of the bill remained to be adjudged—the brand his accusers proposed to put upon his forehead. His final penalty should be the loss of citizenship. It was more than the Governor could bear. He begged an adjournment of the High Court for a conference with his attorneys and it was granted.

He immediately sought the Speaker, who made no effort to conceal the contempt in which he held the trembling petitioner.

"I've come to you, Major Norton," he began falteringly, "in the darkest hour of my life. I've come because I know that you are a brave and generous man. I appeal to your generosity. I've made mistakes in my administration. But I ask you to remember that few men in my place could have done better. I was set to make bricks without straw. I was told to make water run up hill and set at naught the law of gravitation.

"I struck at you personally—yes—but remember my provocation. You made me the target of your merciless ridicule, wit and invective for two years. It was more than flesh and blood could bear without a return blow. Put yourself in my place——"

"I've tried, Governor," Norton interrupted in kindly tones. "And it's inconceivable to me that any man born and bred as you have been, among the best people of the South, a man whose fiery speeches in the Secession Convention helped to plunge this state into civil war—how you could basely betray your own flesh and blood in the hour of their sorest need—it's beyond me! I can't understand it. I've tried to put myself in your place and I can't."

The little ferret eyes were dim as he edged toward the tall figure of his accuser:

"I'm not asking of you mercy, Major Norton, on the main issue. I understand the bitterness in the hearts of these men who sit as my judges to-day. I make no fight to retain the office of Governor, but—major"—his thin voice broke—"it's too hard to brand me a criminal by depriving me of my citizenship and the right to vote, and hurl me from the highest office within the gift of a great people a nameless thing, a man without a country! Come, sir, even if all you say is true, justice may be tempered with mercy. Great minds can understand this. You are the representative to-day of a brave and generous race of men. My life is in ruins—I am at your feet. I have pride. I had high ambitions——"

His voice broke, he paused, and then continued in strained tones:

"I have loved ones to whom this shame will come as a bolt from the clear sky. They know nothing of politics. They simply love me. This final ignominy you would heap on my head may be just from your point of view. But is it necessary? Can it serve any good purpose? Is it not mere wanton cruelty?

"Come now, man to man—our masks are off—my day is done. You are young. The world is yours. This last blow with which you would crush my spirit is too cruel! Can you afford an act of such wanton cruelty in the hour of your triumph? A small man could, yes—but you? I appeal to the best that's in you, to the spark of God that's in every human soul——"

Norton was deeply touched, far more than he dreamed any word from the man he hated could ever stir him. The Governor saw his hesitation and pressed his cause:

"I might say many things honestly in justification of my course in politics; but the time has not come. When passions have cooled and we can look the stirring events of these years squarely in the face—there'll be two sides to this question, major, as there are two sides to all questions. I might say to you that when I saw the frightful blunder I had made in helping to plunge our country into a fatal war, I tried to make good my mistake and went to the other extreme. I was ambitious, yes, but we are confronted with millions of ignorant negroes. What can we do with them? Slavery had an answer. Democracy now must give the true answer or perish——"

"That answer will never be to set these negroes up as rulers over white men!"

Norton raised his hand and spoke with bitter emphasis.

"Even so, in a Democracy with equality as the one fundamental law of life, what are you going to do with them? I could plead with you that in every act of my ill-fated administration I was honestly, in the fear of God, trying to meet and solve this apparently insoluble problem. You are now in power. What are you going to do with these negroes?"

"Send them back to the plow first," was the quick answer.

"All right; when they have bought those farms and their sons and daughters are rich and cultured—what then?"

"We'll answer that question, Governor, when the time comes."

"Remember, major, that you have no answer to it now, and in the pride of your heart to-day let me suggest that you deal charitably with one who honestly tried to find the answer when called to rule over both races.

"I have failed, I grant you. I have made mistakes, I grant you. Won't you accept my humility in this hour in part atonement for my mistakes? I stand alone before you, my bitterest and most powerful enemy, because I believe in the strength and nobility of your character. You are my only hope. I am before you, broken, crushed, humiliated, deserted, friendless—at your mercy!"

The last appeal stirred the soul of the young editor to its depths. He was surprised and shocked to find the man he had so long ridiculed and hated so thoroughly, human and appealing in his hour of need.

He spoke with a kindly deliberation he had never dreamed it possible to use with this man.

"I'm sorry for you, Governor. Your appeal is to me a very eloquent one. It has opened a new view of your character. I can never again say bitter, merciless things about you in my paper. You have disarmed me. But as the leader of my race, in the crisis through which we are passing, I feel that a great responsibility has been placed on me. Now that we have met, with bared souls in this solemn hour, let me say that I have learned to like you better than I ever thought it possible. But I am to-day a judge who must make his decision, remembering that the lives and liberties of all the people are in his keeping when he pronounces the sentence of law. A judge has no right to spare a man who has taken human life because he is sorry for the prisoner. I have no right, as a leader, to suspend this penalty on you. Your act in destroying the civil law, arresting men without warrant and holding them by military force without bail or date of trial, was, in my judgment, a crime of the highest rank, not merely against me—one individual whom you happened to hate—but against every man, woman and child in the state. Unless that crime is punished another man, as daring in high office, may repeat it in the future. I hold in my hands to-day not only the lives and liberties of the people you have wronged, but of generations yet unborn. Now that I have heard you, personally I am sorry for you, but the law must take its course."

"You will deprive me of my citizenship?" he asked pathetically.

"It is my solemn duty. And when it is done no Governor will ever again dare to repeat your crime."

Norton turned away and the Governor laid his trembling hand on his arm:

"Your decision is absolutely final, Major Norton?"

"Absolutely," was the firm reply.

The Governor's shoulders drooped lower as he shuffled from the room and his eyes were fixed on space as he pushed his way through the hostile crowds that filled the corridors of the Capitol.

The Court immediately reassembled and the Speaker rose to make his motion for a vote on the last count in the bill depriving the Chief Executive of the state of his citizenship.

The silence was intense. The crowds that packed the lobby, the galleries, and every inch of the floor of the Senate Chamber expected a fierce speech of impassioned eloquence from their idolized leader. Every neck was craned and breath held for his first ringing words.

To their surprise he began speaking in a low voice choking with emotion and merely demanded a vote of the Senate on the final clause of the bill, and the brown eyes of the tall orator had a suspicious look of moisture in their depths as they rested on the forlorn figure of the little Scalawag. The crowd caught the spirit of solemnity and of pathos from the speaker's voice and the vote was taken amid a silence that was painful.

When the Clerk announced the result and the Chief Justice of the state declared the office of Governor vacant there was no demonstration. As the Lieutenant-Governor ascended the dais and took the oath of office, the Scalawag rose and staggered through the crowd that opened with a look of awed pity as he passed from the chamber.

Norton stepped to the window behind the President of the Senate and watched the pathetic figure shuffle down the steps of the Capitol and slowly walk from the grounds. The sun was shining in the radiant splendor of early spring. The first flowers were blooming in the hedges by the walk and birds were chirping, chattering and singing from every tree and shrub. A squirrel started across the path in front of the drooping figure, stopped, cocked his little head to one side, looked up and ran to cover. But the man with drooping shoulders saw nothing. His dim eyes were peering into the shrouded future.

Norton was deeply moved.

"The judgment of posterity may deal kindlier with his life!" he exclaimed. "Who knows? A politician, a trimmer and a time-server—yes, so we all are down in our cowardly hearts—I'm sorry that it had to be!"

He was thinking of a skeleton in his own closet that grinned at him sometimes now when he least expected it.

Chapter XI

The Unbidden Guest

The night was a memorable one in Norton's life. The members of the Legislature and the leaders of his party from every quarter of the state gave a banquet in his honor in the Hall of the House of Representatives. Eight hundred guests, the flower and chivalry of the Commonwealth, sat down at the eighty tables improvised for the occasion.

Fifty leading men were guests of honor and vied with one another in acclaiming the brilliant young Speaker the coming statesman of the Nation. His name was linked with Hamilton, Jefferson, Webster, Clay and Calhoun. He was the youngest man who had ever been elected Speaker of a Legislative Assembly in American history and a dazzling career was predicted.

Even the newly installed Chief Executive, a hold-over from the defeated party, asked to be given a seat and in a glowing tribute to Norton hailed him as the next Governor of the state.

He had scarcely uttered the words when all the guests leaped to their feet by a common impulse, raised their glasses and shouted:

"To our next Governor, Daniel Norton!"

The cheers which followed were not arranged, they were the spontaneous outburst of genuine admiration by men and women who knew the man and believed in his power and his worth.

Norton flushed and his eyes dropped. His daring mind had already leaped the years. The Governor's chair meant the next step—a seat in the Senate Chamber of the United States. A quarter of a century and the South would once more come into her own. He would then be but forty-nine years old. He would have as good a chance for the Presidency as any other man. His fathers had been of the stock that created the Nation. His great-grandfather fought with Washington and Lafayette. His head was swimming with its visions, while the great Hall rang with his name.

While the tumult was still at its highest, he lifted his eyes for a moment over the heads of the throng at the tables below the platform on which the guests of honor were seated, and his heart suddenly stood still.

Cleo was standing in the door of the Hall, a haunted look in her dilated eyes, watching her chance to beckon to him unseen by the crowd.

He stared at her a moment in blank amazement and turned pale. Something had happened at his home, and by the expression on her face the message she bore was one he would never forget.

As he sat staring blankly, as at a sudden apparition, she disappeared in the crowd at the door. He looked in vain for her reappearance and was waiting an opportune moment to leave, when a waiter slipped through the mass of palms and flowers banked behind his chair by his admirers and thrust a crumpled note into his hand.

"The girl said it was important, sir," he explained.

Norton opened the message and held it under the banquet table as he hurriedly read in Cleo's hand:

> "It's found out—she's raving. The doctor is there. I must see you quick."

He whispered to the chairman that a message had just been received announcing the illness of his wife, but he hoped to be able to return in a few minutes.

It was known that his wife was an invalid and had often been stricken with violent attacks of hysteria, and so the banquet proceeded without interruption. The band was asked to play a stirring piece and he slipped out as the opening strains burst over the chattering, gay crowd.

As his tall figure rose from the seat of honor he gazed for an instant over the sparkling scene, and for the first time in his life knew the meaning of the word fear. A sickening horror swept his soul and the fire died from eyes that had a moment before blazed with visions of ambition. He felt the earth crumbling beneath his feet. He hoped for a way out, but from the moment he saw Cleo beckoning him over the heads of his guests he knew that Death had called him in the hour of his triumph.

He felt his way blindly through the crowd and pushed roughly past a hundred hands extended to congratulate him. He walked by instinct. He couldn't see. The mists of eternity seemed suddenly to have swept him beyond the range of time and sense.

In the hall he stumbled against Cleo and looked at her in a dazed way.

"Get your hat," she whispered.

He returned to the cloakroom, got his hat and hurried back in the same dull stupor.

"Come down stairs into the Square," she said quickly.

He followed her without a word, and when they reached the shadows of an oak below the windows of the Hall, he suddenly roused himself, turned on her fiercely and demanded:

"Well, what's happened?"

The girl was calm now, away from the crowd and guarded by the friendly night. Her words were cool and touched with the least suggestion of bravado. She looked at him steadily:

"I reckon you know——"

"You mean——" He felt for the tree trunk as if dizzy.

"Yes. She has found out——"

"What—how—when?" His words came in gasps of fear.

"About us——"

"How?"

"It was mammy. She was wild with jealousy that I had taken her place and was allowed to sleep in the house. She got to slipping to the nursery at night and watching me. She must have seen me one night at your room door and told her to get rid of me."

The man suddenly gripped the girl's shoulders, swung her face toward him and gazed into her shifting eyes, while his breath came in labored gasps:

"You little yellow devil! Mammy never told that to my wife and you know it; she would have told me and I would have sent you away. She knows that story would kill my baby's mother and she'd have cut the tongue out of her own head sooner than betray me. She has always loved me as her own child—she'd fight for me and die for me and stand for me against every man, woman and child on earth!"

"Well, she told her," the girl sullenly repeated.

"Told her what?" he asked.

"That I was hanging around your room." She paused.

"Well, go on——"

"Miss Jean asked me if it was true. I saw that we were caught and I just confessed the whole thing——"

The man sprang at her throat, paused, and his hands fell limp by his side. He gazed at her a moment, and grasped her wrists with cruel force:

"Yes, that's it, you little fiend—you confessed! You were so afraid you might not be forced to confess that you went out of your way to tell it. Two months ago I came to my senses and put you out of my life. You deliberately tried to commit murder to bring me back. You knew that confession would kill my wife as surely as if you had plunged a knife into her heart. You know that she has the mind of an innocent child—that she can think no evil of any one. You've tried to kill her on purpose, willfully, maliciously, deliberately—and if she dies——"

Norton's voice choked into an inarticulate groan and the girl smiled calmly.

The band in the Hall over their heads ended the music in a triumphant crash and he listened mechanically to the chairman while he announced the temporary absence of the guest of honor:

"And while he is out of the Hall for a few minutes, ladies and gentlemen," he added facetiously, "we can say a lot of fine things behind his back we would have blushed to tell him to his face——"

Another burst of applause and the hum and chatter and laughter came through the open window.

With a cry of anguish, the man turned again on the girl:

"Why do you stand there grinning at me? Why did you do this fiendish thing? What have you to say?"

"Nothing"—there was a ring of exultation in her voice—"I did it because I had to."

Norton leaned against the oak, placed his hands on his temples and groaned:

"Oh, my God! It's a nightmare——"

Suddenly he asked:

"What did she do when you told her?"

The girl answered with indifference:

"Screamed, called me a liar, jumped on me like a wildcat, dug her nails in my neck and went into hysterics."

"And you?"

"I picked her up, carried her to bed and sent for the doctor. As quick as he came I ran here to tell you."

The speaker upstairs was again announcing his name as the next Governor and Senator and the crowd were cheering. He felt the waves of Death roll over and engulf him. His knees grew weak and in spite of all effort he sank to a stone that lay against the gnarled trunk of the tree.

"She may be dead now," he said to himself in a dazed whisper.

"I don't think so!" the soft voice purred with the slightest suggestion of a sneer. She bit her lips and actually laughed. It was more than he could bear. With a sudden leap his hands closed on her throat and forced her trembling form back into the shadows.

"May—God—hurl—you—into—everlasting—hell—for—this!" he cried in anguish and his grip suddenly relaxed.

The girl had not struggled. Her own hand had simply been raised instinctively and grasped his.

"What shall I do?" she asked.

"Get out of my sight before I kill you!"

"I'm not afraid."

The calm accents maddened him to uncontrollable fury:

"And if you ever put your foot into my house again or cross my path, I'll not be responsible for what happens!"

His face was livid and his fists closed with an unconscious strength that cut the blood from the palms of his hands.

"I'm not afraid!" she repeated, her voice rising with clear assurance, a strange smile playing about her full lips.

"Go!" he said fiercely.

The girl turned without a word and walked into the bright light that streamed from the windows of the banquet hall, paused and looked at him, the white rows of teeth shining with a smile:

"But I'll see you again!"

And then, with shouts of triumph mocking his soul, his shoulders drooped, drunk with the stupor and pain of shame, he walked blindly through the night to the Judgment Bar of Life—a home where a sobbing wife waited for his coming.

Chapter XII

The Judgment Bar

He paused at the gate. His legs for the moment simply refused to go any further. A light was burning in his wife's room. Its radiance streaming against the white fluted columns threw their shadows far out on the lawn.

The fine old house seemed to slowly melt in the starlight into a solemn Court of Justice set on the highest hill of the world. Its white boards were hewn slabs of gleaming marble, its quaint old Colonial door the grand entrance to the Judgment Hall of Life and Death. And the judge who sat on the high dais was not the blind figure of tradition, but a blushing little bride he had led to God's altar four years ago. Her blue eyes were burning into the depths of his trembling soul.

His hand gripped the post and he tried to pull himself together, and look the ugly situation in the face. But it was too sudden. He had repented and was living a clean life, and the shock was so unexpected, its coming so unforeseen, the stroke at a moment when his spirits had climbed so high, the fall was too great. He lay a mangled heap at the foot of a precipice and could as yet only stretch out lame hands and feel in the dark. He could see nothing clearly.

A curious thing flashed through his benumbed mind as his gaze fascinated by the light in her room. She had not yet sent for him. He might have passed a messenger on the other side of the street, or he may have gone to the Capitol by another way, yet he was somehow morally sure that no word had as yet been sent. It could mean but one thing—that his wife had utterly refused to believe the girl's story. This would make the only sane thing to do almost impossible. If he could humbly confess the truth and beg for her forgiveness, the cloud might be lifted and her life saved.

But if she blindly refused to admit the possibility of such a sin, the crisis was one that sickened him. He would either be compelled to risk her life with the shock of confession, or lie to her with a shameless passion that would convince her of his innocence.

Could he do this? It was doubtful. He had never been a good liar. He had taken many a whipping as a boy sooner than lie. He had always dared to tell the truth and had felt a cruel free joy somehow in its consequence. He had been reserved and silent in his youth when he had sowed his wild oats before his marriage. He had never been forced to lie about that. No questions had been asked. He had kept his own counsel and that side of his life was a sealed book even to his most intimate friends.

He had never been under the influence of liquor and knew how to be a good fellow without being a fool. The first big lie of his life he was forced to act rather than speak when Cleo had entered his life. This lie had not yet shaped itself into words. And he doubted his ability to carry it off successfully. To speak the truth simply and plainly had become an ingrained habit. He trembled at the possibility of being compelled to deliberately and continuously lie to his wife. If he could only tell her the truth—tell her the hours of anguish he had passed in struggling against the Beast that at last had won the fight—if he could only make her feel to-night the pain, the shame, the loathing, the rage that filled his soul, she must forgive.

But would she listen? Had the child-mind that had never faced realities the power to adjust itself to such a tragedy and see life in its wider relations of sin and sorrow, of repentance and struggle to the achievement of character? There was but one answer:

"No. It would kill her. She can't understand——"

And then despair gripped him, his eyes grew dim and he couldn't think. He leaned heavily on the gate in a sickening stupor from which his mind slowly emerged and his fancy began to play pranks with an imagination suddenly quickened by suffering into extraordinary activity.

A katydid was crying somewhere over his head and a whip-poor-will broke the stillness with his weird call that seemed to rise from the ground under his feet. He was a boy again roaming the fields where stalwart slaves were working his father's plantation. It was just such a day in early spring when he had persuaded Andy to run away with him and go swimming in Buffalo creek. He had caught cold and they both got a whipping that night. He remembered how Andy had yelled so loud his father had stopped. And how he had set his little jaws together, refused to cry and received the worst whipping of his life. He could hear Andy now as he slipped up to him afterward, grinning and chuckling and whispered:

"Lordy, man, why didn't ye holler? You don't know how ter take er whippin' nohow. He nebber hurt me no mo' dan a flea bitin'!"

And then his mind leaped the years. Cleo was in his arms that night at old Peeler's and he was stroking her hair as he would have smoothed the fur of a frightened kitten. That strange impulse was the beginning—he could see it now—and it had grown with daily contact, until the contagious animal magnetism of her nearness became resistless. And now he stood a shivering coward in the dark, afraid to enter his own house and look his wife in the face.

Yes, he was a coward. He acknowledged it with a grim smile—a coward! This boastful, high-strung, self-poised leader of men! He drew his tall figure erect and a bitter laugh broke from his lips. He who had led men to death on battlefields with a smile and a shout! He who had cried in anguish the day Lee surrendered! He who, in defeat, still indomitable and unconquered, had fired the souls of his ruined people and led them through riot and revolution again to victory!—He was a coward now and he knew it, as he stood there alone in the stillness of the Southern night and looked himself squarely in the face.

His heart gave a throb of pity as he recalled the scenes during the war, when deserters and cowards had been led out in the gray dawn and shot to death for something they couldn't help.

It must be a dream. He couldn't realize the truth—grim, hideous and unthinkable. He had won every fight as the leader of his race against overwhelming odds. He had subdued the desperate and lawless among his own men until his word was law. He had rallied the shattered forces of a defeated people and inspired them with enthusiasm. He had overturned the negroid government in the state though backed by a million bayonets in the hands of veteran battle-tried soldiers. He had crushed the man who led these forces, impeached and removed him from office, and hurled him into merited oblivion, a man without a country. He had made himself the central figure of the commonwealth. In the dawn of manhood he had lived already a man's full life. A conquered world at his feet, and yet a little yellow, red-haired girl of the race he despised, in the supreme hour of triumph had laid his life in ruins. He had conquered all save the Beast within and he must die for it—it was only a morbid fancy, yes—yet he felt the chill in his soul.

How long he had stood there doubting, fearing, dreaming, he could form no idea. He was suddenly roused to the consciousness of his position by the doctor who was hurrying from the house. There was genuine surprise in his voice as he spoke slowly and in a very low tone.

Dr. Williams had the habit of slow, quiet speech. He was a privileged character in the town and the state, with the record of a half century of practice. A man of wide reading and genuine culture, he concealed a big heart beneath a brutal way of expressing his thoughts. He said exactly what he meant with a distinctness that was all the more startling because of his curious habit of speaking harsh things in tones so softly modulated that his hearers frequently asked him to repeat his words.

"I had just started to the banquet hall with a message for you," he said slowly.

"Yes—yes," Norton answered vaguely.

"But I see you've come—Cleo told you?"

"Yes—she came to the hall——"

The doctor's slender fingers touched his fine gray beard.

"Really! She entered that hall to-night? Well, it's a funny world, this. We spend our time and energy fighting the negro race in front and leave our back doors open for their women and children to enter and master our life. I congratulate you as a politician on your victory——"

Norton lifted his hand as if to ward off a blow:

"Please! not to-night!"

The doctor caught the look of agony in the haggard face and suddenly extended his hand:

"I wasn't thinking of your personal history, my boy. I was—I was thinking for a moment of the folly of a people—forgive me—I know you need help to-night. You must pull yourself together before you go in there——"

"Yes, I know!" Norton faltered. "You have seen my wife and talked with her—you can see things clearer than I—tell me what to do!"

"There's but one thing you can do," was the gentle answer. "Lie to her—lie—and stick to it. Lie skillfully, carefully, deliberately, and with such sincerity and conviction she's got to believe you. She wants to believe you, of course. I know you are guilty——"

"Let me tell you, doctor——"

"No, you needn't. It's an old story. The more powerful the man the easier his conquest when once the female animal of Cleo's race has her chance. It's enough to make the devil laugh to hear your politicians howl against social and political equality while this cancer is eating the heart out of our society. It makes me sick! And she went to your banquet hall to-night! I'll laugh over it when I'm blue——"

The doctor paused, laughed softly, and continued:

"Now listen, Norton. Your wife can't live unless she wills to live. I've told you this before. The moment she gives up, she dies. It's the iron will inside her frail body that holds the spirit. If she knows the truth, she can't face it. She is narrow, conventional, and can't readjust herself——"

"But doctor, can't she be made to realize that this thing is here a living fact which the white woman of the South must face? These hundreds of thousands of a mixed race are not accidents. She must know that this racial degradation is not merely a thing of to-day, but the heritage of two hundred years of sin and sorrow!"

"The older women know this—yes—but not our younger generation, who have been reared in the fierce defense of slavery we were forced to make before the war. These things were not to be talked about. No girl reared as your wife can conceive of the possibility of a decent man falling so low. I warn you. You can't let her know the truth—and so the only thing you can do is to lie and stick to it. It's queer advice for a doctor to give an honorable man, perhaps. But life is full of paradoxes. My advice is medicine. Our best medicines are the most deadly poisons in nature. I've saved many a man's life by their use. This happens to be one of the cases where I prescribe a poison. Put the responsibility on me if you like. My shoulders are broad. I live close to Nature and the prattle of fools never disturbs me."

"Is she still hysterical?" Norton asked.

"No. That's the strange part of it—the thing that frightens me. That's why I haven't left her side since I was called. Her outburst wasn't hysteria in the first place. It was rage—the blind unreasoning fury of the woman who sees her possible rival and wishes to kill her. You'll find her very quiet. There's a queer, still look in her eyes I don't like. It's the calm before the storm—a storm that may leave death in its trail——"

"Couldn't I deny it at first," Norton interrupted, "and then make my plea to her in an appeal for mercy on an imaginary case? God only knows what I've gone through—the fight I made——"

"Yes, I know, my boy, with that young animal playing at your feet in physical touch with your soul and body in the intimacies of your home, you never had a chance. But you can't make your wife see this. An angel from heaven, with tongue of divine eloquence, can make no impression on her if she once believes you guilty. Don't tell her—and may God have mercy on your soul to-night!"

With a pressure on the younger man's arm, the straight white figure of the old doctor passed through the gate.

Norton walked quickly to the steps of the spacious, pillared porch, stopped and turned again into the lawn. He sat down on a rustic seat and tried desperately to work out what he would say, and always the gray mist of a fog of despair closed in.

For the first time in his life he was confronted squarely with the fact that the whole structure of society is enfolded in a network of interminable lies. His wife had been reared from the cradle in the atmosphere of beauty and innocence. She believed in the innocence of her father, her brothers, and every man who moved in her circle. Above all, she believed in the innocence of her husband. The fact that the negro race had for two hundred years been stirring the baser passions of her men—that this degradation of the higher race had been bred into the bone and sinew of succeeding generations—had never occurred to her child-like mind. How hopeless the task to tell her now when the tragic story must shatter her own ideals!

The very thought brought a cry of agony to his lips:

"God in heaven—what can I do?"

He looked helplessly at the stream of light from her window and turned again toward the cool, friendly darkness.

The night was one of marvellous stillness. The band was playing again in his banquet hall at the Capitol. So still was the night he could hear distinctly the softer strains of the stringed instruments, faint, sweet and thrilling, as they floated over the sleepy old town. A mocking-bird above him wakened by the call of melody answered, tenderly at first, and then, with the crash of cornet and drum, his voice swelled into a flood of wonderful song.

With a groan of pain, Norton rose and walked rapidly into the house. His bird-dog lay on the mat outside the door and sprang forward with a joyous whine to meet him.

He stooped and drew the shaggy setter's head against his hot cheek.

"I need a friend, to-night, Don, old boy!" he said tenderly. And Don answered with an eloquent wag of his tail and a gentle nudge of his nose.

"If you were only my judge!—Bah, what's the use——"

He drew his drooping shoulders erect and entered his wife's room. Her eyes were shining with peculiar brightness, but otherwise she seemed unusually calm. She began speaking with quick nervous energy:

"Dr. Williams told you?"

"Yes, and I came at once." He answered with an unusually firm and clear note of strength. His whole being was keyed now to a high tension of alert decision. He saw that the doctor's way was the only one.

"I don't ask you, Dan," she went on with increasing excitement and a touch of scorn in her voice—"I don't ask you to deny this lie. What I want to know is the motive the little devil had in saying such a thing to me. Mammy, in her jealousy, merely told me she was hanging around your room too often. I asked her if it were true. She looked at me a moment and burst into her lying 'confession.' I could have killed her. I did try to tear her green eyes out. I knew that you hated her and tried to put her out of the house, and I thought she had taken this way to get even with you—but it doesn't seem possible. And then I thought the Governor might have taken this way to strike you. He knows old Peeler, the low miserable scoundrel, who is her father. Do you think it possible?"

"I—don't—know," he stammered, moistening his lips and turning away.

"Yet it's possible"—she insisted.

He saw the chance to confirm this impression by a cheap lie—to invent a story of old Peeler's intimacy with the Governor, of his attempt to marry Lucy, of his hatred of the policy of the paper, his fear of the Klan and of his treacherous, cowardly nature—yet the lie seemed so cheap and contemptible his lips refused to move. If he were going to carry out the doctor's orders here was his chance. He struggled to speak and couldn't. The habit of a life and the fibre of character were too strong. So he did the fatal thing at the moment of crisis.

"I don't think that possible," he said.

"Why not?"

"Well, you see, since I rescued old Peeler that night from those boys, he has been so abjectly grateful I've had to put him out of my office once or twice, and I'm sure he voted for me for the Legislature against his own party."

"He voted for you?" she asked in surprise.

"He told me so. He may have lied, of course, but I don't think he did."

"Then what could have been her motive?"

His teeth were chattering in spite of a desperate effort to think clearly and speak intelligently. He stared at a picture on the wall and made no reply.

"Say something—answer my question!" his wife cried excitedly.

"I have answered, my dear. I said I don't know. I'm stunned by the whole thing."

"You are *stunned?*"

"Yes——"

"Stunned? You, a strong, innocent man, stunned by a weak contemptible lie like this from the lips of such a girl—what do you mean?"

"Why, that I was naturally shocked to be called out of a banquet at such a moment by such an accusation. She actually beckoned to me from the door over the heads of the guests——"

The little blue eyes suddenly narrowed and the thin lips grew hard: "Cleo called you from the door?" she asked.

"Yes."

"You left the hall to see her there?"

"No, I went down stairs."

"Into the Capitol Square?"

"Yes. I couldn't well talk to her before all those guests——"

"Why not?"

The question came like the crack of a pistol. Her voice was high, cold, metallic, ringing. He saw, when too late, that he had made a fatal mistake. He stammered, reddened and then turned pale:

"Why—why—naturally——"

"If you are innocent—why not?"

He made a desperate effort to find a place of safety:

"I thought it wise to go down stairs where I could talk without interruption——"

"You—were—afraid," she was speaking each word now with cold, deadly deliberation, "to take-a-message-from-your-servant-at-the-door-of-a-public banquet-hall——" her words quickened—"then you suspected her possible message! There *was* something between you——"

"My dear, I beg of you——"

He turned his head away with a weary gesture.

She sprang from the side of the bed, leaped to his side, seized him by both arms and fairly screamed in his face:

"Look at me, Dan!"

He turned quickly, his haggard eyes stared into hers, and she looked with slowly dawning horror.

"Oh, my God!" she shrieked. "It's true—it's true—it's true!"

She sprang back with a shiver of loathing, covered her face with her hands and staggered to her bed, sobbing hysterically:

"It's true—it's true—it's true! Have mercy, Lord!—it's true—it's true!" She fell face downward, her frail figure quivering like a leaf in a storm.

He rushed to her side, crying in terror:

"It's not true—it's not true, my dear! Don't believe it. I swear it's a lie—it's a lie—I tell you!"

She was crying in sobs of utter anguish.

He bent low:

"It's not true, dearest! It's not true, I tell you. You mustn't believe it. You can't believe it when I swear to you that it's a lie——"

His head gently touched her slender shoulder.

She flinched as if scorched by a flame, sprang to her feet, and faced him with blazing eyes:

"Don't—you—dare—touch—me——"

"My dear," he pleaded.

"Don't speak to me again!"

"Please——"

"Get out of this room!"

He stood rooted to the spot in helpless stupor and she threw her little body against his with sudden fury, pushing him toward the door. "Get out, I say!"

He staggered back helplessly and awkwardly amazed at her strength as she pushed him into the hall. She stood a moment towering in the white frame of the door, the picture of an avenging angel to his tormented soul.

Through teeth chattering with hysterical emotion she cried:

"Go, you leper! And don't you ever dare to cross this door-sill again—not even to look on my dead face!"

"For God's sake, don't" he gasped, staggering toward her.

But the door slammed in his face and the bolt suddenly shot into its place.

He knocked gently and received no answer. An ominous stillness reigned within. He called again and again without response. He waited patiently for half an hour and knocked once more. An agony of fear chilled him. She might be dead. He knelt, pressed his ear close to the keyhole and heard a long, low, pitiful sob from her bed.

"Thank God——"

He rose with sudden determination. She couldn't be left like that. He would call the doctor back at once, and, what was better still, he would bring her mother, a wise gray-haired little saint, who rarely volunteered advice in her daughter's affairs. The door would fly open at her soft command.

Chapter XIII

An Old Story

The doctor's house lay beyond the Capitol and in his haste Norton forgot that a banquet was being held in his honor. He found himself suddenly face to face with the first of the departing guests as they began to pour through the gates of the Square.

He couldn't face these people, turned in his tracks, walked back to the next block and hurried into an obscure side street by which he could avoid them.

The doctor had not retired. He was seated on his porch quietly smoking, as if he were expecting the call.

"Well, you've bungled it, I see," he said simply, as he rose and seized his hat.

"Yes, she guessed the truth——"

"Guessed?—hardly." The white head with its shining hair slowly wagged. "She read it in those haggard eyes. Funny what poor liars your people have always been! If your father hadn't been fool enough to tell the truth with such habitual persistence, that office of his would never have been burned during the war. It's a funny world. It's the fun of it that keeps us alive, after all."

"Do the best you can for me, doctor," he interrupted. "I'm going for her mother."

"All right," was the cheery answer, "bring her at once. She's a better doctor than I to-night."

Norton walked swiftly toward a vine-clad cottage that stood beside Governor Carteret's place. It sat far back on the lawn that was once a part of the original estate twenty odd years ago. The old Governor during his last administration had built it for Robert Carteret, a handsome, wayward son, whom pretty Jennie Pryor had married. It had been a runaway love match. The old man had not opposed it because of any objection to the charming girl the boy had fallen in love with. He knew that Robert was a wild, headstrong, young scapegrace unfit to be the husband of any woman.

But apparently marriage settled him. For two years after Jean's birth he lived a decent life and then slipped again into hopelessly dissolute habits. When Jean was seven years old he was found dead one night under peculiar circumstances that were never made public. The sweet little woman who had braved the world's wrath to marry him had never complained, and she alone (with one other) knew the true secret of his death.

She had always been supported by a generous allowance from the old Governor and in his last will the vigorous octogenarian had made her his sole heir.

Norton had loved this quiet, patient little mother with a great tenderness since the day of his marriage to her daughter. He had never found her wanting in sympathy or helpfulness. She rarely left her cottage, but many a time he had gone to her with his troubles and came away with a light heart and a clearer insight into the duty that called. Her love and faith in him was one of the big things in life. In every dream of achievement that had fired his imagination during the stirring days of the past months he had always seen her face smiling with pride and love.

It was a bitter task to confess his shame to her—this tender, gracious, uncomplaining saint, to whom he had always been a hero. He paused a moment with his hand on the bell of the cottage, and finally rang.

Standing before her with bowed head he told in a few stammering words the story of his sin and the sorrow that had overwhelmed him.

"I swear to you that for the past two months my life has been clean and God alone knows the anguish of remorse I have suffered. You'll help me, mother?" he asked pathetically.

"Yes, my son," she answered simply.

"You don't hate me?"—the question ended with a catch in his voice that made it almost inaudible.

She lifted her white hands to his cheeks, drew the tall form down gently and pressed his lips:

"No, my son, I've lived too long. I leave judgment now to God. The unshed tears I see in your eyes are enough for me."

"I must see her to-night, mother. Make her see me. I can't endure this."

"She will see you when I have talked with her," was the slow reply as if to herself. "I am going to tell her something that I hoped to carry to the grave. But the time has come and she must know."

The doctor was strolling on the lawn when they arrived.

"She didn't wish to see me, my boy," he said with a look of sympathy. "And I thought it best to humor her. Send for me again if you wish, but I think the mother is best to-night." Without further words he tipped his hat with a fine old-fashioned bow to Mrs. Carteret and hurried home.

At the sound of the mother's voice the door was opened, two frail arms slipped around her neck and a baby was sobbing again on her breast. The white slender hands tenderly stroked the blonde hair, lips bent low and kissed the shining head and a cheek rested there while sob after sob shook the little body. The wise mother spoke no words save the sign language of love and tenderness, the slow pressure to her heart of the sobbing figure, kisses, kisses, kisses on her hair and the soothing touch of her hand.

A long time without a word they thus clung to each other. The sobs ceased at last.

"Now tell me, darling, how can I help you?" the gentle voice said.

"Oh, mamma, I just want to go home to you again and die—that's all."

"You'd be happier, you think, with me, dear?"

"Yes—it's clean and pure there. I can't live in this house—the very air I breathe is foul!"

"But you can't leave Dan, my child. Your life and his are one in your babe. God has made this so."

"He is nothing to me now. He doesn't exist. I don't come of his breed of men. My father's handsome face—my grandfather's record as the greatest Governor of the state—are not merely memories to me. I'll return to my own. And I'll take my child with me. I'll go back where the air is clean, where men have always been men, not beasts——"

The mother rose quietly and took from the mantel the dainty morocco-covered copy of the Bible she had given her daughter the day she left home. She turned its first pages, put her finger on the sixteenth chapter of the Book of Genesis, and turned down a leaf:

"I want you to read this chapter of Genesis which I have marked when you are yourself, and remember that the sympathy of the world has always been with the outcast Hagar, and not with the foolish wife who brought a beautiful girl into her husband's house and then repented of her folly."

"But a negress! oh, my God, the horror, the shame, the humiliation he has put on me! I've asked myself a hundred times why I lived a moment, why I didn't leap from that window and dash my brain out on the ground below—the beast—the beast!"

"Yes, dear, but when you are older you will know that all men are beasts."

"Mother!"

"Yes, all men who are worth while——"

"How can you say that," the daughter cried with scorn, "and remember my father and grandfather? No man passes the old Governor to-day without lifting his hat, and I've seen you sit for hours with my father's picture in your lap crying over it——"

"Yes, dear," was the sweet answer, "these hearts of ours play strange pranks with us sometimes. You must see Dan to-night and forgive. He will crawl on his hands and knees to your feet and beg it."

"I'll never see him or speak to him again!"

"You must—dear."

"Never!"

The mother sat down on the lounge and drew the quivering figure close. Her face was hidden from the daughter's view when she began to speak and so the death-like pallor was not noticed. The voice was held even by a firm will:

"I hoped God might let me go without my having to tell you what I must say now, dearest"—in spite of her effort there was a break and silence.

The little hand sought the mother's:

"You know you can tell me anything, mamma, dear."

"Your father, my child, was not a great man. He died in what should have been the glory of young manhood. He achieved nothing. He was just the spoiled child of a greater man, a child who inherited his father's brilliant mind, fiery temper and willful passions. I loved him from the moment we met and in spite of all I know that he loved me with the strongest, purest love he was capable of giving to any woman. And yet, dearest, I dare not tell you all I discovered of his wild, reckless life. The vilest trait of his character was transmitted straight from sire to son—he would never ask forgiveness of any human being for anything he had done—that is your grandfather's boast to-day. The old Governor, my child, was the owner of more than a thousand slaves on his two great plantations. Many of them he didn't know personally—unless they were beautiful girls——"

"Oh, mother, darling, have mercy on me!"—the little fingers tightened their grip. But the mother's even voice went on remorselessly:

"Cleo's mother was one of his slaves. You may depend upon it, your grandfather knows her history. You must remember what slavery meant, dear. It put into the hands of a master an awful power. It was not necessary for strong men to use this power. The humble daughters of slaves vied with one another to win his favor. Your grandfather was a man of great intellect, of powerful physique, of fierce, ungovernable passions——"

"But my father"—gasped the girl wife.

"Was a handsome, spoiled child, the kind of man for whom women have always died—but he never possessed the strength to keep himself within the bounds of decency as did the older man——"

"What do you mean?" the daughter broke in desperately.

"There has always been a secret about your father's death"—the mother paused and drew a deep breath. "I made the secret. I told the story to save him from shame in death. He died in the cabin of a mulatto girl he had played with as a boy—and—the thing that's hardest for me to tell you, dearest, is that I knew exactly where to find him when he had not returned at two o'clock that morning——"

The white head sank lower and rested on the shoulder of the frail young wife, who slipped her arms about the form of her mother, and neither spoke for a long while.

At last the mother began in quiet tones:

"And this was one of the reasons, my child, why slavery was doomed. The war was a wicked and awful tragedy. The white motherhood of the South would have crushed slavery. Before the war began we had six hundred thousand mulattoes—six hundred thousand reasons why slavery had to die!"

The fire flashed in the gentle eyes for a moment while she paused, and drew her soul back from the sorrowful past to the tragedy of to-day:

"And so, my darling, you must see your husband and forgive. He isn't bad. He carried in his blood the inheritance of hundreds of years of lawless passion. The noble thing about Dan is that he has the strength of character to rise from this to a higher manhood. You must help him, dearest, to do this."

The daughter bent and kissed the gentle lips:

"Ask him to come here, mother——"

She found the restless husband pacing the floor of the pillared porch. It was past two o'clock and the waning moon had risen. His face was ghastly as his feet stopped their dreary beat at the rustle of her dress. His heart stood still for a moment until he saw the smiling face.

"It's all right, Dan," she called softly in the doorway. "She's waiting for you."

He sprang to the door, stooped and kissed the silken gray hair and hurried up the stairs.

Tears were slowly stealing from the blue eyes as the little wife extended her frail arms. The man knelt and bowed his head in her lap, unable to speak at first. With an effort he mastered his voice:

"Say that you forgive me!"

The blonde head sank until it touched the brown:

"I forgive you—but, oh, Dan, dear, I don't want to live any more now——"

"Don't say that!" he pleaded desperately.

"And I've wanted to live so madly, so desperately—but now—I'm afraid I can't."

"You can—you must! You have forgiven me. I'll prove my love to you by a life of such devotion I'll make you forget! All I ask is the chance to atone and make you happy. You must live because I ask it, dear! It's the only way you can give me a chance. And the boy—dearest—you must live to teach him."

She nodded her head and choked back a sob.

When the first faint light of the dawn of a glorious spring morning began to tinge the eastern sky he was still holding her hands and begging her to live.

Chapter XIV

THE FIGHT FOR LIFE

The little wife made a brave fight. For a week there was no sign of a breakdown save an unnatural brightness of the eyes that told the story of struggle within. He gave himself to the effort to help her win. He spent but an hour at the Capitol, left a Speaker *pro tem* in the chair, hurried to his office, gave his orders and by eleven o'clock he was at home, talking, laughing, and planning a day's work that would interest her and bring back the flush to her pale cheeks.

She had responded to his increasing tenderness and devotion with pathetic eagerness. At the beginning of the second week Doctor Williams gave him hope:

"It looks to me, my boy," he said thoughtfully, "that I'm seeing a miracle. I think she's not only going to survive the shock, but, what's more remarkable, she's going to recover her health again. The mind's the source of health and power. We give medicines, of course, but the thought that heals the soul will reach the body. Bah!—the body is the soul anyhow, for all our fine-spun theories, and the mind is only one of the ways through which we reach it——"

"You really think she may be well again?" Norton asked with boyish eagerness.

"Yes, if you can reconcile her mind to this thing, she'll not only live, she will be born again into a more vigorous life. Why not? The preachers have often called me a godless rationalist. But I go them one better when they preach the miracle of a second, or spiritual birth. I believe in the possibility of many births for the human soul and the readjustment of these bodies of ours to the new spirits thus born. If you can tide her over the next three weeks without a breakdown, she will get well."

The husband's eyes flashed:

"If it depends on her mental attitude, I'll make her live and grow strong. I'll give her my body and soul."

"There are just two dangers——"

"What?"

"The first mental—a sudden collapse of the will with which she's making this fight under a reaction to the memories of our system of educated ignorance, which we call girlish innocence. This may come at a moment when the consciousness of these 'ideals' may overwhelm her imagination and cause a collapse——"

"Yes, I understand," he replied thoughtfully. "I'll guard that."

"The other is the big physical enigma——"

"You mean?"

"The possible reopening of that curious abscess in her throat."

"But the specialist assured us it would never reappear——"

"Yes, and he knows just as much about it as you or I. It is one of the few cases of its kind so far recorded in the science of medicine. When the baby was born, the drawing of the mother's neck in pain pressed a bone of the spinal column into the flesh beside the jugular vein. Your specialist never dared to operate for a thorough removal of the trouble for fear he would sever the vein——"

"And if the old wound reopens it will reach the jugular vein?"

"Yes."

"Well—it—won't happen!" he answered fiercely. "It can't happen now——"

"I don't think it will myself, if you can keep at its highest tension the desire to live. That's the magic thing that works the miracle of life in such cases. It makes food digest, sends red blood to the tips of the slenderest finger and builds up the weak places. Don't forget this, my boy. Make her love life, desperately and passionately, until the will to live dominates both soul and body."

"I'll do it," was the firm answer, as he grasped the doctor's outstretched hand in parting.

He withdrew completely from his political work. A Speaker *pro tem* presided daily over the deliberations of the House, and an assistant editor took charge of the paper.

The wife gently urged him to give part of his time to his work again.

"No," he responded firmly and gayly. "The doctor says you have a chance to get well. I'd rather see the roses in your cheeks again than be the President of the United States."

She drew his head down and clung to him with desperate tenderness.

Chapter XV

Cleo's Silence

For two weeks the wife held her own and the doctor grew more confident each day. When Norton began to feel sure the big danger was past his mind became alert once more to the existence of Cleo. He began to wonder why she had not made an effort to see or communicate with him.

She had apparently vanished from the face of the earth. In spite of his effort to minimize the importance of this fact, her silence gradually grew in sinister significance. What did it mean? What was her active brain and vital personality up to? That it boded no good to his life and the life of those he loved he couldn't doubt for a moment. He sent a reporter on a secret mission to Peeler's house to find if she were there.

He returned in three hours and made his report.

"She's at Peeler's, sir," the young man said with a smile.

"You allowed no one to learn the real reason of your visit, as I told you?"

"They never dreamed it. I interviewed old Peeler on the revolution in politics and its effects on the poor whites of the state——"

"You saw her?"

"She seemed to be all over the place at the same time, singing, laughing and perfectly happy."

"Run your interview to-morrow, and keep this visit a profound secret between us."

"Yes, sir."

The reporter tipped his hat and was gone. Why she was apparently happy and contented in surroundings she had grown to loathe was another puzzle. Through every hour of the day, down in the subconscious part of his mind, he was at work on this surprising fact. The longer he thought of it the less he understood it. That she would ever content herself with the dreary existence of old Peeler's farm after her experiences in the town and in his home was preposterous.

That she was smiling and happy under such conditions was uncanny, and the picture of her shining teeth and the sound of her deep voice singing as she walked through the cheap, sordid surroundings of that drab farmhouse haunted his mind with strange fear.

She was getting ready to strike him in the dark. Just how the blow would fall he couldn't guess.

The most obvious thing for her to do would be to carry her story to his political enemies and end his career at a stroke. Yet somehow, for the life of him he couldn't picture her choosing that method of revenge. She had not left him in a temper. The rage and curses had all been his. She had never for a moment lost her self-control. The last picture that burned into his soul was the curious smile with which she had spoken her parting words:

"But I'll see you again!"

Beyond a doubt some clean-cut plan of action was in her mind when she uttered that sentence. The one question now was—"what did she mean?"

There was one thought that kept popping into his head, but it was too hideous for a moment's belief. He stamped on it as he would a snake and hurried on to other possibilities. There was but one thing he could do and that was to await with increasing dread her first move.

Chapter XVI

The Larger Vision

His mind had just settled into this attitude of alert watchfulness toward Cleo when the first danger the doctor dreaded for his wife began to take shape.

The feverish brightness in her eyes grew dimmer and her movements less vigorous. The dreaded reaction had come and the taut strings of weakened nerves could bear the strain no longer.

With a cry of despair she threw herself into his arms:

"Oh, Dan, dear, it's no use! I've tried—I've tried so hard—but I can't do it—I just don't want to live any more!"

He put his hands over the trembling, thin lips:

"Hush, dearest, you mustn't say that—it's just a minute's reaction. You're blue this morning, that's all. It's the weather—a dreary foggy day. The sun will be shining again to-morrow. It's shining now behind the mists if we only remember it. The trees are bare, but their buds are swelling and these days of cold and fog and rain must come to make them burst in glory. Come, let me put your shawl around you and I'll show you how the flowers have pushed up in the sheltered places the past week."

He drew the hands, limp and cold, from his neck, picked up her shawl, tenderly placed it about her shoulders, lifted her in his strong arms, and carried her to the old rose garden behind the house.

Don sniffed his leg, and looked up into his face with surprise at the unexpected frolic. He leaped into the air, barked softly and ran in front to show the way.

"You see, old Don knows the sun is shining behind the clouds, dear!"

She made no answer. The blonde head drooped limply against his breast. He found a seat on the south side of the greenhouse on an old rustic bench his father had built of cedar when he was a boy.

"There," he said cheerfully, as he smoothed her dress and drew her close by his side. "You can feel the warmth of the sun here reflected from the glass. The violets are already blooming along the walks. The jonquils are all gone, and the rose bushes have begun to bud. You mustn't talk about giving up. We haven't lived yet."

"But I'm tired, Dan, tired——"

"It's just for a moment, remember, my love. You'll feel differently to-morrow. The world is always beautiful if we only have eyes to see and ears to hear. Watch that smoke curling straight up from the chimney! That means the clouds are already lifting and the sun will burst through them this afternoon. You mustn't brood, dearest. You must forget the misery that has darkened our world for a moment and remember that it's only the dawn of a new life for us both. We are just boy and girl yet. There's nothing impossible. I'm going to prove to you that my love is the deathless thing in me—the thing that links me to God."

"You really love me so?" she asked softly.

"Give me a chance to prove it. That's all I ask. Men sometimes wait until they're past forty before they begin to sow their wild oats. I am only twenty-five now. This tragic sin and shame has redeemed life. It's yours forever—you must believe me when I say this, dearest——"

"I try," she broke in wearily. "I try, Dan, but it's hard to believe anything now—oh, so hard——"

"But can't you understand, my love, how I have been headstrong and selfish before the shock of my fall brought me to my senses? And that the terror of losing you has taught me how deep and eternal the roots of our love have struck and this knowledge led me into the consciousness of a larger and more wonderful life—can't—can't you understand this, dearest?"

His voice sank to the lowest reverent whisper as he ceased to speak. She stroked his hand with a pathetic little gesture of tenderness.

"Yes, I believe you," she said with a far-away look in her eyes. "I know that I can trust you now implicitly, and what I can't understand is that—feeling this so clearly—still I have no interest in life. Something has snapped inside of me. Life doesn't seem worth the struggle any longer——"

"But it is, dear! Life is always good, always beautiful, and always worth the struggle. We've but to lift our eyes and see. Sin is only our stumbling in the dark as we grope toward the light. I'm going to be a humbler and better man. I am no longer proud and vain. I've a larger and sweeter vision. I feel my kinship to the weak and the erring. Alone in the night my soul has entered into the fellowship of the great Brotherhood through the gates of suffering. You must know this, Jean—you know that it's true as I thus lay my heart's last secret bare to you to-day."

"Yes, Dan," she sighed wearily, "but I'm just tired. I don't seem to recognize anything I used to know. I look at the baby and he don't seem to be mine. I look at you and feel that you're a stranger. I look at my room, the lawn, the street, the garden—no matter where, and I'm dazed. I feel that I've lost my way. I don't know how to live any more."

For an hour he held her hand and pleaded with all the eloquence of his love that she would let him teach her again, and all she could do was to come back forever in the narrow circle her mind had beaten. She was tired and life no longer seemed worth while!

He kissed the drooping eyelids at last and laughed a willful, daring laugh as he gathered her in his arms and walked slowly back into the house.

"You've got to live, my own! I'll show you how! I'll breathe my fierce desire into your soul and call you back even from the dead!"

Yet in spite of all she drooped and weakened daily, and at the end of a fortnight began to complain of a feeling of uneasiness in her throat.

The old doctor said nothing when she made this announcement. He drew his beetling eyebrows low and walked out on the lawn.

Pale and haggard, Norton followed him.

"Well, doctor?" he asked queerly.

"There's only one thing to do. Get her away from here at once, to the most beautiful spot you can find, high altitude with pure, stimulating air. The change may help her. That's all I can say"—he paused, laid his hand on the husband's arm and went on earnestly—"and if you haven't discussed that affair with her, you'd better try it. Tear the old wound open, go to the bottom of it, find the thing that's festering there and root it out if you can—the thing that's caused this break."

The end of another week found them in Asheville, North Carolina.

The wonderful views of purple hills and turquoise sky stretching away into the infinite thrilled the heart of the little invalid.

It was her first trip to the mountains. She never tired the first two days of sitting in the big sun-parlor beside the open fire logs and gazing over the valleys and watching the fleet clouds with their marvelous coloring. The air was too chill in these early days of spring for her to feel comfortable outside. But a great longing began to possess her to climb the mountains and feel their beauty at closer range.

She sat by his side in her room and held his hand while they watched the glory of the first cloud-flecked mountain sunset. The river lay a crooked silver ribbon in the deepening shadows of the valley, while the sky stretched its dazzling scarlet canopy high in heaven above it. The scarlet slowly turned to gold, and then to deepening purple and with each change revealed new beauty to the enraptured eye.

She caught her breath and cried at last:

"Oh, it is a beautiful world, Dan, dear—and I wish I could live!"

He laughed for joy:

"Then you shall, dearest! You shall, of course you shall!"

"I want you to take me over every one of those wonderful purple hills!"

"Yes, dear, I will!"

"I dream as I sit and look at them that God lives somewhere in one of those deep shadows behind a dazzling cloud, and that if we only drive along those ragged cliffs among them we'd come face to face with Him some day——"

He looked at her keenly. There was again that unnatural brightness in her eyes which he didn't like and yet he took courage. The day was a glorious one in the calendar. Hope had dawned in her heart.

"The first warm day we'll go, dear," he cried with the enthusiasm of a boy, "and take mammy and the kid with us, too, if you say so——"

"No, I want just you, Dan. The long ride might tire the baby, and I might wish to stay up there all night. I shall never grow tired of those hills."

"It's sweet, to hear you talk like that," he cried with a smile.

He selected a gentle horse for their use and five days later, when the sun rose with unusual warmth, they took their first mountain drive.

Along the banks of crystal brooks that dashed their sparkling waters over the rocks, up and up winding, narrow roads until the town became a mottled white spot in the valley below, and higher still until the shining clouds they had seen from the valley rolled silently into their faces, melting into the gray mists of fog!

In the midst of one of these clouds, the little wife leaned close and whispered:

"We're in heaven now, Dan—we're passing through the opal gates! I shouldn't be a bit surprised to see Him at any moment up here——"

A lump suddenly rose in his throat. Her voice sounded unreal. He bent close and saw the strange bright light again in her eyes. And the awful thought slowly shaped itself that the light he saw was the shining image of the angel of Death reflected there.

He tried to laugh off his morbid fancy now that she had begun to find the world so beautiful, but the idea haunted him with increasing terror. He couldn't shake off the impression.

An hour later he asked abruptly:

"You have felt no return of the pain in your throat, dear?"

"Just a little last night, but not to-day—I've been happy to-day."

He made up his mind to telegraph to New York at once for the specialist to examine her throat.

The fine weather continued unbroken. Every day for a week she sat by his side and drifted over sunlit valleys, lingered beside beautiful waters and climbed a new peak to bathe in sun-kissed clouds. On the top of one of these peaks they found a farmhouse where lodgers were allowed for the night. They stayed to see the sunrise next morning. Mammy would not worry, they had told her they might spend the night on these mountain trips.

The farmer called them in time—just as the first birds were waking in the trees by their window.

It was a climb of only two hundred yards to reach the top of a great boulder that gave an entrancing view in four directions. To the west lay the still sleeping town of Asheville half hidden among its hills and trees. Eastward towered the giant peaks of the Blue Ridge, over whose ragged crests the sun was climbing.

The young husband took the light form in his strong arms and carried her to the summit. He placed his coat on the rocky ledge, seated her on it, and slipped his arm around the slim waist. There in silence they watched the changing glory of the sky and saw the shadows wake and flee from the valleys at the kiss of the sun.

He felt the moment had come that he might say some things he had waited with patience to speak:

"You are sure, dear, that you have utterly forgiven the great wrong I did you?"

"Yes, Dan," she answered simply, "why do you ask?"

"I just want to be sure, my Jean," he said tenderly, "that there's not a single dark corner of your heart in which the old shadows lurk. I want to drive them all out with my love just as we see the sun now lighting with glory every nook and corner of the world. You are sure?"

The thin lips quivered uncertainly and her blue eyes wavered as he searched their depths.

"There's one thing, Dan, that I'll never quite face, I think"—she paused and turned away.

"What, dear?"

"How any man who had ever bent over a baby's cradle with the tenderness and love I've seen in your face for Tom, could forget the mother who gave the life at his command!"

"I didn't forget, dearest," he said sadly. "I fought as a wounded man, alone and unarmed, fights a beast in the jungle. With her sweet spiritual ideal of love a sheltered, innocent woman can't remember that man is still an animal, with tooth and claw and unbridled passions, that when put to the test his religion and his civilization often are only a thin veneer, that if he becomes a civilized human being in his relations to women it is not by inheritance, for he is yet in the zoölogical period of development—but that it is by the divine achievement of character through struggle. Try, dearest, if you can, to imagine such a struggle. This primeval man, in the shadows with desires inflamed by hunger, meets this free primeval woman who is unafraid, who laughs at the laws of Society because she has nothing to lose. Both are for the moment animals pure and simple. The universal in him finds its counterpart in the universal in her. And whether she be fair or dark, her face, her form, her body, her desires are his—and, above all, she is near—and in that moment with a nearness that overwhelms by its enfolding animal magnetism all powers of the mind to think or reflect. Two such beings are atoms tossed by a storm of forces beyond their control. A man of refinement wakes from such a crash of elemental powers dazed and humiliated. Your lips can speak no word as vile, no curse as bitter as I have hurled against myself——"

The voice broke and he was silent. A little hand pressed his, and her words were the merest tender whisper as she leaned close:

"I've forgiven you, my love, and I'm going to let you teach me again to live. I'll be a very docile little scholar in your school. But you know I can't forget in a moment the greatest single hour that is given a woman to know—the hour she feels the breath of her first born on her breast. It's the memory of that hour that hurts. I won't try to deceive you. I'll get over it in the years to come if God sends them——"

"He will send them—he will send them!" the man broke in with desperate emotion.

Both were silent for several minutes and a smile began to play about the blue eyes when she spoke at last:

"You remember how angry you were that morning when you found a doctor and a nurse in charge of your home? And the great fear that gripped your heart at the first mad cry of pain I gave? I laughed at myself the next moment. And then how I found your hand and wouldn't let you go. The doctor stormed and ordered you out, and I just held on and shook my head, and you stayed. And when the doctor turned his back I whispered in your ear:

"'You won't leave me, Dan, darling, for a single moment—promise me—swear it!'

"And you answered:

"'Yes, I swear it, honey—but you must be very brave—braver than I am, you know'——

"And you begged me to take an anesthetic and I wouldn't, like a little fool. I wanted to know all and feel all if it killed me. And the anguish of your face became so terrible, dear—I was sorrier for you than for myself. And when I saw your lips murmuring in an agony of prayer, I somehow didn't mind it then——"

She paused, looked far out over the hills and continued:

"What a funny cry he gave—that first one—not a real baby cry—just a funny little grunt like a good-natured pig! And how awfully disappointed you were at the shapeless bundle of red flesh that hardly looked human! But I could see the lines of your dear face in his, I knew that he would be even handsomer than his big, brave father and pressed him close and laughed for joy——"

She stopped and sighed:

"You see, Dan, what I couldn't understand is how any man who has felt the pain and the glory of this, with his hand clasped in the hand of the woman he loves, their two souls mirrored in that first pair of mysterious little eyes God sent from eternity—how he could forget the tie that binds——"

He made no effort to interrupt her until the last bitter thought that had been rankling in her heart was out. He was looking thoughtfully over the valley. An eagle poised above the field in the foreground, darted to the stubble with lightning swiftness and rose with a fluttering brown quail in his talons. His shrill cry of triumph rang pitilessly in the stillness of the heights.

The little figure gave an unconscious shiver and she added in low tones:

"I'm never going to speak of this nameless thing again, Dan, but you asked me this morning and I've told you what was in my heart. I just couldn't understand how you could forget——"

"Only a beast could, dearest," he answered with a curl of the lip. "I'm something more than that now, taught by the bitterness of experience. You're just a sweet, innocent girl who has never looked the world as it is in the face. Reared as you were, you can't understand that there's a difference as deep as the gulf between heaven and hell, in the divine love that binds my soul and body and life to you and the sudden passing of a storm of passion. Won't you try to remember this?"

"Yes, dear, I will——"

She looked into his eyes with a smile of tenderness:

"A curious change is coming over you, Dan. I can begin to see it.

There used to be a line of cruelty sometimes about your mouth and a flash of it in your eyes. They're gone. There's something strong and tender, wise and sweet, in their place. If I were an artist I could paint it but I can't just tell you what it is. I used to think the cruel thing I saw in you was the memory of the war. Your eyes saw so much of blood and death and pain and cruelty——"

"Perhaps it was," he said slowly. "War does make men cruel—unconsciously cruel. We lose all sense of the value of human life——"

"No, it wasn't that," she protested, "it was the other thing—the—the—Beast you've been talking about. It's not there any more, Dan—and I'm going to be happy now. I know it, dear——"

He bent and kissed the slender fingers.

"If this old throat of mine just won't bother me again," she added.

He looked at her and turned pale:

"It's bothering you this morning?"

She lifted the delicately shaped head and touched her neck:

"Not much pain, but a sense of fullness. I feel as if I'm going to choke sometimes."

He rose abruptly, a great fear in his heart:

"We'll go back to town at once. The doctor should arrive at three from New York."

"Let's not hurry," she cried smiling. "I'm happy now. You're my old sweetheart again and I'm on a new honeymoon——"

He gazed at the white slender throat. She was looking unusually well. He wondered if this were a trick of the enemy to throw him off his guard. He wondered what was happening in those tiny cells behind the smooth round lines of the beautiful neck. It made him sick and faint to think of the possibility of another attack—just when the fight was over—just when she had begun to smile and find life sweet again! His soul rose in fierce rebellion. It was too horrible for belief. He simply wouldn't believe it!

"All right!" he exclaimed with decision. "We'll stay here till two o'clock, anyhow. We can drive back in three hours. The train will be late—it always is."

Through the long hours of a wonderful spring morning they basked in the sun side by side on a bed of leaves he piled in a sheltered spot on the mountain side. They were boy and girl again. The shadows had lifted and the world was radiant with new glory. They talked of the future and the life of perfect mutual faith and love that should be theirs.

And each moment closer came the soft footfall of an unseen angel.

Chapter XVII

The Opal Gates

The doctor was waiting at the hotel, his keen eyes very serious. He had guessed the sinister meaning of the summons. He was an unusually brusque man—almost rude in his words. He greeted Norton with friendly sympathy and smiled at the radiant face of the wife.

"Well, little mother," he said with grave humor, "we have more trouble. But you're brave and patient. It's a joy to work for you."

"And now," she responded gayly, "you've got to finish this thing, doctor. I don't want any more half-way operations. I'm going to get well this time. I'm happy and I'm going to be strong again."

"Good, we'll get at it right away. I knew you'd feel that way and so I brought with me a great surgeon, the most skillful man I know in New York. I've told him of your case, a very unusual one, and he is going to help me."

The little mouth smiled bravely:

"I'll be ready for the examination in half an hour——"

When the doctors emerged from her room the sun had set behind the dark blue hills and Norton was waiting on the balcony for their report.

The specialist walked slowly to where he was standing. He couldn't move from his tracks. His throat was dry and he had somehow lost the power of speech. He looked into the face of the man of science, read the story of tragedy and a mist closed his eyes.

The doctor took his arm gently:

"I've bad news for you——"

"Yes, I know," was the low answer.

"The truth is best——"

"I want to know it."

"She can't live!"

The tall figure stiffened, there was a moment of silence and when he spoke his words fell slowly with measured intensity:

"There's not a single chance, doctor?"

"Not worth your cherishing. You'd as well know this now and be prepared. We opened and drained the old wound, and both agreed that it is too late for an operation. The flesh that guards the wall of the great vein is a mere shred. She would die under the operation. I can't undertake it."

"And it will not heal again?"

The doctor was silent for a long while and his eyes wandered to the darkening sky where the stars were coming out one by one:

"Who knows but God? And who am I to set bounds to his power?"

"Then there may be a slender chance?" he asked eagerly.

"To the eye of Science—no—yet while life lingers we always hope. But I wouldn't advise you to leave her side for the next ten days. The end, if it comes, will be very sudden, and it will be too late for speech."

A groan interrupted his words and Norton leaned heavily against the balcony rail. The doctor's voice was full of feeling as he continued:

"If you have anything to say to her you'd better say it quickly to be sure that it does not remain unsaid."

"Thank you——"

"I have told her nothing more can be done now until the wound from this draining heals—that when it does she can come to New York for a final decision on the operation."

"I understand."

"We leave to-night on the midnight express——"

"You can do nothing more?"

"Nothing."

A warm pressure of the hand in the gathering twilight and he was gone. The dazed man looked toward the fading sky-line of the southwest at Mt. Pisgah's towering black form pushing his way into the track of the stars and a feeling of loneliness crushed his soul.

He turned abruptly, braced himself for the ordeal and hurried to her room. She was unusually bright and cheerful.

"Why, it didn't hurt a bit, dear!" she exclaimed joyfully. "It was nothing. And when it heals you're to take me to New York for the operation——"

He took her hot hand and kissed it through blinding tears which he tried in vain to fight back.

"They didn't even have to pack that nasty old gauze in it again—were you very much scared waiting out there, Dan?"

"Very much."

She started at the queer note in his voice, caught her hand in his brown locks and pressed his head back in view:

"Why, you're crying—you big foolish boy! You mustn't do that. I'm all right now—I feel much better—there's not a trace of pain or uneasiness. Don't be silly—it's all right, remember."

He stroked the little hand:

"Yes, I'll remember, dearest."

"It should all be healed in three weeks and then we'll go to New York. It'll just be fun! I've always been crazy to go. I won't mind the operation—you'll be with me every minute now till I'm well again."

"Yes, dear, every moment now until—you—are—well."

The last words came slowly, but by a supreme effort of will the voice was held even.

He found mammy, told her the solemn truth, and sent her to hire a nurse for the baby.

"Either you or I must be by her side every minute now, mammy—day and night."

"Yessir, I understand," the dear old voice answered.

Every morning early the nurse brought the baby in for a romp as soon as he waked and mammy came to relieve the tired watcher.

Ten days passed before the end came. Many long, sweet hours he had with her hand in his as the great shadow deepened, while he talked to her of life and death, and immortality.

A strange peace had slowly stolen into his heart. He had always hated and feared death before. Now his fears had gone. And the face of the dim white messenger seemed to smile at him from the friendly shadows.

The change came quietly one night as they sat in the moonlight of her window.

"Oh, what a beautiful world, Dan!" she said softly, and then the little hand suddenly grasped her throat! She turned a blanched face on him and couldn't speak.

He lifted her tenderly and laid her on the bed, rang for the doctor and sent mammy for the baby.

She motioned for a piece of paper—and slowly wrote in a queer, trembling hand:

> "I understand, dearest, I am going—it's all right. I am happy—remember that I love you and have forgiven—rear our boy free from the curse—you know what I mean. I had rather a

thousand times that he should die than this—my brooding spirit will watch and guard."

The baby kissed her sweetly and lisped:
"Good night, mamma!"
From the doorway he waved his chubby little arm and cried again:
"Night, night, mamma!"

The sun was slowly climbing the eastern hills when the end came. Its first rays streamed through the window and fell on his haggard face as he bent and pressed a kiss on the silent lips of the dead.

Chapter XVIII

Questions

The thing that crushed the spirit of the man was not the shock of death with its thousand and one unanswerable questions torturing the soul, but the possibility that his acts had been the cause of the tragedy. Dr. Williams had said to him over and over again:

"Make her will to live and she'll recover!"

He had fought this grim battle and won. She had willed to live and was happy. The world had never seemed so beautiful as the day she died. If the cause of her death lay further back in the curious accident which happened at the birth of the child, his soul was clear of guilt.

He held none of the morbid fancies of the super-sensitive mind that would make a father responsible for a fatal outcome in the birth of a babe. God made women to bear children. The only woman to be pitied was the one who could not know the pain, the joy and the danger of this divine hour.

But the one persistent question to which his mind forever returned was whether the shock of his sin had weakened her vitality and caused the return of this old trouble.

The moment he left the grave on the day of her burial, he turned to the old doctor with this grim question. He told him the whole story. He told him every word she had spoken since they left home. He recounted every hour of reaction and depression, the good and the bad, just as the recording angel might have written it. He ended his recital with the burning question:

"Tell me now, doctor, honestly before God, did I kill her?"

"Certainly not!" was the quick response.

"Don't try to shield me. I can stand the truth. I don't belong to a race of cowards. After this no pain can ever come but that my soul shall laugh!"

"I'm honest with you, my boy. I've too much self-respect not to treat you as a man in such an hour. No, if she died as you say, you had nothing to do with it. The seed of death was hiding there behind that slender, graceful throat. I was always afraid of it. And I've always known that if the pain returned she'd die——"

"You knew that before we left home?"

"Yes. I only hinted the truth. I thought the change might prolong her life, that's all."

"You're not saying this to cheer me? This is not one of your lies you give for medicine sometimes?"

"No"—the old doctor smiled gravely. "No, shake off this nightmare and go back to your work. Your people are calling you."

He made a desperate effort to readjust himself to life, but somehow at the moment the task was hopeless. He had preached, with all the eloquence of the enthusiasm of youth, that life in itself is always beautiful and always good. He found it was easier to preach a thing than to live it.

The old house seemed to be empty, and, strange to say, the baby's voice didn't fill it. He had said to himself that the patter of his little feet and the sound of his laughter would fill its halls, make it possible to live, and get used to the change. But it wasn't so. Somehow the child's laughter made him faint. The sound of his voice made the memory of his mother an intolerable pain. His voice in the morning was the first thing he heard and it drove him from the house. At night when he knelt to lisp his prayers her name was a stab, and when he waved his little hands and said: "Good night, Papa!" he could remember nothing save the last picture that had burned itself into his soul.

He tried to feed and care for a canary she had kept in her room, but when he cocked his little yellow head and gave the loving plaintive cry with which he used to greet her, the room became a blur and he staggered out unable to return for a day.

The silent sympathy of his dog, as he thrust his nose between his hands and wagged his shaggy tail, was the only thing that seemed to count for anything.

"I understand, Don, old boy," he cried, lifting his paw into his lap and slipping his arm around the woolly neck, "you're telling me that you love me always, good or bad, right or wrong. I understand, and it's very sweet to know it. But I've somehow lost the way on life's field, old boy. The night is coming on and I can't find the road home. You remember that feeling when we were lost sometimes in strange countries hunting together, you and I?"

Don licked his hand and wagged his tail again.

He rose and walked through the lawn, radiant now with the glory of spring. But the flowers had become the emblems of Death not Life and their odor was oppressive.

A little black boy, in a ragged shirt and torn trousers, barefooted and bareheaded, stopped at the gate, climbed up and looked over with idle curiosity at his aimless wandering. He giggled and asked:

"Ye don't need no boy fer nothin, do ye?"

The man's sombre eyes suddenly lighted with a look of hate that faded in a moment and he made no reply. What had this poor little ragamuffin, his face smeared with dirt and his eyes rolling with childish mirth, to do with tragic problems which his black skin symbolized! He was there because a greedy race of empire builders had need of his labor. He had remained to torment and puzzle and set at naught the wisdom of statesmen for the same reason. For the first time in his life he asked himself a startling question:

"Do I really need him?"

Before the shock that threw his life into ruins he would have answered as every Southerner always answered at that time:

"Certainly I need him. His labor is indispensable to the South."

But to-day, back of the fire that flashed in his eyes, there had been born a new thought. He was destined to forget it in the stress of the life of the future, but it was there growing from day to day. The thought shaped itself into questions:

"Isn't the price we pay too great? Is his labor worth more than the purity of our racial stock? Shall we improve the breed of men or degrade it? Is any progress that degrades the breed of men progress at all? Is it not retrogression? Can we afford it?"

He threw off his train of thought with a gesture of weariness and a great desire suddenly possessed his heart to get rid of such a burden by a complete break with every tie of life save one.

"Why not take the boy and go?" he exclaimed.

The more he turned the idea over in his mind the more clearly it seemed to be the sensible thing to do.

But the fighting instinct within him was too strong for immediate surrender. He went to his office determined to work and lose himself in a return to its old habits.

He sat down at his desk, but his mind was a blank. There wasn't a question on earth that seemed worth writing an editorial about. Nothing mattered.

For two hours he sat hopelessly staring at his exchanges. The same world, which he had left a few weeks before when he had gone down into the valley of the shadows to fight for his life, still rolled on with its endless story of joy and sorrow, ambitions and struggle. It seemed now the record of the buzzing of a lot of insects. It was a waste of time to record such a struggle or to worry one way or another about it. And this effort of a daily newspaper to write the day's history of these insects! It might be worth the while of a philosopher to pause a moment to record the blow that would wipe them out of existence, but to get excited again over their little squabbles—it seemed funny now that he had ever been such a fool!

He rose at last in disgust and seized his hat to go home when the Chairman of the Executive Committee of his party suddenly walked into his office unannounced. His face was wreathed in smiles and his deep bass voice had a hearty, genuine ring:

"I've big news for you, major!"

The editor placed a chair beside his desk, motioned his visitor to be seated and quietly resumed his seat.

"It's been settled for some time," he went on enthusiastically, "but we thought best not to make the announcement so soon after your wife's death. I reckon you can guess my secret?"

"I give it up," was the listless answer.

"The Committee has voted unanimously to make you the next Governor. Your nomination with such backing is a mere formality. Your election is a certainty——"

The Chairman sprang to his feet and extended his big hand:

"I salute the Governor of the Commonwealth—the youngest man in the history of the state to hold such high office——"

"You mean it?" Norton asked in a stupor.

"Mean it? Of course I mean it! Why don't you give me your hand? What's the matter?"

"You see, I've sort of lost my bearings in politics lately."

The Chairman's voice was lowered:

"Of course, major, I understand. Well, this is the medicine you need now to brace you up. For the first time in my memory a name will go before our convention without a rival. There'll be just one ballot and that will be a single shout that'll raise the roof——"

Norton rose and walked to his window overlooking the Square, as he was in the habit of doing often, turning his back for a moment on the enthusiastic politician.

He was trying to think. The first big dream of his life had come true and it didn't interest him.

He turned abruptly and faced his visitor:

"Tell your Committee for me," he said with slow emphatic voice, "that I appreciate the high honor they would do me, but cannot accept——"

"What!"

"I cannot accept the responsibility."

"You don't mean it?"

"I was never more in earnest."

The Chairman slipped his arm around the editor with a movement of genuine sympathy:

"Come, my boy, this is nonsense. I'm a veteran politician. No man ever did such a thing as this in the history of the state! You can't decline such an honor. You're only twenty-five years old."

"Time is not measured by the tick of a clock," Norton interrupted, "but by what we've lived."

"Yes, yes, we know you've had a great shock in the death of your wife, but you must remember that the people—a million people—are calling you to lead them. It's a solemn duty. Don't say no now. Take a little time and you'll see that it's the work sent to you at the moment you need it most. I won't take no for an answer——"

He put on his hat and started to the door:

"I'll just report to the Committee that I notified you and that you have the matter under consideration."

Before Norton could enter a protest the politician had gone.

His decision was instantly made. This startling event revealed the hopelessness of life under its present conditions. He would leave the South. He would put a thousand miles between him and the scene of the events of the past year. He would leave his home with its torturing memories.

Above all, he would leave the negroid conditions that made his shame possible and rear his boy in clean air.

Chapter XIX

Cleo's Cry

The decision once made was carried out without delay. He placed an editor permanently in charge of his paper, closed the tall green shutters of the stately old house, sold his horses, and bought tickets for himself and mammy for New York.

He paused at the gate and looked back at the white pillars of which he had once been so proud. He hadn't a single regret at leaving.

"A house doesn't make a home, after all!" he sighed with a lingering look.

He took the boy to the cemetery for a last hour beside the mother's grave before he should turn his back on the scenes of his old life forever.

The cemetery was the most beautiful spot in the county. At this period of the life of the South, it was the one spot where every home had its little plot. The war had killed the flower of Southern manhood. The bravest and the noblest boys never surrendered. They died with a shout and a smile on their lips and Southern women came daily now to keep their love watches on these solemn bivouacs of the dead. The girls got the habit of going there to plant flowers and to tend them and grew to love the shaded walks, the deep boxwood hedges, the quiet, sweetly perfumed air. Sweethearts were always strolling among the flowers and from every nook and corner peeped a rustic seat that could tell its story of the first stammering words from lovers' lips.

Norton saw them everywhere this beautiful spring afternoon, the girls in their white, clean dresses, the boys bashful and self-conscious. A throb of pain gripped his heart and he hurried through the wilderness of flowers to the spot beneath a great oak where he had laid the tired body of the first and only woman he had ever loved.

He placed the child on the grass and led him to the newly-made mound, put into his tiny hand the roses he had brought and guided him while he placed them on her grave.

"This is where little mother sleeps, my boy," he said, softly. "Remember it now—it will be a long, long time before we shall see it again. You won't forget——"

"No—dad-ee," he lisped sweetly. "I'll not fordet, the big tree——"

The man rose and stood in silence seeing again the last beautiful day of their life together and forgot the swift moments. He stood as in a trance from which he was suddenly awakened by the child's voice calling him excitedly from another walkway into which he had wandered:

"Dad-ee!" he called again.

"Yes, baby," he answered.

"Oh, come quick! Dad-ee—here's C-l-e-o!"

Norton turned and with angry steps measured the distance between them.

He came upon them suddenly behind a boxwood hedge. The girl was kneeling with the child's arms around her neck, clinging to her with all the yearning of his hungry little heart, and she was muttering half articulate words of love and tenderness. She held him from her a moment, looked into his eyes and cried:

"And you missed me, darling?"

"Oh—C-l-e-o!" he cried, "I thought 'oo'd *nev-er* tum!"

The angry words died in the man's lips as he watched the scene in silence.

He stooped and drew the child away:

"Come, baby, we must go——"

"Tum on, C-l-e-o, we do now," he cried.

The girl shook her head and turned away.

"Tum on, C-l-e-o!" he cried tenderly.

She waved him a kiss, and the child said excitedly:

"Oh, dad-ee, wait!—wait for C-1-e-o!"

"No, my baby, she can't come with us——"

The little head sank to his shoulder, a sob rose from his heart and he burst into weeping. And through the storm of tears one word only came out clear and soft and plaintive:

"C-1-e-o! C-1-e-o!"

The girl watched them until they reached the gate and then, on a sudden impulse, ran swiftly up, caught the child's hand that hung limply down his father's back, covered it with kisses and cried in cheerful, half-laughing tones:

"Don't cry, darling! Cleo will come again!"

And in the long journey to the North the man brooded over the strange tones of joyous assurance with which the girl had spoken.

Chapter XX

The Blow Falls

For a time Norton lost himself in the stunning immensity of the life of New York. He made no effort to adjust himself to it. He simply allowed its waves to roll over and engulf him.

He stopped with mammy and the boy at a brownstone boarding house on Stuyvesant Square kept by a Southern woman to whom he had a letter of introduction.

Mrs. Beam was not an ideal landlady, but her good-natured helplessness appealed to him. She was a large woman of ample hips and bust, and though very tall seemed always in her own way. She moved slowly and laughed with a final sort of surrender to fate when anything went wrong. And it was generally going wrong. She was still comparatively young—perhaps thirty-two—but was built on so large and unwieldy a pattern that it was not easy to guess her age, especially as she had a silly tendency to harmless kittenish ways at times.

The poor thing was pitifully at sea in her new world and its work. She had been reared in a typically extravagant home of the old South where slaves had waited her call from childhood. She had not learned to sew, or cook or keep house—in fact, she had never learned to do anything useful or important. So naturally she took boarders. Her husband, on whose shoulders she had placed every burden of life the day of her marriage, lay somewhere in an unmarked trench on a Virginia battlefield.

She couldn't conceive of any human being enduring a servant that wasn't black and so had turned her house over to a lazy and worthless crew of Northern negro help. The house was never clean, the waste in her kitchen was appalling, but so long as she could find money to pay her rent and grocery bills, she was happy. Her only child, a daughter of sixteen, never dreamed of lifting her hand to work, and it hadn't yet occurred to the mother to insult her with such a suggestion.

Norton was not comfortable but he was lonely, and Mrs. Beam's easy ways, genial smile and Southern weaknesses somehow gave him a sense of being at home and he stayed. Mammy complained bitterly of the insolence and low manners of the kitchen. But he only laughed and told her she'd get used to it.

He was astonished to find that so many Southern people had drifted to New York—exiles of all sorts, with one universal trait, poverty and politeness.

And they quickly made friends. As he began to realize it, his heart went out to the great city with a throb of gratitude.

When the novelty of the new world had gradually worn off a feeling of loneliness set in. He couldn't get used to the crowds on every street, these roaring rivers of strange faces rushing by like the waters of a swollen stream after a freshet, hurrying and swirling out of its banks.

At first he had found himself trying to bow to every man he met and take off his hat to every woman. It took a long time to break himself of this Southern instinct. The thing that cured him completely was when he tipped his hat unconsciously to a lady on Fifth Avenue. She blushed furiously, hurried to the corner and had him arrested.

His apology was so abject, so evidently sincere, his grief so absurd over her mistake that when she caught his Southern drawl, it was her turn to blush and ask his pardon.

A feeling of utter depression and pitiful homesickness gradually crushed his spirit. His soul began to cry for the sunlit fields and the perfumed nights of the South. There didn't seem to be any moon or stars here, and the only birds he ever saw were the chattering drab little sparrows in the parks.

The first day of autumn, as he walked through Central Park, a magnificent Irish setter lifted his fine head and spied him. Some subtle instinct told the dog that the man was a hunter and a lover of his kind. The setter wagged his tail and introduced himself. Norton dropped to a seat, drew the shaggy face into his lap, and stroked his head.

He was back home again. Don, with his fine nose high in the air, was circling a field and Andy was shouting:

"He's got 'em! He's got 'em sho, Marse Dan!"

He could see Don's slim white and black figure stepping slowly through the high grass on velvet feet, glancing back to see if his master were coming—the muscles suddenly stiffened, his tail became rigid, and the whole covey of quail were under his nose!

He was a boy again and felt the elemental thrill of man's first work as hunter and fisherman. He looked about him at the bald coldness of the artificial park and a desperate longing surged through his heart to be among his own people again, to live their life and feel their joys and sorrows as his own.

And then the memory of the great tragedy slowly surged back, he pushed the dog aside, rose and hurried on in his search for a new world.

He tried the theatres—saw Booth in his own house on 23d Street play "Hamlet" and Lawrence Barrett "Othello," listened with rapture to the new Italian Grand Opera Company in the Academy of Music—saw a burlesque in the Tammany Theatre on 14th Street, Lester Wallack in "The School for Scandal" at Wallack's Theatre on Broadway at 13th Street, and Tony Pastor in his variety show at his Opera House on the Bowery, and yet returned each night with a dull ache in his heart.

Other men who loved home less perhaps could adjust themselves to new surroundings, but somehow in him this home instinct, this feeling of personal friendliness for neighbor and people, this passion for house and lawn, flowers and trees and shrubs, for fields and rivers and hills, seemed of the very fibre of his inmost life. This vast rushing, roaring, impersonal world, driven by invisible titanic forces, somehow didn't appeal to him. It merely stunned and appalled and confused his mind.

And then without warning the blow fell.

He told himself afterwards that he must have been waiting for it, that some mysterious power of mental telepathy had wired its message without words across the thousand miles that separated him from the old life, and yet the surprise was complete and overwhelming.

He had tried that morning to write. A story was shaping itself in his mind and he felt the impulse to express it. But he was too depressed. He threw his pencil down in disgust and walked to his window facing the little park.

It was a bleak, miserable day in November—the first freezing weather had come during the night and turned a drizzling rain into sleet. The streets were covered with a thin, hard, glistening coat of ice. A coal wagon had stalled in front of the house, a magnificent draught horse had fallen and a brutal driver began to beat him unmercifully.

Henry Berg's Society had not yet been organized.

Norton rushed from the door and faced the astonished driver:

"Don't you dare to strike that horse again!"

The workman turned his half-drunken face on the intruder with a vicious leer:

"Well, what t'ell——"

"I mean it!"

With an oath the driver lunged at him:

"Get out of my way!"

The big fist shot at Norton's head. He parried the attack and knocked the man down. The driver scrambled to his feet and plunged forward again. A second blow sent him flat on his back on the ice and his body slipped three feet and struck the curb.

"Have you got enough?" Norton asked, towering over the sprawling figure.

"Yes."

"Well, get up now, and I'll help you with the horse."

He helped the sullen fellow unhitch the fallen horse, lift him to his feet and readjust the harness. He put shoulder to the wheel and started the wagon again on its way.

He returned to his room feeling better. It was the first fight he had started for months and it stirred his blood to healthy reaction.

He watched the bare limbs swaying in the bitter wind in front of St. George's Church and his eye rested on the steeples the architects said were unsafe and might fall some day with a crash, and his depression slowly returned. He had waked that morning with a vague sense of dread.

"I guess it was that fight!" he muttered. "The scoundrel will be back in an hour with a warrant for my arrest and I'll spend a few days in jail——"

The postman's whistle blew at the basement window. He knew that fellow by the way he started the first notes of his call—always low, swelling into a peculiar shrill crescendo and dying away in a weird cry of pain.

The call this morning was one of startling effects. It was his high nerve tension, of course, that made the difference—perhaps, too, the bitter cold and swirling gusts of wind outside. But the shock was none the less vivid. The whistle began so low it seemed at first the moaning of the wind, the high note rang higher and higher, until it became the shout of a fiend, and died away with a wail of agony wrung from a lost soul.

He shivered at the sound. He would not have been surprised to receive a letter from the dead after that.

He heard some one coming slowly up stairs. It was mammy and the boy. The lazy maid had handed his mail to her, of course.

His door was pushed open and the child ran in holding a letter in his red, chubby hand:

"A letter, daddy!" he cried.

He took it mechanically, staring at the inscription.

He knew now the meaning of his horrible depression! She was writing that letter when it began yesterday. He recognized Cleo's handwriting at a glance, though this was unusually blurred and crooked. The postmark was Baltimore, another striking fact.

He laid the letter down on his table unopened and turned to mammy:

"Take him to your room. I'm trying to do some writing."

The old woman took the child's hand grumbling:

"Come on, mammy's darlin,' nobody wants us!"

He closed the door, locked it, glanced savagely at the unopened letter, drew his chair before the open fire and gazed into the glowing coals.

He feared to break the seal—feared with a dull, sickening dread. He glanced at it again as though he were looking at a toad that had suddenly intruded into his room.

Six months had passed without a sign, and he had ceased to wonder at the strange calm with which she received her dismissal and his flight from the scene after his wife's death. He had begun to believe that her shadow would never again fall across his life.

It had come at last. He picked the letter up, and tried to guess its meaning. She was going to make demands on him, of course. He had expected this months ago. But why should she be in Baltimore? He thought of a hundred foolish reasons without once the faintest suspicion of the truth entering his mind.

He broke the seal and read its contents. A look of vague incredulity overspread his face, followed by a sudden pallor. The one frightful thing he had dreaded and forgotten was true!

He crushed the letter in his powerful hand with a savage groan:

"God in Heaven!"

He spread it out again and read and reread its message, until each word burned its way into his soul:

> "Our baby was born here yesterday. I was on my way to New York to you, but was taken sick on the train at Baltimore and had to stop. I'm alone and have no money, but I'm proud and happy. I know that you will help me.
>
> "Cleo."

For hours he sat in a stupor of pain, holding this crumpled letter in his hand, staring into the fire.

Chapter XXI

The Call of the Blood

It was all clear now, the mystery of Cleo's assurance, of her happiness, of her acceptance of his going without protest.

She had known the truth from the first and had reckoned on his strength and manliness to draw him to her in this hour.

"I'll show her!" he said in fierce rebellion. "I'll give her the money she needs—yes—but her shadow shall never again darken my life. I won't permit this shame to smirch the soul of my boy—I'll die first!"

He moved to the West side of town, permitted no one to learn his new address, sent her money from the general postoffice, and directed all his mail to a lock box he had secured.

He destroyed thus every trace by which she might discover his residence if she dared to venture into New York.

To his surprise it was more than three weeks before he received a reply from her. And the second letter made an appeal well-nigh resistless. The message was brief, but she had instinctively chosen the words that found him. How well she knew that side of his nature! He resented it with rage and tried to read all sorts of sinister guile into the lines. But as he scanned them a second time reason rejected all save the simplest and most obvious meaning the words implied.

The letter was evidently written in a cramped position. She had missed the lines many times and some words were so scrawled they were scarcely legible. But he read them all at last:

> "I have been very sick since your letter came with the

money. I tried to get up too soon. I have suffered awfully. You see, I didn't know how much I had gone through. Please don't be angry with me for what neither you nor I can help now. I want to see you just once, and then I won't trouble you any more. I am very weak to-day, but I'll soon be strong again.

"Cleo."

It made him furious, this subtle appeal to his keen sense of fatherhood. She knew how tenderly he loved his boy. She knew that while such obligations rest lightly on some men, the tie that bound him to his son was the biggest thing in his life. She had been near him long enough to learn the secret things of his inner life. She was using them now to break down the barriers of character and self-respect. He could see it plainly. He hated her for it and yet the appeal went straight to his heart.

Two things in this letter he couldn't get away from:

"You see, I didn't know how much I had gone through."

He kept reading this over. And the next line:

"Please don't be angry with me for what neither you nor I can help now."

The appeal was so human, so simple, so obviously sincere, no man with a soul could ignore it. How could she help it now? She too had been swept into the tragic situation by the blind forces of Nature. After all, had it not been inevitable? Did not such a position of daily intimate physical contact—morning, noon and night—mean just this? Could she have helped it? Were they not both the victims, in a sense, of the follies of centuries? Had he the right to be angry with her?

His reason answered, no. And again came the deeper question—can any man ever escape the consequences of his deeds? Deeds are of the infinite and eternal and the smallest one disturbs the universe. It slowly began to dawn on him that nothing he could ever do or say could change one elemental fact. She was a mother—a fact bigger than all the forms and ceremonies of the ages. It was just this thing in his history that made his sin against the wife so poignant, both to her and to his imagination. A child was a child, and he had no right to sneak and play a coward in such an hour.

Step by step the woman's simple cry forced its way into the soul and slowly but surely the rags were stripped from pride, until he began to see himself naked and without sham.

The one thing that finally cut deepest was the single sentence: "You see, I didn't know how much I had gone through——"

He read it again with a feeling of awe. No matter what the shade of her olive cheek or the length of her curly hair, she was a mother with all that big word means in the language of men. Say what he might–of her art in leading him on, of her final offering herself in a hundred subtle ways in their daily life in his home—he was still responsible. He had accepted the challenge at last.

And he knew what it meant to any woman under the best conditions, with a mother's face hovering near and the man she loved by her side. He saw again the scene of his boy's birth. And then another picture—a lonely girl in a strange city without a friend—a cot in the whitewashed ward of a city's hospital—a pair of startled eyes looking in vain for a loved, familiar face as her trembling feet stepped falteringly down into the valley that lies between Life and Death!

A pitiful thing, this hour of suffering and of waiting for the unknown.

His heart went out to her in sympathy, and he answered her letter with a promise to come. But on the day he was to start for Baltimore mammy was stricken with a cold which developed into pneumonia. Unaccustomed to the rigors of a Northern climate, she had been careless and the result from the first was doubtful. To leave her was, of course, impossible.

He sent for a doctor and two nurses and no care or expense was spared, but in spite of every effort she died. It was four weeks before he returned from the funeral in the South.

He reached Baltimore in a blinding snowstorm the week preceding Christmas. Cleo had left the hospital three weeks previous to his arrival, and for some unexplained reason had spent a week or ten days in Norfolk and returned in time to meet him.

He failed to find her at the address she had given him, but was directed to an obscure hotel in another quarter of the city.

He was surprised and puzzled at the attitude assumed at this meeting. She was nervous, irritable, insolent and apparently anxious for a fight.

"Well, why do you stare at me like that?" she asked angrily.

"Was I staring?" he said with an effort at self-control.

"After all I've been through the past weeks," she said bitterly, "I didn't care whether I lived or died."

"I meant to have come at once as I wrote you. But mammy's illness and death made it impossible to get here sooner."

"One excuse is as good as another," she retorted with a contemptuous toss of her head.

Norton looked at her in blank amazement. It was inconceivable that this was the same woman who wrote him the simple, sincere appeal a few weeks ago. It was possible, of course, that suffering had embittered her mind and reduced her temporarily to the nervous condition in which she appeared.

"Why do you keep staring at me?" she asked again, with insolent ill-temper.

He was so enraged at her evident attempt to bully him into an attitude of abject sympathy, he shot her a look of rage, seized his hat and without a word started for the door.

With a cry of despair she was by his side and grasped his arm:

"Please—please don't!"

"Change your tactics, then, if you have anything to say to me."

She flushed, stammered, looked at him queerly and then smiled:

"Yes, I will, major—please don't be mad at me! You see, I'm just a little crazy. I've been through so much since I came here I didn't know what I was saying to you. I'm awfully sorry—let me take your hat——"

She took his hat, laid it on the table and led him to a seat.

"Please sit down. I'm so glad you've come, and I thank you for coming. I'm just as humble and grateful as I can be. You must forget how foolish I've acted. I've been so miserable and scared and lonely, it's a wonder I haven't jumped into the bay. And I just thought at last that you were never coming."

Norton looked at her with new astonishment. Not because there was anything strange in what she said—he had expected some such words on his arrival, but because they didn't ring true. She seemed to be lying. There was an expression of furtive cunning in her greenish eyes that was uncanny. He couldn't make her out. In spite of the effort to be friendly she was repulsive.

"Well, I'm here," he said calmly. "You have something to say—what is it?"

"Of course," she answered smilingly. "I have a lot to say. I want you to tell me what to do."

"Anything you like," he answered bluntly.

"It's nothing to you?"

"I'll give you an allowance."

"Is that all?"

"What else do you expect?"

"You don't want to see her?"

"No."

"I thought you were coming for that?"

"I've changed my mind. And the less we see of each other the better. I'll go with you to-morrow and verify the records——"

Cleo laughed:

"You don't think I'm joking about her birth?"

"No. But I'm not going to take your word for it."

"All right, I'll go with you to-morrow."

He started again to the door. He felt that he must leave—that he was smothering. Something about the girl's manner got on his nerves. Not only was there no sort of sympathy or attraction between them but the longer he stayed in her presence the more he felt the desire to choke her. He began to look into her eyes with growing suspicion and hate, and behind their smiling plausibility he felt the power of a secret deadly hostility.

"You don't want me to go back home with the child, do you?" Cleo asked with a furtive glance.

"No, I do not," he replied, emphatically.

"I'm going back—but I'll give her up and let you educate her in a convent on one condition——" "What?" he asked sharply.

"That you let me nurse the boy again and give me the protection and shelter of your home——"

"Never!" he cried.

"Please be reasonable. It will be best for you and best for me and best for her that her life shall never be blackened by the stain of my blood. I've thought it all out. It's the only way——"

"No," he replied sternly. "I'll educate her in my own way, if placed in my hands without condition. But you shall never enter my house again——"

"Is it fair," she pleaded, "to take everything from me and turn me out in the world alone? I'll give your boy all the love of a hungry heart. He loves me."

"He has forgotten your existence——"

"You know that he hasn't!"

"I know that he has," Norton persisted with rising wrath. "It's a waste of breath for you to talk to me about this thing"—he turned on her fiercely:

"Why do you wish to go back there? To grin and hint the truth to your friends?"

"You know that I'd cut my tongue out sooner than betray you. I'd like to scream it from every housetop—yes. But I won't. I won't, because your smile or frown means too much to me. I'm asking this that I may live and work for you and be your slave without money and without price——"

"I understand," he broke in bitterly, "because you think that thus you can again drag me down—well, you can't do it! The power you once had is gone—gone forever—never to return——"

"Then why be afraid? No one there knows except my mother. You hate me. All right. I can do you no harm. I'll never hate you. I'll just be happy to serve you, to love your boy and help you rear him to be a fine man. Let me go back with you and open the old house again——"

He lifted his hand with a gesture of angry impatience:

"Enough of this now—you go your way in life and I go mine."

"I'll not give her up except on my conditions——"

"Then you can keep her and go where you please. If you return home you'll not find me. I'll put the ocean between us if necessary——"

He stepped quickly to the door and she knew it was needless to argue further.

"Come to my hotel to-morrow morning at ten o'clock and I'll make you a settlement through a lawyer."

"I'll be there," she answered in a low tone, "but please, major, before you go let me ask you not to remember the foolish things I said and the way I acted when you came. I'm so sorry—forgive me. I made you terribly mad. I don't know what was the matter with me. Remember I'm just a foolish girl here without a friend——"

She stopped, her voice failing:

"Oh, my God, I'm so lonely, I don't want to live! You don't know what it means for me just to be near you—please let me go home with you!"

There was something genuine in this last cry. It reached his heart in spite of anger. He hesitated and spoke in kindly tones:

"Good night—I'll see you in the morning."

This plea of loneliness and homesickness found the weak spot in his armor. It was so clearly the echo of his own feelings. The old home, with its beautiful and sad memories, his people and his work had begun to pull resistlessly. Her suggestion was a subtle and dangerous one, doubly seductive because it was so safe a solution of difficulties. There was not the shadow of a doubt that her deeper purpose was to ultimately dominate his personal life. He was sure of his strength, yet he knew that the wise thing to do was to refuse to listen.

At ten o'clock next morning she came. He had called a lawyer and drawn up a settlement that only waited her signature.

She had not said she would sign—she had not positively refused. She was looking at him with dumb pleading eyes.

Without a moment's warning the boy pushed his way into the room. Norton sprang before Cleo and shouted angrily to the nurse:

"I told you not to let him come into this room——"

"But you see I des tum——!" the boy answered with a laugh as he darted to the corner.

The thing he dreaded had happened. In a moment the child saw Cleo. There was just an instant's hesitation and the father smiled that he had forgotten her. But the hesitation was only the moment of dazed surprise. With a scream of joy he crossed the room and sprang into her arms:

"Oh, Cleo—Cleo—my Cleo! You've tum—you've tum! Look, Daddy! She's tum—my Cleo!"

He hugged her, he kissed her, he patted her flushed cheeks, he ran his little fingers through her tangled hair, drew himself up and kissed her again.

She snatched him to her heart and burst into uncontrollable sobs, raised her eyes streaming with tears to Norton and said softly:

"Let me go home with you!"

He looked at her, hesitated and then slowly tore the legal document to pieces, threw it in the fire and nodded his consent.

But this time his act was not surrender. He had heard the call of his people and his country. It was the first step toward the execution of a new life purpose that had suddenly flamed in the depths of his darkened soul as he watched the picture of the olive cheek of the woman against the clear white of his child's.

Book Two

ATONEMENT

Chapter I

The New Life Purpose

Norton had been compelled to wait twenty years for the hour when he could strike the first decisive blow in the execution of his new life purpose.

But the aim he had set was so high, so utterly unselfish, so visionary, so impossible by the standards of modern materialism, he felt the thrill of the religious fanatic as he daily girded himself to his task.

He was far from being a religious enthusiast, although he had grown a religion of his own, inherited in part, dreamed in part from the depth of his own heart. The first article of this faith was a firm belief in the ever-brooding Divine Spirit and its guidance in the work of man if he but opened his mind to its illumination.

He believed, as in his own existence, that God's Spirit had revealed the vision he saw in the hour of his agony, twenty years before when he had watched his boy's tiny arms encircle the neck of Cleo, the tawny young animal who had wrecked his life, but won the heart of his child. He had tried to desert his people of the South and awaked with a shock. His mind in prophetic gaze had leaped the years and seen the gradual wearing down of every barrier between the white and black races by the sheer force of daily contact under the new conditions which Democracy had made inevitable.

Even under the iron laws of slavery it was impossible for an inferior and superior race to live side by side for centuries as master and slave without the breaking down of some of these barriers. But the moment the magic principle of equality in a Democracy became the law of life they must all melt or Democracy itself yield and die. He had squarely faced this big question and given his life to its solution.

When he returned to his old home and installed Cleo as his housekeeper and nurse she was the living incarnation before his eyes daily of the problem to be solved—the incarnation of its subtleties and its dangers. He studied her with the cold intellectual passion of a scientist. Nor was there ever a moment's uncertainty or halting in the grim purpose that fired his soul.

She had at first accepted his matter of fact treatment as the sign of ultimate surrender. And yet as the years passed she saw with increasing wonder and rage the gulf between them deepen and darken. She tried every art her mind could conceive and her effective body symbolize in vain. His eyes looked at her, but never saw the woman. They only saw the thing he hated—the mongrel breed of a degraded nation.

He had begun his work at the beginning. He had tried to do the things that were possible. The minds of the people were not yet ready to accept the idea of a complete separation of the races. He planned for the slow process of an epic movement. His paper, in season and out of season, presented the daily life of the black and white races in such a way that the dullest mind must be struck by the fact that their relations presented an insoluble problem. Every road of escape led at last through a blind alley against a blank wall.

In this policy he antagonized no one, but expressed always the doubts and fears that lurked in the minds of thoughtful men and women. His paper had steadily grown in circulation and in solid power. He meant to use this power at the right moment. He had waited patiently and the hour at last had struck.

The thunder of a torpedo under an American warship lying in Havana harbor shook the Nation and changed the alignment of political parties.

The war with Spain lasted but a few months, but it gave the South her chance. Her sons leaped to the front and proved their loyalty to the flag. The "Bloody Shirt" could never again be waved. The negro ceased to be a ward of the Nation and the Union of States our fathers dreamed was at last an accomplished fact. There could never again be a "North" or a "South."

Norton's first brilliant editorial reviewing the results of this war drew the fire of his enemies from exactly the quarter he expected.

A little college professor, who aspired to the leadership of Southern thought under Northern patronage, called at his office.

The editor's lips curled with contempt as he read the engraved card:

"Professor Alexander Magraw"

The man had long been one of his pet aversions. He occupied a chair in one of the state's leading colleges, and his effusions advocating peace at any price on the negro problem had grown so disgusting of late the *Eagle and Phoenix* had refused to print them.

Magraw was nothing daunted. He devoted his energies to writing a book in fulsome eulogy of a notorious negro which had made him famous in the North. He wrote it to curry favor with the millionaires who were backing this African's work and succeeded in winning their boundless admiration. They hailed him the coming leader of "advanced thought." As a Southern white man the little professor had boldly declared that this negro, who had never done anything except to demonstrate his skill as a beggar in raising a million dollars from Northern sentimentalists, was the greatest human being ever born in America!

Outraged public opinion in the South had demanded his expulsion from the college for this idiotic effusion, but he was so entrenched behind the power of money he could not be disturbed. His loud protests for free speech following his acquittal had greatly increased the number of his henchmen.

Norton wondered at the meaning of his visit. It could only be a sinister one. In view of his many contemptuous references to the man, he was amazed at his audacity in venturing to invade his office.

He scowled a long while at the card and finally said to the boy:

"Show him in."

Chapter II

A Modern Scalawag

As the professor entered the office Norton was surprised at his height and weight. He had never met him personally, but had unconsciously formed the idea that he was a scrub physically.

He saw a man above the average height, weighing nearly two hundred, with cheeks flabby but inclined to fat. It was not until he spoke that he caught the unmistakable note of effeminacy in his voice and saw it clearly reflected in his features.

He was dressed with immaculate neatness and wore a tie of an extraordinary shade of lavender which matched the silk hose that showed above his stylish low-cut shoes.

"Major Norton, I believe?" he said with a smile.

The editor bowed without rising:

"At your service, Professor Magraw. Have a seat, sir."

"Thank you! Thank you!" the dainty voice murmured with so marked a resemblance to a woman's tones that Norton was torn between two impulses—one to lift his eyebrows and sigh, "Oh, splash!" and the other to kick him down the stairs. He was in no mood for the amenities of polite conversation, turned and asked bluntly:

"May I inquire, professor, why you have honored me with this unexpected call—I confess I am very curious?"

"No doubt, no doubt," he replied glibly. "You have certainly not minced matters in your personal references to me in the paper of late, Major Norton, but I have simply taken it good-naturedly as a part of your day's work. Apparently we represent two irreconcilable ideals of Southern society——"

"There can be no doubt about that," Norton interrupted grimly.

"Yet I have dared to hope that our differences are only apparent and that we might come to a better understanding."

He paused, simpered and smiled.

"About what?" the editor asked with a frown.

"About the best policy for the leaders of public opinion to pursue to more rapidly advance the interests of the South——"

"And by 'interests of the South' you mean?"

"The best interest of all the people without regard to race or color!"

Norton smiled:

"You forgot part of the pass-word of your order, professor! The whole clause used to read, 'race, color or previous condition of servitude'——"

The sneer was lost on the professor. He was too intent on his mission.

"I have called, Major Norton," he went on glibly, "to inform you that my distinguished associates in the great Educational Movement in the South view with increasing alarm the tendency of your paper to continue the agitation of the so-called negro problem."

"And may I ask by whose authority your distinguished associates have been set up as the arbiters of the destiny of twenty millions of white citizens of the South?"

The professor flushed with amazement at the audacity of such a question:

"They have given millions to the cause of education, sir! These great Funds represent to-day a power that is becoming more and more resistless——"

Norton sprang to his feet and faced Magraw with eyes flashing:

"That's why I haven't minced matters in my references to you, professor. That's why I'm getting ready to strike a blow in the cause of racial purity for which my paper stands."

"But why continue to rouse the bitterness of racial feeling? The question will settle itself if let alone."

"How?"

"By the process of evolution——"

"Exactly!" Norton thundered. "And by that you mean the gradual breaking down of racial barriers and the degradation of our people to a mongrel negroid level or you mean nothing! No miracle of evolution can gloss over the meaning of such a tragedy. The Negro is the lowest of all human forms, four thousand years below the standard of the pioneer white Aryan who discovered this continent and peopled it with a race of empire builders. The gradual mixture of our blood with his can only result in the extinction of National character—a calamity so appalling the mind of every patriot refuses to accept for a moment its possibility."

"I am not advocating such a mixture!" the professor mildly protested.

"In so many words, no," retorted Norton; "yet you are setting in motion forces that make it inevitable, as certain as life, as remorseless as death. When you demand that the patriot of the South let the Negro alone to work out his own destiny, you know that the mere physical contact of two such races is a constant menace to white civilization——"

The professor raised the delicate, tapering hands:

"The old nightmare of negro domination is only a thing with which to frighten children, major, the danger is a myth——"

"Indeed!" Norton sneered. "When our people saw the menace of an emancipated slave suddenly clothed with the royal power of a ballot they met this threat against the foundations of law and order by a counter revolution and restored a government of the wealth, virtue and intelligence of the community. What they have not yet seen, is the more insidious danger that threatens the inner home life of a Democratic nation from the physical contact of two such races."

"And you propose to prevent that contact?" the piping voice asked.

"Yes."

"And may I ask how?"

"By an ultimate complete separation through a process covering perhaps two hundred years——"

The professor laughed:

"Visionary—impossible!"

"All right," Norton slowly replied. "I see the invisible and set myself to do the impossible. Because men have done such things the world moves forward not backward!"

The lavender hose moved stealthily:

"You will advocate this?" the professor asked.

"In due time. The Southern white man and woman still labor under the old delusion that the negro's lazy, slipshod ways are necessary and that we could not get along without him——"

"And if you dare to antagonize that faith?"

"When your work is done, professor, and the glorious results of Evolution are shown to mean the giving in marriage of our sons and daughters, my task will be easy. In the mean time I'll do the work at hand. The negro is still a voter. The devices by which he is prevented from using the power to which his numbers entitle him are but temporary. The first real work before the statesmen of the South is the disfranchisement of the African, the repeal of the Fifteenth Amendment to our Constitution and the restoration of American citizenship to its original dignity and meaning."

"A large undertaking," the professor glibly observed. "And you will dare such a program?"

"I'll at least strike a blow for it. The first great crime against the purity of our racial stock was the mixture of blood which the physical contact of slavery made inevitable.

"But the second great crime, and by far the most tragic and disastrous, was the insane Act of Congress inspired by the passions of the Reconstruction period by which a million ignorant black men, but yesterday from the jungles of Africa, were clothed with the full powers of citizenship under the flag of Democracy and given the right by the ballot to rule a superior race.

"The Act of Emancipation was a war measure pure and simple. By that act Lincoln sought to strike the South as a political power a mortal blow. He did not free four million negroes for sentimental reasons. He destroyed four billion dollars' worth of property invested in slaves as an act of war to save the Union. Nothing was further from his mind or heart than the mad idea that these Africans could be assimilated into our National life. He intended to separate the races and give the Negro a nation of his own. But the hand of a madman struck the great leader down in the hour of his supreme usefulness.

"In the anarchy which followed the assassination of the President and the attempt of a daring coterie of fanatics in Washington to impeach his successor and create a dictatorship, the great crime against Democracy was committed. Millions of black men, with the intelligence of children and the instincts of savages, were given full and equal citizenship with the breed of men who created the Republic.

"Any plan to solve intelligently the problem of the races must first correct this blunder from which a stream of poison has been pouring into our life.

"The first step in the work of separating the races, therefore, must be to deprive the negro of this enormous power over Democratic society. It is not a solution of the problem, but as the great blunder was the giving of this symbol of American kingship, our first task is to take it from him and restore the ballot to its original sanctity."

"Your movement will encounter difficulties, I foresee!" observed the professor with a gracious smile.

He was finding his task with Norton easier than he anticipated. The editor's madness was evidently so hopeless he had only to deliver his ultimatum and close the interview.

"The difficulties are great," Norton went on with renewed emphasis, "but less than they have been for the past twenty years. Until yesterday the negro was the ward of the Nation. Any movement by a Southern state to remove his menace was immediately met by a call to arms to defend the

Union by Northern demagogues who had never smelled powder when the Union was in danger.

"A foolish preacher in Boston who enjoys a National reputation has been in the habit of rousing his hearers to a round of cheers by stamping his foot, lifting hands above his head and yelling:

"'The only way to save the Union now is for Northern mothers to rear more children than Southern mothers!'

"And the sad part of it is that thousands of otherwise sane people in New England and other sections of the North and West believed this idiotic statement to be literally true. It is no longer possible to fool them with such chaff——"

The professor rose and shook out his finely creased trousers until the lavender hose scarcely showed:

"I am afraid, Major Norton, that it is useless for us to continue this discussion. You are quite determined to maintain the policy of your paper on this point?"

"Quite."

"I am sorry. The *Eagle and Phoenix* is a very powerful influence in this state. The distinguished associates whom I represent sent me in the vain hope that I might persuade you to drop the agitation of this subject and join with us in developing the material and educational needs of the South——"

Norton laughed aloud:

"Really, professor?"

The visitor flushed at the marked sneer in his tones, and fumbled his lavender tie:

"I can only deliver to you our ultimatum, therefore——"

"You are clothed with sovereign powers, then?" the editor asked sarcastically.

"If you choose to designate them so—yes. Unless you agree to drop this dangerous and useless agitation of the negro question and give our people a hearing in the columns of your paper, I am authorized to begin at once the publication of a journal that will express the best sentiment of the South——"

"So?"

"And I have unlimited capital to back it."

Norton's eyes flashed as he squared himself before the professor:

"I've not a doubt of your backing. Start your paper to-morrow if you like. You'll find that it takes more than money to build a great organ of public opinion in the South. I've put my immortal soul into this plant. I'll watch your experiment with interest."

"Thank you! Thank you," the thin voice piped.

"And now that we understand each other," Norton went on, "you've given me the chance to say a few things to you and your associates I've been wanting to express for a long time——"

Norton paused and fixed his visitor with an angry stare:

"Not only is the Negro gaining in numbers, in wealth and in shallow 'culture,' and tightening his grip on the soil as the owner in fee simple of thousands of homes, churches, schools and farms, but a Negroid party has once more developed into a powerful and sinister influence on the life of this state! You and your associates are loud in your claims to represent a new South. In reality you are the direct descendants of the Reconstruction Scalawag and Carpetbagger.

"The old Scalawag was the Judas Iscariot who sold his people for thirty pieces of silver which he got by licking the feet of his conqueror and fawning on his negro allies. The Carpetbagger was a Northern adventurer who came South to prey on the misfortunes of a ruined people. A new and far more dangerous order of Scalawags has arisen—the man who boldly preaches the omnipotence of the dollar and weighs every policy of state or society by one standard only, will it pay in dollars and cents? And so you frown on any discussion of the tragic problem the negro's continued pressure on Southern society involves because it disturbs business.

"The unparalleled growth of wealth in the North has created our enormous Poor Funds, organized by generous well-meaning men for the purpose of education in the South. As a matter of fact, this new educational movement had its origin in the same soil that established negro classical schools and attempted to turn the entire black race into preachers, lawyers, and doctors just after the war. Your methods, however, are wiser, although your policies are inspired, if not directed, by the fertile brain of a notorious negro of doubtful moral character.

"The directors of your Poor Funds profess to be the only true friends of the true white man of the South. By a 'true white man of the South' you mean a man who is willing to show his breadth of vision by fraternizing occasionally with negroes.

"An army of lickspittles have begun to hang on the coat-tails of your dispensers of alms. Their methods are always the same. They attempt to attract the notice of the Northern distributors by denouncing men of my type who are earnestly, fearlessly and reverently trying to face and solve the darkest problem the centuries have presented to America. These little beggars have begun to vie with one another not only in denouncing the leaders of public opinion in the South, but in fulsome and disgusting fawning at the feet of the individual negro whose personal influence dominates these Funds."

Again the lavender socks moved uneasily.

"In which category you place the author of a certain book, I suppose?" inquired the professor.

"I paused in the hope that you might not miss my meaning," Norton replied, smiling. "The astounding power for the debasement of public opinion developing through these vast corruption funds is one of the most sinister influences which now threatens Southern society. It is the most difficult of all to meet because its protestations are so plausible and philanthropic.

"The Carpetbagger has come back to the South. This time he is not a low adventurer seeking coin and public office. He is a philanthropist who carries hundreds of millions of dollars to be distributed to the 'right' men who will teach Southern boys and girls the 'right' ideas. So far as these 'right' ideas touch the negro, they mean the ultimate complete acceptance of the black man as a social equal.

"Your chief spokesman of this New Order of Carpetbag, for example, has declared on many occasions that the one thing in his life of which he is most proud is the fact that he is the personal friend of the negro whose influence now dominates your dispensers of alms! This man positively grovels with joy when his distinguished black friend honors him by becoming his guest in New York.

"With growing rage and wonder I have watched the development of this modern phenomenon. I have fought you with sullen and unyielding fury from the first, and you have proven the most dangerous and insidious force I have encountered. You profess the loftiest motives and the highest altruism while the effects of your work can only be the degradation of the white race to an ultimate negroid level, to say nothing of the appalling results if you really succeed in pauperizing the educational system of the South!

"I expected to hear from your crowd when the movement for a white ballot was begun. Through you the society of Affiliated Black League Almoners of the South, under the direction of your inspired negro leader, have sounded the alarm. And now all the little pigs who are feeding on this swill, and all the hungry ones yet outside the fence and squealing to get in, will unite in a chorus that you hope can have but one result—the division of the white race on a vital issue affecting its purity, its integrity, and its future.

"The possible division of my race in its attitude toward the Negro is the one big danger that has always hung its ugly menace over the South. So long as her people stand united, our civilization can be protected against the pressure of the Negro's growing millions. But the moment a serious division of these forces occurs the black man's opportunity will be at hand. The question is, can you divide the white race on this issue?"

"We shall see, major, we shall see," piped the professor, fumbling his lavender tie and bowing himself out.

The strong jaw closed with a snap as Norton watched the silk hose disappear.

Chapter III

His House in Order

Norton knew from the first that there could be no hope of success in such a campaign as he had planned except in the single iron will of a leader who would lead and whose voice lifted in impassioned appeal direct to the white race in every county of the state could rouse them to resistless enthusiasm.

The man who undertook this work must burn the bridges behind him, ask nothing for himself and take his life daily in his hands. He knew the state from the sea to its farthest mountain peak and without the slightest vanity felt that God had called him to this task. There was no other man who could do it, no other man fitted for it. He had the training, bitter experience, and the confidence of the people. And he had no ambitions save a deathless desire to serve his country in the solution of its greatest and most insoluble problem. He edited the most powerful organ of public opinion in the South and he was an eloquent and forceful speaker. His paper had earned a comfortable fortune, he was independent, he had the training of a veteran soldier and physical fear was something he had long since ceased to know.

And his house was in order for the event. He could leave for months in confidence that the work would run with the smoothness of a clock.

He had sent Tom to a Northern university which had kept itself clean from the stain of negro associations. The boy had just graduated with honor, returned home and was at work in the office. He was a handsome, clean, manly, straight-limbed, wholesome boy, the pride of his father's heart, and had shown decided talent for newspaper work.

Andy had long since become his faithful henchman, butler and man of all work. Aunt Minerva, his fat, honest cook, was the best servant he had ever known, and Cleo kept his house.

The one point of doubt was Cleo. During the past year she had given unmistakable signs of a determination to fight. If she should see fit to strike in the midst of this campaign, her blow would be a crushing one. It would not only destroy him personally, it would confuse and crush his party in hopeless defeat. He weighed this probability from every point of view and the longer he thought it over the less likely it appeared that she would take such a step. She would destroy herself and her child as well. She knew him too well now to believe that he would ever yield in such a struggle. Helen was just graduating from a convent school in the Northwest, a beautiful and accomplished girl, and the last thing on earth she could suspect was that a drop of negro blood flowed in her veins. He knew Cleo too well, understood her hatred of negroes too well, to believe that she would deliberately push this child back into a negroid hell merely to wreak a useless revenge that would crush her own life as well. She was too wise, too cunning, too cautious.

And yet her steadily growing desperation caused him to hesitate. The thing he dreaded most was the loss of his boy's respect, which a last desperate fight with this woman would involve. The one thing he had taught Tom was racial cleanness. With a wisdom inspired and guided by the brooding spirit of his mother he had done this thoroughly. He had so instilled into this proud, sensitive boy's soul a hatred for all low association with women that it was inconceivable to him that any decent white man would stoop to an intrigue with a woman of negro blood. The withering scorn, the unmeasured contempt with which he had recently expressed himself to his father on this point had made the red blood slowly mount to the older man's face.

He had rather die than look into this boy's clean, manly eyes and confess the shame that would blacken his life. The boy loved him with a deep, tender, reverent love. His keen eyes had long ago seen the big traits in his father's character. The boy's genuine admiration was the sweetest thing in his lonely life.

He weighed every move with care and deliberately made up his mind to strike the blow and take the chances. No man had the right to weigh his personal career against the life of a people—certainly no man who dared to assume the leadership of a race. He rose from his desk, opened the door of the reporters' room and called Tom.

The manly young figure, in shirt sleeves, pad and pencil in hand, entered with quick, firm step.

"You want me to interview you, Governor?" he said with a laugh. "All right—now what do you think of that little scrimmage at the mouth of the harbor of Santiago yesterday? How's that for a Fourth of July celebration? I ask it of a veteran of the Confederate army?"

The father smiled proudly as the youngster pretended to be taking notes of his imaginary interview.

"You heard, sir," he went on eagerly, "that your old General, Joe Wheeler, was there and in a moment of excitement forgot himself and shouted to his aid:

"'There go the damned Yankees!—charge and give 'em hell!'"

A dreamy look came into the father's eyes as he interrupted:

"I shouldn't be surprised if Wheeler said it—anyhow, it's too good a joke to doubt"—he paused and the smile on his serious face slowly faded.

"Shut the door, Tom," he said with a gesture toward the reporters' room.

The boy rose, closed the door, and sat down near his father's chair:

"Well, Dad, why so serious? Am I to be fired without a chance? or is it just a cut in my wages? Don't prolong the agony!"

"I am going to put you in my chair in this office, my son," the father said in a slow drawl. The boy flushed scarlet and then turned pale.

"You don't mean it—now?" he gasped.

"To-morrow."

"You think I can make good?" The question came through trembling lips and he was looking at his father through a pair of dark blue eyes blurred by tears of excitement.

"You'll do better than I did at your age. You're better equipped."

"You think so?" Tom asked in quick boyish eagerness.

"I know it."

The boy sprang to his feet and grasped his father's hand:

"Your faith in me is glorious—it makes me feel like I can do anything——"

"You can—if you try."

"Well, if I can, it's because I've got good blood in me. I owe it all to you. You're the biggest man I ever met, Dad. I've wanted to say this to you for a long time, but I never somehow got up my courage to tell you what I thought of you."

The father slipped his arm tenderly about the boy and looked out the window at the bright Southern sky for a moment before he slowly answered:

"I'd rather hear that from you, Tom, than the shouts of the rest of the world."

"I'm going to do my level best to prove myself worthy of the big faith you've shown in me—but why have you done it? What does it mean?"

"Simply this, my boy, that the time has come in the history of the South for a leader to strike the first blow in the battle for racial purity by establishing a clean American citizenship. I am going to disfranchise the Negro in this state as the first step toward the ultimate complete separation of the races."

The boy's eyes flashed:

"It's a big undertaking, sir."

"Yes."

"Is it possible?"

"Many say not. That's why I'm going to do it. The real work must come after this first step. Just now the campaign which I'm going to inaugurate to-morrow in a speech at the mass meeting celebrating our victory at Santiago, is the thing in hand. This campaign will take me away from home for several months. I must have a man here whom I can trust implicitly."

"I'll do my best, sir," the boy broke in.

"In case anything happens to me before it ends——"

Tom bent close:

"What do you mean?"

"You never can tell what may happen in such a revolution——"

"It will be a revolution?"

"Yes. That's what my enemies as yet do not understand. They will not be prepared for the weapons I shall use. And I'll win. I may lose my life, but I'll start a fire that can't be put out until it has swept the state—the South"—he paused—"and then the Nation!"

Chapter IV

The Man of the Hour

The editor prepared to launch his campaign with the utmost care. He invited the Executive Committee of his party to meet in his office. The leaders were excited. They knew Norton too well to doubt that he had something big to suggest. Some of them came from distant sections of the state, three hundred miles away, to hear his plans.

He faced the distinguished group of leaders calmly, but every man present felt the deep undercurrent of excitement beneath his words.

"With your coöperation, gentlemen," he began, "we are going to sweep the state this time by an overwhelming majority——"

"That's the way to talk!" the Chairman shouted.

"Four years ago," he went on, "we were defeated for the first time since the overthrow of the negro government under the Reconstruction régime. This defeat was brought about by a division of the whites under the Socialistic program of the Farmers' Alliance. Gradually the black man has forced himself into power under the new régime. Our farmers only wished his votes to accomplish their plans and have no use for him as an officeholder. The rank and file of the white wing, therefore, of the allied party in power, are ripe for revolt if the Negro is made an issue.

The Committee cheered.

"I propose to make the Negro the only issue of this campaign. There will be no half-way measures, no puling hesitation, no weakness, and it will be a fight to the death in the open. The day for secret organizations has gone in Southern history. There is no Black League to justify a reorganization of the Klan. But the new Black League has a far more powerful organization. Its mask is now philanthropy, not patriotism. Its weapon is the lure of gold, not the flash of Federal bayonets. They will fight to divide the white race on this vital issue.

"Here is our danger. It is real. It is serious. But we must meet it. There is but one way, and that is to conduct a campaign of such enthusiasm, of such daring and revolutionary violence if need be, that the little henchmen and sycophants of the Dispensers of the National Poor Funds will be awed into silence.

"The leadership of such a campaign will be a dangerous one. I offer you my services without conditions. I ask nothing for myself. I will accept no honors. I offer you my time, my money, my paper, my life, if need be!"

The leaders rose as one man, grasped Norton's hand, and placed him in command.

No inkling of even the outlines of his radical program was allowed to leak out until the hour of the meeting of the party convention. The delegates were waiting anxiously for the voice of a leader who would sound the note of victory.

And when the platform was read to the convention declaring in simple, bold words that the time had come for the South to undo the crime of the Fifteenth Amendment, disfranchise the Negro and restore to the Nation the basis of white civilization, a sudden cheer like a peal of thunder swept the crowd, followed by the roar of a storm. It died away at last in waves of excited comment, rose again and swelled and rose higher and higher until the old wooden building trembled.

Again and again such assemblies had declared in vague terms for "White Supremacy." Campaign after campaign which followed the blight of negro rule twenty years before had been fought and won on this issue. But no man or party had dared to whisper what "White Supremacy" really meant. There was no fog about this platform. For the first time in the history of the party it said exactly what was meant in so many words.

Thoughtful men had long been weary of platitudes on this subject. The Negro had grown enormously in wealth, in numbers and in social power in the past two decades. As a full-fledged citizen in a Democracy he was a constant menace to society. Here, for the first time, was the announcement of a definite program. It was revolutionary. It meant the revision of the constitution of the Union and a challenge to the negro race, and all his sentimental allies in the Republic for a fight to a finish.

The effect of its bare reading was electric. The moment the Chairman tried to lift his voice the cheers were renewed. The hearts of the people had been suddenly thrilled by a great ideal. No matter whether it meant success or failure, no matter whether it meant fame or oblivion for the man who proposed it, every intelligent delegate in that hall knew instinctively that a great mind had spoken a bold principle that must win in the end if the Republic live.

Norton rose at last to advocate its adoption as the one issue of the campaign, and again pandemonium broke loose—now they knew that he had written it! They suspected it from the first. Instantly his name was on a thousand lips in a shout that rent the air.

He stood with his tall figure drawn to its full height, his face unearthly pale, wreathed in its heavy shock of iron-gray hair and waited, without recognizing the tumult, until the last shout had died away.

His speech was one of passionate and fierce appeal—the voice of the revolutionist who had boldly thrown off the mask and called his followers to battle.

Yet through it all, the big unspoken thing behind his words was the magic that really swayed his hearers. They felt that what he said was great, but that he could say something greater if he would. As he had matured in years he had developed this reserved power. All who came in personal touch with the man felt it instinctively with his first word. An audience, with its simpler collective intelligence, felt it overwhelmingly. Yet if he had dared reveal to this crowd the ideas seething in his brain behind the simple but bold political proposition, he could not have carried them with him. They were not ready for it. He knew that to merely take the ballot from the negro and allow him to remain in physical touch with the white race was no solution of the problem. But he was wise enough to know that but one step could be taken at a time in a great movement to separate millions of blacks from the entanglements of the life of two hundred years.

His platform expressed what he believed could be accomplished, and the convention at the conclusion of his eloquent speech adopted it by acclamation amid a scene of wild enthusiasm.

He refused all office, except the position of Chairman of the Executive Committee without pay, and left the hall the complete master of the politics of his party.

Little did he dream in this hour of triumph the grim tragedy the day's work had prepared in his own life.

Chapter V

A Woman Scorned

As the time drew near for Norton to take the field in the campaign whose fierce passions would mark a new era in the state's history, his uneasiness over the attitude of Cleo increased.

She had received the announcement of his approaching long absence with sullen anger. And as the purpose of the campaign gradually became clear she had watched him with growing suspicion and hate. He felt it in every glance she flashed from the depth of her greenish eyes.

Though she had never said it in so many words, he was sure that the last hope of a resumption of their old relations was fast dying in her heart, and that the moment she realized that he was lost to her would be the signal for a desperate attack. What form the attack would take he could only guess. He was sure it would be as deadly as her ingenuity could invent. Yet in the wildest flight of his imagination he never dreamed the daring thing she had really decided to do.

On the night before his departure he was working late in his room at the house. The office he had placed in Tom's hands before the meeting of the convention. The boy's eager young face just in front of him when he made his speech that day had been an inspiration. It had beamed with pride and admiration, and when his father's name rang from every lip in the great shout that shook the building Tom's eyes had filled with tears.

Norton was seated at his typewriter, which he had moved to his room, writing his final instructions. The last lines he put in caps:

"UNDER NO CONCEIVABLE CIRCUMSTANCES ANNOY ME WITH

ANYTHING THAT HAPPENS AT HOME, UNLESS A MATTER OF IMMEDIATE LIFE AND DEATH. ANYTHING ELSE CAN WAIT UNTIL MY RETURN."

He had just finished this important sentence when the sound of a footstep behind his chair caused him to turn suddenly.

Cleo had entered the room and stood glaring at him with a look of sullen defiance.

By a curious coincidence or by design, she was dressed in a scarlet kimono of the same shade of filmy Japanese stuff as the one she wore in his young manhood. His quick eye caught this fact in a flash and his mind took rapid note of the changes the years had wrought. Their burdens had made slight impression on her exhaustless vitality. Whatever might be her personality or her real character, she was alive from the crown of her red head to the tips of her slippered toes.

Her attitude of tense silence sparkled with this vital power more eloquently than when she spoke with quick energy in the deep voice that was her most remarkable possession.

Her figure was heavier by twenty pounds than when she had first entered his home, but she never produced the impression of stoutness. Her form was too sinuous, pliant and nervous to take on flesh. She was no longer the graceful girl of eighteen whose beauty had drugged his senses, but she was beyond all doubt a woman of an extraordinary type, luxuriant, sensuous, dominant. There was not a wrinkle on her smooth creamy skin nor a trace of approaching age about the brilliant greenish eyes that were gazing into his now with such grim determination.

He wheeled from his machine and faced her, his eyes taking in with a quick glance the evident care with which she had arranged her hair and the startling manner in which she was dressed.

He spoke with sharp, incisive emphasis:

"It was a condition of your return that you should never enter my room while I am in this house."

"I have not forgotten," she answered firmly, her eyes holding his steadily.

"Why have you dared?"

"You are still afraid of me?" she asked with a light laugh that was half a sneer.

"Have I given you any such evidence during the past twenty years?"

There was no bitterness or taunt in the even, slow drawl with which he spoke, but the woman knew that he never used the slow tone with which he uttered those words except he was deeply moved.

She flushed, was silent and then answered with a frown:

"No, you haven't shown any fear for something more than twenty years—until a few days ago."

The last clause she spoke very quickly as she took a step closer and paused.

"A few days ago?" he repeated slowly.

"Yes. For the past week you *have* been afraid of me—not in the sense I asked you just now perhaps"—her white teeth showed in two even perfect rows—"but you have been watching me out of the corners of your eyes—haven't you?"

"Perhaps."

"I wonder why?"

"And you haven't guessed?"

"No, but I'm going to find out."

"You haven't asked."

"I'm going to."

"Be quick about it!"

"I'm going to find out—that's why I came in here to-night in defiance of your orders."

"All right—the quicker the better!"

"Thank you, I'm not in a hurry."

"What do you want?" he demanded with anger.

She smiled tauntingly:

"It's no use to get mad about it! I'm here now, you see that I'm not afraid of you and I'm quite sure that you will not put me out until I'm ready to go——"

He sprang to his feet and advanced on her:

"I'm not so sure of that!"

"Well, I am," she cried, holding his gaze steadily.

He threw up his hands with a gesture of disgust and resumed his seat:

"What is it?"

She crossed the room deliberately, carrying a chair in front of her, sat down, leaned her elbow on his table and studied him a moment, their eyes meeting in a gaze of deadly hostility.

"What is the meaning of this long absence you have planned?"

"I have charge of this campaign. I am going to speak in every county in the state."

"Why?"

"Because I'll win that way, by a direct appeal to the people."

"Why do you want to win?"

"Because I generally do what I undertake."

"Why do you want to do this thing?"

He looked at her in amazement. Her eyes had narrowed to the tiniest lines as she asked these questions with a steadily increasing intensity.

"What are you up to?" he asked her abruptly.

"I want to know why you began this campaign at all?"

"I decline to discuss the question with you," he answered abruptly.

"I insist on it!"

"You wouldn't know what I was talking about," he replied with contempt.

"I think I would."

"Bah!"

He turned from her with a wave of angry dismissal, seized his papers and began to read again his instructions to Tom.

"I'm not such a fool as you think," she began menacingly. "I've read your platform with some care and I've been thinking it over at odd times since your speech was reported."

"And you contemplate entering politics?" he interrupted with a smile.

"Who knows?"

She watched him keenly while she slowly uttered these words and saw the flash of uneasiness cross his face.

"But don't worry," she laughed.

"I'll not!"

"You may for all that!" she sneered, "but I'll not enter politics as you fear. That would be too cheap. I don't care what you do to negroes. I've a drop of their blood in me——"

"One in eight, to be exact."

"But I'm not one of them, except by your laws, and I hate the sight of a negro. You can herd them, colonize them, send them back to Africa or to the devil for all I care. Your program interests me for another reason"—she paused and watched him intently.

"Yes?" he said carelessly.

"It interests me for one reason only—you wrote that platform, you made that speech, you carried that convention. Your man Friday is running for Governor. You are going to take the stump, carry this election and take the ballot from the Negro!"

"Well?"

"I'm excited about it merely because it shows the inside of your mind."

"Indeed!"

"Yes. It shows either that you are afraid of me or that you're not——"

"It couldn't well show both," he interrupted with a sneer.

"It might," she answered. "If you are afraid of me and my presence is the cause of this outburst, all right. I'll still play the game with you and win or lose. I'll take my chances. But if you're not afraid of me, if you've really not been on your guard for twenty years, it means another thing. It means that you've learned your lesson, that the book of the past is closed, and that you have simply been waiting for the time to come to do this thing and save your people from a danger before which you once fell."

"And which horn of the dilemma do you take?" he asked coldly.

"I haven't decided—but I will to-night."

"How interesting!"

"Yes, isn't it?" she leaned close. "With a patience that must have caused you wonder, with a waiting through years as God waits, I have endured your indifference, your coldness, your contempt. Each year I have counted the last that you could resist the call of my body and soul, and at the end of each year I have seen you further and further away from me and the gulf between us deeper and darker. This absence you have planned in this campaign means the end one way or the other. I'm going to face life now as it is, not as I've hoped it might be."

"I told you when you made your bargain to return to this house, that there could be nothing between us except a hate that is eternal——"

"And I didn't believe it! Now I'm going to face it if I must——"

She paused, breathed deeply and her eyes were like glowing coals as she slowly went on:

"I'm not the kind to give up without a fight. I've lived and learned the wisdom of caution and cunning. I'm not old and I've still a fool's confidence in my powers. I'm not quite thirty-nine, strong and sound in body and spirit, alive to my finger tips with the full blood of a grown woman—and so I warn you——"

"You warn me"— he cried with a flush of anger.

"Yes. I warn you not to push me too far. I have negro blood in me, but I'm at least human, and I'm going to be treated as a human being."

"And may I ask what you mean by that?" he asked sarcastically.

"That I'm going to demand my rights."

"Demand?"

"Exactly."

"Your *rights*?"

"The right to love——"

Norton broke into a bitter, angry laugh:

"Are you demanding that I marry you?"

"I'm not quite that big a fool. No. Your laws forbid it. All right—there are higher laws than yours. The law that drew you to me in this room twenty years ago, in spite of all your fears and your prejudices"—she paused and her eyes glowed in the shadows—"I gave you my soul and body then——"

"Gifts I never sought——"

"Yet you took them and I'm here a part of your life. What are you going to do with me? I'm not the negro race. I'm just a woman who loves you and asks that you treat her fairly."

"Treat you fairly! Did I ever want you? Or seek you? You came to me, thrust yourself into my office, and when I discharged you, pushed your way into my home. You won my boy's love and made my wife think you were indispensable to her comfort and happiness. I tried to avoid you. It was useless. You forced yourself into my presence at all hours of the day and night. What happened was your desire, not mine. And when I reproached myself with bitter curses you laughed for joy! And you talk to me to-day of fairness! You who dragged me from that banquet hall the night of my triumph to hurl me into despair! You who blighted my career and sent me blinded with grief and shame groping through life with the shadow of death on my soul! You who struck your bargain of a pound of flesh next to my heart, and fought your way back into my house again to hold me a prisoner for life, chained to the dead body of my shame—you talk to me about fairness—great God!"

He stopped, strangled with passion, his tall figure towering above her, his face livid, his hands clutched in rage.

She laughed hysterically:

"Why don't you strike! I'm not your equal in strength—I dare you to do it—I dare you to do it! I *dare* you—do you hear?"

With a sudden grip she tore the frail silk from its fastenings at her throat, pressed close and thrust her angry face into his in a desperate challenge to physical violence.

His eyes held hers a moment and his hands relaxed:

"I'd like to kill you. I could do it with joy!"

"Why don't you?"

"You're not worth the price of such a crime!"

"You'd just as well do it, as to wish it. Don't be a coward!" Her eyes burned with suppressed fire.

He looked at her with cold anger and his lip twitched with a smile of contempt.

The strain was more than her nerves could bear. With a sob she threw her arms around his neck. He seized them angrily, her form collapsed and she clung to him with blind hysterical strength.

He waited a moment and spoke in quiet determined tones:

"Enough of this now."

She raised her eyes to his, pleading with desperation:

"Please be kind to me just this last hour before you go, and I'll be content if you give no more. I'll never intrude again."

She relaxed her hold, dropped to a seat and covered her face with her hands:

"Oh, my God! Are you made of stone—have you no pity? Through all these years I've gone in and out of this house looking into your face for a sign that you thought me human, and you've given none. I've lived on the memories of the few hours when you were mine. I've sometimes told myself it was just a dream, that it never happened—until I've almost believed it. You've pretended that it wasn't true. You've strangled these memories and told yourself over and over again that it never happened. I've seen you doing this—seen it in your cold, deep eyes. Well, it's a lie! You were mine! You shall not forget it—you can't forget it—I won't let you, I tell you!"

The voice broke again into sobs.

He stood with arms folded, watching her in silence. Her desperate appeal to his memories and his physical passion had only stirred anger and contempt. He was seeing now as he had never noticed before the growing marks of her negroid character. The anger was for her, the contempt for himself. He noticed the growth of her lips with age, the heavy sensual thickness of the negroid type!

It was inconceivable that in this room the sight of her had once stirred the Beast in him to incontrollable madness. There was at least some consolation in the fact that he had made progress. He couldn't see this if he hadn't moved to a higher plane.

He spoke at length in quiet tones:

"I am waiting for you to go. I have work to do to-night."

She rose with a quick, angry movement:

"It's all over, then. There's not a chance that you'll change your mind?"

"Not if you were the last woman on earth and I the last man."

He spoke without bitterness but with a firmness that was final.

"All right. I know what to expect now and I'll plan my own life."

"What do you mean?"

"That there's going to be a change in my relations to your servants for one thing."

"Your relations to my servants?" he repeated incredulously.

"Yes."

"In what respect?"

"I'm not going to take any more insolence from Minerva——"

"Keep out of the kitchen and let her alone. She's the best cook I ever had."

"If I keep this house for you, I demand the full authority of my position. I'll hire the servants and discharge them when I choose."

"You'll do nothing of the kind," he answered firmly.

"Then I demand that you discharge Minerva and Andy at once."

"What's the matter with Andy?"

"I loathe him."

"Well, I like him, and he's going to stay. Anything else?"

"You'll pay no attention to my wishes?"

"I'm master of this house."

"And in your absence?"

"My son will be here."

"All right, I understand now."

"If I haven't made it plain, I'll do so."

"Quite clear, thank you," she answered slowly.

Norton walked to the mantel, leaned his elbow on the shelf for a moment, returned and confronted her with his hands thrust into his pockets, his feet wide apart, his whole attitude one of cool defiance.

"Now I want to know what you're up to? These absurd demands are a blind. They haven't fooled me. There's something else in the back of your devilish mind. What is it? I want to know exactly what you mean?"

Cleo laughed a vicious little ripple of amusement:

"Yes, I know you do—but you won't!"

"All right, as you please. A word from you and Helen's life is blasted. A word from you and I withdraw from this campaign, and another will lead it. Speak that word if you dare, and I'll throw you out of this house and your last hold on my life is broken."

"I've thought of that, too," she said with a smile.

"It will be worth the agony I'll endure," he cried, "to know that I'm free of you and breathe God's clean air at last!"

He spoke the words with an earnestness, a deep and bitter sincerity, that was not lost on her keen ears.

She started to reply, hesitated and was silent.

He saw his advantage and pressed it:

"I want you to understand fully that I know now and I have always known that I am at your mercy when you see fit to break the word you pledged. Yet there has never been a moment during the past twenty years that I've been really afraid of you. When the hour comes for my supreme humiliation, I'll meet it. Speak as soon as you like."

She had walked calmly to the door, paused and looked back:

"You needn't worry, major," she said smoothly, "I'm not quite such a fool as all that. I've been silent too many years. It's a habit I'll not easily break." Her white teeth gleamed in a cold smile as she added:

"Good night."

A hundred times he told himself that she wouldn't dare, but he left home next day with a sickening fear slowly stealing into his heart.

Chapter VI

An Old Comedy

Norton had scarcely passed his gate on the way to catch the train when Cleo left the window, where her keen eyes had been watching, and made her way rapidly to the room he had just vacated.

Books and papers were scattered loosely over his table beside the typewriter which he had, with his usual carelessness, left open.

With a quick decision she seated herself beside the machine and in two hours sufficiently mastered its use to write a letter by using a single finger and carefully touching the keys one by one.

The light of a cunning purpose burned in her eyes as she held up the letter which she had written on a sheet paper with the embossed heading of his home address at the top.

She re-read it, smiling over the certainty of the success of her plan. The letter was carefully and simply worded:

> "My Dear Miss Helen:
>
> "As your guardian is still in Europe, I feel it my duty, and a pleasant one, to give you a glimpse of the South before you go abroad. Please come at once to my home for as long as you care to stay. If I am away in the campaign when you arrive, my son and housekeeper, Cleo, will make you at home and I trust happy.
>
> "With kindest regards, and hoping to see you soon,
>
> "Sincerely,
>
> "Daniel Norton."

The signature she practiced with a pen for half an hour until her imitation was almost perfect and then signed it. Satisfied with the message, she addressed an envelope to "Miss Helen Winslow, Convent of the Sacred Heart, Racine, Wisconsin," sealed and posted it with her own hand.

The answer came six days later. Cleo recognized the post mark at once, broke the seal and read it with dancing eyes:

"MY DEAR MAJOR NORTON:

"I am wild with joy over your kind invitation. As my last examinations are over I will not wait for the Commencement exercises. I am so excited over this trip I just can't wait. I am leaving day after to-morrow and hope to arrive almost as soon as this letter.

"With a heart full of gratitude,

"Your lonely ward,
"HELEN."

Two days later a hack rolled up the graveled walk to the white porch, a girl leaped out and bounded up the steps, her cheeks flushed, her wide open blue eyes dancing with excitement.

She was evidently surprised to find that Cleo was an octoroon, blushed and extended her hand with a timid hesitating look:

"This—this—is Cleo—the major's housekeeper?" she asked.

The quick eye of the woman took in at a glance the charm of the shy personality and the loneliness of the young soul that looked out from her expressive eyes.

"Yes," she answered mechanically.

"I'm so sorry that the major's away—the driver told me——"

"Oh, it's all right," Cleo said with a smile, "he wrote us to make you feel at home. Just walk right in, your room is all ready."

"Thank you so much," Helen responded, drawing a deep breath and looking over the lawn with its green grass, its dense hedges and wonderful clusters of roses in full bloom. "How beautiful the South is—far more beautiful than I had dreamed! And the perfume of these roses—why, the air is just drowsy with their honey! We have gorgeous roses in the North, but I never smelled them in the open before"— she paused and breathed deeply again and again—"Oh, it's fairyland—I'll never want to go!"

"I hope you won't," Cleo said earnestly.

"The major asked me to stay as long as I wished. I have his letter here"— she drew the letter from her bag and opened it—"see what he says: 'Please come at once to my home for as long as you can stay'—now wasn't that sweet of him?"

"Very," was the strained reply.

The girl's sensitive ear caught the queer note in Cleo's voice and looked at her with a start.

"Come, I must show you to your room," she added, hurriedly opening the door for Helen to pass.

The keen eyes of the woman were scanning the girl and estimating her character with increasing satisfaction. She walked with exquisite grace. Her figure was almost the exact counterpart of her own at twenty—Helen's a little fuller, the arms larger but more beautiful. The slender wrists and perfectly moulded hand would have made a painter beg for a sitting. Her eyes were deep blue and her hair the richest chestnut brown, massive and slightly waving, her complexion the perfect white and red of the Northern girl who had breathed the pure air of the fields and hills. The sure, swift, easy way in which she walked told of perfect health and exhaustless vitality. Her voice was low and sweet and full of shy tenderness.

A smile of triumph flashed from Cleo's greenish eyes as she watched her swiftly cross the hall toward the stairs.

"I'll win!" she exclaimed softly.

Helen turned sharply.

"Did you speak to me?" she asked blushing.

"No. I was just thinking aloud."

"Excuse me, I thought you said something to me—"

"It would have been something very nice if I had," Cleo said with a friendly smile.

"Thank you—oh, I feel that I'm going to be so happy here!"

"I hope so."

"When do you think the major will come?"

The woman's face clouded in spite of her effort at self-control:

"It may be a month or more."

"Oh, I'm so anxious to see him! He has been acting for my old guardian, who is somewhere abroad, ever since I can remember. I've begged and begged him to come to see me, but he never came. It was so far away, I suppose. He never even sent me his picture, though I've asked him often. What sort of a man is he?"

Cleo smiled and hesitated, and then spoke with apparent carelessness:

"A very striking looking man."

"With a kind face?"

"A very stern one, clean shaven, with deep set eyes, a firm mouth, a strong jaw that can be cruel when he wishes, a shock of thick iron gray hair, tall, very tall and well built. He weighs two hundred and fifteen now—he was very thin when young."

"And his voice?"

"Gentle, but sometimes hard as steel when he wishes it to be."

"Oh, I'll be scared to death when I see him! I had pictured him just the opposite."

"How?"

"Why, I hardly know—but I thought his voice would be always gentle like I imagine a Southern father's who loved his children very much. And I thought his hair would be blonde, with a kind face and friendly laughing eyes—blue, like mine. His eyes aren't blue?"

"Dark brown."

"I know I'll run when he comes."

"We'll make you feel at home and you'll not be afraid. Mr. Tom will be here to lunch in a few minutes and I'll introduce you."

"Then I must dress at once!"

"The first door at the head of the stairs—your trunk has already been taken up."

Cleo watched the swift, strong, young form mount the stairs.

"It's absolutely certain!" she cried under her breath. "I'll win—I'll win!"

She broke into a low laugh and hurried to set the table in a bower of the sweetest roses that were in bloom. Their languorous odor filled the house.

Helen was waiting in the old-fashioned parlor when Tom's step echoed on the stoop. Cleo hurried to meet him on the porch.

His face clouded with a scowl:

"She's here?"

"Yes, Mr. Handsome Boy," Cleo answered cheerfully. "And lunch is ready—do rub that awful scowl off your face and look like you're glad."

"Well, I'm not—so what's the use? It'll be a mess to have a girl on my hands day and night and I've got no time for it. I wish Dad was here. I know I'll hate the sight of her."

Cleo smiled:

"Better wait until you see her."

"Where is she?"

"In the parlor."

"All right—the quicker a disagreeable job's over the better."

"Shall I introduce you?"

"No, I'll do it myself," he growled, bracing himself for the ordeal.

As he entered the door he stopped short at the vision as Helen sprang to her feet and came to meet him. She was dressed in the softest white filmy stuff, as light as a feather, bare arms and neck, her blue eyes sparkling with excitement, her smooth, fair cheeks scarlet with blushes.

The boy's heart stopped beating in sheer surprise. He expected a frowzy little waif from an orphanage, blear-eyed, sad, soulful and tiresome.

This shining, blushing, wonderful creature took his breath. He stared at first with open mouth, until Cleo's laugh brought him to his senses just as he began to hear Helen's low sweet voice:

"And this is Mr. Tom, I suppose? I am Helen Winslow, your father's ward, from the West—at least he's all the guardian I've ever known."

Tom grasped the warm little hand extended in so friendly greeting and held it in dazed surprise until Cleo's low laughter again roused him.

"Yes—I—I—am delighted to see you, Miss Helen, and I'm awfully sorry my father couldn't be here to welcome you. I—I'll do the best I can for you in his absence."

"Oh, thank you," she murmured.

"You know you're not at all like I expected to find you," he said hesitatingly.

"I hope I haven't disappointed you," she answered demurely.

"No—no"—he protested—"just the opposite."

He stopped and blushed for fear he'd said too much.

"And you're just the opposite from what I'd pictured you since Cleo told me how your father looks."

"And what did you expect?" he asked eagerly.

"A stern face, dark hair, dark eyes and a firm mouth."

"And you find instead?"

Helen laughed:

"I'm afraid you love flattery."

Tom hurried to protest:

"Really, I wasn't fishing for a compliment, but I'm so unlike my father, it's a joke. I get my blonde hair and blue eyes from my mother and my great-grandfather."

Before he knew what was happening Tom was seated by her side talking and laughing as if they had known each other a lifetime.

Helen paused for breath, put her elbow on the old mahogany table, rested her dimpled chin in the palm of her pretty hand and looked at Tom with a mischievous twinkle in her blue eyes.

"What's the joke?" he asked.

"Do you know that you're the first boy I ever talked to in my life?"

"No—really?" he answered incredulously.

"Don't you think I do pretty well?"

"Perfectly wonderful!"

"You see, I've played this scene so many times in my day dreams——"

"And it's like your dream?"

"Remarkably!"

"How?"

"You're just the kind of boy I always thought I'd meet first——"

"How funny!"

"Yes, exactly," she cried excitedly and with a serious tone in her voice that was absolutely convincing. "You're so jolly and friendly and easy to talk to, I feel as if I've known you all my life."

"And I feel the same—isn't it funny?"

They both laughed immoderately.

"Come," the boy cried, "I want to show you my mother's and my grandfather's portraits in the library. You'll see where I get my silly blonde hair, my slightly pug nose and my very friendly ways."

She rose with a laugh:

"Your nose isn't pug, it's just good-humored."

"Amount to the same thing."

"And your hair is very distinguished looking for a boy. I'd envy it, if it were a girl's."

Tom led the way into the big, square library which opened on the pillared porch both on the rear and on the side of the house. Before the fireplace he paused and pointed to his mother's portrait done in oil by a famous artist in New York.

It was life-size and the canvas filled the entire space between the two fluted columns of the Colonial mantel which reached to the ceiling. The woodwork of the mantelpiece was of dark mahogany and the background of the portrait the color of bright gold which seemed to melt into the lines of the massive smooth gilded frame.

The effect was wonderfully vivid and life-like in the sombre coloring of the book-lined walls. The picture and frame seemed a living flame in its dark setting. The portrait was an idealized study of the little mother. The artist had put into his canvas the spirit of the tenderest brooding motherhood. The very curve of her arms holding the child to her breast seemed to breathe tenderness. The smile that played about her delicate lips and blue eyes was ethereal in its fleeting spirit beauty.

The girl caught her breath in surprise:

"What a wonderful picture—it's perfectly divine! I feel like kneeling before it."

"It is an altar," the boy said reverently. "I've seen my father sit in that big chair brooding for hours while he looked at it. And ever since he put those two old gold candlesticks in front of it I can't get it out of my head that he slips in here, kneels in the twilight and prays before it."

"He must have loved your mother very tenderly," she said softly.

"I think he worships her still," the boy answered simply.

"Oh, I could die for a man like that!" she cried with sudden passion.

Tom pointed to his grandfather's portrait:

"And there you see my distinguished features and my pug nose——"

Cleo appeared in the door smiling:

"I've been waiting for you to come to lunch, Mr. Boy, for nearly an hour."

"Well, for heaven's sake, why didn't you let us know?"

"I told you it was ready when you came."

"Forgot all about it."

He was so serenely unconscious of anything unusual in his actions that he failed to notice the smile that continuously played about Cleo's mouth or to notice Andy's evident enjoyment of the little drama as he bowed and scraped and waited on the table with unusual ceremony.

Aunt Minerva, hearing Andy's report of the sudden affair that had developed in the major's absence, left the kitchen and stood in the door a moment, her huge figure completely filling the space while she watched the unconscious boy and girl devouring each other with sparkling eyes.

She waved her fat hand over their heads to Andy, laughed softly and left without their noticing her presence.

The luncheon was the longest one that had been known within the memory of anyone present. Minerva again wandered back to the door, fascinated by the picture they made, and whispered to Andy as he passed:

"Well, fer de Lawd's sake, is dey gwine ter set dar all day?"

"Nobum—'bout er nodder hour, an' he'll go back ter de office."

Tom suddenly looked at his watch:

"Heavens! I'm late. I'll run down to the office and cut the work out for the day in honor of your coming."

Helen rose blushing:

"Oh, I'm afraid I'll make trouble for you."

"No trouble at all! I'll be back in ten minutes."

"I'll be on the lawn in that wilderness of roses. The odor is maddening—it's so sweet."

"All right—and then I'll show you the old rose garden on the other side of the house."

"It's awfully good of you, but I'm afraid I'm taking your time from work."

"It's all right! I'll make the other fellows do it today."

She blushed again and waved her bare arm high over her dark brown hair from the porch as he swung through the gate and disappeared.

In a few minutes he had returned. Through the long hours of a beautiful summer afternoon they walked through the enchanted paths of the old garden on velvet feet, the boy pouring out his dreams and high ambitions, the girl's lonely heart for the first time in life basking in the joyous light of a perfect day.

Andy made an excuse to go in the garden and putter about some flowers just to watch them, laugh and chuckle over the exhibition. He was just in time as he softly approached behind a trellis of climbing roses to hear Tom say:

"Please give me that bud you're wearing?"

"Why?" she asked demurely.

"Just because I've taken a fancy to it."

She blushed scarlet, took the rosebud from her bosom and pinned it on his coat:

"All right—there!"

Andy suppressed a burst of laughter and hurried back to report to Minerva.

For four enchanted weeks the old comedy of life was thus played by the boy and girl in sweet and utter unconsciousness of its meaning. He worked only in the mornings and rushed home for lunch unusually early. The afternoon usually found them seated side by side slowly driving over the quiet country roads. Two battlefields of the Civil War, where his father had led a regiment of troops in the last desperate engagement with Sherman's army two weeks after Lee had surrendered at Appomattox, kept them busy each afternoon for a week.

At night they sat on the moonlit porch behind the big pillars and he talked to her of the great things of life with simple boyish enthusiasm. Sometimes they walked side by side through the rose-scented lawn and paused to hear the love song of a mocking-bird whose mate was busy each morning teaching her babies to fly.

The world had become a vast rose garden of light and beauty, filled with the odors of flowers and spices and dreamy strains of ravishing music.

And behind it all, nearer crept the swift shadow whose tread was softer than the foot of a summer's cloud.

Chapter VII

Trapped

Norton's campaign during its first months was a continuous triumph. The opposition had been so completely stunned by the epoch-making declaration of principles on which he had chosen to conduct the fight that they had as yet been unable to rally their forces. Even the rival newspaper, founded to combat the ideas for which the *Eagle and Phoenix* stood, was compelled to support Norton's ticket to save itself from ruin. The young editor found a source of endless amusement in taunting the professor on this painful fact.

The leader had chosen to begin his tour of the state in the farthest mountain counties that had always been comparatively free from negro influence. These counties were counted as safe for the opposition before the startling program of the editor's party had been announced. Yet from the first day's mass meeting which he had addressed, an enthusiasm had been developed under the spell of Norton's eloquence that had swept the crowds of mountaineers off their feet. They had never been slave owners, and they had no use for a negro as servant, laborer, voter, citizen, or in any other capacity. The idea of freeing the state forever from their baleful influence threw the entire white race into solid ranks supporting his ticket.

The enthusiasm kindled in the mountains swept the foothills, gaining resistless force as it reached the more inflammable feelings of the people of the plains who were living in daily touch with the negro.

Yet amid all the scenes of cheering and enthusiasm through which he was passing daily the heart of the leader was heavy with dread. His mind was brooding over the last scene with Cleo and its possible outcome.

He began to worry with increasing anguish over the certainty that when she struck the blow would be a deadly one. The higher the tide of his triumph rose, the greater became the tension of his nerves. Each day had its appointment to speak. Some days were crowded with three or four engagements. These dates were made two weeks ahead and great expense had been incurred in each case to advertise them and secure record crowds. It was a point of honor with him to make good these dates even to the smallest appointment at a country crossroads.

It was impossible to leave for a trip home. It would mean the loss of at least four days. Yet his anxiety at last became so intense that he determined to rearrange his dates and swing his campaign into the territory near the Capital at once. It was not a good policy. He would risk the loss of the cumulative power of his work now sweeping from county to county, a resistless force. But it would enable him to return home for a few hours between his appointments.

There had been nothing in Tom's reports to arouse his fears. The boy had faithfully carried out his instructions to give no information that might annoy him. His brief letters were bright, cheerful, and always closed with the statement: "Everything all right at home, and I'm still jollying the professor about supporting the cause he hates."

When he reached the county adjoining the Capital his anxiety had reached a point beyond endurance. It would be three days before he could connect with a schedule of trains that would enable him to get home between the time of his hours to speak. He simply could not wait.

He telegraphed to Tom to send Andy to the meeting next day with a bound volume of the paper for the year 1866 which contained some facts he wished to use in his speech in this district.

Andy's glib tongue would give him the information he needed.

The train was late and the papers did not arrive in time. He was compelled to leave his hotel and go to the meeting without them.

An enormous crowd had gathered. And for the first time on his tour he felt hostility in the glances that occasionally shot from groups of men as he passed. The county was noted for its gangs of toughs who lived on the edge of a swamp that had been the rendezvous of criminals for a century.

The opposition had determined to make a disturbance at this meeting and if possible end it with a riot. They counted on the editor's fiery temper when aroused to make this a certainty. They had not figured on the cool audacity with which he would meet such a situation.

When he reached the speaker's stand, the county Chairman whispered:

"They are going to make trouble here to-day."

"Yes?"

"They've got a speaker who's going to demand a division of time."

The editor smiled:

"Really?"

"Yes," the Chairman said, nodding toward a tall, ministerial-looking individual who was already working his way through the crowd. "That's the fellow coming now."

Norton turned and confronted the chosen orator of the opposition, a backwoods preacher of a rude native eloquence whose name he had often heard.

He saw at a glance that he was a man of force. His strong mouth was clean of mustache and the lower lip was shaved to the chin. A long beard covered the massive jaws and his hair reached the collar of his coat. He had been a deserter during the war, and a drunken member of the little Scalawag Governor's famous guard that had attempted to rule the state without the civil law. He had been converted in a Baptist revival at a crossroads meeting place years before and became a preacher. His religious conversion, however, had not reached his politics or dimmed his memory of the events of Reconstruction.

He had hated Norton with a deep and abiding fervor from the day he had escaped from his battalion in the Civil War down to the present moment.

Norton hadn't the remotest idea that he was the young recruit who had taken to his heels on entering a battle and never stopped running until he reached home.

"This is Major Norton?" the preacher asked.

"Yes," was the curt answer.

"I demand a division of time with you in a joint discussion here, sir."

Norton's figure stiffened and he looked at the man with a flush of anger:

"Did you say demand?"

"Yes, sir, I did," the preacher answered, snapping his hard mouth firmly. "We believe in free speech in this county."

Norton placed his hands in his pockets, and looked him over from head to foot:

"Well, you've got the gall of the devil, I must say, even if you do wear the livery of heaven. You demand free speech at my expense! I like your cheek. It cost my committee two hundred dollars to advertise this meeting and make it a success, and you step up at the last moment and demand that I turn it over to your party. If you want free speech, hire your own hall and make it to your heart's content. You can't address this crowd from a speaker's stand built with my money."

"You refuse?"

Norton looked at him steadily for a moment and took a step closer:

"I am trying to convey that impression to your mind. Must I use my foot to emphasize it?"

The long-haired one paled slightly, turned and quickly pushed his way through the crowd to a group awaiting him on the edge of the brush arbor that had been built to shelter the people from the sun. The Chairman whispered to Norton:

"There'll be trouble certain—they're a tough lot. More than half the men here are with him."

"They won't be when I've finished," he answered with a smile.

"You'd better divide with them——"

"I'll see him in hell first!"

Norton stepped quickly on the rude pine platform that had been erected for the speaker and faced the crowd. For the first time on his trip the cheering was given with moderation.

He saw the preacher walk back under the arbor and his men distribute themselves with apparent design in different parts of the crowd.

He lifted his hand with a gesture to stop the applause and a sudden hush fell over the eager, serious faces.

His eye wandered carelessly over the throng and singled out the men he had seen distribute themselves among them. He suddenly slipped his hand behind him and drew from beneath his long black frock coat a big revolver and laid it beside the pitcher of lemonade the Chairman had provided.

A slight stir swept the crowd and the stillness could be felt.

The speaker lifted his broad shoulders and began his speech in an intense voice that found its way to the last man who hung on the edge of the crowd:

"Gentlemen," he began slowly, "if there's any one present who doesn't wish to hear what I have to say, now is the time to leave. This is my meeting, and I will not be interrupted. If, in spite of this announcement, there happens to be any one here who is looking for trouble"—he stopped and touched the shining thing that lay before him—"you'll find it here on the table—walk right up to the front."

A cheer rent the air. He stilled it with a quick gesture and plunged into his speech.

In the intense situation which had developed he had forgotten the fear that had been gnawing at his heart for the past weeks.

At the height of his power over his audience his eye suddenly caught the black face of Andy grinning in evident admiration of his master's eloquence.

Something in the symbolism of this negro grinning at him over the heads of the people hanging breathless on his words sent a wave of sickening fear to his heart. In vain he struggled to throw the feeling off in the midst of his impassioned appeal. It was impossible. For the remaining half hour he spoke as if in a trance. Unconsciously his voice was lowered to a strange intense monotone that sent the chills down the spines of his hearers.

He closed his speech in a silence that was strangling.

The people were dazed and he was halfway down the steps of the rude platform before they sufficiently recovered to break into round after round of cheering.

He had unconsciously made the most powerful speech of his life, and no man in all the crowd that he had hypnotized could have dreamed the grim secret which had been the source of his inspiration.

Without a moment's delay he found Andy, examined the package he brought and hurried to his room.

"Everything all right at home, Andy?" he asked with apparent carelessness.

The negro was still lost in admiration of Norton's triumph over his hostile audience.

"Yassah, you sho did set 'em afire wid dat speech, major!" he said with a laugh.

"And I asked you if everything was all right at home?"

"Oh, yassah, yassah—everything's all right. Of cose, sah, dey's a few little things always happenin'. Dem pigs get in de garden las' week an' et everything up, an' dat ole cow er own got de hollow horn agin. But everything else all right, sah."

"And how's aunt Minerva?"

"Des es big an' fat ez ebber, sah, an' er gittin' mo' unruly every day—yassah—she's gittin' so sassy she try ter run de whole place an' me, too."

"And Cleo?"

This question he asked bustling over his papers with an indifference so perfectly assumed that Andy never guessed his interest to be more than casual, and yet he ceased to breathe until he caught the laughing answer:

"Oh, she's right dar holdin' her own wid Miss Minerva an' I tells her las' week she's lookin' better dan ebber—yassah—she's all right."

Norton felt a sense of grateful relief. His fears had been groundless. They were preposterous to start with. The idea that she might attempt to visit Helen in his absence was, of course, absurd.

His next question was asked with a good-natured, hearty tone:

"And Mr. Tom?"

Andy laughed immoderately and Norton watched him with increasing wonder.

"Right dar's whar my tale begins!"

"Why, what's the matter with him?" the father asked with a touch of anxiety in his voice.

"Lordy, dey ain't nuttin' de *matter* wid him 'tall—hit's a fresh cut!"

Again Andy laughed with unction.

"What is it?" Norton asked with impatience. "What's the matter with Tom?"

"Nuttin' 'tall, sah—nuttin' 'tall— I nebber see 'im lookin' so well in my life. He gets up sooner den I ebber knowed him before. He comes home quicker an' stays dar longer an' he's de jolliest young gentleman I know anywhar in de state. Mo' specially, sah, since dat handsome young lady from de North come down to see us——"

The father's heart was in his throat as he stammered:

"A handsome young lady from the North—I don't understand!"

"Why, Miss Helen, sah, de young lady you invite ter spen' de summer wid us."

Norton's eyes suddenly grew dim, he leaned on the table, stared at Andy, and repeated blankly:

"The young lady I asked to spend the summer with us?"

"Yassah, Miss Helen, sah, is her name—she cum 'bout er week atter you lef——"

"And she's been there ever since?" he asked.

"Yassah, an' she sho is a powerful fine young lady, sah. I don't blame Mister Tom fer bein' crazy 'bout her!"

There was a moment's dead silence.

"So Tom's crazy about her?" he said in a high, nervous voice, which Andy took for a joke.

"Yassah, I'se had some sperience myself, sah, but I ain't nebber seen nuttin' like dis! He des trot long atter her day an' night like a fice. An' de funny thing, sah, is dat he doan' seem ter know dat he's doin' it. Everybody 'bout de house laffin' fit ter kill dersef an' he don't pay no 'tention. He des sticks to her like a sick kitten to a hot brick! Yassah, hit sho's funny! I des knowed you'd bust er laughin' when you sees 'em."

Norton had sunk to a seat too weak to stand. His face was pale and his breath came in short gasps as he turned to the negro, stared at him hopelessly for a moment and said:

"Andy, get me a good horse and buggy at the livery stable—we'll drive through the country to-night. I want to get home right away."

Andy's mouth opened and his eyes stared in blank amazement.

"De Lawd, major, hit's mos' sundown now an' hit's a hundred miles from here home—hit took me all day ter come on de train."

"No, it's only forty miles straight across the country. We can make it to-night with a good horse. Hurry, I'll have my valise packed in a few minutes."

"Do you know de way, sah?" Andy asked, scratching his head.

"Do as I tell you—quick!" Norton thundered.

The negro darted from the room and returned in half an hour with a horse and buggy.

Through the long hours of the night they drove with but a single stop at midnight in a quiet street of a sleeping village. They halted at the well beside a store and watered the horse.

A graveyard was passed a mile beyond the village, and Andy glanced timidly over his shoulder at the white marble slabs glistening in the starlight. His master had not spoken for two hours save the sharp order to stop at the well.

"Dis sho is er lonesome lookin' place!" Andy said with a shiver.

But the man beside him gave no sign that he heard. His eyes were set in a strange stare at the stars that twinkled in the edge of the tree tops far ahead.

Andy grew so lonely and frightened finally at the ominous silence that he pretended to be lost at each crossroads to force Norton to speak.

"I wuz afraid you gone ter sleep, sah!" he said with an apologetic laugh. "An' I wuz erfered dat you'd fall out er de buggy gwine down er hill."

In vain he tried to break the silence. There was no answer—no sign that he was in the same world, save the fact of his body's presence.

The first streak of dawn was widening on the eastern horizon when Norton's cramped legs limped into the gate of his home. He stopped to steady his nerves and looked blankly up at the window of his boy's room. He had given Tom his mother's old room when he had reached the age of sixteen.

Somewhere behind those fluted pillars, white and ghost-like in the dawn, lay the girl who had suddenly risen from the dead to lead his faltering feet up life's Calvary. He saw the cross slowly lifting its dark form from the hilltop with arms outstretched to embrace him, and the chill of death crept into his heart.

The chirp of stirring birds, the dim noises of waking life, the whitening skyline behind the house recalled another morning in his boyhood. He had waked at daylight to go to his traps set at the branch in the edge of the woods behind the barn. The plantation at that time had extended into the town. A fox had been killing his fancy chickens. He had vowed vengeance in his boyish wrath, bought half a dozen powerful steel traps and set them in the fox's path. The prowler had been interrupted the night before and had not gotten his prey. He would return sure.

He recalled now every emotion that had thrilled his young heart as he bounded along the dew-soaked path to his traps.

Before he could see the place he heard the struggles of his captive.

"I've got him!" he shouted with a throb of savage joy.

He leaped the fence and stood frozen to the spot. The fox was a magnificent specimen of his breed, tall and heavy as a setter dog, with beautiful appealing eyes. His fine gray fur was spotched with blood, his mouth torn and bleeding from the effort to break the cruel bars that held his foreleg in their deathlike grip. With each desperate pull the blood spurted afresh and the steel cut deeper into bone and flesh.

The strange cries of pain and terror from the trapped victim had struck him dumb. He had come with murder in his heart to take revenge on his enemy, but when he looked with blanched face on the blood and heard the pitiful cries he rushed to the spot, tore the steel arms apart, loosed the fox, pushed his quivering form from him and gasped:

"Go—go—I'm sorry I hurt you like that!"

Stirred by the memories of the dawn he lived this scene again in vivid anguish, and as he slowly mounted the steps of his home, felt the steel bars of an inexorable fate close on his own throat.

Chapter VIII

Behind the Bars

When Norton reached his room he locked the door and began to pace the floor, facing for the hundredth time the stunning situation which the presence of Helen had created.

To reveal to such a sensitive, cultured girl just as she was budding into womanhood the fact that her blood was tainted with a negro ancestor would be an act so pitifully cruel that every instinct of his nature revolted from the thought.

He began to realize that her life was at stake as well as his boy's. That he loved this son with all the strength of his being and that he only knew the girl to fear her, made no difference in the fundamental facts. He acknowledged that she was his. He had accepted the fact and paid the penalty in the sacrifice of every ambition of a brilliant mind.

He weighed carefully the things that were certain and the things that were merely probable. The one certainty that faced him from every angle was that Cleo was in deadly earnest and that it meant a fight for the supremacy of every decent instinct of his life and character.

Apparently she had planned a tragic revenge by luring the girl to his home, figuring on his absence for three months, to precipitate a love affair before he could know the truth or move to interfere. A strange mental telepathy had warned him and he had broken in on the scene two months before he was expected.

And yet he couldn't believe that Cleo in the wildest flight of her insane rage could have deliberately meant that such an affair should end in marriage. She knew the character of both father and son too well to doubt that such an act could only end in tragedy. She was too cautious for such madness.

What was her game?

He asked himself that question again and again, always to come back to one conclusion. She had certainly brought the girl into the house to force from his reluctant lips her recognition and thus fix her own grip on his life. Beyond a doubt the surest way to accomplish this, and the quickest, was by a love affair between the boy and girl. She knew that personally the father had rather die than lose the respect of his son by a confession of his shame. But she knew with deeper certainty that he must confess it if their wills once clashed over the choice of a wife. The boy had a mind of his own. His father knew it and respected and loved him all the more because of it.

It was improbable as yet that Tom had spoken a word of love or personally faced such an issue. Of the girl he could only form the vaguest idea. It was clear now that he had been stricken by a panic and that the case was not so desperate as he had feared.

One thing he saw with increasing clearness. He must move with the utmost caution. He must avoid Helen at first and find the boy's attitude. He must at all hazards keep the use of every power of body, mind and soul in the crisis with which he was confronted.

Two hours later when Andy cautiously approached his door and listened at the keyhole he was still pacing the floor with the nervous tread of a wounded lion suddenly torn from the forest and thrust behind the bars of an iron cage.

Chapter IX

Andy's Dilemma

Andy left Norton's door and rapped softly at Tom's, tried the lock, found it unfastened, pushed his way quietly inside and called:

"Mister Tom!"

No answer came from the bed and Andy moved closer:

"Mister Tom—Mister Tom!"

"Ah—what's the matter with you—get out!" the sleeper growled.

The negro touched the boy's shoulder with a friendly shake, whispering:

"Yo' Pa's here!"

Tom sat up in bed rubbing his eyes:

"What's that?"

"Yassah, I fotch him through the country and we rid all night——"

"What's the matter?'

"Dat's what I wants ter see you 'bout, sah—an' ef you'll des slip on dem clothes an' meet me in de liberry, we'll hab a little confab an' er council er war——"

The boy picked up a pillow and hurled it at Andy:

"Well, get out, you old rascal, and I'll be down in a few minutes."

Andy dodged the pillow and at the door whispered:

"Yassah, an' don't disturb de major! I hopes ter God he sleep er month when he git started."

"All right, I won't disturb him."

Tom dressed, wondering vaguely what had brought his father home at such an unearthly hour and by such a trip across the country.

Andy, arrayed in a suit of broadcloth which he had appropriated from Norton's wardrobe in his absence, was waiting for Tom with evident impatience.

"Now, what I want to know is," the boy began, "what the devil you mean by pulling me out of bed this time of day?"

Andy chuckled:

"Well, yer see, sah, de major git home kinder sudden like en' I wuz jest er little oneasy 'bout dis here new suit er close er mine——"

"Well, that's not the first suit of his clothes you've swiped—you needn't be scared."

"Scared—who me? Man, I ain't er skeered er yo' Pa."

Minerva banged the dining-room door and Andy jumped and started to run. Tom laughed and seized his arm:

"Oh, don't be a fool! There's no danger."

"Nasah—I knows dey's no danger—but"—he glanced over his shoulder to be sure that the master hadn't come down stairs—"but yer know de ole sayin' is dat indiscretion is de better part er value——"

"I see!" Tom smiled in perfect agreement.

"An' I des has er little indiscretion——"

"Oh, you make me tired, how can I help a coward?"

Andy looked grieved:

"Lordy, Mister Tom—don't say dat, sah. I ain't no coward—I'se des cautious. Ye know I wuz in dat fus' battle er Bull's Run wid de major. I git separated from him in a close place an' hatter move my headquarters. Dey said I wuz er coward den 'cause I run. But twan't so, sah! Twan't cause I wuz er coward. I knowed zactly what I wuz doin'. I run 'cause I didn't hab no wings! I done de very bes' I could wid what I had. An' fuddermo', sah, de fellers dat wuz whar I wuz en' didn't run—dey's all dar yit at Bull's Run! Nasah, I ain't no coward. I des got de indiscretion——"

Another door slammed and Andy dodged.

"What's the matter with you anyhow, you old fool, are you having fits?" Tom cried.

Andy looked around the room cautiously and took hold of the boy's coat:

"You listen to me, Mister Tom. I'se gwine tell yer somfin' now——"

"Well?"

"I ain't er skeered er de major—but he's dangous——"

"Bosh!"

"Dey's sumfin' de matter wid him!"

"Had a few mint juleps with a friend, no doubt."

"Mint juleps! Huh! He kin swim in 'em—dive in 'em an' stay down er whole day an' never come up ter blow his bref—licker don't faze him!"

"It's politics. He's leading this devilish campaign and he's worried over politics."

"Nasah!" Andy protested with a laugh. "Dem fool niggers des well give up—dey ain't gwine ter vote no mo'. De odder feller's doin' all de worryin'. He ain't worrin'——"

"Yes, he is, too," the boy replied. "He put a revolver in his pocket when he started on that trip."

"Yassah!" Andy laughed. "I know, but yer don't understan'. Dat pistol's his flatform!"

"His platform?"

"You ain' hear what he bin er doin' wid dat pistol?"

"No—what ?"

"Man erlive, yer des oughter see 'im yistiddy when I take 'im dem papers ter dat speakin', down in one er dem po' white counties full er Radicals dat vote wid niggers. Er Kermittee comes up an' say dat de Internal Constertooshion er de Nunited States give 'em free Speech an' he gwine ter hear from 'em. De Lordy, man, but his bristles riz! I 'lows ter myself, folks yer sho is thumpin' de wrong watermillion dis time!"

"And what did he say to the Committee?"

"I nebber hear nary word. He des turn 'roun an' step up on dat flatform, kinder peart like, an' yer oughter see 'im open dat meetin'"—Andy paused and broke into a loud laugh.

"How did he open it?" Tom asked with indulgent interest.

Andy scratched his woolly head:

"Well, sah, hit warn't opened wid prayer—I kin tell ye dat! De fust thing he done, he reach back in his britches, kinder kereless lak, an' pull dat big pistol an' lay hit down afore him on de table beside his pitcher er lemonade. Man, you oughter see de eyes er dat crowd er dirty-lookin' po' whites! Dey fairly popped outen der heads! I hump myself an' move out towards de outskirts——"

Tom smiled:

"I bet you did!"

"Oh, I didn't run!" Andy protested.

"Of course not—far be it from you!"

"Nasah, I des tucken drawed out——"

"I understand, just a little caution, so to speak!"

"Yassah—dat's hit! Des tucken drawed out, whar I'd have elbow room in de mergency——"

"In other words," the boy interrupted, "just used a little indiscretion!"

Andy chuckled:

"Yassah! Dat's hit! Well, sah, he pat dat pistol kinder familious like an' say: 'Ef dey's any er you lowlife po' white scoundrels here ter-day that don't want ter hear my speech—git! But ef yer stay an' yer don't feel comfortable, I got six little lead pills here in a box dat'll ease yer pain. Walk right up to de prescription counter!'"

"And they walked right up?"

"Well, sah, dey didn't *crowd up!*—nasah!" Andy paused and laughed immoderately. "An' wid dat he des folded his arms an' look at dat crowd er minute an' his eyes began to spit fire. When I see dat, I feels my very shoes commin' ontied. I sez ter myself, now folks he's gwine ter magnify——"

Tom laughed:

"Magnified, did he?"

The negro's eyes rolled and he lifted his hands in a gesture of supreme admiration:

"De Lordy, man—ef he didn't! He lit inter dem po' white trash lak er thousand er brick——"

"Give 'em what Paddy gave the drum, I suppose?"

"Now yer talkin', honey! Ef he didn't give 'em particular hell!"

"And what happened?"

"Nuttin' happened, chile—dat's what I'm tryin' ter tell ye. Nary one of 'em nebber cheeped. Dey des stood dar an' listened lak er passel er sheep-killin' dogs. Lemme tell ye, honey, politics ain't er worryin' him. De odder fellers doin' all de worrin'. Nasah, dey's sumfin else de matter wid de major——"

"What?"

Andy looked around the room furtively and whispered:

"Dar's a quare look in his eye!"

"Ah, pooh!"

"Hit's des lak I tells ye, Mister Tom. I ain't seed dat quare look in his eye before since de night I see yo' Ma's ghost come down outen dat big picture frame an' walk cross dis hall——"

The boy smiled and looked at the shining yellow canvas that seemed a living thing gleaming in its dark setting:

"I suppose, of course, Andy, you really saw her do that?"

"'Fore God, es sho's I'm talkin' ter you now, she done dat thing—yassah! Hit wus de las' year befo' you come back frum college. De moon wuz shinin' froo dem big windows right on her face, an' I seed her wid my own eyes, all of a sudden, step right down outen dat picture frame an' walk across dis room, huggin' her baby close up in her arms—an' you'se dat very baby, sah!"

The boy was interested in the negro's weird recital in spite of his amusement. He shook his head and said laughingly:

"Andy, you've got the heat——"

"Hit's des lak I tells ye, sah," Andy solemnly repeated. "I stood right dar by dat table froze in my tracks, till I seed her go froo dat do' widout openin' it——"

"Bah!" Tom cried in disgust.

"Dat she did!—an' Miss Minerva she see her do dat same thing once before and tell me about it. But man erlive, when *I* see it, I let off one er dem yells dat wuz hark from de tomb——"

"I bet you did!"

"Yassah, I went froo dat big window dar an' carry de whole sash wid me. De major he take out atter me when he hears de commotion, an' when he kotch me down dar in de fiel' I wuz still wearin' dat sash fer a necktie!"

The boy laughed again:

"And I suppose, of course, he believed all you told him?"

The negro rolled his eyes solemnly to the ceiling and nodded his head:

"Dat he did, sah. When I fust told 'im dat I seed er ghost, he laft fit ter kill hissef——"

The boy nodded:

"I don't doubt it!"

"But mind ye," Andy solemnly continued, "when I tells him what kin' er ghost I seed, he nebber crack anudder smile. He nebber open his mouf ergin fer er whole day. An' dis here's what I come ter tell ye, honey——"

He paused and glanced over his shoulder as if momentarily fearing the major's appearance.

"I thought you'd been telling me?"

"Nasah, I ain't told ye nuttin' yit. When I say what *kin'* er ghost I see—dat quare look come in his eye—de same look dat come dar yistiddy when I tells 'im dat Miss Helen wuz here."

The boy looked at Andy with a sudden start:

"Ah, how could that sweet little girl upset him? He's her guardian's attorney and sent for her to come, of course——"

"I don't know 'bout dat, sah—all I know is dat he went wil' es quick es I tells 'im, an' he bin wil' ever since. Mister Tom, I ain't skeered er de major—but he's dangous!"

"Ah, Andy, you're the biggest fool in the county," the boy answered laughing. "You know my father wouldn't touch a hair of your kinky head."

Andy grinned.

"'Cose not, Mister Tom," he said with unction. "I knows dat. But all de same I gotter keep outen his way wid dis new suit er close till I see 'im smilin'——"

"Always bearing in mind that indiscretion is the better part of value!"

"Yassah—yassah—dat's hit—an' I wants you ter promise you'll stan' by me, sah, till de major's in a good humor."

"All right; if you need me, give a yell."

Tom turned with a smile to go, and Andy caught his sleeve and laughed again:

"Wait—wait er minute, Mister Tom—hold yer hosses. Dey's anodder little thing I wants ye ter help me out erbout. I kin manage de major all right ef I kin des keep outen his sight ter-day wid dis suit er clothes. But de trouble is, I got ter wear 'em, sah—I got er 'pintment wid er lady!"

The boy turned good-naturedly, threw his leg over the corner of the table and raised his eyebrows with a gleam of mischief:

"Oh, a lady! Who is she? Aunt Minerva?"

Andy waved his hands in disgust.

"Dat's des de one hit ain't—nasah! I can't stan' her nohow, Mr. Tom. I des natchally can't stan' er fat 'oman! An' Miss Minerva weighs 'bout three hundred——"

"Oh, not so bad as that, Andy!"

"Yassah, she's er whale! Man, ef we wuz walkin' along tergedder, en she wuz ter slip an' fall she'd sqush de life outen me! I'd nebber know what hit me. An' what makes bad matters wus, I'se er strong suspicion dat she got her eyes sot on me here lately—I des feels it in my bones—she's atter me sho, sah."

Tom broke into a laugh:

"Well, she can't take you by force."

"I don't know 'bout dat, sah. When any 'oman gits her min' sot she's dangous. But when a 'oman big an' black es she make up her min'!"

"Black!" Tom cried, squaring himself and looking Andy over: "Aren't you just a little shady?"

"Who? Me?—nasah! I ain't no black nigger!"

"No?"

"Nasah! I'se what dey calls er tantalizin' brown!"

"Oh, I see!"

"Yassah, I'se er chocolate-colored gemman—an' I nebber could stan' dese here coal-black niggers. Miss Minerva's so black she kin spit ink!"

"And she's 'atter' you?"

"Yassah, an' Miss Minerva's a widder 'oman, an' ye know de Scripter says, 'Beware of widders'——"

"Of course!" Tom agreed.

"I'se er gemman, yer know, Mister Tom. I can't insult er lady, an' dat's de particular reason dat I wants ter percipitate mysef wid my true love before dat big, black 'oman gits her hands on me. She's atter me sho, an' ef she gits me in er close place, what I gwine do, sah?"

Tom assumed a judicial attitude, folded his arms and asked:

"Well, who's the other one?—who's your true love?"

Andy put his hand over his mouth to suppress a snicker:

"Now dat's whar I kinder hesitates, sah. I bin er beatin' de debbil roun' de stump fur de pas' week tryin' ter screw up my courage ter ax ye ter help me. But Mister Tom, you gettin' so big an' dignified I kinder skeered. You got ter puttin' on more airs dan de major——"

"Ah, who is she?" the boy asked brusquely.

Andy glanced at him out of the corners of his rolling eyes:

"Yer ain't gwine laugh at me—is yer?"

With an effort Tom kept his face straight:

"No, I may be just as big a fool some day myself—who is she?"

Andy stepped close and whispered:

"Miss Cleo!"

"Cleo——"

"Yassah."

"Well, you are a fool!" the boy exclaimed indignantly.

"Yassah, I spec I is," Andy answered, crestfallen, "but I des can't hep it, sah."

"Cleo, my nurse, my mammy—why, she wouldn't wipe her foot on you if you were a door-mat. She's almost as white as I am."

"Yassah, I know, an' dat's what make me want her so. She's mine ef I kin git her! Hit des takes one drap er black blood to make er nigger, sah."

"Bah—she wouldn't look at you!"

"I know she holds er high head, sah. She's been eddicated an' all dat—but you listen ter me, honey—she gwine look at me all de same, when I say de word."

"Yes, long enough to laugh."

Andy disregarded the shot, and prinked himself before the mirror:

"Don't yer think my complexion's gettin' little better, sah?"

Tom picked up a book with a smile:

"You do look a little pale today, but I think that's your liver!"

Andy broke into a laugh:

"Nasah. Dat ain't my liver!"

"Must be!"

"Nasah! I got er patent bleacher frum New York dat's gwine ter make me white ef I kin des buy enough of it."

"How much have you used?"

"Hain't used but six bottles yit. Hit costs three dollars a bottle"—he paused and rubbed his hands smoothingly over his head. "Don't yer think my hair's gittin' straighter, sah?"

Tom turned another page of the book without looking up:

"Not so that you could notice it."

"Yassah, 'tis!" Andy laughed, eyeing it sideways in the mirror and making a vain effort to see the back of his head. "I'se er usin' er concoction called 'Not-a-Kink.' Hit costs five dollars a bottle—but man, hit sho is doin' de work! I kin des feel dem kinks slippin' right out."

"There's nothing much the matter with your hair, Andy," Tom said, looking up with a smile, "that's the straightest thing about you. The trouble's inside."

"What de matter wid me inside?"

"You're crooked."

"Who—me?" Andy cried. "Ah, go long, Mister Tom, wid yer projectin'—yer des foolin' wid me"—he came close and busied himself brushing the boy's coat and continued with insinuating unction—"now ef yer des put in one little word fer me wid Miss Cleo——"

"Take my advice, Andy," the boy said seriously, "keep away from her—she'll kill you."

"Not ef you help me out, sah," Andy urged eagerly. "She'll do anything fer you, Mister Tom—she lubs de very ground you walks on—des put in one little word fer me, sah——"

Tom shook his head emphatically:

"Can't do it, Andy!"

"Don't say dat, Mister Tom!"

"Can't do it."

Andy flicked imaginary lint from both sleeves of Tom's coat:

"Now look here, Mister Tom——"

The boy turned away protesting:

"No, I can't do it."

"Lordy, Mister Tom," Andy cried in grieved tones. "You ain't gwine back on me like dat des 'cose yer went ter college up dar in de Norf an' git mixed up wid Yankee notions! Why, you an' me's always been good friends an' partners. What ye got agin me?"

A gleam of mischief slipped into the boy's eyes again as he folded his arms with mock severity:

"To begin with, you're the biggest old liar in the United States——"

"Lordy, Mister Tom, I nebber tell a lie in my life, sah!"

"Andy—Andy!"

The negro held his face straight for a moment and then broke into a laugh:

"Well, sah, I may has *pré-var-i-cated* some times, but dat ain't lyin'—why, all gemmens do dat."

"And look at this suit of clothes," Tom said severely, "that you've just swiped from Dad. You'd steal anything you can get your hands on!"

Andy turned away and spoke with deep grief:

"Mister Tom, you sho do hurt my feelin's, sah—I nebber steal nuttin' in my life."

"I've known you to steal a palm-leaf fan in the dead of winter with snow on the ground."

Andy laughed uproariously:

"Why, man, dat ain't stealin! Who gwine ter want er palm-leaf fan wid snow on de groun'?—dat's des findin' things. You know dey calls me Hones' Andy. When dey ketch me wid de goods I nebber try ter lie outen it lak some fool niggers. I des laugh, 'fess right up, an' hit's all right. Dat's what make 'em call me Hones' Andy, cose I always knows dat honesty's de bes' policy—an' here you comes callin' me a thief—Lordee, Mister Tom, yer sho do hurt my feelin's!"

The boy shook his head again and frowned:

"You're a hopeless old sinner——"

"Who, me, er sinner? Why, man erlive, I'se er pillar in de church!"

"God save the church!"

"I mebbe backslide a little, sah, in de winter time," Andy hastened to admit. "But I'se always de fus' man to de mourners' bench in de spring. I mos' generally leads de mourners, sah, an' when I comes froo an' gits religion over again, yer kin hear me shout er mile——"

"And I bet when the chickens hear it they roost higher the next night!"

Andy ignored the thrust and went on enthusiastically:

"Nasah, de church folks don't call me no sinner. I always stands up fer religion. Don't yer min' de time dat big yaller nigger cum down here from de Norf er castin' circumflexions on our church? I wuz de man dat stood right up in de meetin' an' defends de cause er de Lawd. I haul off an' biff 'im right in the jaw——"

"And you're going to ask Cleo to marry you?"

"I sho' is, sah."

"Haven't you a wife living, Andy?" the boy asked carelessly.

The whites of the negro's eyes suddenly shone as he rolled them in the opposite direction. He scratched his head and turned back to his friendly tormentor with unction:

"Mr. Tom, I'm gwine ter be hones'—cose honesty is de bes' policy. I did marry a lady, sah, but dat wuz er long time ergo. She run away an' lef me an' git married ergin an' I divorced her, sah. She don't pester me no mo' an' I don't pester her. Hit warn't my fault, sah, an' I des put her away ez de Bible sez. Ain't dat all right, sah?"

"Well, it's hardly legal to-day, though it may have been a Biblical custom."

"Yassah, but dat's nuttin' ter do wid niggers. De white folks make de laws an' dey hatter go by 'em. But niggers is niggers, yer know dat yosef, sah."

Tom broke into a laugh:

"Andy, you certainly are a bird!"

The negro joined in the laugh with a joyous chuckle at its close:

"Yassah, yassah—one er dese here great big brown blackbirds! But, Lordy, Mister Tom, yer des foolin' wid me—yer ain't got nuttin' 'gin yer ole partner, barrin' dem few little things?"

"No, barring the few things I've mentioned, that you're a lazy, lying, impudent old rascal—barring these few little things—why—otherwise you're all right, Andy, you're all right!"

The negro chuckled joyfully:

"Yassah—yassah! I knowed yer warn't gwine back on me, Mister Tom." He edged close and dropped his voice to the oiliest whisper: "You'll say dat good word now to Miss Cleo right away, sah?"

The boy shook his head:

"The only thing I'll agree to do, Andy, is to stand by and see you commit suicide. If it's any comfort to you, I'll tell you that she'll kill you."

"Nasah! Don't yer believe it. Ef I kin des escape dat fat 'oman wid my life before she gits me—now dat you'se on my side I kin read my titles clar——"

"Oh, you can get rid of Minerva all right!"

"For de Lord sake, des tell me how!"

Tom bent toward him and spoke in low tones:

"All you've got to do if Minerva gets you in a tight place is to confess your real love and ask her to help you out as a friend."

Andy looked puzzled a moment and then a light broke over his dusky face:

"Dat's a fine plan, Mister Tom. You saved er nigger's life—I'll do dat sho!"

"As for Cleo, I can't do anything for you, but I won't do anything against you."

"Thankee, sah! Thankee, sah!"

When Tom reached the door he paused and said:

"I might consent to consult with the undertaker about the funeral and act as one of your pall-bearers."

Andy waved him away with a suppressed laugh:

"G'way frum here, Mister Tom! G'way frum here!"

The negro returned to the mirror, adjusted his suit and after much effort succeeded in fixing a new scarfpin of a horseshoe design in the centre of the bow of one of Norton's old-fashioned black string ties. He dusted his shoes, smoothed as many of the kinks out of his hair as a vigorous rubbing could accomplish, and put the last touches on his elaborate preparations for a meeting with Cleo that was destined to be a memorable one in her life.

Chapter X

The Best Laid Plans

Andy's plans for a speedy conquest of Cleo were destined to an interruption. Minerva had decided that he was the best man in sight for a husband, and made up her mind to claim her own. She had noticed of late a disposition on his part to dally with Cleo, and determined to act immediately. Breakfast was well under way and she had heard Andy's unctuous laugh in the library with Tom.

She put on her sweeping apron, took up a broom and entered under the pretense of cleaning the room.

Andy was still chuckling with joy over the brilliant plan of escape suggested by Tom. He had just put the finishing touches on his necktie, and was trying on an old silk hat when Minerva's voice caused him to suddenly collapse.

"Say, man, is dat a hat er a bee-gum?" she cried, with a laugh so jolly it would have been contagious but for Andy's terror.

He looked at her, dropped the hat, picked it up and stammered:

"W-w-why—Miss Minerva, is dat you?"

Minerva beamed on him tenderly, placed her broom in the corner and advanced quickly to meet him:

"I knowed ye wuz 'spectin me frum de way yer wuz gettin' ready." She laughed and chuckled with obvious coquetry, adding coyly:

"I knows how yer feel——"

Andy looked for a way of escape. But Minerva was too quick for him. She was a woman of enormous size, fat, jolly and extremely agile for her weight. She carried her two hundred and fifty pounds without apparent effort. She walked with a nervous, snappy energy and could waltz with the grace of a girl of sixteen.

She had reached Andy's side before his dull brain could think of an excuse for going. Her shining coal-black face was aglow with tenderness and the determination to make things easy for him in the declaration of love she had planned that he should make.

"I know how yer feels, Brer Andy," she repeated.

The victim mopped his perspiring brow and stammered:

"Yassam—yassam."

"Yer needn't be so 'barrassed, Mr. Andy," Minerva went on in the most insinuating tones. "Yer kin say what's on yer mind."

"Yassam."

"Come right here and set down er minute."

She seized his hand and drew him with a kittenish skip toward a settee, tripped on a bear rug and would have fallen had not Andy grabbed her.

"De Lord save us!" he gasped. He was trying desperately in his new suit to play the gentleman under difficulties.

Minerva was in ecstasy over his gallantry:

"Yer sho wuz terrified less I git hurt, Mr. Andy," she laughed. "I thought dat bar had me sho."

Andy mopped his brow again and glanced longingly at the door:

"Yassam, I sho wuz terrified—I'm sorry m'am, you'll hatter 'scuse me. Mister Tom's out dar waitin' fer me, an' I hatter go——"

Minerva smilingly but firmly pulled him down on the seat beside her:

"Set right down, Mr. Andy, an' make yoself at home. We got er whole half hour yet 'fore de odder folks come down stairs. Man, don't be so 'barrassed! I knows 'zactly how yer feels. I understand what's de matter wid yer"—she paused, glanced at him out of the corner of her eye, touched him slyly with her elbow, and whispered:

"Why don't yer say what's on yer mind?"

Andy cleared his throat and began to stammer. He had the habit of stammering under excitement, and Tom's plan of escape had just popped into his benumbed brain. He saw the way out:

"Y-y-yas'm—cose, m'am. I got sumfin ter tell ye, Miss M-m-Minerva."

Minerva moved a little closer.

"Yas, honey, I knows what 'tis, but I'se jes' waitin' ter hear it."

He cleared his throat and tried to begin his speech in a friendly business-like way:

"Yassam, I gwine tell yer sho——"

He turned to face her and to his horror found her lips so close she had evidently placed them in position for the first kiss.

He stopped appalled, fidgeted, looked the other way and stammered:

"H-hit sho is powful warm ter-day, m'am!"

"Tain't so much de heat, Brer Andy," she responded tenderly, "as 'tis de humility dat's in de air!"

Andy turned, looked into her smiling face for a moment and they both broke into a loud laugh while he repeated:

"Yassam, de humility—dat's hit! De humility dat's in de air!"

The expression had caught his fancy enormously.

"Yassir, de humility—dat's hit!" Minerva murmured.

When the laughter had slowly died down she moved a little closer and said reassuringly:

"And now, Brer Andy, ez dey's des you an' me here tergedder—ef hits suits yo' circumstantial convenience, hab no reprehenshun, sah, des say what's on yo' min'."

Andy glanced at her quickly, bowed grandiloquently and catching the spirit of her high-flown language decided to spring his confession and ask her help to win Cleo.

"Yassam, Miss Minerva, dat's so. An' ez I allays sez dat honesty is de bes' policy, I'se gwine ter ré-cede ter yo' invitation!"

Minerva laughed with joyous admiration:

"Des listen at dat nigger now! You sho is er talkin' man when yer gits started——"

"Yassam, I bin er tryin' ter tell ye fer de longest kind er time an' ax ye ter help me——"

Minerva moved her massive figure close against him:

"Cose I help you."

Andy edged as far away as possible, but the arm of the settee had caught him and he couldn't get far. He smiled wanly and tried to assume a purely platonic tone:

"Wuz yer ebber in love, Miss Minerva?"

Minerva nudged him slyly:

"Wuz I?"

Andy tried to ignore the hint, lifted his eyes to the ceiling and in far-away tones put the hypothetical case of the friend who needed help:

"Well, des 'spose m'am dat a po' man wuz ter fall in love wid er beautiful lady, fur above him, wid eyes dat shine lak de stars——"

"Oh, g'way frum here, man!" Minerva cried entranced as she broke into a peal of joyous laughter, nudging him again.

The insinuating touch of her elbow brought Andy to a sharp realization that his plan had not only failed to work, but was about to compromise him beyond hope. He hurried to correct her mistake.

"But listen, Miss Minerva—yer don't understand. Would yer be his *friend* an' help him to win her?"

With a cry of joy she threw her huge arms around his neck:

"Would I—Lordy—man!"

Andy tried to dodge her strangle hold, but was too slow and she had him.

He struggled and grasped her arms, but she laughed and held on.

"B-b-but—yer—yer," he stammered.

"Yer needn't say annudder word——"

"Yassam, but wait des er minute," he pleaded, struggling to lower her arms.

"Hush, man," Minerva said good-naturedly. "Cose I knows yer bin er bad nigger—but ye needn't tell me 'bout it now——"

"For Gawd's sake!" Andy gasped, wrenching her arms away at last, "will yer des lemme say one word?"

"Nasah!" she said generously. "I ain't gwine ter let ye say no harsh words ergin yoself. I sho do admire de indelicate way dat yer tells me of yo' love!"

"B-but yer don't understand——"

"Cose I does, chile!" Minerva exclaimed with a tender smile.

Andy made a gesture of despair:

"B-b-but I tries ter 'splain——"

"Yer don't hatter 'splain nuttin' ter me, man—I ain't no spring chicken—I knowed what ye means befo' ye opens yer mouf. Yer tells me dat ye lubs me an' I done say dat I lubs you—an' dat's all dey is to it."

Minerva enfolded him in her ample arms and he collapsed with feeble assent:

"Yassam—yassam."

Chapter XI

A Reconnoitre

Norton slept at last from sheer physical exhaustion and waked at eleven o'clock refreshed and alert, his faculties again strung for action.

He wondered in the clear light of noon at the folly of his panic the night before. The fighting instinct in him had always been the dominant one. He smiled now at his silly collapse and his quick brain began to plan his line of defense.

The girl was in his house, yes. But she had been here in spirit, a living, breathing threat over his life, every moment for the past twenty years. No scene of pain or struggle could come but that he had already lived it a thousand times. There was a kind of relief in facing these phantoms for the first time in flesh and blood. They couldn't be more formidable than the ghosts he had fought.

He shaved and dressed with deliberation—dressed with unusual care—his brain on fire now with the determination to fight and win. The instincts of the soldier were again in command. And the first thing a true soldier did when driven to desperation and surrounded by an overwhelming foe was to reconnoitre, find the strength of his enemy and strike at their weakest spot.

He must avoid Cleo and find the exact situation of Tom and Helen. His safest way was again to cultivate Andy's knowledge of the house in his absence.

He rang for him and waited in vain for his appearance. He rang again and, getting no response, walked down stairs to the door and searched the lawn. He saw Cleo beside a flower bed talking to Helen. He caught a glimpse of the lovely young face as she lifted her eyes and saw him. He turned back quickly into the house to avoid her, and hurried to the library.

Andy had been watching carefully until Norton went through the front door. Sure that he had strolled out on the lawn to see Helen, with a sigh of relief the negro hurried back to the mirror to take another admiring glance at his fine appearance in the new suit.

Norton's sudden entrance completely upset him. He tried to laugh and the effort froze on his lips. He saw that Norton had recognized the stolen suit, but was too excited to see the amusement lurking behind his frown:

"Where were you a while ago, when I was calling?"

"I been right here all mornin', sah," Andy answered with forced surprise.

"You didn't hear that bell?"

"Nasah, nebber hear a thing, sah."

Norton looked at him severely:

"There's a bigger bell going to ring for you one of these days. You like to go to funerals, don't you?"

Andy laughed:

"Yassah—odder folk's funerals—but dey's one I ain't in no hurry to git to——"

"That's the one—where were you when I rang just now?"

The negro looked at his master, hesitated, and a broad, grin overspread his black face. He bowed and chuckled and walked straight up to Norton:

"Yassah, major, I gwine tell yer de honest truf now, cose honesty is de bes' policy. I wuz des embellishin' mysef wid dis here ole suit er close dat ye gimme, sah, an' I wants ter specify my 'preciation, sah, at de generosity wid which yer always treats me, sah. I had a mos' particular reason fer puttin' dis suit on dis mornin'——"

Norton examined the lapel of the coat, his lips twitching to suppress a smile:

"My suit of broadcloth——"

Andy rubbed his hands over the coat in profound amazement:

"Is dis de broadcloth? De Lawd er mussy!"

Norton shook his head:

"You old black hound——"

Andy broke into a loud laugh:

"Yassah, yassah! Dat's me. But, major, I couldn't find the vest!"

"Too bad—shall I get it for you?"

"Nasah—des tell me whar yer put it!"

Norton smiled:

"Did you look in my big cedar box?"

"Thankee, sah—thankee, sah. Yer sho is good ter me, major, an' yer can always 'pend on me, sah."

"Yes, I'm going to send you to the penitentiary for this——"

Andy roared with laughter:

"Yassah—yassah—cose, sah! I kin see myse'f in dat suit er stripes now, but I sho is gwine ter blossom out in dat double-breasted vest fust!"

When the laughter had died away Norton asked in good-natured tones:

"You say I can depend on you, Andy?"

"Dat yer kin, sah—every day in the year—you'se de bes frien' I ebber had in de world, sah."

"Then I want to ask you a question."

"Yassah, I tells yer anything I know, sah."

"I'm just a little worried about Tom. He's too young to get married. Do you think he's been really making love to Miss Helen?"

Norton watched the negro keenly. He knew that a boy would easily trust his secrets to such a servant, and that his sense of loyalty to the young would be strong. He was relieved at the quick reply which came without guile:

"Lawdy, major, he ain't got dat far, sah. I bin er watchin' 'em putty close. He des kinder skimmin' 'round de edges."

"You think so?"

"Yassah!" was the confident reply. "He 'minds me er one er dese here minnows when ye go fishin'. He ain't swallowed de hook yit—he des nibblin'."

Norton smiled, lighted a cigar, and quietly said:

"Go down to the office and tell Mr. Tom that I'm up and wish to see him."

"Yassah—yassah—right away, sah."

Andy bowed and grinned and hurried from the house.

Norton seated himself in an armchair facing the portrait of the little mother. His memory lingered tenderly over the last beautiful days they had spent together. He recalled every smile with which she had looked her forgiveness and her love. He felt the presence of her spirit and took courage.

He lifted his eyes to the sweet, tender face bending over her baby and breathed a prayer for guidance. He wondered if she could see and know in the dim world beyond. Without trying to reason about it, he had grown to believe that she did, and that her soul was near in this hour of his trial.

How like this mother the boy had grown the past year—just her age when he was born. The color of his blonde hair was almost an exact reproduction of hers. And this beautiful hair lent a peculiar distinction to the boy's fine face. He had developed, too, a lot of little ways strikingly like the mother's when a laughing school girl. He smiled in the same flashing way, like a sudden burst of sunlight from behind a cloud. His temper was quick like hers, and his voice more and more seemed to develop the peculiar tones he had loved.

That this boy, around whose form every desire of life had centered, should be in peril was a thought that set his heart to beating with new energy.

He heard his quick step in the hall, rose and laid down his cigar. With a rush Tom was in the room grasping the outstretched hand:

"Glad to see you back, Dad!" he cried, "but we had no idea you were coming so soon."

"I got a little homesick," the father replied, "and decided to come in for a day or two."

"I was awfully surprised at Miss Helen's popping in on us so unexpectedly—I suppose you forgot to tell me about it in the rush of getting away."

"I really didn't expect her to come before my return," was the vague answer.

"But you wrote her to come at once."

"Did I?" he replied carelessly.

"Why, yes, she showed me your letter. I didn't write you about her arrival because you told me under no circumstances, except of life or death, to tell you of anything here and I obeyed orders."

"I'm glad you've made that a principle of your life—stick to it."

"I'm sorry you're away in this dangerous campaign so much, Dad," the boy said with feeling. "It may end your career."

The father smiled and a far-away look stole into his eyes:

"I have no career, my boy! I gave that up years ago and I had to lead this campaign."

"Why?"

The look in the brown eyes deepened:

"Because I am the man to whom our danger has been revealed. I am the man to whom God has given a message—I who have been tried in the fires of hell and fought my way up and out of the pit—only the man who has no ambitions can tell the truth!"

The boy nodded and smiled:

"Yes, I know your hobby——"

"The big tragic truth, that the physical contact of the black race with the white is a menace to our life"—his voice had dropped to a passionate whisper as if he were talking to himself.

A laugh from Tom roused him to the consciousness of time and place:

"But that isn't a speech you meant for me, Dad!"

The father caught his bantering tone with a light reply:

"No."

And then his tall form confronted the boy with a look of deep seriousness:

"To-morrow I enter on the last phase of this campaign. At any moment a fool or a madman may blow my brains out."

Tom gave a start:

"'Dad——"

"Over every mile of that long drive home last night, I was brooding and thinking of you——"

"Of me?"

"Wondering if I had done my level best to carry out the dying commands of your mother——"

He paused, drew a deep breath, looked up tenderly and continued:

"I wish you were settled in life."

The boy turned slightly away and the father watched him keenly and furtively for a moment, and took a step toward him:

"You have never been in love?"

With a shrug and a laugh, Tom dropped carelessly on the settee and crossed his legs:

"Love—hardly!"

The father held his breath until the light answer brought relief and then smiled:

"It will come some day, my boy, and when it hits you, I think it's going to hit hard."

The handsome young head was poised on one side with a serious judicial expression:

"Yes, I think it will—but I guess my ideal's too high, though."

The father spoke with deep emotion:

"A man's ideal can't be too high, my boy!"

Tom didn't hear. His mind was busy with his ideal.

"But if I ever find her," he went on dreamily, "do you know what I'll want?"

"No."

"The strength of Samson!"

"What for?"

He shook his head with a smile:

"To reach over in California, tear one of those big trees up by the roots, dip it in the crater of Vesuvius and write her name in letters of fire across the sky!"

He ended with a wide, sweeping gesture, showing just how he would inscribe it.

"Really!" the father laughed.

"That's how I feel!" he cried, springing to his feet with an emphatic gesture, a smile playing about his firm mouth.

The father slipped his, arm around him:

"Well, if you should happen to do it, be sure to stand in the ocean, because otherwise, you know, if the grass should be dry you might set the world on fire."

The boy broke into a hearty laugh, crossed to the table, and threw his leg carelessly over the corner, a habit he had gotten from his father. When the laugh had died away, he picked up a magazine and said carelessly:

"I guess there's no danger, after all. I'm afraid that the big thing poets sing about is only a myth after all"—he paused, raised his eyes and they rested on his mother's portrait, and his voice became a reverent whisper—"except your love for my mother, Dad—that was the real thing!"

He was looking the other way and couldn't see the cloud of anguish that suddenly darkened his father's face.

"You'll know its meaning some day, my son," was the even reply that came after a pause, "and I only demand of you one thing——"

He laid his hand on the boy's shoulder:

"That the woman you ask to be your wife bear a name without shadow. Good blood is the noblest inheritance that any father or mother ever gave to a child."

"I'm proud of mine, sir!" the boy said, drawing his form erect.

The father's arm stole around the young shoulders and his voice was very low:

"Fools sometimes say, my son, that a man can sow his wild oats and be all the better for it. It's a lie. The smallest deed takes hold on eternity for it may start a train of events that even God can't stop——"

He paused and fought back a cry from the depths of his soul.

"I did something that hurt your mother once"—his voice dropped—"and for twenty years my soul in anguish has begged for forgiveness——"

The boy looked at him in startled sympathy and his own arm instinctively slipped around his father's form as he lifted his face to the shining figure over the mantel:

"But you believe that she sees and understands now?"

Norton turned his head away to hide the mists that clouded his eyes. His answer was uttered with the reverence of a prayer:

"Yes! I've seen her in dreams sometimes so vividly and heard her voice so plainly, I couldn't believe that I was asleep"—his voice stopped before it broke, his arm tightening its hold—"and I know that her spirit broods and watches over you——"

And then he suddenly decided to do the most cruel thing to which his mind had ever given assent. But he believed it necessary and did not hesitate. Only the vague intensity of his eyes showed his deep feeling as he said evenly:

"Ask Miss Helen to come here. You'll find her on the lawn with Cleo."

The boy left the room to summon Helen, and Norton seated himself with grim determination.

Chapter XII

The First Whisper

When Tom reached the lawn Helen was nowhere to be seen. He searched every nook and corner which they had been accustomed to haunt, looked through the rose garden and finally knocked timidly on the door of her room. He was sure at first that he heard a sound within. He dared not open her door and so hurried down town to see if he could find her in one of the stores.

Helen shivering inside had held her breath until his footsteps died away on the stairs.

With heavy heart but swift hands she was packing her trunk. In spite of Cleo's assurances she had been startled and frightened beyond measure by the certainty that Norton had purposely avoided her. She had expected the most hearty welcome. Her keen intuition had scented his hostility though not a word had been spoken.

Cleo, who had avoided Tom, again rapped on her door:

"Just a minute, Miss Helen!"

There was no answer and the woman strained her ear to hear what was happening inside. It couldn't be possible that the girl was really going to leave! Such an act of madness would upset her plans just as they were coming out exactly as she had hoped.

"She can't mean it!" Cleo muttered under her breath. "It's only a fit of petulance!" She didn't dare to give Helen a hint of her clouded birth. That might send her flying. Yet if necessary she must excite her curiosity by a whisper about her parentage. She had already guessed from hints the girl had dropped that her one passionate desire was to know the names of her father and mother. She would be careful, but it was necessary to hold her at all hazards.

She rapped again:

"Please, Miss Helen, may I come in just a minute?"

Her voice was full of pleading. A step was heard, a pause and the door opened. Cleo quickly entered, turned the key and in earnest tones, her eyes dancing excitedly, asked:

"You are really packing your trunk?"

"It's already packed," was the firm answer.

"But you can't mean this——"

"I do."

"I tell you, child, the major didn't see you——"

"He did see me. I caught his eye in a straight, clear look. And he turned quickly to avoid me."

"You have his letter of invitation. You can't think it a forgery?" she asked with impatience.

The girl's color deepened:

"He has evidently changed his mind for some reason."

"Nonsense!"

"I was just ready to rush to meet him and thank him with the deepest gratitude for his invitation. The look on his face when he turned was like a blow."

"It's only your imagination!" Cleo urged eagerly. "He's worried over politics."

"I'm not in politics. No, it's something else—I must go."

Cleo put her hand appealingly on Helen's arm:

"Don't be foolish, child!"

The girl drew away suddenly with instinctive aversion. The act was slight and quick, but not too slight or quick for the woman's sharp eye. She threw Helen a look of resentment:

"Why do you draw away from me like that?"

The girl flushed with embarrassment and stammered:

"Why—you see, I've lived up North all my life, shut up in a convent most of the time and I'm not used—to—colored people——"

"Well, I'm not a negro, please remember that. I'm a nurse and housekeeper, if you please, and there happens to be a trace of negro blood in my veins, but a white soul throbs beneath this yellow skin. I'd strip it off inch by inch if I could change its color"—her voice broke with assumed emotion—it was a pose for the moment, but its apparent genuineness deceived the girl and roused her sympathy.

"I'm sorry if I hurt you," she said contritely.

"Oh, it's no matter."

Helen snapped the lid of her trunk:

"I'm leaving on the first train."

"Oh, come now," Cleo urged impatiently. "You'll do nothing of the kind—the major will be himself to-morrow."

"I am going at once——"

"You're not going!" the woman declared firmly, laying her hand again on the girl's arm.

With a shudder Helen drew quickly away.

"Please—please don't touch me again!" she cried with anger. "I'm sorry, but I can't help it."

With an effort Cleo suppressed her rage:

"Well, I won't. I understand—but you can't go like this. The major will be furious."

"I'm going," the girl replied, picking up the odds and ends she had left and placing them in her travelling bag.

Cleo watched her furtively:

"I—I—ought to tell you something that I know about your life——"

Helen dropped a brush from her hand and quickly crossed the room, a bright color rushing to her cheeks:

"About my birth?"

"You believe," Cleo began cautiously, "that the major is the agent of your guardian who lives abroad. Well, he's not the agent—he *is* your guardian."

"Why should he deceive me?"

"He had reasons, no doubt," Cleo replied with a smile.

"You mean that he knows the truth? That he knows the full history of my birth and the names of my father and mother?"

"Yes."

"He has assured me again and again that he does not——"

"I know that he has deceived you."

Helen looked at her with a queer expression of angry repulsion that she should possess this secret of her unhappy life.

"You know?" she asked faintly.

"No," was the quick reply, "not about your birth; but I assure you the major does. Demand that he tell you."

"He'll refuse——"

"Ask him again, and stay until he does."

"But I'm intruding!" Helen cried, brushing a tear from her eyes.

"No matter, you're here, you're of age, you have the right to know the truth—stay until you learn it. If he slights you, pay no attention to it—stay until you know."

The girl's form suddenly stiffened and her eyes flashed:

"Yes, I will—I'll know at any cost."

With a soft laugh which Helen couldn't hear Cleo hurried from the room.

Chapter XIII

Andy's Proposal

Andy had been waiting patiently for Cleo to leave Helen's door. He had tried in vain during the entire morning to get an opportunity to see her alone, but since Helen's appearance at breakfast she had scarcely left the girl's side for five minutes.

He had slipped to the head of the back stairs, lifted the long flaps of the tail of his new coat and carefully seated himself on the last step to wait her appearance. He smiled with assurance. She couldn't get down without a word at least.

"I'm gwine ter bring things to er head dis day, sho's yer born!" he muttered, wagging his head.

He had been to Norfolk the week before on an excursion to attend the annual convention of his African mutual insurance society, "The Children of the King." While there he had met the old woman who had given him a startling piece of information about Cleo which had set his brain in a whirl. He had long been desperately in love with her, but she had treated him with such scorn he had never summoned the courage to declare his affection.

The advent of Helen at first had made no impression on his slowly working mind, but when he returned from Norfolk with the new clew to Cleo's life he watched the girl with increasing suspicion. And when he saw the collapse of Norton over the announcement of her presence he leaped to an important conclusion. No matter whether his guess was correct or not, he knew enough to give him a power over the proud housekeeper he proposed to exercise without a moment's delay.

"We see now whether she turns up her nose at me ergin," he chuckled, as he heard the door open.

He rose with a broad grin as he saw that at last she was alone. He adjusted his suit with a touch of pride and pulled down his vest with a little jerk he had seen his master use in dressing. He had found the heavy, black, double-breasted vest in the cedar box, but thought it rather sombre when contrasted with a red English hunting jacket the major had affected once in a fashionable fox hunt before the war. The rich scarlet took his fancy and he selected that one instead. He carried his ancient silk hat jauntily balanced in one hand, in the other hand a magnolia in full bloom. The petals of the flower were at least a half-foot long and the leaves longer.

He bowed with an attempt at the easy manners of a gentleman in a gallant effort to attract her attention. She was about to pass him on the stairs without noticing his existence when Andy cleared his throat:

"Ahem!"

Cleo paused with a frown:

"What's the matter? Have you caught cold!" Andy generously ignored her tone, bowed and handed her the magnolia:

"Would you embellish yousef wid dis little posie, m'am ?"

The woman turned on him, drew her figure to its full height, her eyes blazing with wrath, snatched the flower from his hand and threw it in his face.

Andy dodged in time to save his nose and his offering went tumbling down the stairs. He shook his head threateningly when he caught his breath:

"Look a here, m'am, is dat de way yer gwine spessify my welcome?"

"Why, no, I was only thanking you for the compliment!" she answered with a sneer. "How dare you insult me?"

"Insult you, is I?" Andy chuckled. "Huh, if dat's de way ye talk I'm gwine ter say sumfin quick——"

"You can't be too quick!"

Andy held her eye a moment and pointed his index finger in her face:

"Yassam! As de ole sayin' is—I'm gwine take my tex' from dat potion er de Scripter whar de 'Postle Paul pint his 'pistle at de Fenians!—I'se er comin' straight ter de pint."

"Well, come to it, you flat-nosed baboon!" she cried in rage. "What makes your nose so flat, anyhow?"

Andy grinned at her tantalizingly, and spoke with a note of deliberate insult:

"I don't know, m'am, but I spec hit wuz made dat way ter keep hit outen odder folks' business!"

"You impudent scoundrel, how dare you speak to me like this?" Cleo hissed.

A triumphant chuckle was his answer. He flicked a piece of imaginary dust from the rim of his hat, his eyes rolled to the ceiling and he slowly said with a smile:

"Well, yer see, m'am, circumstances alters cases an' dat always makes de altercations! I git holt er a little secret o' yourn dat gimme courage——"

"A secret of mine?" Cleo interrupted with the first flash of surprise.

"Yassam!" was the unctuous answer, as Andy looked over his shoulder and bent to survey the hall below for any one who might possibly be passing.

"Yassam," he went on smoothly, "down ter Norfork. las' week, m'am——"

"Wait a minute!" Cleo interrupted. "Some one might be below. Come to my room."

"Yassam, ob course, I wuz gwine ter say dat in de fust place, but ye didn't gimme time"—he bowed—"cose, m'am, de pleasure's all mine, as de sayin' is."

He placed his silk hat jauntily on his head as they reached the door, and gallantly took hold of Cleo's arm to assist her down the steps.

She stopped abruptly:

"Wait here, I'll go ahead and you can come in a few minutes."

"Sholy, sholy, m'am, I understan' dat er lady allus likes ter make er little preparations ter meet er gemman. I understands. I des stroll out on de lawn er minute."

"The backyard's better," she replied, quietly throwing him a look of scorn.

"Yassam, all right. I des take a little cursory view er de chickens."

"As soon as I'm out of sight, you can come right up."

Andy nodded and Cleo quickly crossed the fifty yards that separated the house from the neat square brick building that was still used as the servants' quarters.

In a few minutes, with his silk hat set on the side of his head, Andy tipped up the stairs and knocked on her door.

He entered with a grandiloquent bow and surveyed the place curiously. Her room was a sacred spot he had never been allowed to enter before.

"Have a seat," Cleo said, placing a chair.

Andy bowed, placed his hat pompously on the table, pulled down his red vest with a jerk and seated himself deliberately.

Cleo glanced at him:

"You were about to tell me something that you heard in Norfolk?"

Andy looked at the door as an extra precaution and smiled blandly:

"Yassam, I happen ter hear down dar dat a long time ergo, mo'rn twenty years, afore I cum ter live here—dat is when I wuz er politicioner—dey wuz rumors 'bout you an' de major when you wuz Mister Tom's putty young nurse."

"Well?"

"De major's wife fin' it out an' die. De major wuz heart-broke, drap everything an' go Norf, an' while he wuz up dar, you claims ter be de mudder of a putty little gal. Now min' ye, I ain't nebber seed her, but dat's what I hears you claims——"

Andy paused impressively and Cleo held his eye in a steady, searching stare. She was trying to guess how much he really knew. She began to suspect that his story was more than half a bluff and made up her mind to fight.

"Claim? No, you fool!" she said with indifferent contempt, "I didn't claim it—I proved it. I proved it to his satisfaction. You may worry some one else with your secret. It doesn't interest me. But I'd advise you to have your life insured before you mention it to the major"— she paused, broke into a light laugh and added: "So that's your wonderful discovery?"

Andy looked at her with a puzzled expression and scratched his head:

"Yassam."

"Then I'll excuse you from wasting any more of your valuable time," Cleo said, rising.

Andy rose and smiled:

"Yassam, but dat ain't all, m'am!"

"No?"

"Nobum. I ain't 'sputin dat de little gal wuz born des lak you say, or des lak, mebbe, de major believes ter dis day"—he paused and leaned over until he could whisper in her ear—"but sposen she die?"

The woman never moved a muscle for an instant. She spoke at last in a half-laughing, incredulous way:

"Suppose she died? Why, what do you mean?"

"Now, mind ye," Andy said, lifting his hands in a persuasive gesture, "I ain't sayin' dat she raly did die—I des say—sposen she die——"

Cleo lost her temper and turned on her tormentor in sudden fury:

"But she didn't! Who dares to tell such a lie? She's living to-day a beautiful, accomplished girl."

Andy solemnly raised his hand again:

"Mind ye, I don't say dat she ain't, I des say *sposen—sposen* she die, an' you git a little orphan baby ter put in her place, twenty years ergo, jis' ter keep yer grip on de major——"

Cleo peered steadily into his face:

"Did you guess that lie?"

He cocked his head to one side and grinned:

"I don't say dat I did, an' I don't say dat I didn't. I des say dat I mought, an' den ergin I moughn't!"

"Well, it's a lie!" she cried fiercely—"I tell you it's an infamous lie!"

"Yassam, dat may be so, but hit's a putty dangous lie fer you, m'am, ef——"

He looked around the room in a friendly, cautious way and continued in a whisper:

"Especially ef de major wuz ter ever git pizened wid it!"

Cleo's voice dropped suddenly to pleading tones:

"You're not going to suggest such an idea to him?"

Andy looked away coyly and glanced back at her with a smile:

"Not ef yer ax me——"

"Well, I do ask you," she said in tender tones. "A more infamous lie couldn't be told. But if such a suspicion were once roused it would be hard to protect myself against it."

"Oh, I des wants ter help ye, m'am," Andy protested earnestly.

"Then I'm sure you'll never suggest such a thing to the major?— I'm sorry I've treated you so rudely, and spoke to you as I did just now."

Andy waved the apology aside with a generous gesture and spoke with large good nature:

"Oh, dat's all right, m'am! Dat's all right! I'm gwine ter show you now dat I'se yer best friend——"

"I may need one soon," she answered slowly. "Things can't go on in this house much longer as they are."

"Yassam!" Andy said reassuringly as he laid his hand on Cleo's arm and bent low. "You kin 'pend on me. I'se always called Hones' Andy."

She shuddered unconsciously at his touch, looked suddenly toward the house and said:

"Go—quick! Mr. Tom has come. I don't want him to see us together."

Andy bowed grandly, took up his hat and tipped down the stairs chuckling over his conquest, and Cleo watched him cross the yard to the kitchen.

"I'll manage him!" she murmured with a smile of contempt.

Chapter XIV

THE FOLLY OF PITY

Norton sat in the library for more than an hour trying to nerve himself for the interview while waiting for Helen. He had lighted and smoked two cigars in rapid succession and grown restless at her delay. He rose, strolled through the house and seeing nothing of either Tom or Helen, returned to the library and began pacing the floor with measured tread.

He had made up his mind to do a cruel thing and told himself over and over again that cruel things are often best. The cruelty of surgery is the highest form of pity, pity expressed in terms of the highest intelligence.

He was sure the boy had not made love to the girl. Helen was no doubt equally innocent in her attitude toward him.

It would only be necessary to tell her a part of the bitter truth and her desire to leave would be a resistless one.

And yet, the longer he delayed and the longer he faced such an act, the more pitiless it seemed and the harder its execution became. At heart a deep tenderness was the big trait of his character.

Above all, he dreaded the first interview with Helen. The idea of the responsibility of fatherhood had always been a solemn one. His love for Tom was of the very beat of his heart. The day he first looked into his face was the most wonderful in all the calendar of life.

He had simply refused to let this girl come into his heart. He had closed the door with a firm will. He had only seen her once when a little tot of two and he was laboring under such deep excitement and such abject fear lest a suspicion of the truth, or any part of the truth, reach the sisters to whom he was entrusting the child, that her personality had made no impression on him.

He vaguely hoped that she might not be attractive. The idea of a girl of his own had always appealed to him with peculiar tenderness, and, unlike most fathers, he had desired that his first-born should be a girl. If Helen were commonplace and unattractive his task would be comparatively easy. It was a mental impossibility for him as yet to accept the fact that she was his—he had seen so little of her, her birth was so unwelcome, her coming into his life fraught with such tragic consequences.

The vague hope that she might prove weak and uninteresting had not been strengthened by the momentary sight of her face. The flash of joy that lighted her sensitive features, though it came across the lawn, had reached him with a very distinct impression of charm. He dreaded the effect at close range.

However, there was no other way. He had to see her and he had to make her stay impossible. It would be a staggering blow for a girl to be told in the dawn of young womanhood that her birth was shadowed by disgrace. It would be a doubly cruel one to tell her that her blood was mixed with a race of black slaves.

And yet a life built on a lie was set on shifting sand. It would not endure. It was best to build it squarely on the truth, and the sooner the true foundation was laid the better. There could be no place in our civilization for a woman of culture and refinement with negro blood in her veins. More and more the life of such people must become impossible. That she should remain in the South was unthinkable. That the conditions in the North were at bottom no better he knew from the experience of his stay in New York.

He would tell her the simple, hideous truth, depend on her terror to keep the secret, and send her abroad. It was the only thing to do.

He rose with a start at the sound of Tom's voice calling her from the stairway.

The answer came in low tones so charged with the quality of emotion that belongs to a sincere nature that his heart sank at the thought of his task.

She had only said the most commonplace thing—"All right, I'll be down in a moment." Yet the tones of her voice were so vibrant with feeling that its force reached him instantly, and he knew that his interview was going to be one of the most painful hours of his life.

And still he was not prepared for the shock her appearance in the shadows of the tall doorway gave. He had formed no conception of the gracious and appealing personality. In spite of the anguish her presence had brought, in spite of preconceived ideas of the inheritance of the vicious nature of her mother, in spite of his ingrained repugnance to the negroid type, in spite of his horror of the ghost of his young manhood suddenly risen from the dead to call him to judgment, in spite of his determination to be cruel as the surgeon to the last—in spite of all, his heart suddenly went out to her in a wave of sympathy and tenderness!

She was evidently so pitifully embarrassed and the suffering in her large, expressive eyes so keen and genuine, his first impulse was to rush to her side with words of comfort and assurance.

The simple white dress, with tiny pink ribbons drawn through its edges, which she wore accentuated the impression of timidity and suffering.

He was surprised to find not the slightest trace of negroid blood apparent, though he knew that a mixture of the sixteenth degree often left no trace until its sudden reversion to a black child.

Her hair was the deep brown of his own in young manhood, the eyes large and tender in their rich blue depths—the eyes of innocence, intelligence, sincerity. The lips were full and fluted, and the chin marked with an exquisite dimple that gave a childlike wistfulness to a face that without it might have suggested too much strength.

Her neck was slightly curved and set on full, strong shoulders with an unconscious grace. The bust was slight and girlish, the arms and figure rounded and beautiful in their graceful fullness.

Her walk, when she took the first few steps into the room and paused, he saw was the incarnation of rhythmic strength and perfect health.

But her voice was the climax of her appeal—low, vibrant, quivering with feeling and full of a subtle quality that convinced the hearer from the first moment of the truth and purity of its owner.

She smiled with evident embarrassment at his silence.

He was stunned for the moment and simply couldn't speak.

"So, I see you at last, Major Norton!" she said as the color slowly stole over her face.

He recovered himself, walked quickly to meet her and extended his hand:

"I must apologize for not seeing you earlier this morning," he said gravely. "I was up all night travelling through the country and slept very late."

As her hand rested in his the girl forgot her restraint and wounded pride at the cold and doubtful reception he had given earlier. Her heart suddenly beat with a desire to win this grave, strong man's love and respect.

With a look of girlish tenderness she hastened to say:

"I want to thank you with the deepest gratitude, major, for your kindness in inviting me here this summer——"

"Don't mention it, child," he interrupted frowning.

"Oh, if you only knew," she went on hurriedly, "how I love the South, how my soul glows under its skies, how I love its people, their old-fashioned ways, their kindness, their hospitality, their high ideals——"

He lifted his hand and the gesture stopped her in the midst of a sentence. He was evidently struggling with an embarrassment that was painful and had determined to end it.

"The time has come, Helen,"—he began firmly—"you're of age that I should tell you the important facts about your birth."

"Yes—yes——" the girl answered in an excited whisper as she sank into a chair and gazed at him fascinated with the terror of his possible revelation.

"I wish I could tell you all," he said, pausing painfully.

"You know—all?"

"Yes, I know."

"My father—my mother—they are living?"

In spite of his effort at self-control Norton was pale and his voice strained. His answers to her pointed questions were given with his face turned from her searching gaze.

"Your mother is living," was the slow reply.

"And my father?"

His eyes were set in a fixed stare waiting for this question, as a prisoner in the dock for the sentence of a judge. His lips gave no answer for the moment and the girl went on eagerly:

"Through all the years that I've been alone, the one desperate yearning of my heart has been to know my father"— the lines of the full lips quivered—"I've always felt somehow that a mother who could give up her babe was hardly worth knowing. And so I've brooded over the idea of a father. I've hoped and dreamed and prayed that he might be living—that I might see and know him, win his love, and in its warmth and joy, its shelter and strength—never be lonely or afraid again——"

Her voice sank to a sob, and Norton, struggling to master his feelings, said:

"You have been lonely and afraid?"

"Utterly lonely! When other girls at school shouted for joy at the approach of vacation, the thought of home and loved ones, it brought to me only tears and heartache. Many a night I've laid awake for hours and sobbed because a girl had asked me about my father and mother. Lonely!—oh, dear Lord! And always I've dried my eyes with the thought that some day I might know my father and sob out on his breast all I've felt and suffered"—she paused, and looked at Norton through a mist of tears—"my father is not dead?"

The stillness was painful. The man could hear the tick of the little French clock on the mantel. How tired his soul was of lies! He couldn't lie to her in answer to this question. And so without lifting his head he said very softly:

"He is also alive."

"Thank God!' the girl breathed reverently. "Oh, if I could only touch his hand and look into his face! I don't care who he is, how poor and humble his home, if it's a log cabin on a mountain side, or a poor white man's hovel in town, I'll love him and cling to him and make him love me!"

The man winced. There was one depth her mind had not fathomed!

How could he push this timid, lonely, haunted creature over such a precipice! He glanced at her furtively and saw that she was dreaming as in a trance.

"But suppose," he said quietly, "you should hate this man when you had met?"

"It's unthinkable," was the quick response. "My father is my father. I'd love him if he were a murderer!"

Again her mind had failed to sound the black depths into which he was about to hurl her. She might love a murderer, but there was one thing beyond all question, this beautiful, sensitive, cultured girl could not love the man who had thrust her into the hell of a negroid life in America! She might conceive of the love of a father who could take human life, but her mind could not conceive the possibility of facing the truth with which he must now crush the soul out of her body. Why had he lied and deceived her at all? The instinctive desire to shield his own blood from a life of ignominy—yes. But was it worth the risk? No—he knew it when it was too late. The steel jaws with their cold teeth were tearing the flesh now at every turn and there was no way of escape.

When he failed to respond, she rose, pressed close and pleaded eagerly:

"Tell me his name! Oh, it's wonderful that you have seen him, heard his voice and held his hand! He may not be far away—tell me——"

Norton shook his head:

"The one thing, child, I can never do."

"You are a father—a father who loves his own—I've seen and know that. A nameless waif starving for a word of love begs it—just one word of deep, real love—think of it! My heart has never known it in all the years I've lived!"

Norton lifted his hand brusquely:

"You ask the impossible. The conditions under which I am acting as your guardian seal my lips."

The girl looked at him steadily:

"Then, you *are* my real guardian?"

"Yes."

"And why have you not told me before?"

The question was asked with a firm emphasis that startled him into a sense of renewed danger.

"Why?" she repeated.

"To avoid questions I couldn't answer."

"You will answer them now?"

"With reservations."

The girl drew herself up with a movement of quiet determination and spoke in even tones:

"My parents are Southern?"

"Yes——"

"My father and, mother were—were"—her voice failed, her head dropped and in an effort at self-control she walked to the table, took a book in her hand and tried to turn its leaves. The hideous question over which she had long brooded was too horrible to put into words. The answer he might give was too big with tragic possibilities. She tried to speak again and couldn't. He looked at her with a great pity in his heart and when at last she spoke her voice was scarcely a whisper:

"My father and mother were married?"

He knew it was coming and that he must answer, and yet hesitated. His reply was low, but it rang through her soul like the stroke of a great bell tolling for the dead:

"No!"

The book she held slipped from the trembling fingers and fell to the floor. Norton walked to the window that he might not see the agony in her sensitive face.

She stood very still and the tears began slowly to steal down her cheeks.

"God pity me!" she sobbed, lifting her face and looking pathetically at Norton. "Why did you let them send me to school? Why teach me to think and feel and know this?"

The low, sweet tones of her wonderful voice found the inmost heart of the man. The misery and loneliness of the orphan years of which she had spoken were nothing to the anguish with which her being now shook.

He crossed the room quickly and extended his hand in a movement of instinctive sympathy and tenderness:

"Come, come, child—you're young and life is all before you."

"Yes, a life of shame and humiliation!"

"The world is wide to-day! A hundred careers are open to you. Marriage is impossible—yes——"

"And if I only wish for marriage?" the girl cried with passionate intensity. "If my ideal is simple and old-fashioned—if all I ask of God is the love of one man—a home—a baby——"

A shadow of pain clouded Norton's face and he lifted a hand in tender warning:

"Put marriage out of your mind once and for all time! It can only bring to you and your loved ones hopeless misery."

Helen turned with a start:

"Even if the man I love should know all?"

"Yes," was the firm answer.

She gazed steadily into his eyes and asked with sharp rising emphasis:

"Why?"

The question brought him squarely to the last blow he must give if he accomplish the thing he had begun. He must tell her that her mother is a negress. He looked at the quivering figure, the white, sensitive, young face with the deep, serious eyes, and his lips refused to move. He tried to speak and his throat was dry. It was too cruel. There must be an easier way. He couldn't strike the sweet uplifted head.

He hesitated, stammered and said:

"I—I'm sorry—I can't answer that question fully and frankly. It may be best, but——"

"Yes, yes—it's best!" she urged.

"It may be best," he repeated, "but I simply can't do it"—he paused, turned away and suddenly wheeled confronting her:

"I'll tell you all that you need to know to-day—you were born under the shadow of a hopeless disgrace——"

The girl lifted her hand as if to ward a blow while she slowly repeated:

"A hopeless—disgrace——"

"Beneath a shadow so deep, no lover's vow can ever lift it from your life. I should have told you this before, perhaps—well, somehow I couldn't"—he paused and his voice trembled—"I wanted you to grow in strength and character first——"

The girl clenched her hands and sprang in front of him:

"That my agony might be beyond endurance? Now you *must* tell me the whole truth!"

Again the appealing uplifted face had invited the blow, and again his heart failed. It was impossible to crush her. It was too horrible. He spoke with firm decision:

"Not another word!"

He turned and walked rapidly to the door. The girl clung desperately to his arm:

"I beg of you! I implore you!"

He paused in the doorway, and gently took her bands:

"Forgive me, child, if I seem cruel. In reality I am merciful. I must leave it just there!"

He passed quickly out.

The girl caught the heavy curtains for support, turned with an effort, staggered back into the room, fell prostrate on the lounge with a cry of despair, and burst into uncontrollable sobs.

Chapter XV

A Discovery

Tom had grown restless waiting for Helen to emerge from the interminable interview with his father. A half dozen times he had walked past the library door only to hear the low hum of their voices still talking.

"What on earth is it all about, I wonder?" he muttered. "Must be telling her the story of his whole life!"

He had asked her to meet him in the old rose garden when she came out. For the dozenth time he strolled in and sat down on their favorite rustic. He could neither sit still nor content himself with wandering.

"What the devil's the matter with me anyhow?" he said aloud. "The next thing I'll be thinking I'm in love—good joke—bah!"

Helen was not the ideal he had dreamed. She had simply brought a sweet companionship into his life—that was all. She was a good fellow. She could walk, ride, run and hold her own at any game he liked to play. He had walked with her over miles of hills and valleys stretching in every direction about town. He had never grown tired of these walks. He didn't have to entertain her. They were silent often for a long time. They sat down beside the roadway, laughed and talked like chums with never a thought of entertaining each other.

In the long rides they had taken in the afternoons and sometimes late in the starlight or moonlight, she had never grown silly, sentimental or tiresome. A restful and homelike feeling always filled him when she was by his side. He hadn't thought her very beautiful at first, but the longer he knew her the more charming and irresistible her companionship became.

"Her figure's a little too full for the finest type of beauty!" he was saying to himself now. "Her arms are splendid, but the least bit too big, and her face sometimes looks too strong for a girl's! It's a pity. Still, by geeminy, when she smiles she *is* beautiful! Her face seems to fairly blossom with funny little dimples—and that one on the chin is awfully pretty! She just misses by a hair being a stunningly beautiful girl!"

He flicked a fly from his boot with a switch he was carrying and glanced anxiously toward the house. "And I must say," he acknowledged judicially, "that she has a bright mind, her tastes are fine, her ideals high. She isn't all the time worrying over balls and dresses and beaux like a lot of silly girls I know. She's got too much sense for that. The fact is, she has a brilliant mind."

Now that he came to think of it, she had a mind of rare brilliance. Everything she said seemed to sparkle. He didn't stop to ask the reason why, he simply knew that it was so. If she spoke about the weather, her words never seemed trivial.

He rose scowling and walked back to the house.

"What on earth can they be talking about all this time?" he cried angrily. Just then his father's tall figure stepped out on the porch, walked its length and entered the sitting-room by one of the French windows.

He sprang up the steps, thrust his head into the hall, and softly whistled. He waited a moment, there was no response, and he repeated the call. Still receiving no answer, he entered cautiously:

"Miss Helen!"

He tipped to the library door and called again:

"Miss Helen!"

Surprised that she could have gone so quickly he rushed into the room, glanced hastily around, crossed to the window, looked out on the porch, heard the rustle of a skirt and turned in time to see her flying to escape.

With a quick dash he headed her off.

Hiding her face she turned and ran the other way for the door through which he had entered.

With a laugh and a swift leap Tom caught her arms.

"Lord, you're a sprinter!" he cried breathlessly. "But I've got you now!" he laughed, holding her pinioned arms tightly.

Helen lifted her tear-stained face:

"Please——"

Tom drew her gently around and looked into her eyes:

"Why—what on earth—you're crying!"

She tried to draw away but he held her hand firmly:

"What is it? What's happened? What's the matter?"

His questions were fired at her with lightning rapidity.

The girl dropped forlornly on the lounge and turned her face away:

"Please go!"

"I won't go—I won't!" he answered firmly as he bent closer.

"Please—please!"

"Tell me what it is?"

Helen held her face resolutely from him.

"Tell me," he urged tenderly.

"I can't!"

She threw herself prostrate and broke into sobs.

The boy wrung his hands helplessly, started to put his arm around her, caught himself in time and drew back with a start. At last he burst out passionately:

"Don't—don't! For heaven's sake don't! It hurts me more than it does you—I don't know what it is but it hurts—it hurts inside and it hurts deep—please!"

Without lifting her head Helen cried:

"I don't want to live any more."

"Oh, is that all?" Tom laughed. "I see, you've stubbed your toe and don't want to live any more!"

"I mean it!' she broke in desperately.

"Good joke!" he cried again, laughing. "You don't want to live any more! Twenty years old and every line of your graceful, young form quivering with the joy of life—you—you don't want to live! That's great!"

The girl lifted her dimmed eyes, looked at him a moment, and spoke the thought that had poisoned her soul—spoke it in hard, bitter accents with a touch of self-loathing:

"I've just learned that my birth is shadowed by disgrace!"

"Well, what have you to do with that?" he asked quickly. "Your whole being shines with truth and purity. What's an accident of birth? You couldn't choose your parents, could you? You're a nameless orphan and my father is the attorney of an old fool guardian who lives somewhere in Europe. All right! The worst thing your worst enemy could say is that you're a child of love—a great love that leaped all bounds and defied the law—a love that was madness and staked all life on the issue! That means you're a child of the gods. Some of the greatest men and women of the world were born like that. Your own eyes are clear. There's no cloud on your beautiful soul——"

Tom paused and Helen lifted her face in rapt attention. The boy suddenly leaped to his feet, turned away and spoke in ecstatic whispers:

"Good Lord—listen at me—why—I'm making love—great Scott—I'm in love! The big thing has happened—to me—to me! I feel the thrill of it—the thing that transforms the world—why—it's like getting religion!"

He strode back and forth in a frenzy of absurd happiness.

Helen, smiling through her tears, asked:

"What are you saying? What are you talking about?"

With a cry of joy he was at her side, her hand tight gripped in his:

"Why, that I'm in love, my own—that I love you, my glorious little girl! I didn't realize it until I saw just now the tears in your eyes and felt the pain of it. Every day these past weeks you've been stealing into my heart until now you're my very life! What hurts you hurts me—your joys are mine—your sorrows are mine!"

Laughing in spite of herself, Helen cried:

"You—don't realize what you're saying!"

"No—but I'm beginning to!" he answered with a boyish smile. "And it goes to my head like wine—I'm mad with its joy! I tell you I love you—I love you! and you love me—you do love me?"

The girl struggled, set her lips grimly and said fiercely:

"No—and I never shall!"

"You don't mean it?"

"I do!"

"You—you—don't love another?"

"No—no!"

"Then you do love me!" he cried triumphantly. "You've just *got* to love me! I won't take any other answer! Look into my eyes!"

She turned resolutely away and he took both hands drawing her back until their eyes met.

"Your lips say no," he went on, "but your tears, your voice, the tremor of your hand and the tenderness of your eyes say yes!"

Helen shook her head:

"No—no—no!"

But the last "no" grew feebler than the first and he pressed her hand with cruel pleading:

"Yes—yes—yes—say it, dear—please—just once." Helen looked at him and then with a cry of joy that was resistless said:

"God forgive me! I can't help it—yes, yes, yes, I love you—I love you!"

Tom snatched her to his heart and held her in perfect surrender. She suddenly drew her arms from his neck, crying in dismay:

"No—no—I don't love you!"

The boy looked at her with a start and she went on quickly:

"I didn't mean to say it—I meant to say—I hate you!"

With a cry of pain she threw herself into his arms, clasping his neck and held him close.

His hand gently stroked the brown hair while he laughed:

"Well, if that's the way you hate—keep it up!"

With an effort she drew back:

"But I mustn't——"

"There!" he said, tenderly drawing her close again. "It's all right. It's no use to struggle. You're mine—mine, I tell you!"

With a determined effort she freed herself:

"It's no use, dear, our love is impossible."

"Nonsense!"

"But you don't realize that my birth is shadowed by disgrace!"

"I don't believe it—I wouldn't believe it if an angel said it. Who dares to say such a thing?"

"Your father!"

"My father?" he repeated in a whisper.

"He has always known the truth and now that I am of age he has told me——"

"Told you what?"

"Just what I said, and warned me that marriage could only bring pain and sorrow to those I love."

"He gave you no facts—only these vague warnings?"

"Yes, more—he told me——"

She paused and moved behind the table:

"That my father and mother were never married."

"Nothing more?" the boy asked eagerly.

"That's enough."

"Not for me!"

"Suppose my father were a criminal?"

"No matter—your soul's as white as snow!"

"Suppose my mother——"

"I don't care who she was—you're an angel!"

Helen faced him with strained eagerness:

"You swear that no stain on my father or mother can ever make the least difference between us?"

"I swear it!" he cried grasping her hand. "Come, you're mine!"

Helen drew back:

"Oh, if I could only believe it——"

"You do believe it—come!"

He opened his arms and she smiled:

"What shall I do!"

"Come!"

Slowly at first, and then with quick, passionate tenderness she threw herself into his arms:

"I can't help it, dearest. It's too sweet and wonderful—God help me if I'm doing wrong!"

"Wrong!" he exclaimed indignantly. "How can it be wrong, this solemn pledge of life and love, of body and soul?"

She lifted her face to his in wonder:

"And you will dare to tell your father?"

"In good time, yes. But it's our secret now. Keep it until I say the time has come for him to know. I'll manage him—promise!"

"Yes! How sweet it is to hear you tell me what to do! I shall never be lonely or afraid again."

The father's footstep on the porch warned of his approach.

"Go quickly!" the boy whispered. "I don't want him to see us together yet—it means too much now—it means life itself!"

Helen moved toward the door, looked back, laughed, flew again into his arms and quickly ran into the hall as Norton entered from the porch.

The boy caught the look of surprise on his father's face, realized that he must have heard the rustle of Helen's dress, and decided instantly to accept the fact.

He boldly walked to the door and gazed after her retreating figure, his back squarely on his father.

Norton paused and looked sharply at Tom:

"Was—that—Helen?"

The boy turned, smiling, and nodded with slight embarrassment in spite of his determined effort at self-control:

"Yes."

The father's keen eyes pierced the boy's:

"Why should she run?"

Tom's face sobered:

"I don't think she wished to see you just now, sir."

"Evidently!"

"She had been crying."

"And told you why?"

"Yes."

The father frowned:

"She has been in the habit of making you her confidant?"

"No. But I found her in tears and asked her the reason for them."

Norton was watching closely:

"She told you what I had just said to her?"

"Vaguely," Tom answered, and turning squarely on his father asked: "Would you mind telling me the whole truth about it?"

"Why do you ask?"

The question came from the father's lips with a sudden snap, so suddenly, so sharply the boy lost his composure, hung his head, and stammered with an attempt at a smile:

"Oh—naturally curious—I suppose it's a secret?"

"Yes—I wish I could tell you, but I can't"—he paused and spoke with sudden decision:

"Ask Cleo to come here."

Chapter XVI

The Challenge

Norton was morally certain now that the boy was interested in Helen. How far this interest had gone he could only guess.

What stunned him was that Tom had already taken sides with the girl. He had not said so in words. But his embarrassment and uneasiness could mean but one thing. He must move with caution, yet he must act at once and end the dangerous situation. A clandestine love affair was a hideous possibility. Up to a moment ago he had held such a thing out of the question with the boy's high-strung sense of honor and his lack of experience with girls.

He was afraid now of both the boy and girl. She had convinced him of her purity when the first words had fallen from her lips. Yet wiser men had been deceived before. The thought of her sleek, tawny mother came with a shudder. No daughter could escape such an inheritance.

There was but one thing to do and it must be done quickly. He would send Helen abroad and if necessary tell her the whole hideous truth.

He lifted his head at the sound of Cleo's footsteps, rose and confronted her. As his deep-set eyes surveyed her he realized that the hour had come for a fight to the finish.

She gazed at him steadily with a look of undisguised hate:

"What is it?"

He took a step closer, planted his long legs apart and met her greenish eyes with an answering flash of rage:

"When I think of your damned impudence, using my typewriter and letterheads to send an invitation to that girl to spend the summer here with Tom at home, and signing my name——"

"I have the right to use your name with her," she broke in with a sneer.

"It will be the last time I'll give you the chance."

"We'll see," was the cool reply.

Norton slowly drew a chair to the table, seated himself and said:

"I want the truth from you now."

"You'll get it. I've never had to lie to you, at least——"

"I've no time to bandy words—will you tell me exactly what's been going on between Tom and Helen during my absence in this campaign?"

"I haven't seen anything!" was the light answer.

His lips moved to say that she lied, but he smiled instead. What was the use? He dropped his voice to a careless, friendly tone:

"They have seen each other every day?"

"Certainly."

"How many hours have they usually spent together?"

"I didn't count them."

Norton bit his lips to keep back an oath:

"How often have they been riding?"

"Perhaps a dozen times."

"They returned late occasionally?"

"Twice."

"How late?"

"It was quite dark——"

"What time?—eight, nine, ten or eleven o'clock?"

"As late as nine one night, half-past nine another—the moon was shining." She said it with a taunting smile.

"Were they alone?"

"Yes."

"You took pains to leave them alone, I suppose?"

"Sometimes"—she paused and looked at him with a smile that was a sneer. "What are you afraid of?"

He returned her gaze steadily:

"Anything is possible of your daughter—the thought of it strangles me!"

Cleo laughed lightly:

"Then all you've got to do is to speak—tell Tom the truth."

"I'll die first!" he fiercely replied. "At least I've taught him racial purity. I've been true to my promise to the dead in this. He shall never know the depths to which I once fell! You have robbed me of everything else in life, this boy's love and respect is all that you've left me"— he stopped, his breast heaving with suppressed passion. "Why—why did you bring that girl into this house?"

"I wished to see her—that's enough. For twenty years, I've lived here as a slave, always waiting and hoping for a sign from you that you were human——"

"For a sign that I'd sink again to your level! Well, I found out twenty years ago that beneath the skin of every man sleeps an ape and a tiger—I fought that battle and won——"

"And I have lost?"

"Yes."

"Perhaps I haven't begun to fight yet."

"I shouldn't advise you to try it. I know now that I made a tragic blunder when I brought you back into this house. I've cursed myself a thousand times that I didn't put the ocean between us. If my boy hadn't loved you, if he hadn't slipped his little arms around your neck and clung to you sobbing out the loneliness of his hungry heart—if I hadn't seen the tears in your own eyes and known that you had saved his life once—I wouldn't have made the mistake that I did. But I gave you my word, and I've lived up to it. I've reared and educated your child and given you the protection of my home——"

"Yes," she broke in, "that you might watch and guard me and know that your secret was safely kept while you've grown to hate me each day with deeper and fiercer hatred—God!—I've wondered sometimes that you haven't killed me!"

Norton's voice sank to a whisper:

"I've wondered sometimes, too"—a look of anguish swept his face—"but I gave you my word, and I've kept it."

"Because you had to keep it!"

He sprang to his feet:

"Had to keep it—you say that to me?"

"I do."

"This house is still mine——"

"But your past is mine!" she cried with a look of triumph.

"Indeed! We'll see. Helen leaves this house immediately."

"She shall not!"

"You refuse to obey my orders?"

"And what's more," she cried with angry menace, "I refuse to allow you to put her out!"

"To *allow*?"

"I said it!"

"So I am your servant? I must ask your permission?—God!——" he sprang angrily toward the bell and Cleo stepped defiantly before him:

"Don't you touch that bell——"

Norton thrust her aside:

"Get out of my way!"

"Ring that bell if you dare!" she hissed.

"Dare?"

The woman drew her form erect:

"If you dare! And in five minutes I'll be in that newspaper office across the way from yours! The editor doesn't love you. To-morrow morning the story of your life and mine will blaze on that first page!"

Norton caught a chair for support, his face paled and he sank slowly to a seat.

Cleo leaned toward him, trembling with passion:

"I'll give you fair warning. There are plenty of negroes to-day your equal in wealth and culture. Do you think they have been listening to their great leader's call to battle for nothing—building fine houses, buying land, piling up money, sending their sons and daughters to college, to come at your beck and call? You're a fool if you do. They are only waiting their chance to demand social equality and get it. Wealth and culture will give it in the end, ballot or no ballot. Once rich, white men and women will come at their command. I've got my chance now to demand my rights of you and do a turn for the negro race. You've got to recognize Helen before your son. I've brought her here for that purpose. With her by my side, I'll be the mistress of this house. Now resign your leadership and get out of this campaign!"

With a stamp of her foot she ended her mad speech in sharp, high tones, turned quickly and started to the door.

Between set teeth Norton growled:

"And you think that I'll submit?"

The woman wheeled suddenly and rushed back to his side, her eyes flaming:

"You've got to submit—you've got to submit—or begin with me a fight that can only end in your ruin! I've nothing to lose, and I tell you now that I'll fight to win, I'll fight to kill! I'll ask no quarter of you and I'll give none. I'll fight with every ounce of strength I've got—body and soul—and if I lose I'll still have strength enough left to pull you into hell with me!"

Her voice broke in a sob, she pulled herself together, straightened her figure and cried:

"Now what are you going to do? What are you going to do? Accept my terms or fight?"

Norton's face was livid, his whole being convulsed as he leaped to his feet and confronted her:

"I'll fight!"

"All right! All right!" she said with hysterical passion, backing toward the door. "I've warned you now—I didn't want to fight—but I'll show you—I'll show you!"

Chapter XVII

A Skirmish

Norton's fighting blood was up, but he was too good a soldier and too good a commander to rush into battle without preparation. Cleo's mask was off at last, and he knew her too well to doubt that she would try to make good her threat. The fire of hate that had flamed in her greenish eyes was not a sudden burst of anger, it had been smoldering there for years, eating its way into the fiber of her being.

There were three courses open.

He could accept her demand, acknowledge Helen to his son, establish her in his home, throw his self-respect to the winds and sink to the woman's level. It was unthinkable! Besides, the girl would never recover from the shock. She would disappear or take her own life. He felt it with instinctive certainty. But the thing which made such a course impossible was the fact that it meant his daily degradation before the boy. He would face death without a tremor sooner than this.

He could defy Cleo and pack Helen off to Europe on the next steamer, and risk a scandal that would shake the state, overwhelm the party he was leading, disgrace him not only before his son but before the world, and set back the cause he had at heart for a generation.

It was true she might weaken when confronted with the crisis that would mean the death of her own hopes. Yet the risk was too great to act on such a possibility. Her defiance had in it all the elements of finality, and he had accepted it as final.

The simpler alternative was a temporary solution which would give him time to think and get his bearings. He could return to the campaign immediately, take Tom with him, keep him in the field every day until the election, ask Helen to stay until his return, and after his victory had been achieved settle with the woman.

It was the wisest course for many reasons, and among them not the least that it would completely puzzle Cleo as to his ultimate decision.

He rang for Andy:

"Ask Mr. Tom to come here."

Andy bowed and Norton resumed his seat.

When Tom entered, the father spoke with quick decision:

"The situation in this campaign, my boy, is tense and dangerous. I want you to go with me to-morrow and stay to the finish."

Tom flushed and there was a moment's pause:

"Certainly, Dad, if you wish it."

"We'll start at eight o'clock in the morning and drive through the country to the next appointment. Fix your business at the office this afternoon, place your men in charge and be ready to leave promptly at eight. I've some important writing to do. I'm going to lock myself in my room until it's done. See that I'm not disturbed except to send Andy up with my supper. I'll not finish before midnight."

"I'll see to it, sir," Tom replied, turned and was gone.

The father had watched the boy with keen scrutiny every moment and failed to catch the slightest trace of resentment or of hesitation. The pause he had made on receiving the request was only an instant of natural surprise.

Before leaving next morning he sent for Helen who had not appeared at breakfast.

She hastened to answer his summons and he found no trace of anger, resentment or rebellion in her gentle face. Every vestige of the shadow he had thrown over her life seem to have lifted. A tender smile played about her lips as she entered the room.

"You sent for me, major?" she asked with the slightest tremor of timidity in her voice.

"Yes," he answered gravely. "I wish you to remain here until Tom and I return. We'll have a conference then about your future."

"Thank you," she responded simply.

"I trust you will not find yourself unhappy or embarrassed in remaining here alone until we return?"

"Certainly not, major, if it is your wish," was the prompt response.

He bowed and murmured:

"I'll see you soon."

Tom waved his hand from the buggy when his father's back was turned and threw her an audacious kiss over his head as the tall figure bent to climb into the seat. The girl answered with another from her finger tips which he caught with a smile.

Norton's fears of Tom were soon at rest at the sight of his overflowing boyish spirits. He had entered into the adventure of the campaign from the moment he found himself alone with his father, and apparently without reservation.

Through every one of his exciting speeches, when surrounded by hostile crowds, the father had watched Tom's face with a subconscious smile. At the slightest noise, the shuffle of a foot, the mutter of a drunken word, or the movement of a careless listener, the keen eyes of the boy had flashed and his right arm instinctively moved toward his hip pocket.

When the bitter struggle had ended, father and son had drawn closer than ever before in life. They had become chums and comrades.

Norton had planned his tour to keep him out of town until after the polls closed on the day of election. They had spent several nights within fifteen or twenty miles of the Capital, but had avoided home.

He had planned to arrive at the speaker's stand in the Capitol Square in time to get the first returns of the election.

Five thousand people were packed around the bulletin board when they arrived on a delayed train.

The first returns indicated that the leader's daring platform had swept the state by a large majority. The negro race had been disfranchised and the ballot restored to its original dignity. And much more had been done. The act was purely political, but its effects on the relations, mental and moral and physical, of the two races, so evenly divided in the South, would be tremendous.

The crowds of cheering men and women felt this instinctively, though it had not as yet found expression in words.

A half-dozen stalwart men with a rush and a shout seized Norton and lifted him, blushing and protesting, carried him on their shoulders through the yelling crowd and placed him on the platform.

He had scarcely begun his speech when Tom, watching his chance, slipped hurriedly through the throng and flew to the girl who was waiting with beating heart for the sound of his footstep.

Chapter XVIII

Love Laughs

When Helen had received a brief note from Tom the night before the election that he would surely reach home the next day, she snatched his picture from the library table with a cry of joy and rushed to her room.

She placed the little gold frame on her bureau, sat down before it and poured out her heart in silly speeches of love, pausing to laugh and kiss the glass that saved the miniature from ruin. The portrait was an exquisite work of art on ivory which the father had commisioned a painter in New York to do in celebration of Tom's coming of age. The artist had caught the boy's spirit in the tender smile that played about his lips and lingered in the corners of his blue eyes, the same eyes and lips in line and color in the dainty little mother's portrait over the mantel.

"Oh, you big, handsome, brave, glorious boy!" she cried in ecstasy. "My sweetheart—so generous, so clean, so strong, so free in soul! I love you—I love you—I love you!"

She fell asleep at last with the oval frame clasped tight in one hand thrust under her pillow. A sound sleep was impossible, the busy brain was too active. Again and again she waked with a start, thinking she had heard his swift footfall on the stoop.

At daybreak she leaped to her feet and found herself in the middle of the room laughing when she came to herself, the precious picture still clasped in her hand.

"Oh, foolish heart, wake up!" she cried with another laugh. "It's dawn, and my lover is coming! It's his day! No more sleep—it's too wonderful! I'm going to count every hour until I hear his step—every minute of every hour, foolish heart!"

She looked out the window and it was raining. The overhanging boughs of the oaks were dripping on the tin roof of the bay window in which she was standing. She had dreamed of a wonderful sunrise this morning. But it didn't matter—the rain didn't matter. The slow, familiar dropping on the roof suggested the nearness of her lover. They would sit in some shadowy corner hand in hand and love all the more tenderly. The raindrops were the drum beat of a band playing the march that was bringing him nearer with each throb. The mocking-bird that had often waked her with his song was silent, hovering somewhere in a tree beneath the thick leaves. She had expected him to call her to-day with the sweetest lyric he had ever sung. Somehow it didn't matter. Her soul was singing the song that makes all other music dumb.

"My love is coming!" she murmured joyfully. "My love is coming!"

And then she stood for an hour in brooding, happy silence and watched the ghostlike trees come slowly out of the mists. To her shining eyes there were no mists. The gray film that hung over the waking world was a bridal veil hiding the blushing face of the earth from the sun-god lover who was on his way over the hills to clasp her in his burning arms!

For the first time in her memory she was supremely happy.

Every throb of pain that belonged to the past was lost in the sea of joy on which her soul had set sail. In the glory of his love pain was only another name for joy. All she had suffered was but the preparation for this supreme good. It was all the more wonderful, this fairy world into which she had entered, because the shadows had been so deep in her lonely childhood.

There really hadn't been any past! She couldn't remember the time she had not known and loved Tom. Love filled the universe, past, present and future. There was no task too hard for her hands, no danger she was not ready to meet. The hungry heart had found its own.

Through the long hours of the day she waited without impatience. Each tick of the tiny clock on the mantel brought him nearer. The hands couldn't turn back! She watched them with a smile as she sat in the gathering twilight.

She had placed the miniature back in its place and sat where her eye caught the smile from his lips when she lifted her head from the embroidery on her lap.

The band was playing a stirring strain in the Square. She could hear the tumult and the shouts of the crowds about the speaker's stand as they read the bulletins of the election. The darkness couldn't hold him many more minutes.

She rose with a soft laugh and turned on the lights, walked to the window, looked out and listened to the roar of the cheering when Norton made his appearance. The band struck up another stirring piece. Yes, it was "Hail to the Chief!" He had come.

She counted the minutes it would take for him to elude his father and reach the house. She pictured the smile on his face as he threaded his way through the throng and started to her on swift feet. She could see him coming with the long, quick stride he had inherited from his father.

She turned back into the room exclaiming:

"Oh, foolish heart, be still!"

She seated herself again and waited patiently, a smile about the corners of her lips and another playing hide and seek in the depths of her expressive eyes.

Tom had entered the house unobserved by any one and softly tipped into the library from the door directly behind her. He paused, removed his hat, dropped it silently into a chair and stood looking at the graceful, beautiful form bending over her work. The picture of this waiting figure he had seen in his day-dreams a thousand times and yet it was so sweet and wonderful he had to stop and drink in the glory of it for a moment.

A joyous laugh was bubbling in his heart as he tipped softly over the thick yielding rug and slipped his hands over her eyes. His voice was the gentlest whisper:

"Guess?"

The white figure slowly rose and her words came in little ripples of gasping laughter as she turned and lifted her arms:

"It's—it's—Tom!"

With a smothered cry she was on his breast. He held her long and close without a word. His voice had a queer hitch in it as he murmured:

"Helen—my darling!"

"Oh, I thought you'd never come!" she sighed, looking up through her tears.

Tom held her off and gazed into her eyes:

"It's been a century since I've seen you! I did my level best when we got into these nearby counties again, but I couldn't shake Dad once this week. He watched me like a hawk and insisted on staying out of town till the very last hour of the election to-day. Did old Andy find out I slipped in last week?"

"No!" she laughed.

"Did Cleo find it out?"

"No."

"You're sure Cleo didn't find out?"

"Sure—but Aunt Minerva did."

"Oh, I'm not afraid of her—kiss me!"

With a glad cry their lips met.

He held her off.

"I'm not afraid of anything!"

With an answering laugh, she kissed him again.

"I'm not afraid of Dad!" he said in tones of mock tragedy. "Once more!"

She gently disengaged herself, asking:

"How did you get away from him so quickly?"

"Oh, he's making a speech to the crowd in the Square proclaiming victory and so"—his voice fell to a whisper—"I flew to celebrate mine!"

"Won't he miss you?"

"Not while he's talking. Dad enjoys an eloquent speech—especially one of his *own*——"

He stopped abruptly, took a step toward her and cried:

"Say! Do you know what the Governor of North Carolina said once upon a time to the Governor of South Carolina?"

Helen laughed:

"What?"

He opened his arms:

"'It strikes me,' said he, 'that it's a long time between drinks!'"

Again her arms flashed around his neck.

"Did you miss me?"

"Dreadfully!" she sighed. "But I've been happy—happy in your love—oh, so happy, dearest!"

"Well, if Dad wins this election to-night," he said, with a boyish smile, "I'm going to tell him. Now's the time—no more slipping and sliding!"—he paused, rushed to the window and looked out—"come, the clouds have lifted and the moon is rising. Our old seat among the roses is waiting."

With a look of utter happiness she slipped her arm in his and they strolled across the lawn.

Chapter XIX

"Fight it Out!"

Cleo had heard the shouts in the square with increasing dread. The hour was rapidly approaching when she must face Norton.

She had deeply regretted the last scene with him when she had completely lost her head. For the first time in her life she had dared to say things that could not be forgiven. They had lived an armed truce for twenty years. She had endured it in the hope of a change in his attitude, but she had driven him to uncontrollable fury now by her angry outburst and spoken words that could not be unsaid.

She realized when too late that he would never forgive these insults. And she began to wonder nervously what form his revenge would take. That he had matured a definite plan of hostile action which he would put into force on his arrival, she did not doubt.

Why had she been so foolish? She asked herself the question a hundred times. And yet the clash was inevitable. She could not see Helen packed off to Europe and her hopes destroyed at a blow. She might have stopped him with something milder than a threat of exposure in his rival's paper. That was the mad thing she had done.

What effect this threat had produced on his mind she could only guess. But she constantly came back to it with increasing fear. If he should accept her challenge, dare her to speak, and, weary of the constant strain of her presence in his house, put her out, it meant the end of the world. She had lived so long in dependence on his will, the thought of beginning life again under new conditions of humiliating service was unthinkable.

She could only wait now until the blow fell, and adjust herself to the situation as best she could. That she had the power to lay his life in ruins and break Tom's heart she had never doubted. Yet this was the one thing she did not wish to do. It meant too much to her.

She walked on the porch and listened again to the tumult in the Square. She had seen Tom enter the house on tip-toe and knew that the lovers were together and smiled in grim triumph. That much of her scheme had not failed! It only remained to be seen whether, with their love an accomplished fact, she could wring from Norton's lips the confession she had demanded and save her own skin in the crash.

Andy had entered the gate and she heard him bustling in the pantry as Tom and Helen strolled on the lawn. The band in the Square was playing their star piece of rag-time music, "A Georgia Campmeeting."

The stirring refrain echoed over the sleepy old town with a weird appeal to-night. It had the ring of martial music—of hosts shouting their victory as they marched. They were playing it with unusual swinging power.

She turned with a gesture of impatience into the house to find Andy. He was carrying a tray of mint juleps into the library.

Cleo looked at him in amazement, suppressed an angry exclamation and asked:

"What's that band playing for?"

"White folks celebratin' de victory!" he replied enenthusiastically, placing the tray on the table.

"It's only seven o'clock. The election returns can't be in yet?"

"Yassam! Hit's all over but de shoutin'!"

Cleo moved a step closer:

"The major has won?"

"Yassam! Yassam!" Andy answered with loud good humor, as he began to polish a glass with a napkin. "Yassam, I des come frum dar. De news done come in. Dey hain't gwine ter 'low de niggers ter vote no mo', 'ceptin they kin read an' write—an' *den* dey won't let 'em!"

He held one of the shining glasses up to the light, examined it with judicial care and continued in tones of resignation:

"Don't make no diffrunce ter me, dough!—I hain't nebber got nuttin' fer my vote nohow, 'ceptin' once when er politicioner shoved er box er cigars at me"—he chuckled—"an' den, by golly, I had ter be a gemman, I couldn't grab er whole handful—I des tuck four!"

Cleo moved impatiently and glared at the tray:

"What on earth did you bring all that stuff for? The whole mob are not coming here, are they?"

"Nobum—nobum! Nobody but de major, but I 'low dat he gwine ter consume some! He's on er high hoss. Dey's 'bout ten thousand folks up dar in de Square. De boys carry de major on dere back to de flatform an' he make 'em a big speech. Dey sho is er-raisin' er mighty humbug. Dey gwine ter celebrate all night out dar, an' gwine ter serenade everybody in town. But de major comin' right home. Dey try ter git him ter stay wid 'em, but he 'low dat he got some 'portant business here at de house."

"Important business here?" she asked anxiously.

"Yassam, I spec him any minute."

Cleo turned quickly toward the door and Andy called:

"Miss Cleo!"

She continued to go without paying any attention and he repeated his call:

"Miss Cleo!"

She paused indifferently, while Andy touched his lips smiling:

"I got my mouf shet!"

"Does it pain you?"

"Nobum!" he laughed.

"Keep it shut!" she replied contemptuously as she again moved toward the door.

"Yassam—yassam—but ain't yer got nuttin' mo' dan dat ter say ter me?"

He asked this question with a rising inflection that might mean a threat.

The woman walked back to him:

"Prove your love by a year's silence——"

"De Lawd er mussy!" Andy gasped. "A whole year?"

"Am I not worth waiting for?" she asked with a smile.

"Yassam—yassam," he replied slowly, "Jacob he wait seben years an' den, by golly, de ole man cheat him outen his gal! But ef yer say so, I'se er waitin', honey——"

Andy placated, her mind returned in a flash to the fear that haunted her:

"He said important business here at once?"

The gate closed with a vigorous slam and the echo of Norton's step was heard on the gravel walk.

"Yassam, dar he is now."

Cleo trembled and hurried to the opposite door:

"If the major asks for me, tell him I've gone to the meeting in the Square."

She passed quickly from the room in a panic of fear. She couldn't meet him in this condition. She must wait a better moment.

Andy, arranging his tray, began to mix three mint juleps, humming a favorite song:

"Dis time er-nudder year,
Oh, Lawd, how long!
In some lonesome graveyard
Woh, Lawd, how long!"

Norton paused on the threshold with a smile and listened to the foolish melody. His whole being was quivering with the power that thrilled from a great act of will. He had just made a momentous decision. His work in hand was done. He had lived for years in an atmosphere poisoned by a yellow venomous presence. He had resolved to be free!—no matter what the cost.

His mind flew to the boy he had grown to love with deeper tenderness the past weeks. The only thing he really dreaded was his humiliation before those blue eyes. But, if the worst came to worst, he must speak. There were things darker than death—the consciousness to a proud and sensitive man that he was the slave to an inferior was one of them. He had to be free—free at any cost. The thought was an inspiration.

With brisk step he entered the library and glanced with surprise at the empty room.

"Tom not come?" he asked briskly.

"Nasah, I ain't seed 'im," Andy replied.

Norton threw his linen coat on a chair, and a dreamy look came into his deep-set eyes:

"Well, Andy, we've made a clean sweep to-day—the old state's white again!"

The negro, bustling over his tray, replied with unction:

"Yassah, dat's what I done tole 'em, sah!"

"All government rests on force, Andy! The ballot is force—physical force. Back of every ballot is a gun——"

He paused, drew the revolver slowly from his pocket and held it in his hand.

Andy glanced up from his tray and jumped in alarm:

"Yassah, dat's so, sah—in dese parts sho, sah!" he ended his speech by a good-natured laugh at the expense of the country that allowed itself to be thus intimidated.

Norton lifted the gleaming piece of steel and looked at it thoughtfully:

"Back of every ballot a gun and the red blood of the man who holds it! No freeman ever yet voted away his right to a revolution——"

"Yassah—dat's what I tells dem niggers—you gwine ter giv 'em er dose er de revolution——"

"Well, it's done now and I've no more use for this thing—thank God!"

He crossed to the writing desk, laid the revolver on its top and walked to the lounge his face set with a look of brooding intensity:

"Bah! The big battles are all fought inside, Andy! There's where the brave die and cowards run—inside——"

"Yassah!—I got de stuff right here fer de *inside*, sah!" he held up the decanter with a grin.

"From to-night my work outside is done," Norton went on moodily. "And I'm going to be free—free! I'm no longer afraid of one of my servants——"

He dropped into a seat and closed his fists with a gesture of intense emotion.

Andy looked at him in astonishment and asked incredulously:

"Who de debbil say you'se er scared of any nigger? Show dat man ter me—who say dat?"

"I say it!" was the bitter answer. He had been thinking aloud, but now that the negro had heard he didn't care. His soul was sick of subterfuge and lies.

Andy laughed apologetically:

"Yassah! Cose, sah, ef you say dat hit's so, why I say hit's so—but all de same, 'twixt you an' me, I knows tain't so!"

"But from to-night!" Norton cried, ignoring Andy as he sprang to his feet and looked sharply about the room:

"Tell Cleo I wish to see her at once!"

"She gone out in de Squar ter hear de news, sah."

"The moment she comes let me know!" he said with sharp emphasis and turned quickly to the door.

"Yassah," Andy answered watching him go with amazement. "De Lawdy, major, you ain't gwine off an' leave dese mint juleps lak dat, is ye?"

Norton retraced a step:

"Yes, from to-night I'm the master of my house and myself!"

Andy looked at the tray and then at Norton:

"Well, sah, yer ain't got no objections to me pizinin' mysef, is ye?"

The master surveyed the grinning servant, glanced at the tray, smiled and said:

"No—you'll do it anyhow, so go as far as you like!"

"Yassah!" the negro laughed as Norton turned again. "An' please, sah, won't yer gimme jes a little advice befo' you go?"

Norton turned a puzzled face on the grinning black one:

"Advice?"

"Yassah. What I wants ter know, major, is dis. Sposen, sah, dat a gemman got ter take his choice twist marryin' er lady dat's forcin' herself on 'im, er kill hissef?"

"Kill her!"

Andy broke into a loud laugh:

"Yassah! but she's er dangous 'oman, sah! She's a fighter from Fightersville—an' fuddermo', sah, I'se engaged to annudder lady at the same time an' I'se in lub wid dat one an' skeered er de fust one."

"Face it, then. Confess your love and fight it out! Fight it out and let them fight it out. You like to see a fight, don't you?"

"Yassah! Oh, yassah," Andy declared bravely. "I likes ter see a fight—I likes ter see de fur fly—but I don't care 'bout furnishin' none er de fur!"

Norton had reached the door when he suddenly turned, the momentary humor of his play with the negro gone from his sombre face, the tragedy of a life speaking in every tone as he slowly said:

"Fight it out! It's the only thing to do—fight it out!"

Andy stared at the retreating figure dazed by the violence of passion with which his master had answered, wondering vaguely what could be the meaning of the threat behind his last words.

Chapter XX

Andy Fights

When Andy had recovered from his surprise at the violence of Norton's parting advice his eye suddenly rested on the tray of untouched mint juleps.

A broad smile broke over his black countenance:

"Fight it out! Fight it out!" he exclaimed with a quick movement toward the table. "Yassah, I'm gwine do it, too, I is!"

He paused before the array of filled glasses of the iced beverage, saluted silently, and raised one high over his head to all imaginary friends who might be present. His eye rested on the portrait of General Lee. He bowed and saluted again. Further on hung Stonewall Jackson. He lifted his glass to him, and last to Norton's grandfather in his blue and yellow colonial regimentals. He pressed the glass to his thirsty lips and waved the julep a jovial farewell with the palm of his left hand as he poured it gently but firmly down to the last drop.

He smacked his lips, drew a long breath and sighed:

"Put ernuff er dat stuff inside er me, I kin fight er wil'cat! Yassah, an' I gwine do it. I gwine ter be rough wid her, too! Rough wid her, I is!"

He seized another glass and drained half of it, drew himself up with determination, walked to the door leading to the hall toward the kitchen and called:

"Miss Minerva!"

Receiving no answer, he returned quickly to the tray and took another drink:

"Rough wid her—dat's de way—rough wid her!"

He pulled his vest down with a vicious jerk, bravely took one step, paused, reached back, picked up his glass again, drained it, and walked to the door.

"Miss Minerva!" he called loudly and fiercely.

From the kitchen came the answer in tender tones:

"Yas—honey!"

Andy retreated hastily to the table and took another drink before the huge but smiling figure appeared in the doorway.

"Did my true love call?" she asked softly.

Andy groaned, grasped a glass and quickly poured another drink of Dutch courage down. "Yassam, Miss Minerva, I thought I hear yer out dar——"

Minerva giggled as lightly as she could, considering her two hundred and fifty pounds:

"Yas, honey, hit's little me!"

Andy had begun to feel the bracing effects of the two full glasses of mint juleps. He put his hands in his pockets, walked with springing strides to the other end of the room, returned and squared himself impressively before Minerva. Before he could speak his courage began to fail and he stuttered:

"M-M-M-Miss Minerva!"

The good-humored, shining black face was raised in sharp surprise:

"What de matter wid you, man, er hoppin' roun' over de flo' lak er flea in er hot skillet?"

Andy saw that the time had come when he must speak unless he meant to again ignominiously surrender. He began boldly:

"Miss Minerva! I got somethin' scandalous ter say ter you!"

She glared at him, the whites of her eyes shining ominously, crossed the room quickly and confronted Andy:

"Don't yer dar' say nuttin' scandalizin' ter me, sah!"

His eyes fell and he moved as if to retreat. She nudged him gently:

"G'long, man, what is it?"

He took courage:

"I got ter 'fess ter you, m'am, dat I'se tangled up wid annuder 'oman!"

The black face suddenly flashed with wrath, and her figure was electric with battle. The very pores of her dusky skin seemed to radiate war.

"Who bin tryin' ter steal you?" she cried. "Des sho' her ter me, an' we see who's who!"

Andy waved his hands in a conciliatory self-accusing gesture:

"Yassam—yassam! But I make er fool outen myse'f about her—hit's Miss Cleo!"

"Cleo!" Minerva gasped, staggering back until her form collided with the table and rattled the glasses on the tray. At the sound of the tinkling glass, she turned, grasped a mint julep, and drank the whole of it at a single effort.

Andy, who had been working on a figure in the rug with the toe of his shoe during his confession, looked up, saw that she had captured his inspiration, and sprang back in alarm.

Minerva paused but a moment for breath and rushed for him:

"Dat yaller Jezebel!—tryin' ter fling er spell over you—but I gwine ter save ye, honey!"

Andy retreated behind the lounge, his ample protector hot on his heels:

"Yassam!" he cried, "but I don't want ter be saved!"

Before he had finished the plea, she had pinned him in a corner and cut off retreat.

"Of course yer don't!" she answered generously. "No, po' sinner ever does. But don't yer fret, honey, I'se gwine ter save ye in spite er yosef! Yer needn't ter kick, yer needn't ter scramble, now's de time ye needs me, an I'se gwine ter stan' by ye. Nuttin' kin shake me loose now!"

She took a step toward him and he vainly tried to dodge. It was useless. She hurled her ample form straight on him and lifted her arms for a generous embrace:

"Lordy, man, dat make me lub yer er hundred times mo!"

Andy made up his mind in a sudden burst of courage to fight for his life. If she once got those arms about him he was gone. He grasped them roughly and stayed the onset:

"Yassam!" he answered warningly. "But I got ter 'fess up ter you now de whole truf. I bin er deceivin' you 'bout myself. I'se er bad nigger, Miss Minerva, an' I hain't worthy ter be you' husban'!"

"G'long, chile, I done know dat all de time!" she laughed.

Andy walled his eyes at her uneasily, and she continued:

"But I likes ter hear ye talk humble dat a way—hit's a good sign."

He shook his head impatiently:

"But ye don't know what I means!"

"Why, of cose I does!" she replied genially. "I always knowed dat I wuz high above ye. I'se black, but I'se pure ez de drivellin' snow. I always knowed, honey, dat ye wern't my equal. But ye can't help dat. I'se er born 'ristocrat. My mudder was er African princess. My grandmudder wuz er queen—an' I'se er cook!"

Andy stamped his foot with angry impatience:

"Yassam—but ye git dat all wrong!"

"Cose, you' Minerva understan's when ye comes along side er yo' true love dat ye feels humble——"

"Nobum! Nobum!" he broke in emphatically—"ye got dat all wrong—all wrong!" He paused, drew a chair to the table and motioned her to a seat opposite.

"Des lemme tell ye now," he continued with determined kindness. "Ye see I got ter 'fess de whole truf ter you. Tain't right ter fool ye."

Minerva seated herself, complacently murmuring:

"Yassah, dat's so, Brer Andy."

He leaned over the table and looked at her a moment solemnly:

"I gotter 'fess ter you now, Miss Minerva, dat I'se always bin a bad nigger—what dey calls er pizen bad nigger—I'se er wife beater!"

Minerva's eyes walled in amazement:

"No?"

"Yassam," he went on seriously. "When I wuz married afore I got de habit er beatin' my wife!"

"Beat her?"

Andy shook his head dolefully:

"Yassam. Hit's des lak I tell ye. I hates ter 'fess hit ter you, m'am, but I formed de habit, same ez drinkin' licker—I beat her! I des couldn't keep my hands offen her. I beat her scandalous! I pay no tenshun to her hollerin!—huh!— de louder she holler, 'pears lak de harder I beat her!"

"My, my, ain't dat terrible!" she gasped.

"Yassam——"

"Scandalous!"

"Dat it is——"

"Sinful!"

"Jes so!" he agreed sorrowfully.

"But man!" she cried ecstatically, "dat's what I calls er husband!"

"Hey?"

"Dat's de man fer me!"

He looked at her in dismay, snatched the decanter, poured himself a straight drink of whiskey, gulped it down, leaned over the table and returned to his task with renewed vigor:

"But I kin see, m'am, dat yer don't know what I means! I didn't des switch 'er wid er cowhide er de buggy whip! I got in er regular habit er lammin' her wid anything I git hold of—wid er axe handle or wid er fire shovel——"

"Well, dat's all right," Minerva interrupted admiringly. "She had de same chance ez you! I takes my chances. What I wants is er husban'—a husban' dat's got de sand in his gizzard! Dat fust husban' er mine weren't no good 'tall—nebber hit me in his life but once—slap me in de face one day, lak dat!"

She gave a contemptuous imitation of the trivial blow with the palms of her hands.

"An' what'd you do, m'am?" Andy asked with sudden suspicion.

"Nuttin' 'tall!" she said with a smile. "I des laf, haul off, kinder playful lak, an' knock 'im down wid de flatiron——"

Andy leaped to his feet and walked around the table toward the door:

"Wid de flatiron!" he repeated incredulously.

"Didn't hit 'im hard!" Minerva laughed. "But he tumble on de flo' lak er ten-pin in er bowlin' alley. I stan' dar waitin' fer 'im ter git up an' come ergin, an' what ye reckon he done?"

"I dunno, m'am," Andy sighed, wiping the perspiration from his forehead.

Minerva laughed joyously at the memory of the scene:

"He jump up an' run des lak er turkey! He run all de way down town, an' bless God ef he didn't buy me a new calico dress an' fotch hit home ter me. He warn't no man at all! I wuz dat sorry fer 'im an' dat ershamed er him I couldn't look 'im in de face ergin. I gits er divorce frum him——"

She paused, rose, and looked at Andy with tender admiration:

"But, Lordy, honey, you an' me's gwine ter have joyful times!"

Andy made a break for the door but she was too quick for him. With a swift swinging movement, astonishing in its rapidity for her size, she threw herself on him and her arms encircled his neck:

"I'se yo' woman an' you'se my man!" she cried with a finality that left her victim without a ray of hope. He was muttering incoherent protests when Helen's laughing voice came to his rescue:

"Oho!" she cried, with finger uplifted in a teasing gesture.

Minerva loosed her grip on Andy overwhelmed with embarrassment, while he crouched behind her figure crying:

"'Twa'n't me, Miss Helen—'twa'n't me!"

Helen continued to laugh while Andy grasped the tray and beat a hasty retreat.

Helen approached Minerva teasingly:

"Why, Aunt Minerva!"

The big, jovial black woman glanced at her:

"G'way, chile—g'way frum here!"

"Aunt Minerva, I wouldn't have thought such a thing of you!" Helen said demurely.

Minerva broke into a jolly laugh and faced her tormentor:

"Yassum, honey, I spec hit wuz all my fault. Love's such foolishness—yer knows how dat is yosef!"

A look of rapture overspread Helen's face

"Such a sweet, wonderful foolishness, Aunt Minerva!"—she paused and her voice was trembling when she added—"It makes us all akin, doesn't it?"

"Yassam, an' I sho' is glad ter see you so happy!"

"Oh, I'm too happy, Aunt Minerva, it frightens me"—she stopped, glanced at the door, drew nearer and continued in low tones: "I've just left Tom out there on the lawn, to ask you to do something for me."

"Yassam."

"I want you to tell the major our secret to-night. He'll be proud and happy in his victory and I want him to know at once."

The black woman shook her head dubiously:

"Tell him yosef, honey!"

"But I'm afraid. The major frightens me. When I look into his deep eyes I feel that he has the power to crush the soul out of my body and that he will do it if I make him very angry."

"Dat's 'cause yer deceives him, child."

"Please tell him for us, Aunt Minerva! Oh, you've been so good to me! For the past weeks I've been in heaven. It seems only a day instead of a month since he told me his love and then it seems I've lived through all eternity since I first felt his arms about me. Sitting out there in the moonlight by his side I forget that I'm on earth, forget that there's a pain or a secret in it. I'm just in heaven. I have to pinch myself to see if it's real"—she smiled and pinched her arm—"I'm afraid I'll wake up and find it only a dream!"

"Well, yer better wake up just er minute an' tell de major—Mister Tom got ter have it out wid him."

"Yes, I know, and that's what scares me. Won't you tell him for us right away? Get him in a good humor, make him laugh, say a good word for us and then tell him. Tell him how useless it will be to oppose us. He can't hold out long against Tom, he loves him so."

"Mr. Tom want me ter tell de major ter-night? He ax yer ter see me?"

"No. He doesn't know what I came for. I just decided all of a sudden to come. I want to surprise him. He is going to tell his father himself to-night. But somehow I'm afraid, Aunt Minerva. I want you to help us. You will, won't you?"

The black woman shook her head emphatically:

"Nasah, I ain't gwine ter git mixed up in dis thing!"

"Aunt Minerva!"

"Nasah—I'se skeered!"

"Ah, please?"

"Nasah!"

"Please——"

"Na, na, na!"

"Aunt Minerva——"

"Na——"

The girl's pleading eyes were resistless and the black lips smiled:

"Cose I will, chile! Cose I will—I'll see 'im right away. I'll tell him de minute I lays my eyes on 'im."

She turned to go and ran squarely into Norton as he strode into the room. She stopped and stammered:

"Why—why—wuz yer lookin' fer me, major?"

Norton gazed at her a moment and couldn't call his mind from its painful train of thought. He spoke finally with sharp accent:

"No. I want to see Cleo."

Helen slipped behind Minerva:

"Stay and tell him now. I'll go."

"No, better wait," was her low reply, as she watched Norton furtively. "I don't like de way his eyes er spittin' fire."

Norton turned to Minerva sharply:

"Find Cleo and tell her I wish to see her immediately!"

"Yassah—yassah!" Minerva answered, nervously, whispering to Helen: "Come on, honey—git outen here—come on!"

Helen followed mechanically, glancing timidly back over her shoulder at Norton's drawn face.

Chapter XXI

The Second Blow

Norton could scarcely control his eagerness to face the woman he loathed. Every nerve of his body tingled with the agony of his desire to be free.

He was ready for the end, no matter what she might do. The time had come in the strong man's life when compromise, conciliation, and delay were alike impossible. He cursed himself and his folly to-night that he had delayed so long. He had tried to be fair to the woman he hated. His sense of justice, personal honor, and loyalty to his pledged word, had given her the opportunity to strike him the blow she had delivered through the girl. He had been more than fair and he would settle it now for all time.

That she was afraid to meet him was only too evident from her leaving the house on his return. He smiled grimly when he recalled the effrontery with which she had defied him at their last meeting.

Her voice, sharp and angry, rang out to Andy at the back door.

Norton's strong jaw closed with a snap, and he felt his whole being quiver at the rasping sound of her familiar tones. She had evidently recovered her composure and was ready with her usual insolence.

She walked quickly into the room, and threw her head up with defiance:

"Well ?"

"Why have you avoided me to-night?"

"Have I?"

"I think so."

Cleo laughed sneeringly:

"You'll think again before I'm done with you!"

She shook her head with the old bravado, but the keen eyes of the man watching saw that she was not sure of her ground.

He folded his arms and quietly began:

"For twenty years I have breathed the air poisoned by your presence. I have seen your insolence grow until you have announced yourself the mistress of my house. You knew that I was afraid of your tongue, and thought that a coward would submit in the end. Well, it's over. I've held my hand for the past four weeks until my duty to the people was done. I've been a coward when I saw the tangled web of lies and shame in which I floundered. But the past is past. I face life to-night as it is"—his voice dropped—"and I'm going to take what comes. Your rule in my house is at an end——"

"Indeed!"

"Helen leaves here to-morrow morning and *you* go."

"Really?"

"I've made a decent provision for your future—which is more than you deserve. Pack your things!"

The woman threw him a look of hate and her lips curved with scorn:

"So—you have kindly allowed me to stay until your campaign was ended. Well, I've understood you. I knew that you were getting ready for me. I'm ready for you."

"And you think that I will allow you to remain in my house after what has passed between us?"

"Yes, you will," she answered smiling. "I'm not going to leave. You'll have to throw me into the street. And if you do, God may pity you, I'll not. There's one thing you fear more than a public scandal!"

Norton advanced and glared at her:

"What?"

"The hatred of the boy you idolize. I dare you to lay your hands on me to put me out of this house! And if you do, Tom will hear from my lips the story of the affair that ended in the death of his mother. I'll tell him the truth, the whole truth, and then a great deal more than the truth——"

"No doubt!" he interrupted.

"But there'll be enough truth in all I say to convince him beyond a doubt. I promise you now"—she dropped her voice to a whisper—"to lie to him with a skill so sure, so cunning, so perfect, no denial you can ever make will shake his faith in my words. He loves me and I'll make him believe me. When I finish my story he ought to kill you. There's one thing you can depend on with his high-strung and sensitive nature and the training you have given him in racial purity—when he hears my story, he'll curse you to your face and turn from you as if you were a leper. I'll see that he does this if it's the last and only thing I do on this earth!"

"And if you do——"

"Oh, I'm not afraid!" she sneered, holding his eye with the calm assurance of power. "I've thought it all over and I know exactly what to say."

He leaned close:

"Now listen! I don't want to hurt you but you're going out of my life. Every day while I've sheltered you in this house you have schemed and planned to drag me down again to your level. You have failed. I am not going to risk that girl's presence here another day—and *you* go!"

As he spoke the last words he turned from her with a gesture of final dismissal. She tossed her head in a light laugh and calmly said:

"You're too late!"

He stopped in his tracks, his heart chilled by the queer note of triumph in her voice. Without turning or moving a muscle he asked:

"What do you mean?"

"Tom is already in love with Helen!"

He wheeled and hurled himself at her:

"What?"

"And she is desperately in love with him"—she stopped and deliberately laughed again in his face—"and I have known it for weeks!"

Another step brought his trembling figure towering over her:

"I don't believe you!" he hissed.

Cleo walked leisurely to the door and smiled:

"Ask the servants if you doubt my word." She finished with a sneer. "I begged you not to fight, major!"

He stood rooted to the spot and watched her slowly walk backward into the hall. It was a lie, of course. And yet the calm certainty with which she spoke chilled his soul as he recalled his own suspicions. He must know now without a moment's delay and he must know the whole truth without reservation.

Before he approached either Tom or Helen there was one on whom he had always relied to tell the truth. Her honest black face had been the one comfort of his life through the years of shadow and deceit. If Minerva knew she would tell him.

He rushed to the door that led to the kitchen and called:

"Minerva!"

The answer came feebly:

"Yassah."

"Come here!"

He had controlled his emotions sufficiently to speak his last command with some degree of dignity.

He walked back to the table and waited for her coming. His brain was in a whirl of conflicting, stunning emotion. He simply couldn't face at once the appalling possibilities such a statement involved. His mind refused to accept it. As yet it was a lie of Cleo's fertile invention, and still his reason told him that such a lie could serve no sane purpose in such a crisis. He felt that he was choking. His hand involuntarily went to his neck and fumbled at his collar.

Minerva's heavy footstep was heard and he turned sharply:

"Minerva!"

"Yassah"—she answered, glancing at him timidly. Never had she seen his face so ghastly or the look in his eye so desperate. She saw that he was making an effort at self-control and knew instinctively that the happiness of the lovers was at stake. It was too solemn a moment for anything save the naked truth and her heart sank in pity and sympathy for the girl she had promised to help.

"Minerva," he began evenly, "you are the only servant this house who has never lied to me"—he took a step closer. "Are Tom and Miss Helen lovers?"

Minerva fumbled her apron, glanced at his drawn face, looked down on the floor and stammered:

"De Lordy, major——"

"Yes or no!" he thundered.

The black woman moistened her lips, hesitated, turned her honest face on his and said tremblingly: "Yassah, dey is!"

His eyes burned into hers:

"And you, too, have known this for weeks?"

"Yassah. Mister Tom ax me not ter tell ye——"

Norton staggered to a seat and sank with a groan of despair, repeating over and over again in low gasps the exclamation that was a sob and a prayer:

"Great God!—Great God!"

Minerva drew near with tender sympathy. Her voice was full of simple, earnest pleading:

"De Lordy, major, what's de use? Young folks is young folks, an' love's love. What ye want ter break 'em up fer—dey's so happy! Yer know, sah, ye can't mend er butterfly's wing er put er egg back in de shell. Miss Helen's young, beautiful, sweet and good—won't ye let me plead fer 'em, sah?"

With a groan of anguish Norton sprang to his feet:

"Silence—silence!"

"Yassah!"

"Go—find Miss Helen—send her to me quickly. I don't want to see Mr. Tom. I want to see her alone first."

Minerva had backed out of his way and answered plaintively:

"Yassah."

She paused and extended her hand pleadingly:

"You'll be easy wid 'em, sah?"

He hadn't heard. The tall figure slowly sank into the chair and his shoulders drooped in mortal weariness.

Minerva shook her head sadly and turned to do his bidding.

Norton's eyes were set in agony, his face white, his breast scarcely moving to breathe, as he waited Helen's coming. The nerves suddenly snapped—he bowed his face in his hands and sobbed aloud:

"Oh, dear God, give me strength! I can't—I can't confess to my boy!"

Chapter XXII

The Test of Love

Norton made a desperate effort to pull himself together for his appeal to Helen. On its outcome hung the possibility of saving himself from the terror that haunted him. If he could tell the girl the truth and make her see that a marriage with Tom was utterly out of the question because her blood was stained with that of a negro, it might be possible to save himself the humiliation of the full confession of their relationship and of his bitter shame.

He had made a fearful mistake in not telling her this at their first interview, and a still more frightful mistake in rearing her in ignorance of the truth. No life built on a lie could endure. He was still trying desperately to hold his own on its shifting sands, but in his soul of souls he had begun to despair of the end. He was clutching at straws. In moments of sanity he realized it, but there was nothing else to do. The act was instinctive.

The girl's sensitive mind was the key to a possible solution. He had felt instinctively on the day he told her the first fact about the disgrace of her birth, vague and shadowy as he had left it, that she could never adjust herself to the certainty that negro blood flowed in her veins. He had observed that her aversion to negroes was peculiarly acute. If her love for the boy were genuine, if it belonged to the big things of the soul, and were not the mere animal impulse she had inherited from her mother, he would have a ground of most powerful appeal. Love seeks not its own. If she really loved she would sink her own life to save his.

It was a big divine thing to demand of her and his heart sank at the thought of her possible inheritance from Cleo. Yet he knew by an instinct deeper and truer than reason, that the ruling power in this sensitive, lonely creature was in the spirit, not the flesh. He recalled in vivid flashes the moments he had felt this so keenly in their first pitiful meeting. If he could win her consent to an immediate flight and the sacrifice of her own desires to save the boy! It was only a hope—it was a desperate one—but he clung to it with painful eagerness.

Why didn't she come? The minutes seemed hours and there were minutes in which he lived a life.

He rose nervously and walked toward the mantel, lifted his eyes and they rested on the portrait of his wife.

"'My brooding spirit will watch and guard!'"

He repeated the promise of her last scrawled message. He leaned heavily against the mantel, his eyes burning with an unusual brightness.

"Oh, Jean, darling," he groaned, "if you see and hear and know, let me feel your presence! Your dear eyes are softer and kinder than the world's to-night. Help me, I'm alone, heartsick and broken!"

He choked down a sob, walked back to the chair and sank in silence. His eyes were staring into space, his imagination on fire, passing in stern review the events of his life. How futile, childish and absurd it all seemed! What a vain and foolish thing its hope and struggles, its dreams and ambitions! What a failure for all its surface brilliance! He was standing again at the window behind the dais of the President of the Senate, watching the little drooping figure of the Governor staggering away into oblivion, and his heart went out to him in a great tenderness and pity. He longed to roll back the years that he might follow the impulse he had felt to hurry down the steps of the Capitol, draw the broken man into a sheltered spot, slip his arms about him and say:

"Who am I to judge? You're my brother—I'm sorry! Come, we'll try it again and help one another!"

The dream ended in a sudden start. He had heard the rustle of a dress at the door and knew without lifting his head that she was in the room.

Only the slightest sound had come from her dry throat, a little muffled attempt to clear it of the tightening bands. It was scarcely audible, yet his keen ear had caught it instantly, not only caught the excitement under which she was struggling, but in it the painful consciousness of his hostility and her pathetic desire to be friends.

He rose trembling and turned his dark eyes on her white uplifted face.

A feeling of terror suddenly weakened her knees. He was evidently not angry as she had feared. There was something bigger and more terrible than anger behind the mask he was struggling to draw over his mobile features.

"What has happened, major?" she asked in a subdued voice.

"That is what I must know of you, child," he replied, watching her intently.

She pressed closer with sudden desperate courage, her voice full of wistful friendliness:

"Oh, major, what have I done to offend you? I've tried so hard to win your love and respect. All my life I've been alone in a world of strangers, friendless and homesick——"

He lifted his hand with a firm gesture:

"Come, child, to the point! I must know the truth now. Tom has made love to you?"

She blushed:

"I—I—wish to see Tom before I answer——"

Norton dropped his uplifted arm with a groan:

"Thank you," he murmured in tones scarcely audible. "I have your answer!"—he paused and looked at her curiously—"And you love him?"

The girl hesitated for just an instant, her blue eyes flashed and she drew her strong, young figure erect:

"Yes! And I'm proud of it. His love has lifted me into the sunlight and made the world glorious—made me love everything in it—every tree and every flower and every living thing that moves and feels——"

She stopped abruptly and lifted her flushed face to his:

"I've learned to love you, in spite of your harshness to me—I love you because you are his father!"

He turned from her and, then wheeled suddenly, his face drawn with pain:

"Now, I must be frank, I must be brutal. I must know the truth without reservation—how far has this thing gone?"

"I—I—don't understand you!"

"Marriage is impossible! I told you that and you must have realized it."

Her head drooped:

"You said so——"

"Impossible—utterly impossible! And you know it"—he drew a deep breath. "What—what are your real relations?"

"My—real—relations?" she gasped.

"Answer me now, before God! I'll hold your secret sacred—your life and his may depend on it"—his voice dropped to a tense whisper. "Your love is pure and unsullied?"

The girl's eyes flashed with rage:

"As pure and unsullied as his dead mother's for you!"

"Thank God!" he breathed. "I believe you—but I had to know, child! I had to know—there are big, terrible reasons why I had to know."

A tear slowly stole down Helen's flushed cheeks as she quietly asked:

"Why—why should you insult and shame me by asking that question?"

"My knowledge of your birth."

The girl smiled sadly:

"Yet you might have guessed that I had learned to cherish honor and purity before I knew I might not claim them as my birthright!"

"Forgive me, child," he said contritely, "if in my eagerness, my fear, my anguish, I hurt you. But I had to ask that question! I had to know. Your answer gives me courage"—he paused and his voice quivered with deep intensity—"you really love Tom?"

"With a love beyond words."

"The big, wonderful love that comes to the human soul but once?"

"Yes!"

His eyes were piercing to the depths now:

"With the deep, unselfish yearning that asks nothing for itself and seeks only the highest good of its beloved?"

"Yes—yes," she answered mechanically and, pausing, looked again into his burning eyes: "but you frighten me—" she grasped a chair for support, recovered herself and went on rapidly—"you mustn't ask me to give him up—I won't give him up! Poor and friendless, with a shadow over my life and everything against me, I have won him and he's mine! I have the right to his love—I didn't ask to be born. I must live my own life. I have as much right to happiness as you. Why must I bear the sins of my father and mother? Have I broken the law? Haven't I a heart that can ache and break and cry for joy?"

He allowed the first paroxysm of her emotion to spend itself before he replied, and then in quiet tones said:

"You must give him up!"

"I won't! I won't, I tell you!" she said through her set teeth as she suddenly swung her strong, young form before him. "I won't give him up! His love has made life worth living and I'm going to live it! I don't care what you say—he's mine—and you shall not take him from me!"

Norton was stunned by the fiery intensity with which her answer had been given. There was no mistaking the strength of her character. Every vibrant note of her voice had rung with sincerity, purity, the justice of her cause, and the consciousness of power. He was dealing with no trembling schoolgirl's mind, filled with sentimental dreams. A woman, in the tragic strength of a great nature, stood before him. He felt this greatness instinctively and met it with reverence. It could only be met thus, and as he realized its strength, his heart took fresh courage. His own voice became tender, eager, persuasive:

"But suppose, my dear, I show you that you will destroy the happiness and wreck the life of the man you love?"

"Impossible! He knows that I'm nameless and his love is all the deeper, truer and more manly because he realizes that I am defenseless."

"But suppose I convince you?"

"You can't!"

"Suppose," he said in a queer tone, "I tell you that the barrier between you is so real, so loathsome——"

"Loathsome?" she repeated with a start.

"So loathsome," he went on evenly, "that when he knows the truth, whether he wishes it or not, he will instinctively turn from you with a shudder."

"I won't believe it!"

"Suppose I prove to you that marriage would wreck both your life and his"—he gazed at her with trembling intensity—"would you give him up to save him?"

She held his eye steadily:

"Yes—I'd die to save him!"

A pitiful stillness followed. The man scarcely moved. His lips quivered and his eyes grew dim. He looked at her pathetically and motioned her to a seat.

"And if I convince you," he went on tenderly, "you will submit yourself to my advice and leave America?"

The blue eyes never flinched as she firmly replied:

"Yes. But I warn you that no such barrier can exist."

"Then I must prove to you that it does." He drew a deep breath and watched her. "You realize the fact that a man who marries a nameless girl bars himself from all careers of honor?"

"The honor of fools, yes—of the noble and wise, no!"

"You refuse to see that the shame which shadows a mother's life will smirch her children, and like a deadly gangrene at last eat the heart out of her husband's love?"

"My faith in him is too big——"

"You can conceive of no such barrier?"

"No!"

"In the first rush of love," he replied kindly, "you feel this. Emotion obscures reason. But there are such barriers between men and women."

"Name one!"

His brow clouded, his lips moved to speak and stopped. It was more difficult to frame in speech than he had thought. His jaw closed with firm decision at last and he began calmly:

"I take an extreme case. Suppose, for example, your father, a proud Southern white man, of culture, refinement and high breeding, forgot for a moment that he was white and heard the call of the Beast, and your mother were an octoroon—what then?"

The girl flushed with anger:

"Such a barrier, yes! Nothing could be more loathsome. But why ask me so disgusting a question? No such barrier could possibly exist between us!"

Norton's eyes were again burning into her soul as he asked in a low voice:

"Suppose it does?"

The girl smiled with a puzzled look:

"Suppose it does? Of course, you're only trying to prove that such an impossible barrier might exist! And for the sake of argument I agree that it would be real"—she paused and her breath came in a quick gasp. She sprang to her feet clutching at her throat, trembling from head to foot— "What do you mean by looking at me like that?"

Norton lowered his head and barely breathed the words:

"That is the barrier between you!"

Helen looked at him dazed. The meaning was too big and stupefying to be grasped at once.

"Why, of course, major," she faltered, "you just say that to crush me in the argument. But I've given up the point. I've granted that such a barrier may exist and would be real. But you haven't told me the one between us."

The man steeled his heart, turned his face away and spoke in gentle tones:

"I am telling you the pitiful, tragic truth—your mother is a negress——"

With a smothered cry of horror the girl threw herself on him and covered his mouth with her hand, half gasping, half screaming her desperate appeal:

"Stop! don't—don't say it!— take it back! Tell me that it's not true—tell me that you only said it to convince me and I'll believe you. If the hideous thing is true—for the love of God deny it now! If it's true—lie to me"—her voice broke and she clung to Norton's arms with cruel grip—"lie to me! Tell me that you didn't mean it, and I'll believe you—truth or lie, I'll never question it! I'll never cross your purpose again—I'll do anything you tell me, major"—she lifted her streaming eyes and began slowly to sink to her knees—"see how humble—how obedient I am! You don't hate me, do you? I'm just a poor, lonely girl, helpless and friendless now at your feet"—her head sank into her hands until the beautiful brown hair touched the floor—"have mercy! have mercy on me!"

Norton bent low and fumbled for the trembling hand. He couldn't see and for a moment words were impossible.

He found her hand and pressed it gently:

"I'm sorry, little girl! I'd lie to you if I could—but you know a lie don't last long in this world. I've lied about you before—I'd lie now to save you this anguish, but it's no use—we all have to face things in the end!"

With a mad cry of pain, the girl sprang to her feet and staggered to the table:

"Oh, God, how could any man with a soul—any living creature, even a beast of the field—bring me into the world—teach me to think and feel, to laugh and cry, and thrust me into such a hell alone! My proud father—I could kill him!"

Norton extended his hands to her in a gesture of instinctive sympathy:

"Come, you'll see things in a calm light to-morrow. You are young and life is all before you!"

"Yes!" she cried fiercely, "a life of shame—a life of insult, of taunts, of humiliation, of horror! The one thing I've always loathed was the touch of a negro——"

She stopped suddenly and lifted her hand, staring with wildly dilated eyes at the nails of her finely shaped fingers to find if the telltale marks of negro blood were there which she had seen on Cleo's. Finding none, the horror in her eyes slowly softened into a look of despairing tenderness as she went on:

"The one passionate yearning of my soul has been to be a mother—to feel the breath of a babe on my heart, to hear it lisp my name and know a mother's love—the love I've starved for—and now, it can never be!"

She had moved beyond the table in her last desperate cry and Norton followed with a look of tenderness:

"Nonsense," he cried persuasively, "you're but a child yourself. You can go abroad where no such problem of white and black race exists. You can marry there and be happy in your home and little ones, if God shall give them!"

She turned on him savagely:

"Well, God shall not give them! I'll see to that! I'm young, but I'm not a fool. I know something of the laws of life. I know that Tom is not like you"—she turned and pointed to the portrait on the wall—"he is like his great-grandfather! Mine may have been——"

Her voice choked with passion. She grasped a chair with one hand and tore at the collar of her dress with the other. She had started to say "mine may have been a black cannibal!" and the sheer horror of its possibility had strangled her. When she had sufficiently mastered her feelings to speak she said in a strange muffled tone:

"I ask nothing of God now—if I could see Him, I'd curse Him to His face!"

"Come, come!" Norton exclaimed, "this is but a passing ugly fancy—such things rarely happen——"

"But they do happen!" she retorted slowly. "I've known one such tragedy, of a white mother's child coming into the world with the thick lips, kinky hair, flat nose and black skin of a cannibal ancestor! She killed herself when she was strong enough to leap out the window"—her voice dropped to a dreamy chant—"yes, blood will tell—there's but one thing for me to do! I wonder, with the yellow in me, if I'll have the courage."

Norton spoke with persuasive tenderness:

"You mustn't think of such madness! I'll send you abroad at once and you can begin life over again——"

Helen suddenly snatched the chair to which she had been holding out of her way and faced Norton with flaming eyes:

"I don't want to be an exile! I've been alone all my miserable orphan life! I don't want to go abroad and die among strangers! I've just begun to live since I came here! I love the South—it's mine—I feel it—I know it! I love its blue skies and its fields—I love its people—they are mine! I think as you think, feel as you feel——"

She paused and looked at him queerly:

"I've learned to honor, respect and love you because I've grown to feel that you stand for what I hold highest, noblest and best in life"—the voice died in a sob and she was silent.

The man turned away, crying in his soul:

"O God, I'm paying the price now!"

"What can I do!" she went on at last. "What is life worth since I know this leper's shame? There are millions like me, yes. If I could bend my back and be a slave there are men and women who need my services. And there are men I might know—yes—but I can't—I can't! I'm not a slave. I'm not bad. I can't stoop. There's but one thing!"

Norton's face was white with emotion:

"I can't tell you, little girl, how sorry I am"—his voice broke. He turned, suddenly extended his hand and cried hoarsely: "Tell me what I can do to help you—I'll do anything on this earth that's within reason!"

The girl looked up surprised at his anguish, wondering vaguely if he could mean what he had said, and then threw herself at him in a burst of sudden, fierce rebellion, her voice, low and quivering at first, rising to the tragic power of a defiant soul in combat with overwhelming odds:

"Then give me back the man I love—he's mine! He's mine, I tell you, body and soul! God—gave—him—to—me! He's your son, but I love him! He's my mate! He's of age—he's no longer yours! His time has come to build his own home—he's mine—not yours! He's my life—and you're tearing the very heart out of my body!"

The white, trembling figure slowly crumpled at his feet.

He took both of her bands, and lifted her gently:

"Pull yourself together, child. It's hard, I know, but you begin to realize that you must bear it. You must look things calmly in the face now."

The girl's mouth hardened and she answered with bitterness:

"Yes, of course—I'm nobody! We must consider you"—she staggered to a chair and dropped limply into it, her voice a whisper—"we must consider Tom—yes—yes—we must, too—I know that——"

Norton pressed eagerly to her side and leaned over the drooping figure:

"You can begin to see now that I was right," he pleaded. "You love Tom—he's worth saving—you'll do as I ask and give him up?"

The sensitive young face was convulsed with an agony words could not express and the silence was pitiful. The man bending over her could hear the throb of his own heart. A quartet of serenaders celebrating the victory of the election stopped at the gate and the soft strains of the music came through the open window. Norton felt that he must scream in a moment if she did not answer. He bent low and softly repeated:

"You'll do as I ask now, and give him up?"

The tangled mass of brown hair sank lower and her answer was a sigh of despair:

"Yes!"

The man couldn't speak at once. His eyes filled. When he had mastered his voice he said eagerly:

"There's but one way, you know. You must leave at once without seeing him."

She lifted her face with a pleading look:

"Just a moment—without letting him know what has passed between us—just one last look into his dear face?"

He shook his head kindly:

"It isn't wise——"

"Yes, I know," she sighed. "I'll go at once."

He drew his watch and looked at it hurriedly:

"The first train leaves in thirty minutes. Get your hat, a coat and travelling bag and go just as you are. I'll send your things——"

"Yes—yes,"—she murmured.

"I'll join you in a few days in New York and arrange your future. Leave the house immediately. Tom mustn't see you. Avoid him as you cross the lawn. I'll have a carriage at the gate in a few minutes."

The little head sank again:

"I understand."

He looked uncertainly at the white drooping figure. The serenaders were repeating the chorus of the old song in low, sweet strains that floated over the lawn and stole through the house in weird ghost-like echoes. He returned to her chair and bent over her:

"You won't stop to change your dress, you'll get your hat and coat and go just as you are—at once?"

The brown head nodded slowly and he gazed at her tenderly:

"You've been a brave little girl to-night,"—he lifted his hand to place it on her shoulder in the first expression of love he had ever given. The hand paused, held by the struggle of the feelings of centuries of racial pride and the memories of his own bitter tragedy. But the pathos of her suffering and the heroism of her beautiful spirit won. The hand was gently lowered and pressed the soft, round shoulder.

A sob broke from the lonely heart, and her head drooped until it lay prostrate on the table, the beautiful arms outstretched in helpless surrender.

Norton staggered blindly to the door, looked back, lifted his hand and in a quivering voice, said:

"I can never forget this!"

His long stride quickly measured the distance to the gate, and a loud cheer from the serenaders roused the girl from her stupor of pain.

In a moment they began singing again, a love song, that tore her heart with cruel power.

"Oh, God, will they never stop" she cried, closing her ears with her hands in sheer desperation.

She rose, crossed slowly to the window and looked out on the beautiful moonlit lawn at the old rustic seat where her lover was waiting. She pressed her hand on her throbbing forehead, walked to the center of the room, looked about her in a helpless way and her eye rested on the miniature portrait of Tom. She picked it up and gazed at it tenderly, pressed it to her heart, and with a low sob felt her way through the door and up the stairs to her room.

Chapter XXIII

The Parting

Tom had grown impatient, waiting in their sheltered seat on the lawn for Helen to return. She had gone on a mysterious mission to see Minerva, laughingly refused to tell him its purpose, but promised to return in a few minutes. When half an hour had passed without a sign he reconnoitered to find Minerva, and to his surprise she, too, had disappeared.

He returned to his trysting place and listened while the serenaders sang their first song. Unable to endure the delay longer he started to the house just as his father hastily left by the front door, and quickly passing the men at the gate, hurried down town.

The coast was clear and he moved cautiously to fathom, if possible, the mystery of Helen's disappearance. Finding no trace of her in Minerva's room, he entered the house and, seeing nothing of her in the halls, thrust his head in the library and found it empty. He walked in, peeping around with a boyish smile expecting her to leap out and surprise him. He opened the French window and looked for her on the porch. He hurried back into the room with a look of surprised disappointment and started to the door opening on the hall of the stairway. He heard distinctly the rustle of a dress and the echo on the stairs of the footstep he knew so well.

He gave a boyish laugh, tiptoed quickly to the old-fashioned settee, dropped behind its high back and waited her coming.

Helen had hastily packed a travelling bag and thrown a coat over her arm. She slowly entered the library to replace the portrait she had taken, kissed it and started with feet of lead and set, staring eyes to slip through the lawn and avoid Tom as she had promised.

As she approached the corner of the settee the boy leaped up with a laugh:

"Where have you been?"

With a quick movement of surprise she threw the bag and coat behind her back. Luckily he had leaped so close he could not see.

"Where've you been?" he repeated.

"Why, I've just come from my room," she replied with an attempt at composure.

"What have you got your hat for?"

She flushed the slightest bit:

"Why, I was going for a walk."

"With a veil—at night—what have you got that veil for?"

The boyish banter in his tones began to yield to a touch of wonder.

Helen hesitated:

"Why, the crowds of singing and shouting men on the streets. I didn't wish to be recognized, and I wanted to hear what the speakers said."

"You were going to leave me and go alone to the speaker's stand?"

"Yes. Your father is going to see you and I was nervous and frightened and wanted to pass the time until you were free again"—she paused, looked at him intently and spoke in a queer monotone—"the negroes who can't read and write have been disfranchised, haven't they?"

"Yes," he answered mechanically, "the ballot should never have been given them."

"Yet there's something pitiful about it after all, isn't there, Tom?" She asked the question with a strained wistfulness that startled the boy.

He answered automatically, but his keen, young eyes were studying with growing anxiety every movement of her face and form and every tone of her voice:

"I don't see it," he said carelessly.

She laid her left hand on his arm, the right hand still holding her bag and coat out of sight.

"Suppose," she whispered, "that you should wake up to-morrow morning and suddenly discover that a strain of negro blood poisoned your veins—what would you do?"

Tom frowned and watched her with a puzzled look:

"Never thought of such a thing!"

She pressed his arm eagerly:

"Think—what would you do?"

"What would I do?" he repeated in blank amazement.

"Yes."

His eyes were holding hers now with a steady stare of alarm. The questions she asked didn't interest him. Her glittering eyes and trembling hand did. Studying her intently he said lightly:

"To be perfectly honest, I'd blow my brains out."

With a cry she staggered back and threw her hand instinctively up as if to ward a blow:

"Yes—yes, you would—wouldn't you?"

He was staring at her now with blanched face and she was vainly trying to hide her bag and coat.

He seized her arms:

"Why are you so excited? Why do you tremble so?"—he drew the arm around that she was holding back—"What is it? What's the matter?"

His eye rested on the bag, he turned deadly pale and she dropped it with a sigh.

"What—what—does this mean?" he gasped "You are trying to leave me without a word?"

She staggered and fell limp into a seat:

"Oh, Tom, the end has come, and I must go!"

"Go!" he cried indignantly, "then I go, too!"

"But you can't, dear!"

"And why not?"

"Your father has just told me the whole hideous secret of my birth—and it's hopeless!"

"What sort of man do you think I am? What sort of love do you think I've given you? Separate us after the solemn vows we've given to each other! Neither man nor the devil can come between us now!"

She looked at him wistfully:

"It's sweet to hear such words—though I know you can't make them good."

"I'll make them good," he broke in, "with every drop of blood in my veins—and no coward has ever borne my father's name—it's good blood!"

"That's just it—and blood will tell. It's the law of life and I've given up."

"Well, I haven't given up," he protested, "remember that! Try me with your secret—I laugh before I hear it!"

With a gleam of hope in her deep blue eyes she rose trembling:

"You really mean that? If I go an outcast you would go with me?"

"Yes—yes."

"And if a curse is branded on my forehead you'll take its shame as yours?"

"Yes."

She laid her hand on his arm, looked long and yearningly into his eyes, and said:

"Your father has just told me that I am a negress—my mother is an octoroon!"

The boy flinched involuntarily, stared in silence an instant, and his form suddenly stiffened:

"I don't believe a word of it! My father has been deceived. It's preposterous!"

Helen drew closer as if for shelter and clung to his hand wistfully:

"It does seem a horrible joke, doesn't it? I can't realize it. But it's true. The major gave me his solemn word in tears of sympathy. He knew both my father and mother. I am a negress!"

The boy's arm unconsciously shrank the slightest bit from her touch while he stared at her with wildly dilated eyes and spoke in a hoarse whisper:

"It's impossible! It's impossible—I tell you!"

He attempted to lift his hand to place it on his throbbing forehead. Helen clung to him in frantic grief and terror:

"Please, please—don't shrink from me! Have pity on me! If you feel that way, for God's sake don't let me see it—don't let me know it—I—I—can't endure it! I can't——"

The tense figure collapsed in his arms and the brown head sank on his breast with a sob of despair. The boy pressed her to his heart and held her close. He felt her body shiver as he pushed the tangled ringlets back from her high, fair forehead and felt the cold beads of perspiration. The serenaders at the gate were singing again—a negro folk-song. The absurd childish words which he knew so well rang through the house, a chanting mockery.

"There, there," he whispered tenderly, "I didn't shrink from you, dear. I couldn't shrink from you—you only imagined it. I was just stunned for a moment. The blow blinded me. But it's all right now, I see things clearly. I love you—that's all—and love is from God, or it's not love, it's a sham——"

A low sob and she clung to him with desperate tenderness.

He bent his head close until the blonde hair mingled with the rich brown:

"Hush, my own! If a single nerve of my body shrank from your little hand, find it and I'll tear it out!"

She withdrew herself slowly from his embrace, and brushed the tears from her eyes with a little movement of quiet resignation:

"It's all right. I'm calm again and it's all over. I won't mind now if you shrink a little. I'm really glad that you did. It needed just that to convince me that your father was right. Our love would end in the ruin of your life.

I see it clearly now. It would become to you at last a conscious degradation. *That* I couldn't endure."

"I have your solemn vow," he interrupted impatiently, "you're mine! I'll not give you up!"

She looked at him sadly:

"But I'm going, dear, in a few minutes. You can't hold me—now that I know it's for the best."

"You can't mean this?"

She clung to his hand and pressed it with cruel force:

"Don't think it isn't hard. All my life I've been a wistful beggar, eager and hungry for love. In your arms I had forgotten the long days of misery. I've been happy—perfectly, divinely happy! It will be hard, the darkness and the loneliness again. But I can't drag you down, my sweetheart, my hero! Your life must be big and brilliant. I've dreamed it thus. You shall be a man among men, the world's great men—and so I am going out of your life!"

"You shall not!" the boy cried fiercely. "I tell you I don't believe this hideous thing—it's a lie, I tell you —it's a lie, and I don't care who says it! Nothing shall separate us now. I'll go with you to the ends of the earth and if you sink into hell, I'll follow you there, lift you in my arms and fight my way back through its flames!"

She smiled at him tenderly:

"It's beautiful to hear you say that, dearest, but our dream has ended!"

She stooped, took up the bag and coat, paused and looked into his face with the hunger and longing of a life burning in her eyes:

"But I shall keep the memory of every sweet and foolish word you have spoken, every tone of your voice, every line of your face, every smile and trick of your lips and eyes! I know them all. The old darkness will not be the same. I have loved and I have lived. A divine fire has been kindled in my soul. I can go into no world so far I shall not feel the warmth of your love, your kisses on my lips, your strong arms pressing me to your heart—the one true, manly heart that has loved me. I shall see your face forever though I see it through a mist of tears—good-by!"

The last word was the merest whisper.

The boy sprang toward her:

"I won't say it—I won't—I won't!"

"But you must!"

He opened his arms and called in tones of compelling anguish:

"Helen!"

The girl's lips trembled, her eyes grew dim, her fingers were locked in a cruel grip trying to hold the bag which slipped to the floor. And then with a cry she threw herself madly into his arms:

"Oh, I can't give you up, dearest! I can't—I've tried—but I can't!"

He held her clasped without a word, stroking her hair, kissing it tenderly and murmuring little inarticulate cries of love.

Norton suddenly appeared in the door, his face blanched with horror. With a rush of his tall figure he was by their side and hurled them apart:

"My God! Do you know what you're doing?"

He turned on Tom, his face white with pain:

"I forbid you to ever see or speak to this girl again!"

Tom sprang back and confronted his father:

"Forbid!"

Helen lifted her head:

"He's right, Tom."

"Yes," the father said with bated breath, "in the name of the law—by all that's pure and holy, by the memory of the mother who bore you and the angels who guard the sanctity of every home, I forbid you!"

The boy squared himself and drew his figure to its full height:

"You're my father! But I want you to remember that I'm of age. I'm twenty-two years old and I'm a man! Forbid? How dare you use such words to me in the presence of the woman I love?"

Norton's voice dropped to pitiful tenderness:

"You—you—don't understand, my boy. Helen knows that—I'm right. We have talked it over. She has agreed to go at once. The carriage will be at the door in a moment. She can never see you again"—he paused and lifted his hand solemnly above Tom's head—"and in the name of Almighty God I warn you not to attempt to follow her——"

He turned quickly, picked up the fallen bag and coat and added:

"I'll explain all to you at last if I must."

"Well, I won't hear it!" Tom cried in rage. "I'm a free agent! I won't take such orders from you or any other man!"

The sound of the carriage wheels were heard on the graveled drive at the door.

Norton turned to Helen and took her arm:

"Come, Helen, the carriage is waiting."

With a sudden leap Tom was by his side, tore the bag and coat from his hand, hurled them to the floor and turned on his father with blazing eyes:

"Now, look here, Dad, this thing's going too far! You can't bulldoze me. There's one right no American man ever yields without the loss of his self-respect—the right to choose the woman he loves. When Helen leaves this house, I go with her! I'm running this thing now—your carriage needn't wait."

With sudden decision he rushed to the porch and and called:

"Driver!"

"Yassah."

"Go back to your stable—you're not wanted."

"Yassah."

"I'll send for you if I want you—wait a minute till I tell you."

Norton's head drooped and he blindly grasped a chair.

Helen watched him with growing pity, drew near and said softly:

"I'm sorry, major, to have brought you this pain——"

"You promised to go without seeing him!" he exclaimed bitterly.

"I tried. I only gave up for a moment. I fought bravely. Remember now in all you say to Tom that I am going—that I know I must go——"

"Yes, I understand, child," he replied brokenly, "and my heart goes out to you. Mine is heavy to-night with a burden greater than I can bear. You're a brave little girl. The fault isn't yours—it's mine. I've got to face it now"—he paused and looked at her tenderly. "You say that you've been lonely—well, remember that in all your orphan life you never saw an hour as lonely as the one my soul is passing through now! The loneliest road across this earth is the way of sin."

Helen watched him in amazement: "The way of sin—why——"

Tom's brusque entrance interrupted her. With quick, firm decision he took her arm and led her to the door opening on the hall:

"Wait for me in your room, dear," he said quietly. "I have something to say to my father."

She looked at him timidly:

"You won't forget that he is your father, and loves you better than his own life?"

"I'll not forget."

She started with sudden alarm and whispered:

"You haven't got the pistol that you brought home to-day from the campaign, have you?"

"Surely, dear——"

"Give it to me!" she demanded.

"No."

"Why?" she asked pleadingly.

"I've too much self-respect."

She looked into his clear eyes:

"Forgive me, dear, but I was so frightened just now. You were so violent. I never saw you like that before. I was afraid something might happen in a moment of blind passion, and I could never lift my head again——"

"I'll not forget," he broke in, "if my father does. Run now, dear, I'll join you in a few minutes."

A pressure of the hand, a look of love, and she was gone. The boy closed the door, quickly turned and faced his father.

Chapter XXIV

Father and Son

Norton had ignored the scene between Helen and Tom and his stunned mind was making a desperate fight to prepare for the struggle that was inevitable.

The thing that gave him fresh courage was the promise the girl had repeated that she would go. Somehow he had grown to trust her implicitly. He hadn't time as yet to realize the pity and pathos of such a trust in such an hour. He simply believed that she would keep her word. He had to win his fight now with the boy without the surrender of his secret. Could he do it? It was doubtful, but he was going to try. His back was to the wall.

Tom took another step into the room and the father turned, drew his tall figure erect in an instinctive movement of sorrowful dignity and reserve and walked to the table.

All traces of anger had passed from the boy's handsome young face and a look of regret had taken its place. He began speaking very quietly and reverently:

"Now, Dad, we must face this thing. It's a tragedy for you perhaps——"

The father interrupted:

"How big a tragedy, my son, I hope that you may never know——"

"Anyhow," Tom went on frankly, "I am ashamed of the way I acted. But you're a manly man and you can understand."

"Yes."

"I know that all you've done is because you love me——"

"How deeply, you can never know."

"I'm sorry if I forgot for a moment the respect I owe you, the reverence and love I hold for you—I've always been proud of you, Dad—of your stainless name, of the birthright you have given me—you know this——"

"Yet it's good to hear you say it!"

"And now that I've said this, you'd as well know first as last that any argument about Helen is idle between us. I'm not going to give up the woman I love!"

"Ah, my boy——"

Tom lifted his hand emphatically:

"It's no use! You needn't tell me that her blood is tainted—I don't believe it!"

The father came closer:

"You *do* believe it! In the first mad riot of passion you're only trying to fool yourself."

"It's unthinkable, I tell you! and I've made my decision"—he paused a moment and then demanded:

"How do you know her blood is tainted?"

The father answered firmly:

"I have the word both of her mother and father."

"Well, I won't take their word. Some natures are their own defense. On them no stain can rest, and I stake my life on Helen's!"

"My boy——"

"Oh, I know what you're going to say—as a theory it's quite correct. But it's one thing to accept a theory, another to meet the thing in your own heart before God alone with your life in your hands."

"What do you mean by that?" the father asked savagely.

"That for the past hour I've been doing some thinking on my own account."

"That's just what you haven't been doing. You haven't thought at all. If you had, you'd know that you can't marry this girl. Come, come, my boy, remember that you have reason and because you have this power that's bigger than all passion, all desire, all impulse, you're a man, not a brute——"

"All right," the boy broke in excitedly, "submit it to reason! I'll stand the test—it's more than you can do. I love this girl—she's my mate. She loves me and I am hers. Haven't I taken my stand squarely on Nature and her highest law?"

"No!"

"What's higher? Social fictions—prejudices?"

The father lifted his head:

"Prejudices! You know as well as I that the white man's instinct of racial purity is not prejudice, but God's first law of life—the instinct of self-preservation! The lion does not mate with the jackal!"

The boy flushed angrily:

"The girl I love is as fair as you or I."

"Even so," was the quick reply, "we inherit ninety per cent of character from our dead ancestors! Born of a single black progenitor, she is still a negress. Change every black skin in America to-morrow to the white of a lily and we'd yet have ten million negroes—ten million negroes whose blood relatives are living in Africa the life of a savage."

"Granted that what you say it true—and I refuse to believe it—I still have the right to live my own life in my own way."

"No man has the right to live life in his own way if by that way he imperil millions."

"And whom would I imperil?"

"The future American. No white man ever lived who desired to be a negro. Every negro longs to be a white man. No black man has ever added an iota to the knowledge of the world of any value to humanity. In Helen's body flows sixteen million tiny drops of blood—one million black—poisoned by the inheritance of thousands of years of savage cruelty, ignorance, slavery and superstition. The life of generations are bound up in you. In you are wrapt the onward years. Man's place in nature is no longer a myth. You are bound by the laws of heredity—laws that demand a nobler not a baser race of men! Shall we improve the breed of horses and degrade our men? You have no right to damn a child with such a legacy!"

"But I tell you I'm not trying to—I refuse to see in her this stain!"

The father strode angrily to the other side of the room in an effort to control his feelings:

"Because you refuse to think, my boy!" he cried in agony. "I tell you, you can't defy these laws! They are eternal—never new, never old—true a thousand years ago, to-day, to-morrow and on a million years, when this earth is thrown, a burnt cinder, into God's dust heap. I can't tell you what I feel—it strangles me!"

"No, and I can't understand it. I feel one thing, the touch of the hand of the woman I love; hear one thing, the music of her voice——"

"And in that voice, my boy, I hear the crooning of a savage mother! But yesterday our negroes were brought here from the West Soudan, black, chattering savages, nearer the anthropoid ape than any other living creature. And you would dare give to a child such a mother? Who is this dusky figure of the forest with whom you would cross your blood? In old Andy there you see him to-day, a creature half child, half animal. For thousands of years beyond the seas he stole his food, worked his wife, sold his child, and ate his brother—great God, could any tragedy be more hideous than our degradation at last to his racial level!"

"It can't happen! It's a myth!"

"It's the most dangerous thing that threatens the future!" the father cried with desperate earnestness. "A pint of ink can make black gallons of water. The barriers once down, ten million negroes can poison the source of life and character for a hundred million whites. This nation is great for one reason only—because of the breed of men who created the Republic! Oh, my boy, when you look on these walls at your fathers, don't you see this, don't you feel this, don't you know this?"

Tom shook his head:

"To-night I feel and know one thing. I love her! We don't choose whom we love——"

"Ah, but if we are more than animals, if we reason, we do choose whom we marry! Marriage is not merely a question of personal whim, impulse or passion. It's the one divine law on which human society rests. There are always men who hear the call of the Beast and fall below their ideals, who trail the divine standards of life in the dust as they slink under the cover of night——"

"At least, I'm not trying to do that!"

"No, worse! You would trample them under your feet at noon in defiance of the laws of man and God! You're insane for the moment. You're mad with passion. You're not really listening to me at all—I feel it!"

"Perhaps I'm not——"

"Yet you don't question the truth of what I've said. You can't question it. You just stand here blind and maddened by desire, while I beg and plead, saying in your heart: 'I want this woman and I'm going to have her.' You've never faced the question that she's a negress—you can't face it, and yet I tell you that I know it's true!"

The boy turned on his father and studied him angrily for a moment, his blue eyes burning into his, his face flushed and his lips curled with the slightest touch of incredulity:

"And do you really believe all you've been saying to me?"

"As I believe in God!"

With a quick, angry gesture he faced his father:

"Well, you've had a mighty poor way of showing it! If you really believed all you've been saying to me, you wouldn't stop to eat or sleep until every negro is removed from physical contact with the white race. And yet on the day that I was born you placed me in the arms of a negress! The first human face on which I looked was hers. I grew at her breast. You let her love me and teach me to love her. You keep only negro servants. I grow up with them, fall into their lazy ways, laugh at their antics and see life through their eyes, and now that my life touches theirs at a thousand points of contact, you tell me that we must live together and yet a gulf separates us! Why haven't you realized this before? If what you say about Helen is true, in God's name—I ask it out of a heart quivering with anguish—why haven't you realized it before? I demand an answer! I have the right to know!"

Norton's head was lowered while the boy poured out his passionate protest and he lifted it at the end with a look of despair:

"You have the right to know, my boy. But the South has not a valid answer to your cry. The Negro is not here by my act or will, and their continued presence is a constant threat against our civilization. Equality is the law of life and we dare not grant it to the negro unless we are willing to descend to his racial level. We cannot lift him to ours. This truth forced me into a new life purpose twenty years ago. The campaign I have just fought and won is the first step in a larger movement to find an answer to your question in the complete separation of the races—and nothing is surer than that the South will maintain the purity of her home! It's as fixed as her faith in God!"

The boy was quiet a moment and looked at the tall figure with a queer expression:

"Has she maintained it?"

"Yes."

"Is her home life clean?"

"Yes."

"And these millions of children born in the shadows—these mulattoes?"

The older man's lips trembled and his brow clouded:

"The lawless have always defied the law, my son, North, South, East and West, but they have never defended their crimes. Dare to do this thing that's in your heart and you make of crime a virtue and ask God's blessing on it. The difference between the two things is as deep and wide as the gulf between heaven and hell."

"My marriage to Helen will be the purest and most solemn act of my life——"

"Silence, sir!" the father thundered in a burst of uncontrollable passion, as he turned suddenly on him, his face blanched and his whole body trembling. "I tell you once for all that your marriage to this girl is a physical and moral impossibility! And I refuse to argue with you a question that's beyond all argument!"

The two men glared at each other in a duel of wills in which steel cut steel without a tremor of yielding. And then with a sudden flash of anger, Tom turned on his heel crying:

"All right, then!"

With swift, determined step he moved toward the door. The father grasped the corner of the table for support:

"Tom!"

His hands were extended in pitiful appeal when the boy stopped as if in deep study, turned, looked at him, and walked deliberately back:

"I'm going to ask you some personal questions!"

In spite of his attempt at self-control, Norton's face paled. He drew himself up with an attempt at dignified adjustment to the new situation, but his hands were trembling as he nervously repeated:

"Personal questions?"

"Yes. There's something very queer about your position. Your creed forbids you to receive a negro as a social equal?"

"Yes."

The boy suddenly lifted his head:

"Why did you bring Helen into this house?"

"I didn't bring her."

"You didn't invite her?"

"No."

"She says that you did."

"She thought so."

"She got an invitation?"

"Yes."

"Signed with your name?"

"Yes, yes."

"Who dared to write such a letter without your knowledge?"

"I can't tell you that."

"I demand it!"

Norton struggled between anger and fear and finally answered in measured tones:

"It was forged by an enemy who wished to embarrass me in this campaign."

"You know who wrote it?"

"I suspect."

"You don't *know*?"

"I said, I suspect," was the angry retort.

"And you didn't kill him?"

"In this campaign my hands were tied."

The boy, watching furtively his father's increasing nervousness and anger, continued his questions in a slower, cooler tone:

"When you returned and found her here, you could have put her out?"

"Yes," Norton answered tremblingly, "and I ought to have done it!"

"But you didn't?"

"No."

"Why?"

The father fumbled his watch chain, moved uneasily and finally said with firmness:

"I am Helen's guardian!"

The boy lifted his brows:

"You are supposed to be his attorney only. Why did you, of all men on earth, accept such a position?"

"I felt that I had to."

"And the possibility of my meeting this girl never occurred to you? You, who have dinned into my ears from childhood that I should keep myself clean from the touch of such pollution—why did you take the risk?"

"A sense of duty to one to whom I felt bound."

"Duty?"

"Yes."

"It must have been deep—what duty?"

Norton lifted his hand in a movement of wounded pride:

"My boy!"

"Come, come, Dad, don't shuffle; this thing's a matter of life and death with me and you must be fair——"

"I'm trying——"

"I want to know why you are Helen's guardian, exactly why. We must face each other to-day with souls bare—why are you her guardian?"

"I—I—can't tell you."

"You've got to tell me!"

"You must trust me in this, my son!"

"I won't do it!" the boy cried, trembling with passion that brought the tears blinding to his eyes. "We're not father and son now. We face each other man to man with two lives at stake—hers and mine! You can't ask me to trust you! I won't do it—I've got to know!"

The father turned away:

"I can't betray this secret even to you, my boy."

"Does any one else share it?"

"Why do you use that queer tone? What do you mean?" The father's last question was barely breathed.

"Nothing," the boy answered with a toss of his head. "Does any one in this house suspect it?"

"Possibly."

Again Tom paused, watching keenly:

"On the day you returned and found Helen here, you quarrelled with Cleo?"

Norton wheeled with sudden violence:

"We won't discuss this question further, sir!"

"Yes, we will," was the steady answer through set teeth. "Haven't you been afraid of Cleo?"

The father's eyes were looking into his now with a steady stare:

"I refuse to be cross-examined, sir!"

Tom ignored his answer:

"Hasn't Cleo been blackmailing you?"

"No—no."

The boy held his father's gaze until it wavered, and then in cold tones said:

"You are not telling me the truth!"

Norton flinched as if struck:

"Do you know what you are saying. Have you lost your senses?"

Tom held his ground with dogged coolness:

"*Have* you told me the truth?"

"Yes."

"It's a lie!"

The words were scarcely spoken when Norton's clenched fist struck him a blow full in the face.

A wild cry of surprise, inarticulate in fury, came from the boy's lips as he staggered against the table. He glared at his father, drew back a step, his lips twitching, his breath coming in gasps, and suddenly felt for the revolver in his pocket.

With a start of horror the father cried:

"My boy!"

The hand dropped limp, he leaned against the table for support and sobbed:

"O God! Let me die!"

Norton rushed to his side, his voice choking with grief:

"Tom, listen!"

"I won't listen!" he hissed. "I never want to hear the sound of your voice again!"

"Don't say that—you don't mean it!" the father pleaded.

"I do mean it!"

Norton touched his arm tenderly:

"You can't mean it, Tom. You're all I've got in the world. You mustn't say that. Forgive me—I was mad. I didn't know what I was doing. I didn't mean to strike you. I forgot for a moment that you're a man, proud and sensitive as I am——"

The boy tore himself free from his touch and crossed the room with quick, angry stride and turned:

"Well, you'd better not forget it again"—he paused and drew himself erect. "You're my father, but I tell you to your face that I hate and loathe you——"

The silver-gray head drooped:

"That I should have lived to hear it!"

"And I want you to understand one thing," Tom went on fiercely, "if an angel from heaven told me that Helen's blood was tainted, I'd demand proofs! You have shown none, and I'm not going to give up the woman I love!"

Norton supported himself by the table and felt his way along its edges as if blinded. His eyes were set with a half-mad stare as he gripped Tom's shoulders:

"I love you, my boy, with a love beyond your ken, a love that can be fierce and cruel when God calls, and sooner than see you marry this girl, I'll kill you with my own hands if I must!"

The answer came slowly:

"And you can't guess what's happened?"

"Guess—what's—happened!" the father repeated in a whisper. "What do you mean?"

"That I'm married already!"

With hands uplifted, his features convulsed, the father fell back, his voice a low piteous shriek:

"Merciful God!—No!"

"Married an hour before you dragged me away in that campaign!" he shouted in triumph. "I knew you'd never consent and so I took matters into my own hands!"

With a leap Norton grasped the boy again and shook him madly:

"Married already? It's not true, I tell you! It's not true. You're lying to me—lying to gain time—it's not true!"

"You wish me to swear it?"

"Silence, sir!" the father cried in solemn tones. "You are my son—this is my house—I order you to be silent!"

"Before God, I swear it's true! Helen is my lawful——"

"Don't say it! It's false—you lie, I tell you!" Again the father shook him with cruel violence, his eyes staring with the glitter of a maniac.

Tom seized the trembling hands and threw them from his shoulders with a quick movement of anger:

"If that's all you've got to say, sir, excuse me, I'll go to my wife!"

He wheeled, slammed the door and was gone.

The father stared a moment, stunned, looked around blankly, placed his hands over his ears and held them, crying:

"God have mercy!"

He rushed to a window and threw it open. The band was playing "For He's a Jolly Good Fellow!" The mocking strains rolled over his prostrate soul. He leaned heavily against the casement and groaned:

"My God!"

He slammed the sash, staggered back into the room, lifted his eyes in a leaden stare at the portrait over the mantel, and then rushed toward it with uplifted arms and streaming eyes:

"It's not true, dearest! Don't believe it—it's not true, I tell you! It's not true!"

The voice sank into inarticulate sobs, he reeled and fell, a limp, black heap on the floor.

Chapter XXV

The One Chance

The dim light began to creep into the darkened brain at last. Norton's eyes opened wider and the long arms felt their way on the floor until they touched a rug and then a chair. He tried to think what had happened and why he was lying there. It seemed a dream, half feverish, half restful. His head was aching and he was very tired.

"What's the matter?" he murmured, unable to lift his head.

He was whirling through space again and the room faded. Once before in his life had he been knocked insensible. From the trenches before Petersburg in the last days of the war he had led his little band of less than five hundred ragged, half-starved tatterdemalions in a mad charge against the line in front. A bomb from a battery on a hilltop exploded directly before them. He had been thrown into the air and landed on a heap of dead bodies, bruised and stunned into insensibility. He had waked feeling the dead limbs and wondering if they were his own.

He rubbed his hands now, first over his head, and then over each limb, to find if all were there. He felt his body to see if a bomb had torn part of it away.

And then the light of memory suddenly flashed into the darkened mind and he drew himself to his knees and fumbled his way to a chair.

"Married? Married already!" he gasped. "O, God, it can't be true! And he said, 'married an hour before you dragged me away in that campaign'"—it was too hideous! He laughed in sheer desperation and again his brain refused to work. He pressed his hands to his forehead and looked about the room, rose, staggered to the bell and rang for Andy.

When his black face appeared, he lifted his bloodshot eyes and said feebly:

"Whiskey——"

The negro bowed:

"Yassah!"

He pulled himself together and tried to walk. He could only reel from one piece of furniture to the next. His head was on fire. He leaned again against the mantel for support and dropped his head on his arm in utter weariness:

"I must think! I must think!"

Slowly the power to reason returned.

"What can I do? What can I do?" he kept repeating mechanically, until the only chance of escape crept slowly into his mind. He grasped it with feverish hope.

If Tom had married but an hour before leaving on that campaign, he hadn't returned until to-day. But had he? It was, of course, a physical possibility. From the nearby counties, he could have ridden a swift horse through the night, reached home and returned the next day without his knowing it. It was possible, but not probable. He wouldn't believe it until he had to.

If he had married in haste the morning he had left town and had only rejoined Helen to-night, it was no marriage. It was a ceremony that had no meaning. In law it was void and could be annulled immediately. But if he were really married in all that word means—his mind stopped short and refused to go on.

He would cross that bridge when he came to it. But he must find out at once and he must know before he saw Tom again.

His brain responded with its old vigor under the pressure of the new crisis. One by one his powers returned and his mind was deep in its tragic problem when Andy entered the room with a tray on which stood a decanter of whiskey, a glass of water and two small empty glasses.

The negro extended the tray. Norton was staring into space and paid no attention.

Andy took one of the empty glasses and clicked it against the other. There was still no sign of recognition until he pushed the tray against Norton's arm and cleared his throat:

"Ahem! Ahem!"

The dazed man turned slowly and looked at the tray and then at the grinning negro:

"What's this?"

Andy's face kindled with enthusiasm:

"Dat is moonshine, sah—de purest mountain dew—yassah!"

"Whiskey?"

"Yassah," was the astonished reply, "de whiskey you jis ring fer, sah!"

"Take it back!"

Andy could not believe his ears. The major was certainly in a queer mood. Was he losing his mind? There was nothing to do but obey. He bowed and turned away:

"Yassah."

Norton watched him with a dazed look and cried suddenly:

"Where are you going?"

"Back!"

"Stop!"

Andy stopped with a sudden jerk:

"Yassah!"

"Put that tray down on the table!"

The negro obeyed but watched his master out of the corners of his eye:

"Yassah!"

Again Norton forgot Andy's existence, his eyes fixed in space, his mind in a whirl of speculation in which he felt his soul and body sinking deeper. The negro was watching him with increasing suspicion and fear as he turned his head in the direction of the table.

"What are you standing there for?" he asked sharply.

"You say stop, sah."

"Well, get away—get out!" Norton cried with sudden anger.

Andy backed rapidly:

"Yassah!"

As he reached the doorway Norton's command rang so sharply that the negro spun around on one foot:

"Wait!"

"Y—yas—sah!"

The master took a step toward the trembling figure with an imperious gesture:

"Come here!"

Andy approached gingerly, glancing from side to side for the best way of retreat in case of emergency:

"What's the matter with you?" Norton demanded.

Andy laughed feebly:

"I—I—I dunno, sah; I wuz des wonderin' what's de matter wid you, sah!"

"Tell me!"

The negro's teeth were chattering as he glanced up:

"Yassah! I tell all I know, sah!"

Norton fixed him with a stern look:

"Has Tom been back here during the past four weeks?"

"Nasah!" was the surprised answer, "he bin wid you, sah!"

The voice softened to persuasive tones:

"He hasn't slipped back here even for an hour since I've been gone?"

"I nebber seed him!"

"I didn't ask you," Norton said threateningly, "whether you'd 'seed' him"—he paused and dropped each word with deliberate emphasis—"I asked you if you knew whether he'd been here?"

Andy mopped his brow and glanced at his inquisitor with terror:

"Nasah, I don't know nuttin', sah!"

"Haven't you lied to me?"

"Yassah! yassah," the negro replied in friendly conciliation. "I has pér-var-i-cated sometimes—but I sho is tellin' you de truf dis time, sah!"

The master glared at him a moment and suddenly sprang at his throat, both hands clasping his neck with a strangling grip. Andy dropped spluttering to his knees.

"You're lying to me!" Norton growled. "Out with the truth now"—his grip tightened—"out with it, or I'll choke it out of you!"

Andy grasped the tightening fingers and drew them down:

"Fer Gawd's sake, major, doan' do dat!"

"Has Tom been back here during the past weeks to see Miss Helen?"

Andy struggled with the desperate fingers:

"Doan' do dat, major—doan' do dat! I ain't holdin' nuttin' back—I let it all out, sah!"

The grip slackened:

"Then out with the whole truth!"

"Yassah. Des tell me what ye wants me ter say, sah, an' I sho say hit!"

"Bah! You miserable liar!" Norton cried in disgust, hurling him to the floor, and striding angrily from the room. "You're all in this thing, all of you! You're all in it—all in it!"

Andy scrambled to his feet and rushed to the window in time to see him hurry down the steps and disappear in the shadows of the lawn. He stood watching with open mouth and staring eyes:

"Well, 'fore de Lawd, ef he ain't done gone plum crazy!"

Chapter XXVI

Between Two Fires

So intent was Andy's watch on the lawn, so rapt his wonder and terror at the sudden assault, he failed to hear Cleo's step as she entered the room, walked to his side and laid her hand on his shoulder:

"Andy——"

With a loud groan he dropped to his knees:

"De Lawd save me!"

Cleo drew back with amazement at the prostrate figure:

"What on earth's the matter?"

"Oh—oh, Lawd," he shivered, scrambling to his feet and mopping his brow. "Lordy, I thought de major got me dat time sho!"

"You thought the major had you?" Cleo cried incredulously.

Andy ran back to the window and looked out again:

"Yassam—yassam! De major try ter kill me—he's er regular maniacker—gone wild——"

"What about?"

The black hands went to his throat:

"Bout my windpipes, 'pears like!"

"What did he do?"

"Got me in de *gills*!"

"Why?"

"Dunno," was the whispered answer as he peered out the window. "He asked me if Mr. Tom been back here in de past fo' weeks——"

"Asked if Tom had been back here?"

"Yassam!"

"What a fool question, when he's had the boy with him every day! He must have gone crazy."

"Yassam!" Andy agreed with unction as he turned back into the room and threw both hands high above his head in wild gestures. "He say we wuz all in it! Dat what he say—we wuz all in it! *All* in it!"

"In what?"

"Gawd knows!" he cried, as his hands again went to his neck to feel if anything were broken, "Gawd knows, but he sho wuz gittin' inside er me!"

Cleo spoke with stern appeal:

"Well, you're a man; you'll know how to defend yourself next time, won't you?"

"Yassam!—yas, m'am!" Andy answered boldly. "Oh, I fit 'im! Don't you think I didn't fight him! I fit des lak er wild-cat—yassam!"

The woman's eyes narrowed and her voice purred:

"You're going to stand by me now?"

"Dat I is!" was the brave response.

"You'll do anything for me?"

"Yassam!"

"Defend me with your life if the major attacks me to-night?"

"Dat I will!"

Cleo leaned close:

"You'll die for me?"

"Yassam! Yassam—I'll *die* fer you—I'll die fer ye; of cose I'll *die* for ye! B-b-but fer Gawd's sake what ye want wid er dead nigger?"

Andy leaped back in terror as Norton's tall figure suddenly appeared in the door, his rumpled iron-gray hair gleaming in the shadows, his eyes flashing with an unnatural light. He quickly crossed the room and lifted his index finger toward Cleo:

"Just a word with you——"

The woman's hands met nervously, and she glanced at Andy:

"Very well, but I want a witness. Andy can stay."

Norton merely glanced at the negro "Get out!"

"Yassah!"

"Stay where you are!" Cleo commanded.

"Y—yassam"—Andy stammered, halting.

"Get out!" Norton growled.

Andy jumped into the doorway at a single bound:

"Done out, sah!"

The major lifted his hand and the negro stopped:

"Tell Minerva I want to see her."

Andy hastened toward the hall, the whites of his eyes shining:

"Yassah, but she ain't in de kitchen, sah!"

"Find her and bring her here!" Norton thundered. His words rang like the sudden peal of a gun at close quarters.

Andy jumped:

"Yassah, yassah, I fetch her! I fetch her!" As he flew through the door he repeated humbly:

"I fetch her, right away, sah—right away, sah!"

Cleo watched his cowardly desertion with lips curled in scorn.

Chapter XXVII

A Surprise

For a while Norton stood with folded arms gazing at Cleo, his eyes smouldering fires of wonder and loathing. The woman was trembling beneath his fierce scrutiny, but he evidently had not noted the fact. His mind was busy with a bigger problem of character and the possible depths to which a human being might fall and still retain the human form. He was wondering how a man of his birth and breeding, the heir to centuries of culture and refinement, of high thinking and noble aspirations, could ever have sunk to the level of this yellow animal—this bundle of rags and coarse flesh! It was incredible! His loathing for her was surpassed by one thing only—his hatred of himself.

He was free in this moment as never before. In the fearlessness of death soul and body stood erect and gazed calmly out on time and eternity.

There was one thing about the woman he couldn't understand. That she was without moral scruple—that she was absolutely unmoral in her fundamental being—he could easily believe. In fact, he could believe nothing else. That she would not hesitate to defy every law of God or man to gain her end, he never doubted for a moment. But that a creature of her cunning and trained intelligence could deliberately destroy herself by such an act of mad revenge was unreasonable. He began dimly to suspect that her plans had gone awry. How completely she had been crushed by her own trap he could not yet guess.

She was struggling frantically now to regain her composure but his sullen silence and his piercing eyes were telling on her nerves. She was on the verge of screaming in his face when he said in low, intense tones:

"You did get even with me—didn't you?"

"Yes!"

"I didn't think *you* quite capable of this!"

His words were easier to bear than silence. She felt an instant relief and pulled herself together with a touch of bravado:

"And now that you see I am, what are you going to do about it?"

"That's my secret," was the quiet reply. "There's just one thing that puzzles me!"

"Indeed!"

"How you could willfully and deliberately do this beastly thing?"

"For one reason only, I threw them together and brought about their love affair——"

"Revenge—yes," Norton interrupted, "but the boy—you don't hate him—you can't. You've always loved him as if he were your own——"

"Well, what of it?"

"I'm wondering——"

"What?"

His voice was low, vibrant but quiet:

"Why, if your mother instincts have always been so powerful and you've loved my boy with such devotion"—the tones quickened to sudden menace—"why you were so willing to give up your own child that day twenty years ago?"

He held her gaze until her own fell:

"I—I—don't understand you," she said falteringly.

He seized her with violence and drew her squarely before him:

"Look at me!" he cried fiercely. "Look me in the face!" He paused until she slowly lifted her eyes to his and finally glared at him with hate. "I want to see your soul now if you've got one. There's just one chance and I'm clutching at that as a drowning man a straw."

"Well?" she asked defiantly.

Norton's words were hurled at her, each one a solid shot:

"Would you have given up that child without a struggle—if she had really been your own?"

"Why—what—do you—mean?" Cleo asked, her eyes shifting.

"You know what I mean. If Helen is really your child, why did you give her up so easily that day?"

"Why?" she repeated blankly.

"Answer my question!"

With an effort she recovered her composure:

"You know why! I was mad. I was a miserable fool. I did it because you asked it. I did it to please you, and I've cursed myself for it ever since."

Norton's grip slowly relaxed, and he turned thoughtfully away. The woman's hand went instinctively to the bruises he had left on her arms as she stepped back nearer the door and watched him furtively.

"It's possible, yes!" he cried turning again to face her suddenly. "And yet if you are human how could you dare defy the laws of man and God to bring about this marriage?"

"It's not a question of marriage yet," she sneered. "You've simply got to acknowledge her, that's all. That's why I brought her here. That's why I've helped their love affair. You're in my power now. You've got to tell Tom that Helen is my daughter, and yours—his half sister! Now that they're in love with one another you've got to do it!"

Norton drew back in amazement:

"You mean to tell me that you don't know that they are married?"

With a cry of surprise and terror, the woman leaped to his side, her voice a whisper:

"Married? Who says they are married?"

"Tom has just said so."

"But they are not married!" she cried hysterically. "They can't marry!"

Norton fixed her with a keen look:

"They are married!"

The woman wrung her hands nervously:

"But you can separate them if you tell them the truth. That's all you've got to do. Tell them now—tell them at once!"

Never losing the gaze with which he was piercing her soul Norton said in slow menacing tones:

"There's another way!"

He turned from her suddenly and walked toward the desk. She followed a step, trembling.

"Another way"—she repeated.

Norton turned:

"An old way brave men have always known—I'll take it if I must!"

Chilled with fear Cleo glanced in a panic about the room and spoke feebly:

"You—you—don't mean——"

Minerva and Andy entered cautiously as Norton answered:

"No matter what I mean, it's enough for you to know that I'm free—free from you—I breathe clean air at last!"

Minerva shot Cleo a look:

"Praise God!"

Cleo extended a hand in pleading:

"Major——"

"That will do now!" he said sternly. "Go!"

Cleo turned hurriedly to the door leading toward the stairs.

"Not that way!" Norton called sharply. "Tom has no further need of your advice. Go to the servants' quarters and stay there. I am the master of this house to-night!"

Cleo slowly crossed the room and left through the door leading to the kitchen, watching Norton with terror. Minerva broke into a loud laugh and Andy took refuge behind her ample form.

Chapter XXVIII

Via Dolorosa

Minerva was still laughing at the collapse of her enemy and Andy sheltering himself behind her when a sharp call cut her laughter short:

"Minerva!"

"Yassah"—she answered soberly.

"You have been a faithful servant to me," Norton began, "you have never lied——"

"An' I ain't gwine ter begin now, sah."

He searched her black face keenly:

"Did Tom slip back here to see Miss Helen while I was away on this last trip?"

Minerva looked at Andy, fumbled with her apron, started to speak, hesitated and finally admitted feebly:

"Yassah!"

Andy's eyes fairly bulged:

"De Lordy, major, I didn't know dat, sah!"

Norton glanced at him:

"Shut up!"

"You ain't gwine ter be hard on 'em, major?" Minerva pleaded.

He ignored her interruption and went on evenly:

"How many times did he come?"

"Twice, sah."

"He sho come in de night time den!" Andy broke in. "I nebber seed 'im once!"

Norton bent close:

"How long did he stay?"

Minerva fidgeted, hesitated again and finally said:

"Once he stay about er hour——"

"And the other time?"

She looked in vain for a way of escape, the perspiration standing in beads on her shining black face:

"He stay all night, sah."

A moment of stillness followed. Norton's eyes closed, and his face became a white mask. He breathed deeply and then spoke quietly:

"You—you knew they were married?"

"Yassah!" was the quick reply. "I seed 'em married. Miss Helen axed me, sah."

Andy lifted his hands in solemn surprise and walled his eyes at Minerva:

"Well, 'fore Gawd!"

Another moment of silence and Andy's mouth was still open with wonder when a call like the crack of a revolver suddenly rang through the room:

"Andy!"

The negro dropped to his knees and lifted his hands:

"Don't do nuttin' ter me, sah! 'Fore de Lawd, major, I 'clare I nebber knowed it! Dey fool me, sah—I'd a tole you sho!"

Norton frowned:

"Shut your mouth and get up."

"Yassah!" Andy cried. "Hit's shet an' I'se up!"

He scrambled to his feet and watched his master.

"You and Minerva go down that back stairway into the basement, fasten the windows and lock the doors."

Andy's eyes were two white moons in the shadows as he cried through chattering teeth:

"G—g—odder mighty—what—what's de matter, major?"

"Do as I tell you, quick!"

Andy dodged and leaped toward the door:

"R—right away, sah!"

"Pay no attention to anything Mr. Tom may say to you——"

"Nasah," Andy gasped. "I pay no 'tension ter nobody, sah!"

"When you've fastened everything below, do the same on this floor and come back here—I want you."

"Y-y-yas—sah! R-r-r-right a-way, sah!"

Andy backed out, beckoning frantically to Minerva. She ignored him and watched Norton as he turned toward a window and looked vaguely out. As Andy continued his frantic calls she slipped to the doorway and whispered:

"G'long! I be dar in er minute. You po' fool, you can't talk nohow. You're skeered er de major. I'm gwine do my duty now, I'm gwine ter tell him sumfin' quick——"

Norton wheeled on her with sudden fury:

"Do as I tell you! Do as I tell you!"

Minerva dodged at each explosion, backing away. She paused and extended her hand pleadingly:

"Can't I put in des one little word, sah?"

"Not another word!" he thundered, advancing on her—"Go!"

"Yassah!"

"Go! I tell you!"

Dodging again, she hurried below to join Andy. Norton turned back into the room and stood staring at something that gleamed with sinister brightness from the top of the little writing desk. An electric lamp with crimson shade seemed to focus every ray of light on the shining steel and a devil in the shadows pointed a single finger and laughed:

"It's ready—just where you laid it!"

He took a step toward the desk, stopped and gripped the back of the settee, steadied himself, and glared at the thing with fascination. He walked unsteadily to the chair in front of the desk and stared again. His hand moved to grasp the revolver and hesitated. And then, the last thought of pity strangled, he gripped the handle, lifted it with quick familiar touch, grasped the top clasp, loosed the barrel, threw the cylinder open and examined the shells, dropped them into his hand and saw that there were no blanks. One by one he slowly replaced them, snapped the cylinder in place and put the weapon in his pocket.

He glanced about the room furtively, walked to each of the tall French windows, closed the shutters and carefully drew the heavy draperies. He turned the switch of the electric lights, extinguishing all in the room save the small red one burning on the desk. He would need that in a moment.

He walked softly to the foot of the stairs and called:

"Tom!"

Waiting and receiving no answer he called again:

"Tom! Tom!"

A door opened above and the boy answered:

"Well?"

"Just a word, my son," the gentle voice called.

"I've nothing to say, sir! We're packing our trunks to leave at once."

"Yes, yes, I understand," the father answered tenderly. "You're going, of course, and it can't be helped—but just a minute, my son; we must say good-by in a decent way, you know—and—I've something to show you before you go"—the voice broke—"you—won't try to leave without seeing me?"

There was a short silence and the answer came in friendly tones:

"I'll see you. I'll be down in a few minutes."

The father murmured:

"Thank God!"

He hurried back to the library, unlocked a tiny drawer in the desk, drew out a plain envelope from which he took the piece of paper on which was scrawled the last message from the boy's mother. His hand trembled as he read and slowly placed it in a small pigeon-hole.

He took his pen and began to write rapidly on a pad of legal cap paper.

While he was still busy with his writing, in obedience to his orders, Andy and Minerva returned. They stopped at the doorway and peeped in cautiously before entering. Astonished and terrified to find the room so dimly lighted they held a whispered conference in the hall:

"Better not go in dar, chile!" Andy warned.

"Ah, come on, you fool!" Minerva insisted. "He ain't gwine ter hurt us!"

"I tell ye he's wild—he's gone crazy, sho's yer born! I kin feel dem fingers playin' on my windpipe now!"

"What's he doin' dar at dat desk?" Mwnerva asked.

"He's writin' good-by ter dis world, I'm tellin' ye, an' hit's time me an' you wuz makin' tracks!"

"Ah, come on!" the woman urged.

Andy hung back and shook his head:

"Nasah—I done bin in dar an' got my dose!"

"You slip up behin' him an' see what he's writin'," Minerva suggested.

"Na, you slip up!"

"You're de littlest an' makes less fuss," she argued.

"Yes, but you'se de biggest an' you las' de longest in er scrimmage——"

"Ah, go on!" she commanded, getting behind Andy and suddenly pushing him into the room.

He rushed back into her arms, but she pushed him firmly on:

"G'long, I tell ye, fool, an' see what he's doin'. I back ye up."

Andy balked and she pressed him another step:

"G'long!"

He motioned her to come closer, whispering:

"Ef yer gwine ter stan' by me, for de Lawd's sake stan' by me—don't stan' by de do'!"

Seeing that retreat was cut off and he was in for it, the negro picked his way cautiously on tip-toe until he leaned over the chair and tried to read what his master was writing.

Norton looked up suddenly:

"Andy!"

He jumped in terror:

"I—I—didn't see nuttin', major! Nasah! I nebber seed a thing, sah!"

Norton calmly lifted his head and looked into the black face that had been his companion so many years:

"I want you to see it!"

"Oh!" Andy cried with surprised relief, "you wants me to see hit"—he glanced at Minerva and motioned her to come nearer. "Well, dat's different, sah. Yer know I wouldn't er tried ter steal er glimpse of it ef I'd knowed ye wuz gwine ter show it ter me. I allers is er gemman, sah!"

Norton handed him the paper:

"I taught you to read and write, Andy. You can do me a little service to-night—read that!"

"Yassah—yassah," he answered, pompously, adjusting his coat and vest. He held the paper up before him, struck it lightly with the back of his hand and cleared his throat:

"Me an' you has bin writin' fer de newspapers now 'bout fifteen years—yassah"—he paused and hurriedly read the document. "Dis yo' will, sah? An' de Lawd er mussy, 'tain't more'n ten lines. An' dey hain't nary one er dem whereases an' haremditaments aforesaids, like de lawyers puts in dem in de Cote House—hit's des plain writin'"—he paused again—"ye gives de house, an' ten thousand dollars ter Miss Helen an' all yer got ter de Columnerzation Society ter move de niggers ter er place er dey own!"—he paused again and walled his eyes at Minerva. "What gwine come er Mr. Tom?"

Norton's head sank:

"He'll be rich without this! Sign your name here as a witness," he said shortly, picking up the pen.

Andy took the pen, rolled up his sleeve carefully, bent over the desk, paused and scratched his head:

"Don't yer think, major, dat's er terrible pile er money ter fling loose 'mongst er lot er niggers?"

Norton's eyes were dreaming again and Andy went on insinuatingly: "Now, wouldn't hit be better, sah, des ter pick out one good *reliable* nigger dat yer knows pussonally—an' move him?"

Norton looked up impatiently:

"Sign it!"

"Yassah! Cose, sah, you knows bes', sah, but 'pears ter me lak er powerful waste er good money des flingin' it broadcast!"

Norton lifted his finger warningly and Andy hastened to sign his name with a flourish of the pen. He looked at it admiringly:

"Dar now! Dey sho know dat's me! I practise on dat quereque two whole mont's——"

Norton folded the will, placed it in an envelope, addressed it and lifted his drawn face:

"Tell the Clerk of the Court that I executed this will to-night and placed it in this desk"—his voice became inaudible a moment and went on—"Ask him to call for it to-morrow and record it for me."

Minerva, who had been listening and watching with the keenest interest, pressed forward and asked in a whisper:

"Yassah, but whar's you gwine ter be? You sho ain't gwine ter die ter-night?"

Norton quietly recovered himself and replied angrily:

"Do I look as if I were dying?"

"Nasah!—But ain't dey no way dat I kin help ye, major? De young folks is gwine ter leave, sah——"

"They are not going until I'm ready!" was the grim answer.

"Nasah, but dey's gwine," the black woman replied tenderly. "Ye can't stop 'em long. Lemme plead fur 'em, sah! You wuz young an' wild once, major"—the silvery gray head sank low and the white lips quivered—"you take all yer money frum Mister Tom—what he care fer dat now wid love singin' in his heart? Young folks is young folks——"

Norton lifted his head and stared as in a dream.

"Won't ye hear me, sah? Can't I go upstairs an' speak de good word ter Mister Tom now an' tell him hit's all right?"

A sudden idea flashed into Norton's mind.

The ruse would be the surest and quickest way to get Tom into the room alone.

"Yes, yes," he answered, glancing at her. "You can say that to him now——"

Minerva laughed:

"I kin go right up dar to his room now an' tell 'im dat you're er waitin' here wid yer arms open an' yer heart full er love an' fergiveness?"

"Yes, go at once"—he paused—"and keep Miss Helen there a few minutes. I want to see him first—you understand——"

"Yassah! yassah!" Minerva cried, hastening to the door followed by Andy. "I understands, I understands"—she turned on Andy. "Ye hear dat, you fool nigger? Ain't I done tole you dat hit would all come out right ef I could des say de good word? Gloree! We gwine ter hab dat weddin' all over agin! You des wait till yer seen dat cake I gwine ter bake——"

With a quick turn she was about to pass through the door when Andy caught her sleeve:

"Miss Minerva!"

"Yas, honey!"

"Miss Minerva," he repeated, nervously glancing at Norton, "fer Gawd's sake don't you leave me now! You'se de only restful pusson in dis house!'

With a triumphant laugh Minerva whispered:

"I'll be right back in a minute, honey!"

Norton had watched with apparent carelessness until Minerva had gone. He sprang quickly to his feet, crossed the room and spoke in an excited whisper:

"Andy!"

"Yassah!"

"Go down to that front gate and stay there. Turn back anybody who tries to come in. Don't you allow a soul to enter the lawn."

"I'll do de best I kin, sah," he replied hastening toward the door.

Norton took an angry step toward him:

"You do exactly as I tell you, sir!"

Andy jumped and replied quickly:

"Yassah, but ef dem serenaders come back here you know dey ain't gwine pay no 'tensun ter no nigger talkin' to 'em—dat's what dey er celebratin' erbout——"

Norton frowned and was silent a moment:

"Say that I ask them not to come in."

"I'll tell 'em, sah, but I spec I'll hatter climb er tree 'fore I explains hit to 'em—but I tell 'em, sah—yassah."

As Andy slowly backed out, Norton said sternly:

"I'll call you when I want you. Stay until I do!"

"Yassah," Andy breathed softly as he disappeared trembling and wondering.

Chapter XXIX

The Dregs in the Cup

Norton walked quickly to the window, drew back the draperies, opened the casement and looked out to see if Andy were eavesdropping. He watched the lazy figure cross the lawn, glancing back at the house. The full moon, at its zenith, was shining in a quiet glory, uncanny in its dazzling brilliance.

He stood drinking in for the last time the perfumed sweetness and languor of the Southern night. His senses seemed supernaturally acute. He could distinctly note the odors of the different flowers that were in bloom on the lawn. A gentle breeze was blowing from the path across the old rose garden. The faint, sweet odor of the little white carnations his mother had planted along the walks stole over his aching soul and he was a child again watching her delicate hands plant them, while grumbling slaves protested at the soiling of her fingers. She was looking up with a smile saying:

"I love to plant them. I feel that they are my children then, and I'm making the world sweet and beautiful through them!"

Had he made the world sweeter and more beautiful?

He asked himself the question sternly.

"God knows I've tried for twenty years—and it has come to this!"

The breeze softened, the odor of the pinks grew fainter and the strange penetrating smell of the hedge of tuberoses swept in from the other direction with the chill of Death in its breath.

His heart rose in rebellion. It was too horrible, such an end of life! He was scarcely forty-nine years old. Never had the blood pulsed through his veins with stronger throb and never had his vision of life seemed clearer and stronger than to-day when he had faced those thousands of cheering men and hinted for the first time his greater plans for uplifting the Nation's life.

The sense of utter loneliness overwhelmed his soul. The nearest being in the universe whose presence he could feel was the dead wife and mother.

His eye rested on the portrait tenderly:

"We're coming, dearest, to-night!"

For the first time his spirit faced the mystery of eternity at close range. He had long speculated in theories of immortality and brooded over the problem of the world that lies but a moment beyond the senses.

He had clasped hands with Death now and stood face to face, calm and unafraid. His mind quickened with the thought of the strange world into which he would be ushered within an hour. Would he know and understand? Or would the waves of oblivion roll over the prostrate body without a sign? It couldn't be! The hunger of immortality was too keen for doubt. He would see and know! The cry rose triumphant within. He refused to perish with the moth and worm. The baser parts of his being might die—the nobler must live. There could be no other meaning to this sublimely cruel and mad decision to kill the body rather than see it dishonored. His eye caught the twinkle of a star through the branches of a treetop. His feet would find the pathway among those shining worlds! There could be no other meaning to the big thing that throbbed and ached within and refused to be content to whelp and stable here as a beast of the field. Pride, Honor, Aspiration, Prayer, meant this or nothing!

"I've made blunders here," he cried, "but I'm searching for the light and I'll find the face of God!"

The distant shouts of cheering hosts still celebrating in the Square brought his mind to earth with a sickening shock. He closed the windows, and drew the curtains. His hands clutched the velvet hangings in a moment of physical weakness and he steadied himself before turning to call Tom.

Recovering his composure in a measure, his hand touched the revolver in his pocket, the tall figure instinctively straightened and he walked rapidly toward the hall. He had barely passed the centre of the room when the boy's voice distinctly echoed from the head of the stairs:

"I'll be back in a minute, dear!"

He heard the door of Helen's room close softly and the firm step descend the stairs. The library door opened and closed quickly, and Tom stood before him, his proud young head lifted and his shoulders squared.

The dignity and reserve of conscious manhood shone in every line of his stalwart body and spoke in every movement of face and form.

"Well, sir," he said quietly. "It's done now and it can't be helped, you know."

Norton was stunned by the sudden appearance of the dear familiar form. His eyes were dim with unshed tears. It was too hideous, this awful thing he had to do! He stared at him piteously and with an effort walked to his side, speaking in faltering tones that choked between the words:

"Yes, it's done now—and it can't be helped"—he strangled and couldn't go on—"I—I—have realized that, my son—but I—I have an old letter from your mother—that I wanted to show you before you go—you'll find it on the desk there."

He pointed to the desk on which burned the only light in the room.

The boy hesitated, pained by the signs of deep anguish in his father's face, turned and rapidly crossed the room.

The moment his back was turned, Norton swiftly and silently locked the door, and with studied carelessness followed.

The boy began to search for the letter:

"I don't see it, sir."

The father, watching him with feverish eyes, started at his voice, raised his hand to his forehead and walked quickly to his side:

"Yes, I—I—forgot—I put it away!"

He dropped limply into the chair before the desk, fumbled among the papers and drew the letter from the pigeon-hole in which he had placed it.

He held it in his hand, shaking now like a leaf, and read again the scrawl that he had blurred with tears and kisses. He placed his hand on the top of the desk, rose with difficulty and looked for Tom. The boy had moved quietly toward the table. The act was painfully significant of their new relations. The sense of alienation cut the broken man to the quick. He could scarcely see as he felt his way to the boy's side and extended the open sheet of paper without a word.

Tom took the letter, turned his back on his father and read it in silence.

"How queer her handwriting!" he said at length.

Norton spoke in strained muffled tones:

"Yes—she—she was dying when she scrawled that. The mists of the other world were gathering about her. I don't think she could see the paper"— the voice broke, he fought for self-control and then went on— "but every tiny slip of her pencil, each little weak hesitating mark etched itself in fire on my heart"—the voice stopped and then went on—"you can read them?"

"Yes."

The father's long trembling finger traced slowly each word:

"'Remember that I love you and have forgiven——'"

"Forgiven what?" Tom interrupted.

Norton turned deadly pale, recovered himself and began in a low voice:

"You see, boy, I grew up under the old régime. Like a lot of other fellows with whom I ran, I drank, gambled and played the devil—you know what that meant in those days——"

"No, I don't," the boy interrupted. "That's just what I don't know. I belong to a new generation. And you've made a sort of exception of me even among the men of to-day. You taught me to keep away from women. I learned the lesson. I formed clean habits, and so I don't know just what you mean by that. Tell me plainly."

"It's hard to say it to you, my boy!" the older man faltered.

"I want to know it."

"I—I mean that twenty years ago it was more common than now for youngsters to get mixed up with girls of negroid blood——"

The boy shrank back:

"You!—great God!"

"Yes, she came into my life at last—a sensuous young animal with wide, bold eyes that knew everything and was not afraid. That sentence means the shame from which I've guarded you with such infinite care——"

He paused and pointed again to the letter, tracing its words:

"'Rear our boy free from the curse!'—you—you—see why I have been so desperately in earnest?"—Norton bent close with pleading eagerness: "And that next sentence, there, you can read it? 'I had rather a thousand times that he should die than this—My brooding spirit will watch and guard'—he paused and repeated—"'that he should die'—you—you—see that?"

The boy looked at his father's trembling hand and into his glittering eyes with a start:

"Yes, yes, but, of course, that was only a moment's despair—no mother could mean such a thing."

Norton's eyes fell, he moved uneasily, tried to speak again and was silent. When he began his words were scarcely audible:

"We must part now in tenderness, my boy, as father and son—we—we—must do that you know. You—you forgive me for striking you to-night?"

Tom turned away, struggled and finally answered:

"No."

The father followed eagerly:

"Tell me that it's all right!"

The boy's hand nervously fumbled at the cloth on the table:

"I—I—am glad I didn't do something worse!"

"Say that you forgive me! Why is it so hard?"

Tom turned his back:

"I don't know, Dad, I try, but—I—just can't!"

The father's hand touched the boy's, arm timidly:

"You can never understand, my son, how my whole life has been bound up in you! For years I've lived, worked, and dreamed and planned for you alone. In your young manhood I've seen all I once hoped to be and have never been. In your love I've found the healing of a broken heart. Many a night I've gone out there alone in that old cemetery, knelt beside your mother's grave and prayed her spirit to guide me that I might at least lead your little feet aright——"

The boy moved slightly and the father's hand slipped limply from his, he staggered back with a cry of despair, and fell prostrate on the lounge:

"I can endure anything on this earth but your hate, my boy! I can't endure that —I can't—even for a moment!"

His form shook with incontrollable grief as he lay with his face buried in his outstretched arms.

The boy struggled with conflicting pride and love, looked at the scrawled, tear-stained letter he still held in his hand and then at the bowed figure, hesitated a moment, and rushed to his father's side, knelt and slipped his arm around the trembling figure:

"It's all right, Dad! I'll not remember—a single tear from your eyes blots it all out!"

The father's hand felt blindly for the boy's and grasped it desperately:

"You won't remember a single harsh word that I've said?"

"No—no—it's all right," was the soothing answer, as he returned the pressure.

Norton looked at him long and tenderly:

"How you remind me of *her* to-night! The deep blue of your eyes, the trembling of your lips when moved, your little tricks of speech, the tear that quivers on your lash and never falls and the soul that's mirrored there"—he paused and stroked the boy's head—"and her hair, the beaten gold of honeycomb!"

His head sank and he was silent.

The boy again pressed his hand tenderly and rose, drawing his father to his feet:

"I'm sorry to have hurt you, Dad. I'm sorry that we have to go—good-by!"

He turned and slowly moved toward the door. Norton slipped his right hand quickly to the revolver, hesitated, his fingers relaxed and the deadly thing dropped back into his pocket as he sank to his seat with a groan:

"Wait! Wait, Tom!"

The boy stopped.

"I—I've got to tell it to you now!" he went on hoarsely. "I—I tried to save you this horror—but I couldn't—the way was too hard and cruel."

Tom took a step and looked up in surprise:

"The way—what way?"

"I couldn't do it," the father cried. "I just couldn't—and so I have to tell you."

The boy spoke with sharp eagerness:

"Tell me what?"

"Now that I know you are married in all that word means and I have failed to save you from it—I must give you the proofs that you demand. I must prove to you that Helen *is* a negress——"

A sudden terror crept into the young eyes:

"You—you have the proofs?"

"Yes!" the father nodded, placing his hand on his throat and fighting for breath. He took a step toward the boy, and whispered:

"Cleo—is—her mother!"

Tom flinched as if struck a blow. The red blood rushed to his head and he blanched with a death-like pallor:

"And you have been afraid of Cleo?"

"Yes."

"Why?"

The father's head was slowly lowered and his hands moved in the slightest gesture of dumb confession.

A half-articulate, maniac cry and the boy grasped him with trembling hands, screaming in his face:

"God in Heaven, let me keep my reason for just a moment!—So—you—are—Helen's——"

The bowed head sank lower.

"Father!"

Tom reeled, and fell into a chair with a groan:

"Lord have mercy on my lost soul!"

Norton solemnly lifted his eyes:

"God's full vengeance has fallen at last! You have married your own——"

The boy sprang to his feet covering his face:

"Don't! Don't! Helen doesn't know?"

"No."

"She mustn't!" he shivered, looking wildly at his father. "But why, why—oh, dear God, why didn't you kill me before I knew!"

He sank back into the chair, his arms outstretched across the table, his face hidden in voiceless shame.

The father slowly approached the prostrate figure, bent low and tenderly placed his cheek against the blonde head, soothing it with trembling touch. For a long while he remained thus, with no sound breaking the stillness save the sobs that came from the limp form.

And then Norton said brokenly:

"I tried, my boy, to end it for us both without your knowing just now when your back was turned, but I couldn't. It seemed too cowardly and cruel! I just couldn't"—he paused, slowly drew the revolver from his pocket and laid it on the table.

The boy felt the dull weight of the steel strike the velvet cover and knew what had been done without lifting his head.

"Now you know," the father added, "what we both must do."

Tom rose staring at the thing on the dark red cloth, and lifted his eyes to his fathers:

"Yes, and hurry! Helen may come at any moment."

He had barely spoken when the knob of the door turned. A quick knock was heard at the same instant and Helen's voice rang through the hall:

"Tom! Tom!"

Norton grasped the pistol, thrust it under the table-cover and pressed the boy toward the door:

"Quick! Open it, at once!"

Tom stared in a stupor, unable to move until his father shook his arm:

"Quick—open it—let her in a moment—it's best."

He opened the door and Helen sprang in breathlessly.

Chapter XXX

The Mills of God

Norton had dropped into a seat with apparent carelessness, while Tom stood immovable, his face a mask. The girl looked quickly from one to the other, her breath coming in quick gasps.

She turned to Tom:

"Why did you lock the door—what does it mean?"

Norton hastened to answer, his tones reassuringly simple:

"Why, only that we wished to be alone for a few moments——"

"Yes, we understand each other now," Tom added.

Helen's eyes flashed cautiously from one to the other:

"I heard a strange noise"—she turned to the boy—"and, oh, Tom, darling, I was so frightened! I thought I heard a struggle and then everything became so still. I was wild—I couldn't wait any longer!"

"Why, it was really nothing," Tom answered her bravely smiling. "We—we did have a little scene, and lost our temper for a moment, but you can see for yourself it's all right now. We've thrashed the whole thing out and have come to a perfect understanding!"

His words were convincing but not his manner. He hadn't dared to look her in the face. His eyes were on the rug and his foot moved nervously.

"You are not deceiving me?" she asked trembling.

The boy appealed to his father:

"Haven't we come to a perfect understanding, Dad?"

Norton rose:

"Perfect, my son. It's all right, now, Helen."

"Just wait for me five minutes, dear," Tom pleaded.

"Can't I hear what you have to say?"

"We prefer to be alone," the father said gravely.

Again her eyes flashed from one to the other and rested on Tom. She rushed to him and laid her hand appealingly on his arm:

"Oh, Tom, dear, am I not your wife?" the boy's head drooped—"must you have a secret from me now?"

"Just a few minutes," Norton pleaded, "that's a good girl!"

"Only a few minutes, Helen," Tom urged.

"Please let me stay. Why were you both so pale when I came in?"

Father and son glanced at each other over her head. Norton hesitated and said:

"You see we are perfectly calm now. All bitterness is gone from our hearts. We are father and son again."

"Why do you look so queerly at me? Why do you look so strangely at each other?"

"It's only your imagination, dear," Tom said.

"No, there's something wrong," Helen declared desperately. "I feel it in the air of this room—in the strange silence between you. For God's sake tell me what it means! Surely, I have the right to know"—she turned suddenly to Norton—"You don't hate me now, do you, major?"

The somber brown eyes rested on her in a moment of intense silence and he slowly said:

"I have never hated you, my child!"

"Then what is it?" she cried in anguish, turning again to Tom. "Tell me what I can do to help you! I'll obey you, dearest, even if it's to lay my life down. Don't send me away. Don't keep this secret from me. I feel its chill in my heart. My place is by your side—tell me how I can help you!"

Tom looked at her intently:

"You say that you will obey me?"

"Yes—you are my lord and master!"

He seized her hand and led her to the door:

"Then wait for me just five minutes."

She lifted her head pleadingly:

"You will let me come to you then?"

"Yes."

"You won't lock the door again?"

"Not now."

While Tom stood immovable, with a lingering look of tenderness she turned and passed quickly from the room.

He closed the door softly, steadied himself before loosing the knob and turned to his father in a burst of sudden rebellion:

"Oh, Dad! It can't be true! It can't be true! I can't believe it. Did you look at her closely again?"

Norton drew himself wearily to his feet and spoke with despairing certainty:

"Yes, yes, as I've looked at her a hundred times with growing wonder."

"She's not like you——"

"No more than you, my boy, and yet you're bone of my bone and flesh of my flesh—it can't be helped——"

He paused and pointed to the revolver:

"Give it to me!"

The boy started to lift the cloth and the father caught his arm:

"But first—before you do," he faltered. "I want you to tell me now with your own lips that you forgive me for what I must do—and then I think, perhaps, I can—say it!"

Their eyes met in a long, tender, searching gaze:

"I forgive you," he softly murmured.

"Now give it to me!" the father firmly said, stepping back and lifting his form erect.

The boy felt for the table, fumbled at the cloth, caught the weapon and slowly lifted it toward his father's extended hand. He opened his eyes, caught the expression of agony in the drawn face, the fingers relaxed and the pistol fell to the floor. He threw himself blindly on his father, his arms about his neck:

"Oh, Dad, it's too hard! Wait—wait—just a moment!"

The father held him close for a long while. His voice was very low when he spoke at last:

"There's no appeal, my boy! The sin of your father is full grown and has brought forth death. Yet I was not all to blame. We are caught to-night in the grip of the sins of centuries. I tried to give my life to the people to save the children of the future. My shame showed me the way as few men could have seen it, and I have set in motion forces that can never be stopped. Others will complete the work that I have begun. But our time has come——"

"Yes, yes, I understand!"

The father's arms pressed the son in a last long embrace:

"What an end to all my hopes! Oh, my boy, heart of my heart!"

Tom's hand slowly slipped down and caught his father's:

"Good-by, Dad!"

Norton held the clasp with lingering tenderness as the boy slowly drew away, measured four steps and calmly folded his arms, his head erect, his broad young shoulders squared and thrown far back.

Cleo, who had crept into the hall, stood behind the curtains of the inner door watching the scene with blanched face.

The father walked quickly to the revolver, picked it up, turned and lifted it above his head.

With a smothered cry Cleo sprang into the room—but she was too late. Norton had quickly dropped the pistol to the level of the eye and fired.

A tiny red spot flamed on the white skin of the boy's forehead, the straight figure swayed, and pitched forward face down on the rug.

The woman staggered back, cowering in the shadows.

The father knelt beside the quivering form, clasped his left hand in Tom's, placed the revolver to his temple and fired. The silver-gray head sank slowly against the breast of the boy as a piercing scream from Helen's lips rang through the silent hall.

Chapter XXXI

Sin Full Grown

The sensitive soul of the girl had seen the tragedy before she rushed into the library. At the first shot she sprang to her feet, her heart in her throat. The report had sounded queerly through the closed doors and she was not sure. She had entered the hall, holding her breath, when the second shot rang out its message of death.

She was not the woman who faints in an emergency. She paused just a moment in the door, saw the ghastly heap on the floor and rushed to the spot.

She tore Tom's collar open and placed her ear over his heart:

"O God! He's alive—he's alive!"

She turned and saw Cleo leaning against the table with blanched face and chattering teeth.

"Call Andy and Aunt Minerva—and go for the doctor!— his heart's beating—quick—the doctor—he's alive—we may save him!"

She knelt again on the floor, took Tom's head in her lap, wiped the blood from the clean, white forehead, pressed her lips to his and sobbed:

"Come back, my own—it's I—Helen, your little wife—I'm calling you—you can't die—you're too young and life's too dear. We've only begun to live, my sweetheart! You shall not die!"

The tears were raining on his pale face and her cries had become little wordless prayers when Andy and Minerva entered the room.

She nodded her head toward Norton's motionless body:

"Lift him on the lounge!"

They moved him tenderly:

"See if his heart's still beating," she commanded.

Andy reverently lowered his dusky face against the white bosom of his master. When he lifted it the tears had blinded his eyes:

"Nobum," he said slowly, "he's done dead!"

The tick of the little French clock on the mantel beneath the mother's portrait rang with painful clearness.

Helen raised her hand to Minerva:

"Open the windows and let the smoke out. I'll hold him in my arms until the doctor comes."

"Yassum——"

Minerva drew the heavy curtains back from the tall windows, opened the casements and the perfumed air of the beautiful Southern night swept into the room.

A cannon boomed its final cry of victory from the Square and a rocket, bursting above the tree-tops, flashed a ray of red light on the white face of the dead.

Chapter XXXII

Confession

When Dr. Williams entered the room Helen was still holding Tom's head in her lap.

He had stirred once with a low groan.

"The major is dead, but Tom's alive, doctor!" she cried through her tears. "He's going to live, too—I feel it—I know it—tell me that it's so!"

The lips trembled pitifully with the last words.

The doctor felt the pulse and was silent.

"It's all right? He's going to live—isn't he?" she asked pathetically.

"I can't tell yet, my child," was the calm answer.

He examined the wound and ran his hand over the blonde hair. His fingers stopped suddenly and he felt the head carefully. He bent low, parted the hair and found a damp blood mark three inches above the line of the forehead.

"See!" he cried, "the ball came out here. His head was thrown far back, the bullet struck the inner skull bone at an angle and glanced."

"What does it mean?" she asked breathlessly.

The doctor smiled:

"That the brain is untouched. He is only stunned and in a swoon. He'll be well in two weeks."

Helen lifted her eyes and sobbed:

"O God!"

She tried to bend and kiss Tom's lips, her body swayed and she fell backward in a dead faint.

Andy and Minerva carried her to her room, left Cleo to minister to her and returned to help the doctor.

He examined Norton's body to make sure that life was extinct and placed the body on an improvised bed on the floor until he should regain his senses.

In half an hour Tom looked into the doctor's face:

"Why, it's Doctor Williams?"

"Yes."

"What—what's happened?"

"It's only a scratch for you, my boy. You'll be well in a few days——"

"Well in a few days"—he repeated blankly. "I can't get well! I've got to die"—his head dropped and he caught his breath.

The doctor waited for him to recover himself to ask the question that was on his lips. He had gotten as yet no explanation of the tragedy save Cleo's statement that the major had shot Tom and killed himself. He had guessed that the ugly secret in Norton's life was in some way responsible.

"Why must you die, my boy?" he asked kindly.

Tom opened his eyes in a wild stare:

"Helen's my wife—we married secretly without my father knowing it. He has just told me that Cleo is her mother and I have married my own——"

His voice broke and his head sank.

The doctor seized the boy's hand and spoke eagerly:

"It's a lie, boy! It's a lie! Take my word for it——"

Tom shook his head.

"I'll stake my life on it that it's a lie"— the old man repeated—"and I'll prove it—I'll prove it from Cleo's lips!"

"You—you—can do it!" the boy said hopelessly, though his eyes flashed with a new light.

"Keep still until I return!" the doctor cried, "and I'll bring Cleo with me."

He placed the revolver in his pocket and hastily left the room, the boy's eyes following him with feverish excitement.

He called Cleo into the hall and closed Helen's door.

The old man seized her hand with a cruel grip:

"Do you dare tell me that this girl is your daughter?"

She trembled and faltered:

"Yes!"

"You're a liar!" he hissed. "You may have fooled Norton for twenty years, but you can't fool me. I've seen too much of this sort of thing. I'll stake my immortal soul on it that no girl with Helen's pure white skin and scarlet cheeks, clean-cut features and deep blue eyes can have in her body a drop of negro blood!"

"She's mine all the same, and you know when she was born," the woman persisted.

He could feel her body trembling, looked at her curiously and said:

"Come down stairs with me a minute."

Cleo drew back:

"I don't want to go in that room again!"

"You've got to come!"

He seized her roughly and drew her down the stairs into the library.

She gripped the door, panting in terror. He loosed her hands and pushed her inside before the lounge on which the body of Norton lay, the cold wide-open eyes staring straight into her face.

She looked a moment in abject horror, shivered and covered her eyes:

"Oh, my God, let me go!"

The doctor tore her hands from her face and confronted her. His snow-white beard and hair, his tense figure and flaming anger seemed to the trembling woman the image of an avenging fate as he solemnly cried:

"Here, in the presence of Death, with the all-seeing eye of God as your witness, and the life of the boy you once held in your arms hanging on your words, I ask if that girl is your daughter?"

The greenish eyes wavered, but the answer came clear at last:

"No——"

"I knew it!" the doctor cried. "Now the whole truth!"

The color mounted Tom's cheeks as he listened.

"My own baby died," she began falteringly, "I was wild with grief and hunted for another. I found Helen in Norfolk at the house of an old woman whom I knew, and she gave her to me——"

"Or you stole her—no matter"—the doctor interrupted—"Go on."

Helen had slipped down stairs, crept into the room unobserved and stood listening.

"Who was the child's mother?" the doctor demanded.

Cleo was gasping for breath:

"The daughter of an old fool who had disowned her because she ran away and married a poor white boy—the husband died—the father never forgave her. When the baby was born the mother died, too, and I got the child from the old nurse—she's pure white—there's not a stain of any kind on her birth!"

With a cry of joy Helen knelt and drew Tom into her arms:

"Oh, darling, did you hear it—oh, my sweetheart, did you hear it?"

The boy's head sank on her breast and he breathed softly:

"Thank God!"

Chapter XXXIII

Healing

The years brought their healing to wounded hearts. Tom Norton refused to leave his old home. He came of a breed of men who had never known how to quit. He faced the world and with grim determination took up the work for the Republic which his father had begun.

With tireless voice his paper pleads for the purity of the race. Its circulation steadily increases and its influence deepens and widens.

The patter of a baby's feet again echoes through the wide hall behind the white fluted columns. The young father and mother have taught his little hands to place flowers on the two green mounds beneath the oak in the cemetery. He is not old enough yet to understand, and so the last time they were there he opened his eyes wide at his mother's tears and lisped:

"Are 'oo hurt, mama?"

"No, my dear, I'm happy now."

"Why do 'oo cry?"

"For a great man I knew a little while, loved and lost, dearest—your grandfather for whom we named you."

Little Dan's eyes grew very serious as he looked again at the flower-strewn graves and wondered what it all meant.

But the thing which marks the Norton home with peculiar distinction is that since the night of his father's death, Tom has never allowed a negro to cross the threshold or enter its gates.

The End